NO
WITNESSES

Also by Ridley Pearson
in Thorndike Large Print ®

The Angel Maker
Hard Fall

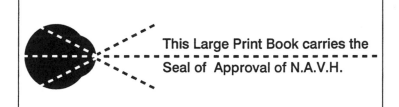

This Large Print Book carries the
Seal of Approval of N.A.V.H.

NO WITNESSES

RIDLEY PEARSON

Thorndike Press • Thorndike, Maine

Published in 1995 by arrangement with Hyperion.

The individuals and incidents portrayed in this novel are fictitious. Any resemblance to actual incidents, or individuals living or dead, is purely coincidental.

Thorndike Large Print ® Basic Series.

The tree indicium is a trademark of Thorndike Press.

The text of this Large Print edition is unabridged.
Other aspects of the book may vary from the original edition.

Set in 16 pt. News Plantin by Minnie B. Raven.

Printed in the United States on permanent paper.

Library of Congress Cataloging in Publication Data

Pearson, Ridley.
    No witnesses : a novel / Ridley Pearson.
        p.   cm.
    ISBN 0-7862-0355-2 (lg. print : hc)
    1. Large type books. I. Title.
    [PS3566.E234N6   1995]
    813'.54—dc20   94-37390

Dedication

Every so often there is that rare experience that profoundly alters one's life. In receiving the Raymond Chandler Fulbright Award, I was afforded a year at Oxford, with access to that institution's unparalleled libraries, as well as Raymond Chandler's personal letters and manuscripts. It was at Wadham College, up staircase Kings Arms eleven, that I researched and outlined both *The Angel Maker* and this novel, *No Witnesses*. The ten months spent at Wadham College, under the auspices of the Fulbright Foundation, have never left me, nor will they. For both Colleen and me, these months remain sacred.

This book is dedicated to Mr. Graham C. Greene, who on the centennial of Raymond Chandler's birth elected not to dedicate a statue or a park bench to the great author, but to leave a living legacy in the form of funding a private Fulbright through the Chandler estate. This award has now been enjoyed by several British and American writers and has created its own legacy by changing all our lives.

This book is also dedicated to Dr. Tim Binyon, Dr. Robin Fiddian, Mr. Jeffry Hackney,

Sir Claus Mosner, and all the Fellows of Wadham College, Oxford; and to Captain John Franklin and the Fulbright Foundation, London, England; Ms. Karen Adams and the Fulbright Commission, Washington, D.C.

What you gave me is irreplaceable.

Acknowledgments

The author wishes to express a special debt of gratitude to Ian and Annette Cumming and Leucadia National Corporation. Also to James and Wendy Daverman, and Alex and Gina Macdonald, Marino Tomacelli, and all the gang at Kailuum.

Technical research would not have been possible without the generosity of the following:

Washington State: Dr. Donald Reay, chief pathologist, King County medical examiner; Dr. Christian Harris, forensic psychiatrist; Judge Robert Lasnik, King County Superior Court; Judge Mike Rikert, Skagit County Superior Court; Mr. Thomas Bass, president, The Exchange; Dr. Phillip I. Tarr, M.D., assistant professor (pediatrics), Division of Gastroenterology, University of Washington; Lieutenant Dave Reichert, King County police; Sergeant Don Cameron, Homicide, Seattle Police Department.

England: Mr. Bill Tupman, Center for Police Studies, University of Exeter; Dr. Jack Wright, HM Prison and Youth Custody Centre, Grendon Underwood, Aylesbury; Richard Baker, Metropolitan Police, London; Detective Inspector

Adrian Maybank, New Scotland Yard; Detective Inspector Phil Gulliford; Inspector Thomas M. Seamon, Philadelphia Police Department, Police Studies Fulbright; Nick Roditi, Hampstead, London; John D. Drysdale, Robert Flemings Holdings Limited, London; Shelagh James-Hudson, Bicester, Oxon; Carole Blake and Julian Friedman; Mary Peterson, office assistance; Judy McLean, manuscript preparation; Colleen Daly, editorial assistance.

*The author wishes to thank Brian DeFiore,
who edited this manuscript.*

Thanks also to Albert Zuckerman and Steve Ross.

ONE

And now for the good part.

This was where Lou Boldt threw out all convention, where the textbooks took a backseat to experience, and where he found out who in the lecture hall was listening and who was asleep.

He raised his voice. Boldt was a big man and his words bellowed clear back to the make-out seats without the need of the mike clipped to his tie. "Everything I've told you in the past few weeks concerning evidence, investigative procedure, chain of custody, and chain of command is worthless." A few heads snapped up — more than he had expected. "Worthless unless you learn to read the crime scene, to know the victim, to listen to and trust your own instincts. To feel with your heart as much as think with your head. To find a balance between the two. If it was all in the head, then we would not need detectives; the lab technicians could do it all. Conversely, if it was all in the heart — if we could simply empathize with the suspect and say, 'Yup, you did it' — then who would need the lab nerds?" A few of the studious types busily flipped pages. Boldt informed them, "You won't find any of this in your textbooks. That's just the point. All the textbooks in the world are not going to clear a case — only the *investigator* can. Evidence and information is *nothing* without a human being to analyze, organize, and interpret it. That's you. That's me. There comes a time when all the information must be set aside; there comes a time when passion and instinct take over. It's the stuff that can't be taught; but it *can* be learned. Heart and mind — one's worthless without the other." He paused here, wondering if these peach-fuzz students could see beyond the forty-four-year-old, slightly paunchy homicide cop in the wrinkled khakis and the tattered sport coat that hid a pacifier in its side pocket.

At the same time, he listened to his own words reverberating through the lecture hall, wondering how much he dare tell them. Did he tell them about the nightmares, the divorces, the ulcers and the politics? The hours? The salary? The penetrating numbness with which the veterans approached a crime scene?

Light flooded an aisle as a door at the rear of the hall swung open and a lanky kid wearing oversize jeans and a rugby shirt hurried toward the podium, casting a stretched shadow. Reaching Boldt, he passed the sergeant a pink telephone memo. A sea of students looking on, Boldt unfolded and read it.

Volunteer Park, after class. I'll wait fifteen minutes. — D.M.

12

Volunteer Park? he wondered, his curiosity raised. Why not the offices? Daphne Matthews was anything but dramatic. As the department's forensic psychologist, she was cool, controlled, studied, patient. Articulate, strong, intelligent. But not dramatic — not like this. The curious faces remained fixed on him. "A love letter," he said, winning a few laughs. But not many: Cops weren't expected to be funny — something else they would have to learn.

Volunteer Park is perched well above Seattle's downtown cluster of towering high-rises and the gray-green curve of Elliott Bay that sweeps out into the island-riddled estuary of Puget Sound. A large reservoir, acting as a reflecting pond, is terraced below the parking lot and lookout that fronts the museum, a building under reconstruction for months on its way to housing the city's Asian Collection. Boldt parked his aging department-issued four-door Chevy three spaces away from the red Prelude that Daphne Matthews maintained showroom clean. She was not to be found in her car.

The water tower's stone facade rose several stories to his left. Well-kept beds of flowering shrubs and perennials surrounded its footing, like gems in a setting. The grass was a phenomenal emerald green, — unique, he thought, to Seattle and Portland. Maybe Ireland, too; he had never been. Summer was just taking hold. Every living thing seemed poised for change. The sky was a patch quilt of azure blue and cotton white, the clouds moving in swiftly from the west, low and fast. A visitor might think rain, but a local knew better. Not tonight. Cold maybe, if it cleared.

He spotted an unfamiliar male face behind the iron grate of one of the tower's upper viewing windows and waited a minute for this person and his companion to descend and leave the structure. Once they were gone, he chose the stairway to his right, ascending a narrow chimney of steep steps wedged between the brick rotunda to his right and the riveted steel hull of the water tank to his left. The painted tank and the tower that surrounded it were enormous, perhaps forty or fifty feet high and half again as wide. With each step, Boldt's heart pounded heavier. He was not in the best shape; or maybe it was because she had elected to step outside the system, and that could not help but intrigue him; or maybe it was personal and had nothing whatsoever to do with the shop. He and Daphne had been close once — too close for what was allowed of a married man. They still were close, but mention of that one night together never passed their lips. A month earlier she had surprised him by telling him about a new relationship. After Bill Gates, Owen Adler was the reigning bachelor prize of the Northwest, having gone from espresso cart to the fastest-growing beverage and food business in the western region. He leased his own plane, owned a multimillion-dollar estate overlooking Shilshole Marina, and now, quite possibly, owned the heart and affections of Daphne Matthews. Had her note been worded any other way, had she not chosen such an isolated location, Boldt would have been convinced that her request was nothing more than some lover butterflies.

In another two hours, Volunteer Park would be a drug and sex bazaar. Despite its view, the tower was not a place frequented by the pin-striped set. She had clearly chosen it carefully. Daphne was not given to acts of spontaneity. She desired a clandestine meeting — and he had to wonder why.

He reached the open-air lookout at the top of the tower. It had a cement floor and evenly spaced viewing windows crosshatched with heavy-gauge steel to prevent flyers from testing their wings, or projectiles from landing on passersby.

Daphne held her arms crossed tightly, accentuating an anxiety uncommon in her. Her brown hair spilled over her face hiding her eyes, and when she cleared it, he saw fear where there was usually the spark of excitement. Her square-shouldered, assertive posture collapsed in sagging defeat.

She wore the same blue slacks and cotton sweater he had seen her wearing at work. She had not been to her houseboat yet. "What is it?" he asked, worried by this look of hers.

Her chin cast a shadow hiding the scar on her neck. She did not answer immediately. "It's a potential *black hole*," she explained — a difficult if not impossible case to solve, and with political overtones. And then he understood: She had bypassed the proper procedures to give him a chance to sidestep this investigation before he formally inherited it at the cop shop. Why she would have a *black hole* in the first place confused him. The department's psychologist did not lead investigations; she kept cops from swallowing barrels, and profiled the loonies that kept Boldt and the others chasing body bags. She assisted in interrogations. She could take any side of any discussion and make a convincing argument out of it. She was the best listener he knew.

She handed him a fax — the first of what appeared to be several that she removed from a briefcase.

SOUP IS MOTHER'S CHOICE. NOT ALWAYS.

She told him, "That was the first threat he received."

"Adler," Boldt said, filling in the blank.

She nodded, her hair trailing her movements. Daphne Matthews had grace, even when frightened. "It's an ad slogan they use."

"Innocuous enough," he said.

She handed him the next saying, "Yes, but not for long."

**SUICIDE OR MURDER. TAKE YOUR PICK.
NO COPS. NO PRESS. NO TRICKS,
OR YOU WILL CARRY WITH YOU
THE LIVES OF THE INNOCENT.**

"It could be nothing," Boldt said, though his voice belied this.

"That's exactly what *he* said," she replied angrily, lumping them together.

Boldt did not want to be lumped in with Owen Adler. "I'll give you one thing: When you say *black hole*, you mean *black hole*." Faxed threats? he thought. In the top left of the page of thermal paper, he read a date and time in tiny typeface. To the right: "Page 1 of 1." Good luck tracing this, he thought.

She handed him a third. He did not want it.

"Quite a collection," he said. Boldt's nerves unraveled from time to time, and when it happened, he defaulted to stupid one-liners that seldom won a laugh.

**IF ADLER FOODS IS OUT OF
BUSINESS WITHIN 30 DAYS,
AND <u>ALL</u> OF THE MONEY IS GONE,
AND YOU ARE DEAD AND BURIED, THERE
WILL BE NO SENSELESS KILLING.
THE CHOICE IS YOURS.**

"How many days has it been?" It was the first question that popped into his head, though

17

it was answered by the date in the corner. He counted the weeks in his head. The thirty days had expired.

"You see the way he worded it?" Looking down at her feet, she spoke softly, dreamy and terrified. Her lover was the target of these threats, and despite her training, she clearly was not prepared for how to handle it. "The more common threat would be: 'If Adler Foods is *not* out of business within thirty days . . .' You see the difference?"

Her bailiwick, not his, he felt tempted to remind her. "Is that significant?" He played along because she had FRAGILE written all over her.

"To me it's significant. So is the attempt in each fax to place the blame firmly with Owen: It's his decision; his choice." When she looked up at him, he saw that she held back tears.

"Daffy —" he offered, stepping closer.

"Owen and I are not going to see each other — socially — for a while. Me being police and all." She wanted it to sound casual, but failed. "We have to take him seriously now."

Boldt felt a chill. "Do we?"

She handed him another.

I AM WAITING. I SUGGEST YOU DO NOT.
YOU WILL HAVE TO LIVE
WITH YOUR CHOICE.
OTHERS WILL NOT BE SO LUCKY.

18

"It's the first time he's mentioned himself," Boldt noted.

She handed him the last of the group. "That one was sent four days ago. This one arrived this morning."

YOUR INDECISION IS COSTLY. IT CAN, AND WILL, GET <u>MUCH</u> <u>WORSE</u> THAN THIS.

Below this on the fax was a copy of a newspaper article.

"*Today's* paper," she explained.

The headline read: INFECTIONS BAFFLE DOCTORS — *Two Children Hospitalized.*

He read the short article quickly.

"The girl is improving. The boy is *not*," she told him. " 'It can, and will, get *much worse* than this,' " she quoted.

He looked up. "This is his offer of proof? Is that what you're thinking?"

"He means to be taken seriously."

"I don't get it," he complained, frustrated. "Why didn't you bring this in sooner?"

"Owen didn't want to believe it." She took back the faxes possessively. Her hand trembled. "The second one warns against involving us."

She meant cops. She meant that the reason for them meeting here, and not in the fifth-floor offices, was that she still was not sure how to handle this.

"An Adler employee," Boldt said. "Past or present, an employee is the most likely."

19

"Owen has Fowler working on it."

She meant Kenny Fowler, formerly of Major Crimes, now Adler's chief of security. Boldt liked Kenny Fowler, and said so. Better yet, he was good police — or had been at one time. She nodded and toyed with a silver ring fashioned into a porpoise that she wore on her right hand.

"I misjudged him," she said so quietly that Boldt leaned in to hear as she repeated herself. Daphne was not one to mumble.

"Are you okay?"

"Sure," she lied.

A *black hole.* Absorbing energy. Admitting no light — pure darkness. He realized that he had already accepted it, and he wanted to blame her for knowing him so well.

"Talk to me," he said, nervous and irritated.

"You're right about it being an employee. That's the highest percentage bet. But typically it involves extortion, not suicide demands. Howard Taplin, Owen's counsel, wants it handled internally, where there's no chance of press leakage, no police involvement, nothing to violate the demands." This sounded a little too much like the party line, and it bothered him. It was not like her to voice the opinions of others as her own, and he had to wonder what kind of man Howard Taplin was that he seemed to carry so much influence with her. "That's why I have to be so careful in dealing with you. Taplin wants Fowler to handle this internally. Owen overruled this morning. He suggested this meeting — opening a dialogue. But it was *not* an easy decision."

"We can't be sure this newspaper story is his doing," Boldt told her. "He may have just seized upon a convenient headline."

"Maybe." She clearly believed otherwise, and Boldt trusted Daphne's instincts. Heart and mind; he was reminded of his lecture.

"What's Fowler doing about it?" Boldt asked.

"He doesn't know about this meeting. Not yet. He, like Taplin, advised against involving us. He's looking to identify a disgruntled employee — but he's been on it a month now. He's had a few suspects, but none of them has panned out. His loyalty is to the company. Howard Taplin writes his paychecks, not Owen — if you follow me."

Boldt's irritation surfaced. "If this news story *is* his doing, I'd say we're a little late."

"I'm to blame. Owen asked me for my professional opinion. I classified the threats as low-risk. I thought whoever it was was blowing smoke. Proper use of the language. The faxes are sent by portable computer from pay phones. Fowler traced the last two to pay phones on Pill Hill. That's a decent enough neighborhood. What that tells us is that in all probability we're dealing with an *educated, affluent, white male* between the ages of *twenty-five* and *forty.* The demands seemed so unrealistic that I assumed this person was venting some anger —

21

nothing more. Owen went along with that. He put Kenny on it and tried to forget it. I screwed this up, Lou." She crossed her arms tightly again and her breasts rode high in the cradle. Again she quoted, " 'It can, and will, get *much worse* than this.' "

Her voice echoed slightly in the cavernous enclosure, circling inside his thoughts like horses on a carousel.

A *black hole.* His now.

"You want me to look into it, I'll look into it," he offered reluctantly.

"Unofficially."

"You know I can't do that, Daffy."

"Please."

"I'm not a rent-a-cop. Neither are you. We're fifth-floor. You know the way it works."

"Please!"

"I can't do that *for very long,*" he qualified.

"Thank you."

"If either of these kids dies, Daffy —" He left it dangling there, like one of the many broken cobwebs suspended from the cement ceiling.

"I know." She avoided his gaze.

"You'll share *everything* with me. No stone-walling."

"Agreed."

"Well . . . maybe not *everything,*" he corrected.

It won a genuine smile from her, and he was glad for that — though it deserted her as quickly as it had come. His frantic footfalls on the formed stairs sounded like the beating of bats' wings as he descended at a run.

The newspaper article had listed one of the hospitals. For Lou Boldt, the victim was where every investigation began.

TWO

Boldt stood at the foot of the bed in the Harborview Medical Clinic's ICU ward. Slater Lowry lay unconscious, the repository of a half-dozen tubes, the source for the weakened signals charted on a variety of green video monitors. KIRO's morning news had picked up the story of a "mysterious infection." There had been no mention of Owen Adler or the threatening faxes.

The boy was a towhead with a short, turned-up nose and monkey ears he would hopefully grow into. The hospital gown fit him awkwardly, riding up tightly against his neck; Boldt glanced toward the door, then to the large viewing window, and found himself alone with the boy. He reached out and tugged the white seam to a moonlike crescent at the boy's collarbone. Better now. Despite the child's beauty, he did not sleep peacefully. His was a tormented unconsciousness. This room was too bright, too clinical for a child: more an operating theater with a bed in it. Too many machines, too much tile and stainless steel — a place to die rather than to recover. No window to the outside, nothing human about it whatsoever. It

24

had been created to be sterile, and had greatly succeeded.

"Hold on," Boldt whispered encouragingly, willing him stronger, unable to fight off the thought that this might be his own son just as easily. That this condition had been *inflicted* on him by a complete stranger so repulsed Boldt that he, too, felt briefly nauseated and sought a chair where there was none to be found.

Miles. His two-year-old. All the clichés held true: The sun rose and set on the boy; the light of his life. And what if? What then? How does a parent stand idly by at a hospital bedside and watch a child shrink from this earth? Who deserves that? A sickening energy invaded him. He shuddered and pulled at the gauze mask that suffocated him.

There was no consideration of ducking this one, *black hole* or not. It qualified as "crimes against persons," and as such, was to be handled by Homicide. It was his; he owned it. He *wanted* this case now — eager, like a boxer climbing into the ring.

Pressed into the wall, concentrating on the boy — *the victim* — a greenish haze clouded the room. Boldt had heard all the stories of cops who could place themselves into the head of the killer. Not him: He was no mind reader, but an observer. An evidence hound. His strength was not so much intuition as an uncanny ability to listen to the *victim*. Empathy. In this

25

regard, he had what the others did not.

But for the moment he was stumped. The victim typically brought along a crime scene, a foundation of physical evidence from which Boldt built a case. Slater Lowry offered him nothing. Or did he? the detective wondered, stepping closer to the bed again. True, the crime scene was now well separated from the victim. But there was, in fact, an intended weapon: this bacteria or virus. Boldt called down to the basement of this same building and after a long hold connected with Dr. Ronald Dixon — "Dixie" — pathologist and chief medical examiner for all of King County. A man recruited by San Francisco, Los Angeles, New York at twice the salary, twice the vacation; a man who stayed at half the salary and half the vacation and ten times the friends. Boldt asked Dixie to join him, and without any questions Dixie agreed. There was, quite possibly, a crime scene somewhere. Somehow the food eaten by Slater Lowry had been contaminated, intentional or not.

Waiting, Boldt fell victim to his own active imagination. He pictured a man's hands injecting a piece of fruit with a syringe; he saw a fast-food chef worker squeezing several drops of fluid onto a roll. He saw a cannery, a thousand cans an hour whirling down roller chutes and a single square inch of a stainless steel cutter somewhere in the maze holding a green fuzzy mold that the swing-shift cleaners had failed to notice.

It was this last thought that caught him. What if Adler Foods *was* responsible? What if these faxes were merely a ruse to cover up a massive blunder, a contaminated product — *their own product?* What if Daphne had been used — manipulated. What if she were the real victim?

Suspicion. He lived with it, always casting as wide a net as possible, encompassing every possibility, distasteful or not. He worked systematically, methodically following up each thought, each suspicion. He processed, considered, weighed, tested, and then compared with whatever evidence was available.

"It's a strain of cholera." It was Dixie's voice. He was reading the boy's chart. A youthful face for a fifty-year-old. Somewhat oriental eyes. Dixie was a big man like Boldt. Thinning brown hair juxtaposed by bushy eyebrows. He wore a gold wedding ring and a black rubber watch. Wide shoulders that hunched forward from years of leaning over a stainless steel slab.

"I've gotten a couple of calls about this," he informed Boldt. They had worked maybe two hundred crime scenes together. "The girl, Lori Chin, is much improved. She's going to pull through."

"Who's on this?"

"State Health investigates infectious diseases. CDC, if it's a real bastard."

"It's a real bastard," Boldt said, staring at the boy. "It's unofficial."

"No, it's cholera. Cholera is quite official."

"How did he get it?" Boldt asked.

Dixie referenced the boy's chart. "They have names, you know? Numbers really: the strains. They can be followed that way — tracked." Boldt felt his eye twitch. Dixie continued: "It's a particularly virulent strain, this one, whatever it is. Normally, cholera responds to rehydration. Antibiotics can speed the recovery but this strain is resistant to the usual antibiotics. Theoretically," he said, sounding suddenly detached, "antibiotics are not necessary for recovery. This boy is dying from shock, Lou. His dehydration progressed too far, and when rehydrated he showed a temporary recovery and then went into severe shock that has resulted in organ failure. Acute tubular necrosis of the kidneys, which will result in renal failure and fluid overload. And something called ARDS — adult respiratory distress syndrome, which can occur in children — also the result of rehydration shock. ARDS causes pulmonary failure."

"He's going to pull through," Boldt stated emphatically.

Dixie shifted uneasily, returning the chart to a plastic file holder on the wall. "No," Dixie corrected. "He's not going to pull out of this, Lou."

Boldt heard the words, but would not allow them to register. His eyes flashed darkly at his friend. "How'd he *get* it?" Boldt repeated, teeth clenched.

"Listen, there are bacterial outbreaks like this

28

all the time. Maybe not cholera, but plenty just the same. You don't hear about most of them, only the sensational ones. Typically, it doesn't take State Health very long to identify the source: a restaurant, a fish stand. It goes down pretty quickly. But this one's a bastard. An uncommon strain of an uncommon bacteria. They're unlikely to track down the source before IDing the strain."

"What if I knew the source?" Boldt asked. "What if I think I knew the source?" Boldt modified.

Dixie bore down on him intensely. "Then we've got to move on this, Lou."

"I'll need some techs. I'll need a cover — something to fool the neighbors."

"I can help with that." Dixie pointed urgently to the door. He said, "After you."

Boldt glanced back at Slater Lowry. The nausea had grown into a knot.

THREE

Less than ninety minutes later, at 11:30 A.M., a RID-ALL Pest Control van turned left past a pair of green recycling bins into the driveway of 1821 Cascadia. Dixie had arranged it; State Health used the van for low-profile inquiries exactly like this.

Boldt parked his Chevy on the street. He wore a RID-ALL windbreaker and carried a brushed aluminum clipboard clasped in his big fist. The neighbors were certain to have heard of Slater Lowry's illness. This small effort to disguise police involvement — an involvement that remained unofficial and went strictly against the blackmailer's demands — seemed well worth the short delay it had caused. Inside the van four State Health field technicians, outfitted in what amounted to environmental space suits, awaited a go-ahead from Boldt.

He introduced himself to a strikingly handsome woman and displayed his police identification. Pointing to the logo silk-screened onto the jacket he explained, "Just a precaution against curious neighbors."

"A precaution against what?" she asked, immediately suspicious.

"If you have a minute?"

She apologized and showed him inside.

She gave her name as Betty, closing the door behind him. Germanic ancestry, in her late thirties, she had boyish blond hair, bright blue eyes, and wore fashion jeans and a T-shirt bearing Van Gogh's *Irises*. She had small, high breasts, square shoulders, and a straight spine. A brave intensity flashed in her eyes. She wasn't one to be pushed around, he noted. She showed him into a baby boomer's living room: hardwood floor, cream canvas couches, a brick fireplace, surround-sound speakers.

She offered him tea and he accepted. He wanted her comfortable. He wanted her calm.

A few minutes later she returned with the tea and explained, "A man from the State Health Department called me late yesterday. He asked a lot of questions. Which restaurants we frequented, markets. That sort of thing. I can understand State Health. But what's the interest of the police?"

"The van in the drive," he said, "it's State Health."

"But *you* are not," she fired back. She looked up as she poured. "You visited Slater this morning." He nodded. "I keep track. I don't want the press bothering him."

"I have a two-year-old," he said, though it sounded stupid once he heard it.

"Why?" she asked sternly. "Why the visit? What are you doing here?"

"It's unofficial, my interest —" he explained. This wasn't easy for him. He wanted to break it to her gently, but she was all business. Her boy was critical. A cop was sitting on her couch. How would Liz have reacted? Her jaw muscles tightened and the teapot danced slightly under her direction. He was relieved to see this. The exterior was hard, but the inside was human.

"What department are you with, Sergeant?"

There it was, he thought. She'd gone and done it. He could dodge it — answer a question with a question — he knew the tricks. *Most* of them. But he owed her.

"Homicide." It came out more like a confession.

She blinked furiously, placed the tea down, and excused herself. After several excruciating minutes she returned with reddened eyes. "Okay, what's going on?" she asked heatedly. Angry. Her eyes a hard blue ice.

"We don't know."

"Bullshit! He's *my* boy. You tell me, damn it! You tell me everything." She hesitated. "Homicide?" she asked.

"We investigate all *crimes against persons*. That may — only *may* — be what we have here."

She crossed her arms tightly. "Meaning?"

"We can't confirm any of this."

"Any of *what?*" she fumed.

He explained it in general terms: A company had received threats; those threats included a reference to Slater's illness; there may or may not be a connection; State Health field technicians were on call in the van outside hoping for her permission to look for any such connection.

"It's entirely up to you, but I'll tell you honestly: We need your cooperation and we need your candor. We don't want anyone else joining Slater in the hospital."

"May I call my husband?"

"You may call your husband. You may throw me out." She rose and headed toward the kitchen door. He hurried, "*Or* you can give me a go-ahead."

It stopped her. She looked exhausted all of a sudden. "You don't want me to call him."

"I want to control this, to keep it controlled. If he's upset, if he has to leave the office, he'll say something. You see? That's out of my control. That worries me."

"What's his name?" she asked. "Your boy?" She moved back toward the couch. She was distant. Dazed.

"Miles," he answered. "I love jazz. My wife and I like jazz."

"Yes," she said. "They're wonderful, aren't they? Children." She looked up and they met eyes. Hers were pooled. "It's a beautiful name: Miles."

The search was its own kind of terror. The van disgorged the four technicians — two women and two men — wearing green jumpsuits, Plexiglas goggles, and elbow-length orange rubber gloves with a space-age silver material covering the palms and fingers to protect against sharpies. They wore high rubber boots. Paper filters covered their mouths. Technomonsters.

Lou Boldt and Betty Lowry looked on as these aliens methodically searched and stripped the kitchen from the deep freeze to the dustpan. The contents of every food cabinet, the pantry, and the home's two refrigerators were removed, examined, sorted, inventoried, or returned. The occasional item was confiscated to a thick, glassine bag that was then sealed, labeled, and placed inside a bright red plastic bag that read *Contaminated Waste* in a winding chain of bold, black lettering. The crew's leader kept a careful inventory. At a future date the great state of Washington would replace or return these items. What Betty Lowry was to do in the interim was not discussed. A narrow bottle of horseradish. A can of chocolate syrup. Two yogurts long past their sale date.

Every toilet bowl in the house was wiped down with paper tissues bearing stenciled numbers. Each was bagged separately.

Betty Lowry cradled herself in tightly crossed arms as she watched the desecration of her home. The crew worked silently and efficiently, the effect disarming. Boldt experienced her sense of violation and wondered which side he was on. The technicians spoke to each other using a clipped, highly specialized verbiage that further isolated them.

The last kitchen item to be bagged and labeled was the electric can opener. As they moved outside to work the trash, they left behind a kitchen stripped of its character. The teapot was gone from the stove. The entire disposal unit had been removed from the sink, along with a part of the faucet nozzle, leaving the immediate need of a plumber — something not discussed. The salt and pepper shakers were gone. The coffee grinder had been labeled and bagged — removed — as if Slater Lowry had been drinking a cup of home brew on the day he took ill. It suddenly looked like a real estate model home. A distraught but brave Betty Lowry glared up at Boldt, blaming him. He offered a look of concern, but made no apology.

She stood away from him as they listened uncomfortably to the crew's rummaging through the trash like a bunch of rats. At one point she mumbled, "It was picked up a couple days ago. They won't find anything." Boldt nodded, but he didn't stop them. They had been cued to pay particular attention for any Adler Foods products. So far, not one had been found.

Forty-five minutes after it had arrived, the van drove away, having cut a swath through Betty Lowry's home and her life, taking off like a thief with oversize red bags of discarded garbage, and leaving her with only a multipage yellow receipt bearing some scribbles and the familiarity of her own signature.

The last room to be searched was Slater's bedroom. Boldt and Betty Lowry watched the van depart from this window. There were sports posters and a well-traveled basketball, a Macintosh computer and a *Webster's* dictionary. In the closet was a shoe box filled with army men and another filled with trading cards. Three pairs of sneakers and a pair of soccer shoes. A model of the Space Shuttle, incomplete.

She picked up the model and held it at eye level.

"He'll finish that one of these days," Boldt encouraged.

"Are you *finished?*" she asked angrily.

Boldt detested these acts of violation. He resented discovery of a victim's closely guarded secrets, the intensely private side of a person's life that often surfaced at death: the drugs, pornography, handcuffs, hidden bottles, home videotapes, and inappropriate phone numbers. His detectives on the fifth floor got a lot of mileage out of such things, finding needed humor wherever possible. Uncomfortable miles for Lou Boldt. A victim surrendered all rights, knowingly or unknowingly, but it didn't make it any easier. If *he* died suddenly, he didn't want some dog-tired detective discovering his manuscript and parading it about. He knew damn well that the fifth floor would be tossing jokes around about "Johann Sebastian Boldt." They would be humming mockingly. He cringed.

When she opened the front door, anxious to be rid of him, Boldt spotted the city's recycle truck blocking his car. For a moment it felt to him like just another delay, another hurry-up-and-wait inconvenience. A cop's life. At the last possible second he saw beyond all that.

He hollered at the workman, interrupting him before he dumped the plastic barrel. Boldt hurried out to the street and plunged his face into the first of the three large containers. He dug his way through the crushed aluminum cans. "Okay," he said, giving this over to the worker and returning to curbside, where a confused and bewildered Betty Lowry joined him.

"In here?" she asked, joining Boldt in his search, though unaware of what he might be looking for.

Boldt noisily stirred the discarded jars with his pen; they clanged like dull bells. The worker hovered behind him and complained, "I can't hang here all day."

"Leave it," Boldt ordered, waving the man off and adding at the last moment: "She lost her engagement ring."

"Good luck," the man called back.

Two of the jars near the bottom wore labels containing the Adler Foods logo and the script *Redi Spaghetti*. Boldt, beside himself with excitement, intentionally slowed down, increasingly precise and careful. This was where a cop made mistakes — oddly, enthusiasm was an enemy. The third bin contained the Lowrys' discarded cans. He dug down. Dog food. Clam chowder. Tuna fish. Green chilies. He hooked a can well within the bin, and carried it aloft on the end of his pen like a New Year's noisemaker. He jerked his wrist and it spun. The label came off, like a colorful flag. That same logo: Adler Foods. Mom's Chicken Soup. "Ah!" he allowed in a moment of triumph. "Soup," Boldt said.

"It was cold over the weekend, remember?" she reminded in a nervously apologetic tone. "Slater *loves* all the 'Mom's' soups," she added, sounding like an ad.

The can stopped spinning. Boldt felt hot all of a sudden. He asked her hoarsely, "Where did you buy the soup? Do you shop a certain grocery? One in particular?"

"Foodland," she replied, without hesitation. It was the immediacy of her answer, her certainty, that pleased and convinced Boldt most of all.

"Foodland," he repeated. It was a regional chain. "Which one?"

"Broadway."

"You're sure?" It was the cop in him that asked that; it just spilled out.

"Of course."

"When?"

"When?" she asked.

"The soup," he emphasized.

"Oh, God, I don't know. This week? Last week? I'm in that store five days a week. Is that bad?" she asked, catching his expression.

"Do you save receipts? Pay by check?"

She slumped, "No to both."

Boldt nodded. "It's okay. It's okay."

Evidence! That was his only real thought. Evidence! The fuel that drove the engine of any investigation.

He kept evidence bags in the trunk of his car. He captured the cans and bottles into separate bags. Trophies. He told her the crew would be back for the bins, and reminded her one last time about the need for confidentiality.

She nodded and stuck her hand out for him to shake.

Hers was ice-cold.

He called ahead to the lab on the way downtown. But first, and much more important, he would have to convince the lieutenant.

FOUR

Boldt dropped the evidence at the police lab on the second floor of the Public Safety Building with specific instructions that the lab techs follow procedure concerning the handling of infectious diseases. The anticipated difficulty arose when Bernie Lofgrin asked him for the case number. No case number, no lab work.

"What if I recorded my Costa for you?"

"You already owe me Scott Hamilton's *Radio City*." Lofgrin wore thick glasses that enlarged his eyes. He was balding.

"Both of them, then. Plus Hashim's *Guys and Dolls*."

Lofgrin grinned. "We'll go ahead and start the workup without the number, but if you want the results —"

"I'll be down with the number within the hour."

"Sure you will," Lofgrin replied sarcastically.

"What's up?" Boldt asked his friend.

"Shoswitz is on a tear. Rankin is all over him about the clearance rate."

"That's *my* clearance rate," Boldt said knowingly. "Or lack of it."

"That's what I'm telling you."

40

Boldt thanked him for the warning and hurried upstairs.

Lieutenant Phil Shoswitz oversaw three squad sergeants, of whom Boldt was the most senior, the most experienced and, until recently, had the highest clearance rate. Boldt had five detectives under him; the other two squad leaders had four each. Shoswitz reported to Captain Carl Rankin, a political captain and a real asshole most of the time. This kept the lieutenant ever vigilant. His crew had homicides to work. They tracked them in "the Book," a cardboard-bound, thumb-worn ledger that sat at its own table outside the coffee room with a pen Scotch-taped to a worn string at its side. When you were assigned a case, it went into the Book under your name. When the case went "down" — when it was cleared — it received a check in the right-hand column. The sergeant's job was to keep those check marks coming. The lieutenant's job was to ride the sergeants. Boldt's squad had turned in an extremely respectable 72 last year: Seventy-two percent of all homicides and crimes against persons investigated by their squad had cleared. A clearance was defined as any investigation ending in an arrest, a warrant for arrest, or compelling evidence against a particular suspect whose whereabouts remained unknown. The clearance rate had nothing to do with how many cases went to trial or how many of those resulted in convictions or sentences, or how many of those sentences actually resulted in time spent in a correctional facility. It was merely a yardstick of how well a sergeant and his squad conducted their investigations. It was also the figure used for crime statistics, and therefore a figure the public eventually took note of. The last six months had not served Boldt well. There had been a double homicide down by the docks — three months now and still unsolved. A *black hole*. There was an apparent swan dive off the Fremont Bridge, a paraplegic who no way in hell threw herself to her death. A *black hole*. There was a two-week-old torture/homicide that wasn't going anywhere. Another two hit-and-runs, both in the same neighborhood. A drive-by shooting, drug-related. All unsolved: *black holes*. Boldt's squad had drawn the tough investigations — sometimes it worked out that way. You answered the phone, you took a call; you took whatever case was there. You signed into the Book. With his squad's clearance rate in the low 50s, there was hell to pay for Boldt. They needed a couple of domestics, a suicide or two — some "slam dunks" — and they might possibly pull that number up into the low 60s by Christmas.

Lately, the other squads seemed to have the luck. David Pasquini's squad was batting an unbelievable mid-80s, and this with a couple of knucklehead detectives on his squad. Pasquini was strutting around like a peacock these days.

Boldt, on the other hand, was spending a lot of time out of the office.

Bringing an absolute surefire *black hole* to the lieutenant at a time like this was asking for it. But Boldt needed that case number. Shoswitz was having a tough ride with a bad case of hemorrhoids that everyone on the fifth floor knew about.

"You have that fucking look in your eye," Shoswitz said. His office was decorated in baseball memorabilia and cheap trophies. He had big brown eyes, a narrow face, and the anxious movements of a used-car salesman. His shirt collar was a half size too big.

"I've got a live one. I need a case number for the second floor."

"Evidence? Don't tell me someone in your squad actually came up with some evidence!" He moved around the room judiciously.

Boldt saw Wednesday's paper on a chair. He opened it to page 7 and spread it on Shoswitz's desk, tapping the article. Shoswitz read.

"Adler Foods has received some convincing threats. Part of the demands include our staying out of it," Boldt observed.

"Adler Foods is huge," Shoswitz said, the concern very real in his voice.

"There's the very real possibility that these illnesses are our criminal's way of making himself be taken seriously."

"So we keep it out of the Book," Shoswitz observed.

43

"I'd like to be detailed," Boldt said, requesting he be assigned solely to this one investigation and his other responsibilities reassigned.

"I can justify that." Shoswitz was not going to fight him, was not going to nag him about clearance rates or internal politics. He was, in effect, throwing himself to the lions, and doing so without complaint or comment.

"You'll want LaMoia and Gaynes, so I'll give the squad over to Danielson. That should starch some shorts." Danielson was a newcomer to Boldt's Homicide squad, and not particularly well liked, though he had earned the support and respect of his sergeant and lieutenant.

"How long can we sit on it?" Boldt asked.

"A day or two. Rankin will have to be told eventually, and by then, you'll have to have something more than this," he said, pointing at the newspaper.

"This is one time I'd really like to be wrong," Boldt said honestly.

A patrolman knocked on Shoswitz's door and opened it, informing Boldt that the lab had just called up for him.

The lieutenant and sergeant met eyes, and the lieutenant said plaintively, "Tell Bernie it's not going in the Book. He has a problem with that, he can call me."

The lab smelled medicinal, with a hint of cordite and the bitter taste of shorting electricity.

Lofgrin's glasses gave him eyes that looked

like boiled eggs sliced in half. He had an oily face and wild hair — what was left of it.

"I need to know if any of the jars or cans had been tampered with," Boldt said, following at a brisk pace across the lab.

"The jars are out," Lofgrin declared, explaining, "we would need the *lids* to detect tampering. Probably would miss it even then. The cans," he said, pointing ahead, "are a different story."

"Can you test the jars for cholera?"

"Can, and will. But it won't be today. And honestly, we're unlikely to get much of anything. The bacteria will not survive in a dry jar. Even in the soup, it has a shelf life of only a few days at the outside. But obviously, we'll still try. An early jump won't help with these."

"When?"

"Eight to ten working days. Five days at the earliest; two weeks at the outside."

Weeks? Boldt wondered. He grabbed Lofgrin by the arm, pulled him aside, and spoke in a whisper. "It's not going in the Book, Bernie. It's one of *those*. I don't have weeks."

Lofgrin searched Boldt's eyes and then fixed his attention on Boldt's tight grip, which loosened immediately. He said, "We may be able to get some help with this. First, let's see what we've *got*, okay?"

"We've got two down that we know of. Alive, but not well."

"Understood."

They each took a seat on a stool in front of the lab counter where Boldt's prized evidence — two soup cans and a spaghetti jar — awaited them. A loose-leaf reference manual lay open alongside. "The labels match. No forgery or nothing; they're the real thing. Dimensions, too," he added, tapping the reference book. "Got the specs on everything from Milky Ways to Lean Cuisine in here. Adler uses the same size can for all his soups."

"You dusted them," Boldt said, noticing the white smudges on the outside of the cans.

"Dusted one, but I'll fume the others," Lofgrin said, referring to SuperGlu fumes that had been used for the last decade to develop latent prints on surfaces that offered difficult imaging. "Nothing of interest," he added. "Smudges. Let's check 'em for continuity," Lofgrin delivered in his most professorial tone.

His initial inspection of the cans' surfaces was accomplished with a magnifying glass. "Seems archaic," Lofgrin said, "I know." He used the glass carefully and methodically, rotating the can slowly beneath a strong light. When he placed the glass down and clipped a special set of magnifiers to his glasses, Boldt asked him, "Got something?"

"Hmm," Lofgrin answered, pushing his face to the can. "May be." Carrying the can, he led Boldt to an elaborate instrument that turned out to be a microscope. He spent several minutes setting it up. Then, spinning the can slowly, he raised the piggybacked pair of glasses and pressed his greasy face to the black rubber viewfinder. Boldt instinctively stepped closer. Lofgrin said to the machine, "Hello there!"

"Bernie?"

He said softly, "There's a solder plug in the seam." He reached up and spun a dial without taking his eyes away. "It's small. Couple millimeters is all. Carefully done. The color is off. FDA outlawed the use of lead in seams some time ago. They're all a ferrous-based alloy now. This plug shows up despite the attempts to sand it smooth and blend it into the seam."

Lofgrin looked up.

"It would have been beneath — that is hidden by — the label. Drill it, inject whatever your pleasure, plug it, reapply the label, and you've got one hell of a surprise. We detect the lead or the flux in a chromatograph, if I'm right."

"Tampered?" Boldt asked.

He offered Boldt a look. Magnified to twenty times its normal size, Boldt could make out the slightly discolored plug of gray metal surrounded by obvious scratch marks from sanding.

"Hiding his work like that — that's thinking," Lofgrin said.

Boldt did not want to face someone so thought-out.

"Blackmail?" Lofgrin asked.

Boldt nodded. "That's why it's not going in the Book."

"Drilling tin cans and plugging them with

47

solder. You find this Tin Man, I gotta think he's got some kind of background in microbiology or chemistry. Might be a jeweler. Might be in electronics." It was customary to invent nicknames. Boldt's stomach turned with the image of a person hunched over a soup can and injecting it with a hypodermic needle.

He poked the can with his pen. "This is what I'm looking for? A soup can that looks like every other soup can?"

"I'm a big help, aren't I? That's what they pay me for."

Boldt did not want to face a grocery store full of food — shelves stacked high with cans, any one of which might be poisoned — but that was where he was now headed: the Foodland supermarket on Broadway.

"Where the hell are you going in such a hurry?" Lofgrin called after him. "We've got paperwork to complete," he objected.

Boldt stopped and turned at the door, far enough away that Bernie Lofgrin could not detain him. "Never keep a crime scene waiting," he said, quoting one of Lofgrin's favorite expressions.

He finally had his crime scene.

FIVE

It was just after three-thirty on that same June
Thursday when Boldt pulled the worn Chevy
into the expanse of asphalt fronting the Foodland
on Broadway. Before going inside, he called
State Health and was told that a search of the
second victim's home had turned up nothing
useful. Lori Chin's mother did remember serving her daughter soup, but not the same brand,
and there were no Adler Foods products found
in the home or in the trash. Boldt remained
focused on the evidence connecting Slater Lowry
to Adler's chicken soup.

He climbed out of the Chevy and locked it
and walked toward the supermarket's automatic
doors, passing abandoned shopping carts that
carried two-color ads in their kiddie baskets
announcing this week's specials. Eggplant was
nearly a dime cheaper per pound than where
Boldt shopped. The sixteen-ounce spaghetti
sauce was a bargain. Boldt did most of the
marketing and all of the laundry; he split the
child care with Liz, who handled finances, some
ironing, housecleaning, and their social calendar.

He suspected this was a crime scene. Daphne
had reached him on the cell phone only minutes

earlier, confirming that the product-run number stamped on the lid of the Adler soup can found in Betty Lowry's recycle crate was indeed a valid lot number and one that would have recently been on sale in the greater Seattle area. The investigation was beginning to take shape in his mind, which was a little bit like the morning rush hour on I-5: too many ideas entering all at once and not enough lanes to accommodate them. But the basic structure seemed clear enough: either the blackmailer was working from within Adler Foods, or from without. Both concepts would have to be pursued — each differently, and both quite delicately.

More important to the moment was that the blackmailer had managed — in person or indirectly — to place a contaminated can of soup on a shelf in this store. That much was fact. Boldt traveled the aisles of this store now, first as the victim: the unknowing patron on an afternoon shop, Betty Lowry, busily hunting down provisions. And then again as the criminal: alert for security cameras, store personnel, lines of sight, and placement of product. It was not so much an investigative technique as it was a result of his dedication to the evidence. He broke out in a sweat as he threw himself fully into this identity, even going so far as to carry a can of Hormel Chili that he intended to place among the shelved cans of Adler Soup just to see how difficult it might be to do so without being seen by human or camera.

He stalked the aisles, aware of his own rapid breathing, the sound of his synthetic soles on the vinyl flooring, the slight chill from the store's vigorous air-conditioning that conflicted with his own perspiration. He was aware of each and every person, immediately visible or not. Patrons. Employees. Checkers. He passed the morning cereals, where dozens of faces stared out at him: sports legends, cartoon characters, the All-American Mom, dinosaurs, astronauts. He, the center of attention, the focus of their combined sales efforts. "Take me." "Buy this one!" "Twenty-five percent *more!*" Loud, despite the insipid Muzak.

The security cameras appeared tricky if not impossible to avoid. There was a multicamera device over aisle 5 with three lenses that rotated and then stopped every ten seconds like an inverted gun turret. Each lens slightly larger than the last, and only one was recording at any one time, made apparent by a red light beneath the lens. The three combined to afford a manager or security personnel everything from a wide-angle to a close-up on the various aisles. Two more such turrets oversaw the butcher counter, meat display, the wines, and wall coolers, respectively. These units had clearly been installed with an eye toward the most expensive items, which suggested to Boldt that the soup aisle might possibly have *less* security. Boldt timed each of these other two camera turrets. They were also on fixed rotations, ten seconds

51

apart, but were not synchronized in their start-and-stop times: difficult, but not impossible, for a fast hand to beat. The trick was to find that moment in the pattern when view of the soup aisle, number 4, would be lost briefly to a blind spot. After eight minutes of wandering the store — his attention split among all three, like a juggler — Boldt identified just such a moment. Eight minutes later the blind spot repeated. Clockwork. Predictable. Fallible. Enough time to plant a tainted can of soup.

Foodland made sense as a crime scene.

Large mirrors were mounted high on three of the four walls, with the fourth given to glass overlooking the parking lot and admitting light. Boldt assumed the business office could be found behind one of these mirrors, and, if so, then the blackmailer additionally threw himself open to being spotted as a shoplifter.

The concept of a shoplifter made Boldt realize that the blackmailer would not be spotted as such. Would a customer returning an item to a shelf attract any attention? Customers changed their minds constantly. Shelves were cluttered with misplaced items. It was a regular part of the grocery business — straightening and re-stocking shelves. He sagged: Slipping an item *onto* a shelf was unlikely to create any suspicion.

Boldt rounded the corner, taking in the registers and the glaring copies of the tabloids to his right: BAT HAS FACE OF MAN — STUNNED SCIENTISTS SAY, "SMART AS A WHIP!" He checked his watch: one minute to go until the blind spot. He glanced up at the mirrors, wondering if anyone had a clear look at the soups. Wondering once again if anyone would even take notice of a product being returned.

Thirty seconds.

He turned down aisle 4, the can of chili in hand. Soup everywhere. The Adler Soup was up ahead to his right. Five seconds. One quick glance over his shoulder. A single shopper, but she was facing away; she would, in fact, screen any sight of him from the checkers and bag boys at the registers. Regimented rows of Campbell's Soup cans, lined up for Andy Warhol. Late afternoon, there were some cans missing from nearly every variety, which made Boldt realize that time of day was important to the blackmailer. Adler Soup, a local product and an all-organic line, was a popular seller, and there were more cans missing from these shelves than any other brand. Time! Boldt's heart pumped hard — for these brief few seconds he was the Tin Man, and he found it unsettling. He slipped his can of Hormel Chili into place alongside Mom's Chicken Soup. He walked on, blood pounding loudly in his ears, heat prickling his skin. He marched through a sea of yellow-clad enchiladas wearing Mexican sombreros that blurred past him like the sharpened points of a picket fence.

He had done it.

He had poisoned a person. A stranger. No

connection to be made.

No one the wiser.

No witnesses.

Lee Hyundai — "like the car," he said — was the supermarket's day manager, a man in his midthirties but already balding. He squinted through a pair of wire-rimmed glasses, displaying a nervous energy that might not have been his natural temperament. Cops made innocent people nervous and guilty ones cautious. It often interfered with Boldt's work. It did now.

On the wall of Boldt's office cubicle hung a needlepoint that Liz had given him for Christmas in their second year of marriage, when hand-made gifts were all they could afford. In blue lettering on a white background it read: *There is no such thing as The Perfect Crime.* There were those who could and did take issue with such a statement — plenty of crimes went unsolved. The Book was full of *black holes* that never had, and never would, clear. And yet he still clung to this as truth. He relied upon it to see him through, to get him out of bed in the morning. A *black hole* was the product of his own vulnerability, his own failures, not the intractability of his adversary's powers.

There is no such thing as The Perfect Crime, thought Boldt.

Hyundai educated him about the process of food distribution, from the moment a shipment arrived in the store to the closing of the automatic doors. Soup arrived from a wholesale distributor in sealed cardboard boxes. Case lots — no partial cases. Hyundai made it a policy not to accept opened or damaged cases because it usually meant a dented can or two, and he couldn't sell dented cans. "People are weird about even the slightest ding in something. I'm telling you, if it is not *perfect*, it stays on the shelf. Cereal, soup. I don't care what it is."

"Are the cases stored somewhere — temporarily — in a back room, perhaps?"

"Sure."

"Show me?"

"Sure."

He led Boldt through the store into a loading dock area that served as a staging zone. Meats and produce and dairy went to giant walk-ins, some of which were built directly behind the shelved product — beer and soda mostly. A conveyor system and dumbwaiter transported the nonperishables to an enormous basement. Boldt looked around, stunned by the quantity he saw — row after row, stacks of cases of every conceivable product. "I hate carrying this much inventory," Hyundai said. "Cheaper in these quantities, though."

"Some of these cases are open," Boldt pointed out. "Quite a few, in fact."

"Sure. We're constantly restocking."

Boldt would ask for an employee list before he left. Not now, but later, when he would claim it was "routine." The list would be checked against Adler employees past and present and against the Criminal Identification Bureau's computerized database of state felons. Maybe the FBI would get a copy as well. Alone, down here in this basement, placing a tainted can would be effortless. Boldt assumed the employee list would draw a blank — blackmail was rarely so simply solved.

"How bad is your shoplifting?" he asked, steering the man away from any thought of open cases.

"We've hired a new security company. All the latest stuff."

If the blackmailer worked for a security company, he would know the store's surveillance weaknesses better than anyone.

Where is he, right now? Boldt wondered.

He questioned Hyundai about his soup distributor, wondering privately how hard it could be to open a case, substitute a can, and reglue it. That kind of deceit was certain to go unnoticed. He was told it was the same wholesale distributor he had worked with for years, but that the distributor had switched truckers a couple of months ago. Boldt scribbled notes, his thoughts and suspicions branching continually. He tried to keep each thought separate, to give each full consideration, and yet never to lose that thread that might lead to another, more promising possibility. These mental gymnastics continued, as did his questions. He felt exhausted and must have looked it. Hyundai interrupted, offering an espresso. *Espresso in the grocery store!* Boldt thought. He said no, he didn't drink the stuff.

"Tears a hole in my stomach."

"Too bad," Hyundai said.

"It's simpler," Boldt replied.

Hyundai steered them toward the deli and ordered himself "a tall double with shavings." There ought to be a handbook, Boldt was thinking. The man signed the receipt and handed it back to the attendant.

"If I knew the nature of your investigation, perhaps I'd be able to help more," Hyundai suggested.

Boldt flashed a false smile that said, Answer the questions, don't ask them. Hyundai received the message, returning to a description of the surveillance system.

"The name of the new company?" Boldt asked.

"Shop-Alert."

Boldt flipped another page in his notebook.

There was always a time in any investigation when he sensed the enormity of the case. The limitless possibilities. It was the first, brief glimpse of the *black hole* opening up to swallow him.

Hyundai knew his facts and figures: average number of customers, daily and weekly; average purchase amount: $42.50; the demographics of his customers; figures skewed by this particular neighborhood, for it leaned toward the college crowd. *Scribble, scribble,* Boldt caught it all, useful or not. He could, and would, throw most of it out later, but not until he had taken the time to review it.

The veins of the leaf were many: Each required one or more detectives to chase down leads. Boldt would be awake a good part of the night writing it up. Up early to start it over. Somewhere in this city, as Boldt stood questioning Hyundai, the Tin Man could be twisting his drill into the seam of yet another can of soup. Somewhere, a Slater Lowry was dying to eat it.

Confused, Boldt asked the man about the numbers printed on the lid of the can and whether or not anyone in Hyundai's employ would catch it if a can suddenly showed up with a different number. He was told they would not. As long as the UPC bar code remained the same — and it would from one product run to the next — there would be nothing to alert them. "Even a label change would be likely to carry the same UPC code," Hyundai concluded.

A bell rang in Boldt's head, a way to ensure that no more cans of tainted chicken soup reached the public. Tossed out insignificantly by Hyundai, it went into Boldt's notebook in thick bold letters: *A Label Change.*

He was still writing this down when the bell tolled again, causing a surge of excitement in his chest.

"What's that? Repeat that," Boldt stuttered.

Hyundai stiffened; he didn't appreciate repeating himself. "I was talking about the automated checking system," he said. "The registers itemize every sale. I can tell you which brands sell on which days. Mondays, for instance, are big on dairy products; Wednesdays, we do a lot of cigarettes — don't ask me why; and Fridays we can't keep beer or fish in the store."

"You said 'each sale,' " Boldt reminded. "Let me get this straight: I come in here and buy a shopping cart full of groceries and you track *every item?*"

"Sure."

"I come back three days later and you can tell me what I bought?" He was thinking: *right down to a can of soup!*

"Sure. No problem. Computers. Register tapes. We got it."

"And if I paid by check, would you know it?"

"Sure. Cash. Check. Credit card. We keep records of all forms of payment. Sure."

Boldt needed to know when Betty Lowry had purchased her can of Mom's Chicken Soup. This would provide him a way to work backward with the distributor, and even possibly the security company's surveillance videos. Timing was everything. Tracking bank checks and payment by credit card would also give him a chance to identify other customers who might have witnessed the blackmailer in the act. This, he realized, was the trail to follow. *A crime scene.*

Boldt received a page and placed a call downtown. Dixie had come through: State Health had identified the particular strain of cholera and had traced it to the Infectious Diseases lab at King County Hospital. Excited by this news, Boldt reached out and shook the man's hand vigorously, anxious to be going.

A stunned Lee Hyundai was left standing there with a drained espresso in hand, shouting after the detective, "What did I say? What did I say?"

SIX

Dr. Brian Mann had an energetic handshake, eyes glassy with exhaustion, brown curly hair, and a disheveled look to which Boldt could relate. He led the detective through the Infectious Diseases lab at King County Hospital and into a small corner office littered with reading material. A computer terminal hummed in the far corner. Boldt was overly sensitive to such noise. There was also a phone, its receiver discolored from activity.

"Neither of us has much time, Sergeant, so I'll get right to it. You and everybody else would like to know where this strain of cholera originated, and I can answer that now." Mann had pulled a twenty-hour shift, and he looked it. He pointed into his lab. "We're the only ones in the city — in the state, for that matter — with that strain, cholera-395."

This was what Dixon had told Boldt: a single source for the offending bacteria. Another possible crime scene.

"We believe these contaminations were intentional," Boldt said. "You understand the need for confidentiality."

"Exactly what the hell are you saying?"

"Product tampering — food product tampering. It was a can of soup. Chicken soup."

"Protein base," Mann mumbled, nodding. And then to explain himself, "The cholera needs a protein base to survive. Soup would provide that." He rubbed his eyes. "What's this world coming to?"

Boldt was thinking that this man could be the bastard behind it all. His lab. His cholera. Why not? Except that Dixie swore by Mann, and that was good enough for Boldt.

"How many have access to the cholera? To the lab?" he questioned.

"Too many," Mann said. "Coffee?"

"No thanks."

"Anything?"

"Tea would be nice."

"Give me a minute, will you? I pulled some stuff for you to read." He stood. Boldt called out, "No cream. No sugar."

"Be right back."

A lot of what Boldt read was over his head, but some was not. He was distracted, in part by the fact that this was a children's research hospital. In the last forty-eight hours, he had seen precious little of his boy. Liz, too, for that matter. When he was away from Miles for too long, he missed him in a way that until the boy's birth he had never experienced, and would never have expected. It was a chemical longing, like an addict after his fix.

"Make any sense of that?" Mann asked, setting

down Boldt's tea in a Styrofoam cup. Liz would not drink out of Styrofoam cups anymore.

The tea tasted terrible, but Boldt choked it down for the caffeine. "If I'm the person doing this, why do I choose cholera?"

Dr. Mann considered this a long time. When he finally spoke, it was cautiously, a man unfamiliar and uncomfortable with being inside the mind of a stranger. "It depends on what you hope to accomplish. I would guess he considered three choices — a poison, a viral contaminate, a bacterial contaminate. The toxins, the poisons — strychnine, or something like what we saw in the Sudafed product tampering — can and will be immediately detected in the blood of the victim. If you're just looking to kill a few people, then that's the poison of choice, I would think. Most of your other choices, if you're talking *food* products, will give themselves away, either by producing a gas you can smell or a taste that warns you immediately what you're into. Also, *all* of the more common of these would be immediately detected in the state lab. If it was me, I too would choose cholera if available. What's interesting about cholera is that labs around here once tested for it, but many don't any longer. This gets political, I'm afraid; this enters into health care and insurance costs, and believe me, you don't want to get me started. But the point is, this is the exact area where reduced health care costs are felt. The lab has to cut something and they cut right here. We see virtually *no* cholera up here. Dropping that test is justifiable at every level of bureaucracy. Don't tell that to these two kids, mind you."

"You'd miss the cholera. Is that what you're saying?"

"It would take longer to type — which is what happened. If *I* wanted to make a few people real sick, if I wanted to use something that would take awhile to detect, confuse the authorities, then I'd look to something like this strain of cholera."

"A scare technique?" Boldt took out his notebook and pen.

"Could be." Mann tasted his coffee. He grimaced, but drank it. "Is it?"

Boldt did not answer.

"Make this company look bad?" Mann glanced up. Again, Boldt did not answer. "Which company? Or can't you say?"

"Adler Foods," Boldt answered. He wrote the product-run number on a page of his notepad, tore it out, and handed it to Mann. "They're clearing the shelves of this product-run number as we speak. The number will be announced on the news tonight, and in the papers for the next couple of days. At this point the public won't be told exactly *why* there's a recall."

"Why not tell them?"

"The individual has warned against police involvement. And there's also a concern about

64

copycats. It's the biggest risk with product tampering. We want to keep the actual tampering, the connection to these kids, out of the press just as long as possible. A lot more people are at risk if we don't. We *know* that. In a British food-tampering case, after word of the contamination hit the press, police faced fourteen hundred reports of similar tamperings."

Mann winced. "Fourteen *hundred?*"

The two men shared an uncomfortable silence. "You won't hear it from me," Mann said. Boldt looked out the window at the crowded sea of houses. How many cans of contaminated soup might they miss? How many were sitting in a kitchen pantry ready to go off like time bombs?

"I'll need the names of everyone who has access to the lab," Boldt informed him.

"One of *my* people?" Mann asked defensively. "That strain is marked clear as day."

"But a person can't just walk in and take it," Boldt suggested.

"Why not?"

"You're kidding, I hope."

"Not a bit. This is a university lab. Dozens of people pass through every day, many of them complete strangers to one another. Students. Grad students. Researchers. We get visitors from all over the world. Every walk of life. Every look you can imagine. It's a *teaching* hospital. Men, women, young, old, black, white, Asian, Hispanic, African, Middle Eastern, you name it. Every week of the year. Sometimes there are a half-dozen techs working in that lab, sometimes one or even none."

"Just walk in and take it?" Boldt asked, astonished.

"If you know what you're looking for."

"I don't believe it."

"Try it."

"What?"

"Go ahead and try it." Mann pushed back his chair and came to his feet. He eyed Boldt as would a haberdasher. "Not bad. That's the look you need: the run-down professor thing. I'm telling you, just go ahead and try it." The doctor clearly said this as his chance to remove his lab workers from suspicion.

He grabbed his lab coat from a hook on the back of the door and offered it to Boldt, and Boldt put it on. It was a little snug. Mann said, "If you look like you know what you're doing, you're in. Confidence is everything. It's in a half-size refrigerator on the right. If I'm your man, I go in at lunchtime, because the place is deserted at lunch. It's a little late for that — but that's all the better for your test. Straight to the fridge. You're looking for a petri dish." He scrambled and found an empty dish by the computer that was filled with paper clips. "Like this, but containing a tan gelatin with florid spots. You're looking for one marked cholera or *V. cholerae*, INABA strain, and a number.

"Anyone asks you a question, you say you're

66

working the third floor. You're looking for some vibrio cholera. You watch: They'll *hand it* to you if you're polite."

"I gotta see this," Boldt said.

"Out through this lab, down the hall, first door on your right."

By the time Boldt was in the hall, he could once again feel himself as the would-be thief. With each step he felt a little more nervous. There were three people perched on metal stools working at the lab counter. Wearing goggles and plastic gloves, they appeared focused on their work. The place was littered with hundreds of glass flasks, plastic petri dishes, test tubes, and other lab equipment. A mess. He headed directly to the small refrigerator, stooped, and pulled open the door. No one said a word. He caught himself expecting it, but it never happened. The refrigerator shelves were crammed with petri dishes. He picked one up, inspected it, and dropped it as it came apart.

The woman nearest him glanced over at him. An attractive Asian woman in her mid-twenties. She smiled at him and returned to her work. He returned the fallen dish and sorted through the others. Way in the back he found it, marked with a black grease pen: *V. cholerae-395.* He took it, shut the refrigerator door, and walked out.

Just like that.

His heartbeat was back to normal by the

67

time he reached Dr. Mann.

"Well?"

"You're right: If I hadn't done that myself, I never would have believed it." He handed Mann the petri dish.

Mann studied the dish, spinning it in his hand.

"And once he has it?" Boldt asked, removing the uncomfortable lab coat, taking notes again.

"Not much to it. He probably has some microbiology under his belt — early college level. Some agar — a petri dish containing a protein base; some broth — the book would have a recipe; an incubator — but could build something — a light box might work. Doesn't need much, I'm afraid. It's all pretty easy. It looks real complex and the language is fairly complex, but the actual mechanics of growing a culture are relatively simple. It's covered in both high school and college chemistry."

"Anything else I should know?" Boldt tried. "Limited shelf life?"

"Not terribly. Cholera's a pretty good choice. Salmonella would have been obvious to whoever opened the can because of gases — bacterial odor. But cholera? No odor or gases to speak of. And if it *isn't* someone at the university, someone who knows specifically about cholera-395 — and there couldn't be more than a handful who do — then this guy probably didn't know what a powerful punch it packed. Three ninety-five is a resistant strain. Probably didn't know what he was getting. And unless and until you *do* put this in the press, he may not even be aware he may kill people with it."

Boldt felt the wind knocked out of him. "Kill?"

"It's a research strain, 395. It doesn't react to the more common antibiotics. That's why these kids became so ill. It's in the material," he said, indicating Boldt's pile of literature. "Their youth may help them — we're lucky there."

"It's lethal, and it's just sitting in there in a refrigerator?"

"I know. I know. But it's true of much of what's in there: This is Infectious Diseases. We're working to *cure* people here."

"Am I the only one who sees irony in that?"

"The Lowry boy went critical a couple hours ago," Mann informed him.

Again, Boldt couldn't catch his breath. He could picture the boy as clear as day: the sunken eyes, the strange color to his skin. It made him sick to his stomach. He put down the tea.

"Sorry," Mann said.

"I've got a two-year-old," Boldt explained.

"Me, a boy five, a girl three," Mann said, pointing to color photographs by the computer.

"We're on the back side of the curve, I'm afraid, even with the research work on 395. I'd like to tell you that they will be okay, but I can't because it isn't necessarily true."

Boldt said, "The girl is doing better."

Mann said, "We get lucky now and then." He hesitated, "There's something else you should know — your lab people should be aware of this, but in case they are not: *Vibrio cholerae* degrades rather rapidly. At room temperature, it will die on the shelf inside these soup cans. With a high enough inoculum, there should be sufficient organisms to cause disease for the first five to seven days. After that, the organisms will die, which means they may go undetected by your lab. Just so you know."

"You're telling me these are time bombs with a shelf life. We won't be able to prove they were contaminated?"

"Not after the first five to seven days. After that, the bug is dead and your tests will return negative." The doctor added, "The bright side is that after a week on the shelf it won't harm anyone."

Boldt was devastated by this. Providing evidence of the contamination in a court of law might prove difficult if not impossible. He thanked the man for his time and they shook hands.

On his way out, Boldt leaned his head into the lab and looked down at the half-refrigerator, unlocked and available for the killer.

This triggered a thought, and he returned to Mann, who hung up the phone. He said, "Will you lock that refrigerator for me?"

"Just arranging that." He pointed to the phone.

As Boldt passed the lab, a woman's voice called out: "Did you get what you need?" It was the young Asian woman, her eyes stretched open by the clear safety goggles, a wire loop held in her hand and sparking in the flames of a Bunsen burner.

"Yes," he said with a slightly raised voice, loud enough to carry above the whine of a centrifuge.

"Good," she said brightly.

"Not really," Boldt replied. He turned and left, negotiating his way through a labyrinth of hospital corridors so similar in appearance that someone had painted color bars on the floor to direct you — only Boldt didn't know which colors led where. Like this case. He finally reached the main lobby, and then headed off at a run out into the parking lot, out into the unexpected rain, pouring rain, buckets of rain, out without an umbrella or even a newspaper to hold over his head. Sometimes he hated this city.

SEVEN

The meeting with Owen Adler was due to begin promptly at three. For the sake of security and privacy, it was to take place aboard Adler's yacht. Earlier that Friday morning, Boldt had assigned Detective John LaMoia to obtain a list of Mann's students and faculty who had regular access to the Infectious Diseases lab. He also asked for employee lists from Foodland, Shop-Alert Security, and Wagner Wholesale, the distributor that supplied Lee Hyundai's Foodland store. In an attempt to link motive with opportunity, these lists would be cross-checked with that of Adler's employees.

Shilshole Marina was a clutter of masts alive with the clanging slap of nylon line on hollow-core aluminum. Wind whistled across the steel stays. Stinging rain struck the launch's Plexiglas shield and drummed on the blue canvas awning as the craft carried Boldt and Daphne through choppy water to the waiting motor cruiser. It was temporarily moored in the lee of the gray stone boulders that created the breakwater protecting the man-made inlet from the sound. The multidecked, fifty-five-foot cruiser could have made a landing at the dock, but Adler was taking no chances that he or any of his passengers might be seen meeting with the police.

"It looked so nice earlier," she called across the noise of the twin engines. She was not herself. Nervous, perhaps to see Adler professionally and in the company of others.

"Is he crazy?" Boldt shouted.

Her eyebrows danced. She knew whom he meant. She hollered back, "He's *disturbed*." She reached up and took hold of her hair, keeping it from whipping her face. "We want to look for suicides when we get this employee list — a spouse, a relative. And bankruptcy. Those are his immediate demands."

"It's personal?" he asked.

"Love, money, and *revenge*," she said, quoting the three most common reasons humans killed each other. "We may have a possible paranoid schizophrenic on our hands," she warned. "And then again, he may be a cold-blooded psychopath." The wind suddenly felt colder to Boldt.

"I'd like to bring in Dr. Richard Clements. He's BSU." She meant the Behavioral Sciences Unit of the FBI. Boldt knew she had used Clements in past investigations. He had never met the man.

The low charcoal clouds grew oppressively lower. Boldt loosened his collar and chewed down two Maalox.

"You all right?" She crossed unsteadily and

flopped down onto the cushion beside him. Her hair whipped in the wind. "Are you okay?" she asked more intimately, pressed up against him.

"The boy is worse, I hear," he said.

She reached out and laid her hand gently on the lower sleeve of his sport jacket and squeezed his forearm.

The launch engines slowed, and as the launch pulled alongside, a woman crew member tossed a line. Daphne climbed the ladder, followed by Boldt. The launch sped away, cutting into the angry green water, ripping open a crease of white foam.

"Lousy weather," the woman offered. She was in her twenties with an athletic figure, nice legs, and quite crisp green eyes. She wore khaki shorts, white and blue canvas deck shoes, and an aquamarine T-shirt damp on her shoulders.

They descended into a spacious, well-appointed living room. Owen Adler stood to the side of the steep ladder and offered his hand to Daphne to guide her down the steep steps. "Welcome aboard," he said to Boldt.

Adler was a boyish forty-five, with graying hair at the temples, wire-rimmed glasses, French cuffs, and silver cuff links. He stood just under six feet but carried himself much taller. He wore soft brown Italian loafers, linen pants, and a faint pink pinpoint cotton shirt with a starched collar. His handshake was firm, his

74

dark eyes attentive.

Adler and Daphne sat on opposite ends of a small chintz couch. Adler's attorney and chief operating officer, Howard Taplin, took the cushioned chair to Adler's immediate right. Taplin was a wiry man with drawn features, a trimmed mustache, and intense gray eyes. He wore a gray suit and black wing tips and the kind of high, thin socks that required garters. Boldt sat between Taplin and Kenny Fowler. Fowler had once served on the police force in Major Crimes, working the gangland wars. Boldt saw him occasionally at the Big Joke, where Boldt played happy-hour piano. Fowler carried a deliberate intensity in his eyes. He wore his dark hair slicked back and kept himself impeccably groomed. He fancied himself a ladies' man, though the rumors had always been that he chased the cheerleading age. Boldt knew well the man's reputation for an explosive disposition and frank honesty. Fowler shook hands strongly with Boldt and asked him about Liz and Miles. He always remembered to ask. He had a couple of new teeth in front and a tiny scar on his lower lip. Boldt wondered what the other guy looked like: Fowler was the workout type and wore tailored clothes to prove it.

As Adler opened the meeting, the cruiser left the protection of the jetty, entering some rougher water. But as the speed increased, the ride smoothed. The cabin was impressively soundproofed. A male crew member delivered a pitcher of iced tea and extra glasses with sprigs of mint and wedges of lemon. A plate of cookies circulated.

Adler said, "We want to welcome your assistance and expertise, Sergeant. This is a horrible situation, and we will cooperate in whatever way required to resolve this just as quickly as possible. I want to say right up front that we're aware we may have impeded your efforts by waiting to contact you as we did." He glanced at both Daphne and Howard Taplin. "And I should add that we still feel strongly about keeping the involvement of the police as low-profile as possible. With these contaminations, whoever this is has proved he means business, and we would just as soon be *perceived* as adhering to his demands — all of his demands."

"Agreed," Boldt replied. "Where do we stand with the recall?"

"We've issued a full recall for the product run in question. Kenny is continuing to quietly search for a possible employee who might carry a grudge. You two will want to coordinate on that, I'm sure."

"We will *not* give in to terrorism," Taplin interrupted.

Adler did not appreciate the intrusion. "What Tap means," he said addressing Boldt, "is that we would *prefer* to catch this person than enter into negotiations."

"And some of us would *prefer* to keep the

76

police out," Taplin said. "Nothing personal," he added coolly, passing Boldt the most recent fax.

THE CHOICE IS YOURS.
MORE SUFFERING — AND WORSE —
UNLESS YOU OBEY.
DO NOT CLEAR THE SHELVES,
AND NO POLICE OR PRESS OR
HUNDREDS WILL DIE.
BEEN TO PORTLAND LATELY?

"Portland?" Boldt asked, worried.

"We have calls in to all the hospitals," Fowler explained.

Daphne took the fax and reread it, saying partly to herself, partly to the gathering, "He's getting more wordy. That's a good sign. He's opening up." The others listened. Boldt felt cold. She reread it yet again. "No contractions; he's well educated. And he uses the word *obey*, not *cooperate* — that's interesting."

Taplin said, "You see our position?"

"Damned if we do, damned if we don't," Fowler said.

"What do you advise?" Adler asked. "We will cooperate however we can. We would like to place another run of soup back out there — but not if we're risking more poisonings."

"Can you keep the chicken soup off the shelves, but stock them with something else?" Boldt inquired.

"It's our highest-velocity product," Taplin complained.

"My take," Daphne offered, "is that we should accede to the specific demands while taking every precaution possible to prevent this from happening again. What about product re-design?"

Boldt explained, "If the blackmailer is working in one of your production facilities, a label or product redesign might tell us so. If he — or she — has access to the new materials then we know it's inside work." He added, "And it doesn't go against any of the demands."

"Way ahead of you," Taplin crowed. "Six to eight working days to print new labels *if* we already had a new design, which we do not. Two to three weeks for a new design. In terms of container redesign — moving to something tamper-proof — we're looking both domestic and abroad, but best guess is anywhere from two to twenty months to facilitate such an overhaul."

Fowler contributed, "We're aware of the product-tampering cases that have lasted years, Lou, 'kay? But from what I can tell, they seem to *always* involve extortion. These are strange demands we're getting, and with the time limit already exceeded, it somehow doesn't seem too real that this nut house is going to hang in there for all that long. You follow? Whatever he's got cooking — you'll pardon the pun — I don't think we can wait around a couple months to put the soup in jars or something. 'Kay? So I advised to move forward with the new labels but not to hold our breath or nothing."

"What about changing the glue to water-insoluble," Boldt suggested. "This guy is drilling the cans *beneath* the label. If we make it impossible to soak off a label, and yet he is still able to contaminate the cans, we narrow the field of where to look inside your company."

Fowler said, "It would have to be someone stealing labels from, or working on, the line."

"Exactly."

"That's very good!" exclaimed Adler, jotting a note onto a legal pad. "And it's a simple change," he said to Taplin, who nodded.

"As few people as possible should know about the glue change," Boldt encouraged.

"We can arrange this with virtually no one involved," Adler said.

"We might piss him off," Fowler cautioned.

"He's threatened *hundreds* if we challenge him," Taplin reminded.

Boldt considered how much to reveal and then informed them, "The lab tests suggest that there is no direct evidence indicating that the label was either soaked or steamed off the can. There's a high probability that the blackmailer is working with fresh labels — new labels."

"And that means the production line, the loading dock, or the printers," Fowler offered.

"Storage?" Boldt asked.

Taplin answered, "We're a *just-in-time* operation. Printing inventory is kept to a ten-day lead time."

Making a note, Fowler said, "It should be added to the list."

Adler addressed Boldt, "If it's all right with you, Sergeant, I think Kenny should handle all the in-house aspects of this investigation. We operate on a family concept. Police would be noticed, and would be talked about immediately —"

"And given his threats, we certainly don't want that," Daphne agreed.

Fowler said, "We've had some employee-related thefts lately. I can use that as an excuse for asking around."

They all agreed on this: The police would remain involved, but well in the background.

"If we're to meet again," Adler suggested, addressing Boldt and Daphne, "I suggest we arrange it by fax and not telephone, and that we stay with remote locations."

"How soon can you make the glue change?"

"Overnight. A day at the outside," Taplin said, his mood improved.

"Is there anything else that might help us?" Boldt asked. Adler glanced over at Taplin, who glared back at him.

Adler said to Daphne, "Perhaps you could show the sergeant the rest of the yacht. A few minutes is all."

There was an awkward moment of hesitation,

after which the two stood.

She led Boldt forward through a deck dining room to a trio of private quarters and Adler's floating study, equipped with both cellular phone and fax machine.

"What's going on in there?" he asked.

"Owen can smooth over any flap. Give him a few minutes."

"Tell me about Taplin."

"Bright, protective, loyal. Longtime friend of Owen. Runs a lot of the day-to-day. Owen credits him with much of their success, but that says as much about Owen as it does about Howard Taplin. It's Owen's baby; always has been."

He noticed a caller-ID box connected into the fax machine line. The device would display the phone number of any incoming fax. "Fowler," Boldt said, pointing it out.

"It's a good idea, isn't it?"

"If he shares the results with us," Boldt said, adding, "which I somehow doubt. Taplin would clearly rather handle this without us. And as you said: Taplin is the one writing Kenny's paychecks."

"Owen will give you anything you want, Lou."

"Is that the inside track?"

She did not like his comment.

"Time," she declared. She guided him back to the meeting, where the others were waiting. Boldt and Daphne sat down.

Adler said, "We had a scare in the mideighties. Not cholera — salmonella. But it *was* our soup line."

"A *scare?*" Boldt asked.

"Not an intentional contamination — nothing like that. Some bad poultry in our soup. But four people were hospitalized and there were lawsuits."

Taplin added, "Let me clarify. We were *not* held liable. It was not us, but one of our suppliers. It was a state health department matter. I see no reason to make any comparison."

Boldt said, "We'll want any files you've got on this."

Adler said, "Of course." But Taplin stiffened. He opened his mouth to object and Adler interrupted him, saying to Boldt, "*Whatever* you need."

EIGHT

Dressed in a dull green surgical smock and wearing a white paper mask over his mouth and nose, Boldt took up a vigil at Slater Lowry's hospital bedside, his presence approved by both the medical staff and the boy's mother, whose mask was damp with tears below the eyes.

The boy's father had collapsed an hour earlier when Slater's condition had been downgraded from serious to critical, and was presently under sedation in a room down the hall. The woman's green surgical smock was wrinkled from where her husband had clutched it for hours.

Slater Lowry was dying of organ failure.

It seemed impossible to Boldt that with the boy having been admitted to the hospital, with his having been diagnosed and treated, that his condition could degenerate so quickly. Gunshot wounds, knife wounds, strangulations, and burns — Boldt had learned to live with all of these over his twenty-plus years of police service. But he did not accept what was happening to this boy.

He felt hypnotized by the steady drip of the IV, by the peaks and valleys of the green lines crawling across the monitors. Slater's skin was a pasty white, and a light sheen of perspiration made it glisten. His mother dabbed him dry, but it did not last long. Slater Lowry was burning up with fever despite the fluids and antibiotics. Slater Lowry was leaving.

"If we could only trade places," the woman had mumbled to Boldt an hour earlier. He knew that she meant her son and her, though Boldt thought she might have wished that he could switch places with her — that this would be his son, Miles, lying there, and she the visitor. Since that comment not a word had passed between them. The glances they shared needed no explanations. She blamed Boldt for this, without meaning to. And without meaning to, Lou Boldt accepted it.

As the hours passed, as Friday slipped into Saturday, as the doctors and nurses came and went, Boldt imagined this boy a young man, the young man an adult. He envisioned the successes and failures, the joys and heartbreaks that compromised his own life, and he loaned these to Slater Lowry believing that a borrowed dream was better than none at all.

At two in the morning the father returned to the room, dulled and incoherent in his few attempts to share. Boldt rose to leave them, but the woman said, "Stay if you want," and Boldt sat back down. He was not certain what drew him to this boy or this woman or this room, and he knew firsthand the trials of taking a personal interest in the victims — a detective needed a certain degree of distance — but he kept his seat and stayed. For some reason he found it impossible to leave.

At two-forty, several of the electronic monitors sounded alarms at once, and Boldt's pulse quickened as Slater Lowry's faded. A team of nurses and physicians swarmed the boy's bedside. Their work silenced the alarms, and twenty minutes later, with the boy stabilized, the doctor held a private conference with the parents. After that, Boldt remained outside the room, viewing the boy through the glass window that communicated with the nurses' station, where the monitor signals were repeated on small television screens tucked beneath the counter. Inside the room there was only enough space for three chairs, and Boldt's was now occupied by a woman minister who prayed quietly, her chair pulled close alongside the bed, the boy's limp hand clutched between her own, her lips moving in silent prayer. Boldt realized there were to be no more beaches for Slater Lowry, no more late-summer nights, no more smiles or complaints or singing or trading football cards — no more birthdays.

The nurses offered Boldt a seat and offered him coffee. When a third woman reminded him the cafeteria was open twenty-four hours, he turned and snapped, "It's him that needs you, not me!" And there was no time to apologize to her, for the monitor alarms called out for a second time, ringing in Boldt's ears like church bells.

The moment of death, recorded as 3:11 A.M. Saturday, June 30, played out before Boldt in an eerie and hollow silence. The monitors cried out the truth, though Boldt clung to hope. He encouraged the boy to recovery, a spectator rooting from the sidelines. The nurses and doctors once again rushed to revive the boy, but for all their efforts, all the technology, there were no miracles left.

The parents hugged tightly in terror; the minister stepped out of the way and closed her eyes.

In the midst of a silent scream, Betty Lowry glanced over her shoulder and met eyes with Boldt through the window, and though only a fraction of a second, he saw that her pain and hope had given way to the disbelief of acceptance.

The boy's final heartbeat was followed by a series of straight green lines in a race across the screens — chasing the next patient.

The doctor turned and offered apologetic eyes filled with sympathy and compassion.

Boldt imagined this boy huddled over his model of the Space Shuttle, eyes curious and sparked with challenge. He imagined the excited expressions in his own son's eyes, and hoped never to lose him, never to count him among the statistics.

"No more," Boldt whispered aloud, his promise fogging the glass, his right hand gripped in a fist. A promise made from the most sincere, the most private place in his heart.

A promise soon to be broken.

Boldt arrived home sometime after four. His entrance awakened Miles. Liz rolled over in bed and admonished, "You caused it. You handle it." She gathered the sheets around her like a cocoon and her head sank back into the pillow, and he felt a desperate urge to make love with her. To erase the death of that young boy.

For forty-five minutes Miles would have nothing of going back to sleep. He finally did so, clutched in the warm arms of his father, who subsequently fell asleep sitting up on the living room couch. At six-thirty Boldt was once again awakened, this time by his son struggling to be free. Late, he rose quickly from the couch and crashed to the floor when his legs and back failed him. Miles ran into their bedroom. Liz appeared in her underwear and said in a groggy voice, "If you're alive, please move your right hand." She pulled off his shoes, rubbed his feet, and helped him to stand.

He made coffee and toast for her and poured himself a bowl of granola, waiting for his pot of tea to steep. Miles was assisted by his father in smearing part of a banana and some instant oatmeal over most of his face. Liz appeared at twenty to eight wearing jeans and a T-shirt — weekend clothes. Boldt felt tempted to explain his evening to her but didn't know where to start. He was a mass of confusion, fatigue, and frustration. He glanced at the wall clock. Late.

"I miss you," he heard her say sometime during his frantic efforts to change shirts and shave. He had been a lousy father and an even worse husband these past four days, and though he wasn't keeping score, he feared maybe she was.

Back in the kitchen with her, the two of them talked over each other as they hurried through a running list that included shopping that had to be done, oil that needed changing, the plumber that had overcharged for shoddy work, a dental appointment Boldt had missed, and then, dropped as a bombshell, Liz said, "I'm two months late."

"Late?"

"My period. I'm two months late."

"Months?" he asked, stunned.

"That's the usual way it happens."

"Two months late." He made it a statement. Liz wiped her son's chin.

"And?" Boldt asked.

"And what?"

"When are you going to the doctor?"

"I'm going to buy one of those in-home kits first."

"When are you going to do the test?" He had unknowingly stepped closer to her. They stood only inches apart, their voices gentle. He took her by the waist. The world seemed a miraculous place to him. A place where one child lost was so quickly replaced by another.

"When would you like me to?" she asked.

"Will you wait?"

"Of course I will."

"I'll bring Chinese." Her favorite. "And beer," he added.

"Better make it nonalcoholic."

"I can't believe this."

"I'm thirty-eight, love. It's a long road between here and there. It may be nothing, don't forget."

"I love you," he said.

"Those are nice words to hear."

He squeezed her waist. "I miss you, too."

"You don't look very good," she said honestly. She meant that he was old for this. She meant that he belonged behind a desk with regular hours, or maybe she was suggesting that he might have to quit the department — again — if a child came.

"Never felt better," he lied.

"Go on," she said, amused, shoving him gently toward the door.

"Chinese," he reminded her. "Seven o'clock. I'll call."

"Like last night?" She obviously couldn't resist saying this, and he couldn't blame her — but he did.

"I'll call. I promise."

Her eyes apologized to him. And there seemed in this expression of hers an appreciation of him — of their shared feelings, of their mutual efforts to define and maintain some semblance of a life together, and perhaps even for his part in creating the child that might be within her at this very moment.

"Seven," she confirmed.

"And if it's a boy," Boldt added, "I have a name for him."

Following the eight o'clock shift change, when Boldt's skeleton crew, weekend squad replaced Pasquini's, inheriting a gang shooting and an assault-with-intent in a bar-fight-turned-knifing, Boldt was officially detailed to the Tin Man. His duties as squad leader were to be passed to Chris Danielson, his squad's newcomer. Boldt needed LaMoia and Gaynes for his own purposes; Frank Herbert was available to Danielson. Guccianno was on vacation leave for another ten days.

They called Danielson "Hollywood" because of his Vuarnet sunglasses and ostrich boots. He was a handsome black man who carried a chip on his shoulder the size of Rhode Island because he owned the highest individual clearance rate ever recorded in the books. Danielson kept to himself, rarely socializing in any of the cop bars or at functions. He was ambitious, maybe too ambitious for his peers. The complaints were that he avoided the phone, avoided the Book, allowing others in the squad to pick up his slack. Pasquini had passed him off to

Boldt's squad for this very reason, but Boldt was glad to have him. Danielson liked *black holes*. He thrived on attempting to clear those cases where others had failed — and he was good at it, which also accounted for his unpopularity: a newcomer beating the veterans at their own game.

"I'd rather be assigned to whatever it is you're on, Sarge," he complained.

"I'm giving you the entire squad," Boldt said.

"Don't want it."

"You got it," Boldt informed him sternly.

"You could use me on this," Danielson attempted.

Danielson had no way of knowing what case Boldt was being detailed to, other than by rumor, and this attempt to milk the sergeant for information fell on deaf ears.

"You're a problem solver, Chris. We all are, but you especially. Some guys come by it naturally. Women, too: Gaynes is a natural. You pick up the *black holes* other people drop — some of them you even clear. Well, now you get all the *black holes* you want, and a lot you don't. You run a squad and every case is yours. You problem solve on a magnitude, on a level that I think is important for you to see."

"What's more important, solving this case of yours or shuffling a lot of paper? You *need* me, Sarge. This is my kind of case, this one you're on."

Danielson had a nose for it, that was all. He understood the look in Boldt's eye and he knew from the hours that Boldt was keeping, from the long meetings with Shoswitz behind closed doors, and most of all from the lack of any entry in the Book that this was one of the ones that came around once in ten years, this was a career maker. Boldt could tell all this by just looking at him. "It's a ball-buster, Chris," he advised him. "This is one of those that if you *don't* clear it, it breaks you. You put a month, six months, a year, six years into it, and it never goes down. Guys eat barrels over cases like this. Believe me: I've had them before."

"Cross killer," Danielson said. He knew all of Boldt's cases. Knew them so well it bothered Boldt, it embarrassed him.

"Sometimes you get lucky."

"You could have made captain in two years after that case," Danielson observed, reminding Boldt of Liz's arguments.

"But instead I took a leave of absence. That should tell you something."

"You took two *years*. That's hardly a leave."

"My point exactly. The squad is yours. The shit-eating clearance rate is yours. Do with it what you will."

"I don't *want* it!" he complained, knowing there were others who would kill for it.

"Maybe that's why it's yours." Danielson's eyes registered disgust and contempt. "Someday you'll thank me," Boldt said.

Danielson hesitated and cautioned ominously, "Someday I'll outrank you."

"But may I remind you that you don't today, Detective." Boldt handed him an enormous stack of files and said, "Careful of your back. They're heavy."

Boldt spent the rest of his Saturday trying to shake the memories of Slater Lowry's death and to organize the manpower and paperwork necessary to compare the Adler employee lists to the various other lists he had requested.

At 7:05 that evening, with the smell of egg rolls and ginger sweetening the air, Liz came out of the bathroom sobbing and carrying a long plastic tab with what looked like blue litmus paper glowing on its tip. That strip of plastic seemed strangely removed from the real world. It existed someplace that Boldt did not.

"I'm sorry," he offered, gathering her in his arms. He swallowed away the lump in his throat and tried to think of something positive to say. Anything. But his voice remained silent. She pressed her face tightly into the crook of his neck, and he felt her shake. Her face was warm. Her breath blew hotly against his neck.

"I'm pregnant!" she informed him, sobbing, as it turned out, for joy. She waved the plastic strip like a flag announcing her motherhood. Boldt kissed her fingers. He kissed her forehead, her nose, and found her lips. She walked him awkwardly to the bedroom and nudged the door shut with her toe. Miles was lost in a set of wooden blocks.

"Maybe we should practice once, just to make sure," Boldt suggested.

She said something into his ear but he didn't understand it over the roar of his own heartbeat.

By the time they got to the egg rolls, they were cold and the fake beer was warming, but there were smiles all around. For these brief few minutes, Boldt forgot the Tin Man.

But not for long. He was working through his third report by the time he realized Liz had gone to bed. Interrupted by her crying, he saw the bedroom lights were out, and it quickly registered that these were clearly not tears of joy. As Boldt went in to comfort her, he wondered at the obsessed man he had become, and if he would ever be any different. "I'm here," he whispered, sitting down beside her, laying a hand upon her back.

"I don't think so," she answered, her face aimed away from him. "But you were for a while."

"I was for a while," he agreed, though it pained him to do so. "It's a start," he tried, but they both knew it was not. They had been here before. They had never left.

"I'm scared."

"Me too." But for different reasons, he thought.

She fell asleep with silver tears still clinging

94

to her reddened cheeks. And Boldt slept beside her that night, still dressed in his street clothes, snuggled in tight where the warmth of her filled him with an all-encompassing peace.

NINE

"This is the last time," Owen Adler whispered in the dark, the bed and the houseboat shifting imperceptibly. On Sunday mornings, Lake Union was active early. Seaplanes and outboard engines competed noisily in the distance. "It really is. It *has* to be." His voice was sad.

"I know." Daphne rolled over, pressing her bare chest against his and curling onto him like a snake onto a branch, and kissed Owen wetly on the mouth. "I hate it," she confessed. She knew that this time it was for real — with her being police, they could not risk violating the demands. Maybe, she told herself, it helped explain why the sex had been lifeless. Maybe it offered her a way for her to win access to his files.

She told him. "I would like to take a look at your files. The New Leaf contamination you told us about."

"Tap will help you with that."

She did not want to involve Howard Taplin, or any other Adler employee; she did not want any filters between her and the information. And besides, she thought, such involvement presented too great a risk. "The thing is," she

96

explained, "within your company Howard Taplin is as high-profile as you are. If he goes requesting a bunch of files, and the blackmailer is an insider, we take too big a risk that he or she might cotton on to police involvement. And I imagine that if Taplin gets a file himself rather than asking his secretary for it, that would raise as much suspicion."

"Probably right."

"And now that this person has proved what he's capable of, I have no desire to test his threat of killing hundreds. We can't afford any hint of our involvement in the investigation." She allowed this to sink in and suggested, "I was thinking I could go in after hours. Nice and quiet. All alone, when no employees are around. Get what I need, make copies, and get out."

"Whatever you want." He held her tightly, and she could feel his fear in the embrace.

"I want it over," she said.

A long time passed before he said, "You don't expect something like this. And when it comes you wonder why you ever bothered with any of it. A month ago you and I were so close, and now I feel a distance in you — I feel your professionalism. Not that I'm complaining. You can't believe what a relief it is to have you working on this, to have the police finally involved — despite the threats. I waited too long. I made mistakes — and I do *not* want to hear you blame yourself again — that's *not* what I mean. Belief in my own instincts is what built this company. When those instincts fail you, it rattles the foundations."

"Self-doubt is destructive. You can't dwell on it."

"You can't help but dwell on it," he said.

Wind whistled through the houseboat. Sometimes that noise sounded peaceful to her, but today it sounded ominous. She heard a light chop striking the pier, and in the distance the hum of traffic on the interstate. "Do you think it's an employee?" she asked.

"I'm *afraid* it's one. There's a difference." He added, "And it frosts me, because as clichéd as it sounds, we're a family, and this kind of betrayal is the worst kind imaginable. But the evidence certainly seems to point that way."

"I think it's connected to New Leaf — to these salmonella poisonings," she told him. "That's the psychologist speaking," she said.

"I'd like to run away with you," he confessed. "Leave it all. Wake up on some island and make love and drink beer."

"You'd last about two days. When was the last time you took time off?"

"That's what I mean."

"You don't know how to take time off."

"You could teach me."

She wormed her way fully atop him, and slid slowly against him until he was aroused. "We could teach each other," she said.

"I'm a quick learner." He kissed her, and

she felt herself responding to him. There were times he made her body feel seventeen again, the way it reacted. Her desire had little to do with penetration or friction — she wanted inside his skin, she wanted some kind of union with his soul. It was a feeling she did not fully understand, and that somehow made it all the more attractive to her. Too often she understood too much.

She said, "Quickness is *not* something that could be stuck on you. You are anything but quick."

"Do you honestly think I would choose work over you?"

"I'm not sure it's your choice. A person's behavior can change — but I'm not sure the person ever does."

He took the lobe of her ear in his lips and nibbled there. "I'll send you flowers every day," he promised. "And every day I'll wish I were here. And as soon as this is over, I'll leave Corky with Mrs. Crutch and we'll hole up in a hotel somewhere and make up for lost time."

"That's quite an incentive program."

They made love after that — a quiet, peaceful union that made up for their earlier frenetic effort. There was nothing frantic about it, but instead it felt to her that they briefly found one another — purely — the way she hoped for.

Her dreams were peaceful for the first time in weeks, and when she awakened he was gone, having left behind a heart drawn in lipstick on the bathroom mirror, and the scrawled words, "Miss you already." There had been a time, in her early twenties, that such sugary sentiments would have provoked an uncomfortable reaction in her, but on this day, both older and wiser, she relished them: There was nothing quite like the feeling of being wanted and needed.

She decided not to clean the mirror until this investigation was over — her own childish reaction. This would serve as her reminder, her purpose.

In the kitchen she found his master key and his note to her explaining the Mansion's security system, including the code needed for the keypad. She picked up the key and it felt cool in her hand.

As it warmed, she felt convinced of its importance.

TEN

Boldt's attempts at sleep proved restless and unforgiving. His appetite abandoned him and he found himself back on a routine of antacids and warm milk. On the fifth floor he was the recipient of cautious looks and deliberate avoidance maneuvers. He thought of the child on the way to the grave. He thought of the child inside his wife — and none of it made any sense to him. Where he strived for order and understanding, none was to be found.

At the office the initial reports were not good. Using computers, the Adler employee lists had been electronically compared to those of Foodland and Shop-Alert, in hopes of finding a disgruntled employee who had switched jobs and was now repaying Adler. But no overlaps were found. Every detective assigned a *black hole* hoped for a lucky break, an unexpected, quick solution, and Boldt was no exception. It was not something he talked about, but nonetheless this hope was harbored secretly inside him. With this news, coupled with the loss of Slater Lowry, any such hopes were abandoned.

This negative news was soon balanced by something more promising: Cash register receipt tapes from the Broadway Foodland supermarket that included purchases of Adler soup products had been sorted and printed out for the two-week period prior to Slater Lowry's illness. These cash register tapes were shown to Betty Lowry, who despite the loss of her son, or perhaps because of it, seemed eager to help. Hours later she notified Boldt that she recognized a receipt that included the purchase of soup, soy sauce, and a wooden spoon. It was the wooden spoon she remembered most of all. The receipt indicated payment in cash, which also fit her buying habits.

Using the date and time from this receipt, Boldt notified Shop-Alert Security and requested they search their store surveillance videos for the twenty-four-hour period prior to and including Betty Lowry's purchase of Mom's Chicken Soup.

Redmond, Washington, a forty-minute drive from the city in good traffic, was home to Microsoft and other technocracies. It's boom in the eighties was partly responsible for the unwanted Californication that had spawned the unprecedented traffic, fast-food joints, air pollution, and Armani suits.

Shop-Alert's interior appeared to have been constructed of materials found at Saturday-morning hardware store sales. All artificial everything: faux wood paneling, adjustable Tru-Grain shelves. Overhead fluorescent lighting caused human skin to take on the pale green hue that Boldt associated with tainted meat. The individual office cubicles were cramped and dark despite the lighting, in part because of a brown-purple carpeting that absorbed light like a black hole. And he thought that it was dirty enough that heretofore undiscovered life forms probably lived down inside it.

Money saved by this tacky interior had been spent instead on state-of-the-art electronics heaped and stacked and connected in a spaghetti of multicolored wires, keyboards, and screens.

Boldt had already forgotten the name of the computer nerd who had met him in the lobby. Ron something — or was it Jon? He was a particularly unattractive human with no social graces, so stereotypical that Boldt hated himself for having expected someone like this. He talked through his nose and blinked continually. Maybe it was Don. He looked to be about twelve years old. His loafers had tassels and he had a Motorola pager strapped to his belt. It made Boldt want to throw his own away.

"Foodland is part of our StopLifters program. Let me explain. When we receive the videos from our StopLifters stores, stores like Foodland, before we analyze them we transfer the data to OM disk — optical magnetic. Kind of like CD-ROM, only more flexible to our needs. That allows us to turn over the videotape — zero it and send it back out there for use in one of our client's systems while we retain the original images. Phase one of our analysis is handled here," he said, directing Boldt's attention to a dozen young people studying black-and-white television screens showing store interiors, "reviewing the in-store images, alert for shoplifters or taggers."

"Taggers?"

"Price-tag switchers. It used to be pulling a price tag off of one, lesser-valued item and attaching it to another of higher value. The tagger pockets the difference in savings. Because of nonremovable and now optical pricing systems, the taggers are more sophisticated than they used to be: They arrive in-store with pre-printed UPC-code labels on their person. They attach these fraudulent pricing mechanisms to the package of their choice and leave the store having paid a *serious* discount, usually only on one or two big-ticket items, mixed in with many smaller purchases. This makes it difficult for the checkers to spot the game. That's what we call any of these techniques: 'games.' "

Original, Boldt thought.

"Another benefit to our clients of our transferring the tapes to OM disks is that we are able to catalogue months, even years, of a store's history, making it possible for us to present a very serious legal case against repeat offenders. Typically they move from store to store, too smart to keep hitting the same place. But the advantage of being a Shop-Alert StopLifters client is that we're essentially building a database of offenders, giving us a much better shot at

104

moving these offenses past the probationary sentence and really *slam-dunking* these bastards."

I'll never use that expression again, Boldt thought. He said, "What have you got for me?"

Don(?) led the detective over to an unoccupied viewing station amid the others, where a folded piece of paper with the hand-scrawled word *Reserved* had been placed. He sat Boldt down in the chair directly before the large monitor. Don explained, "A real advantage of the OM disk format is taking the signal digital. We can not only enhance and zoom but we have the ability to instantly jump position without suffering through fast-forward or rewind. If you think of it as picking up the needle on an LP record and moving it to the song you want to hear, and comparing that to a cassette tape where you have to wait for the thing to fast-forward, you'll see what I mean. We can jump an hour, a minute, twenty seconds ahead or behind by simply dialing in the specific time request. We can cut and paste to other disks and build the records of these offenders I was talking about, or we can highlight a particularly vulnerable area of a store by clipping together shots of lost angles. It's really very versatile."

"I'm not buying anything," Boldt reminded him.

"Right." He turned a vivid red and toyed

105

with his smudged glasses.

"What's your name again?" Boldt finally asked.

"Gus."

"Gus?"

"That's right."

Gus sat down alongside Boldt. He worked a computer keyboard as fast and as delicately as Boldt's grandmother used to knit. "Your request was easy," he bragged. "You told us which aisle and what to look for. Without that, it might have taken us a day or more. I think I may have your offender, although I'm not familiar with this particular game — placing product onto a shelf. What's your interest in this anyway?"

"Corporate espionage," Boldt lied, making it up on the spot and feeling self-conscious until the technofreak grinned enthusiastically as if he'd been let in on something.

"Cool," he said. "What I've done is catalogue the images I have found so far and placed them in chronological order. Here's the first image in the progression. This is the entrance door to Foodland as caught by one of our cameras."

On the screen was displayed a slightly fuzzy black-and-white image that showed a pair of automatic doors. The left door swung open admitting a person wearing a gimme cap and a dark jacket. Medium height and weight. He (she?) turned into the store and walked off the screen.

"That's our first look," Gus muttered. "Not much."

The bottom right of the screen was date- and time-coded. The suspect had entered Foodland at 5:02 P.M. on June 21. Clearly a busy time of day for the store. And late in the day, when the shelves were more likely to have room for the killer's substitution. Boldt experienced a pang of anxiety: Was this the Tin Man?

"Our next decent hit is three minutes later. And you should know something here, Lieutenant." Boldt didn't bother to correct the mistaken rank. "Your average shopper — your *innocent* shopper — ends up all over these videos. But except for a flash here and there, this mark has avoided the cameras for nearly three minutes. And that's not easy. Granted, Shop-Alert didn't install the Foodland system — we only analyze their images, and it isn't the greatest system, but even so, to *avoid* these cameras is something of an art form. It requires prolonged study of the facility, and even at that, a hell of a lot of luck. Of course, dress has a lot to do with it. You'll note the dark clothing and the hat. Dark clothing in saturated black-and-white video — in this kind of light, as you can see — tends to absorb too much light, throwing off the gray-scale balance on the areas immediately around it, causing a graininess like a shadow that renders the image difficult to evaluate. The dark clothing makes it difficult to see her face."

"Her?" Boldt asked. "She looks a little androgynous to me."

"A woman, I think so, yes."

Gus consulted a time log on a clipboard in front of him, then keyed in a set of numbers. "For the time being, we're going to jump ahead two minutes and fifty seconds to show you this." He hit the ENTER key. A new image appeared, ran for only half a second, and then, as he struck another key, was freeze-framed. It was this same person in another area of an aisle. The person's head turned slightly, which was where Gus stopped it. "I'm going to zoom and enhance now. It takes a second or two for the screen to refresh at each phase." Using a computer mouse, Gus dragged a box around the face. This box then filled the entire screen. Box by box the electronically enhanced enlargements continued, and the suspect's head grew ever larger. The tighter the image, the fuzzier it grew, because "enhancement can't keep pace with enlargement," as Gus explained. By the time the process was completed, much of what was on the screen was only made discernible by Boldt's imagination and the images that had come before. He wasn't even sure what he was looking at.

"Lower head and neck," Boldt guessed.

"Exactly right, Lieutenant." The boy sounded impressed. He typed additional instructions into the machine and sat back. "Now let's run that again." He ran it several times, like instant replay, before Boldt saw it.

"The bounce to the hat?" Boldt asked.

"It's oversize. And the way it bounces means there's a lot of hair up inside there."

"You're good at this," Boldt complimented.

"We spend enough time at it." Gus drew a box around the woman's ear, and the computer began a series of enhancements. At the same time, the sequence played in slow motion, backed up, and played again repeatedly. Gus slowed the motion even further. "There!" he declared excitedly — and a little too loudly for Boldt's ear. "It's our only real chance to see it." He pointed to the earlobe, where a square black mark winked at them.

Boldt studied the repetition for several passes, and Gus had the good sense to keep quiet and let the detective have some room. Boldt finally tested, "A freckle? A mole? I'm not sure I see the importance."

"Lower earlobe," the boy hinted. This was a contest.

"Pierced ears!" Boldt said loudly, briefly drawing the attention of the other video attendants in the room. "No earring, but that's a hole in the ear! Even so, that hardly indicates a woman."

"Added to the height of the individual and the apparent weight of hair inside that hat —"

"It *may* be a woman!" Boldt stated. "I'll

109

give you that," although this shattered his image of the Tin Man, whom he had assumed to be male. "I need to follow her every movement."

The technician showed him all the images in which the female suspect was captured by the cameras. At no point did she reveal her face. "Here's where we vote her All-Pro," Gus said. "There are only a few shoplifters as good. Note her position to the camera. She's in aisle 4: soup and vegetables. Positioned this way, she fully blocks any chance we might have of seeing her specific actions. She checks her watch — see that?" He replayed the moment. "And now she's gone from our view for over seven seconds. By the time we pick her up again, she has moved quickly down the aisle. She bumps into that man with the cart, there — see that? — and by the time we pick her up again, she is paying cash, head still down, for a candy bar, and she's gone. The thing is, checking her watch: She had the cameras timed."

"A woman?" Boldt asked uneasily. *The Tin Man?* he wondered.

"Now check this out. This is beautiful!" the technician said enthusiastically. The screen blanked to a deep blue. When an image re-appeared again, it showed aisle 4. The technician blocked a segment using a white box, tripped a key, and leaned back. The area zoomed and enlarged several times, the shelves moving increasingly closer, the products — soup cans —

more easily identified: Adler soup cans. "This is where the woman was standing," he explained. He split the screen into two similar images and said: "Before and after. See the difference? She's not a lifter after all; we've got *nothing* on her!"

The right-hand screen showed five soup cans that were not present in the earlier image.

"Five?" Boldt asked in a panic.

"Something wrong?" the young man queried.

"She's not a lifter at all," he repeated.

"Is it possible?" Boldt muttered.

"Five cans of soup?" the young man asked, misunderstanding the question. "You should see some of the clothing that's been used, the amount of stuff they can hide. We offer a seminar on clothing used in shoplifting — you wouldn't believe some of the stuff!"

Boldt could only account for two, possibly three, cans: the Chin girl and Slater Lowry. So where were the other three cans?

"Listen up," Boldt announced to his squad: LaMoia, Gaynes, Danielson, and Frank Herbert.

Herbert, fifty, stood five feet five with a pot belly that made him equally wide. His balding head was spot-shined. Lieutenant Shoswitz stood by the door.

Homicide's situation room contained a half-dozen Formica desks, a retractable projection screen, and a large Wipe-It board that at the

111

moment contained several profanities and a graphic cartoon.

Boldt briefed them on the case, taking them through his visit to Shop-Alert and the discovery of several unaccounted-for soup cans. He had been on the phone the entire afternoon; his voice was hoarse. Or maybe that was nerves.

"We're missing two to three cans: Lori Chin's mother doesn't have any on her shelf, so I'm guessing there are still three at large. The surveillance video has given us a window of time during which the suspect was inside the store, making the drop," Boldt continued. "Thanks to a computerized cash register system, we can identify any bank check or credit card purchases and then trace them back to whoever made that purchase. We've identified thirty-four people who we *know* were shopping inside this Foodland supermarket at the exact same time as our suspect. We have also identified eleven customers who purchased the Adler chicken soup within the twenty-four hours that followed the contaminated cans' being placed on the shelves.

"Here's the drill: First, I've attempted to contact these eleven individuals, but I only reached three. Your job is to do a follow-up. You proceed to their homes, collect any cans — treated as evidence, don't forget — and conduct a thorough interview to make sure no cans were given away or placed somewhere that's been forgotten about."

112

Boldt said, "If we get lucky — if we locate these extra cans — then, beginning tomorrow morning, I want each of you to contact and interview these thirty-four others who were present at Foodland during the time of the drop." He added as a footnote: "Obviously, this case gets our priority, although technically you're not detailed to it, so you'll have to stay current on the Book as well. It's a lot of work, I know." He continued, "These shoppers — and *anyone they were with* — are all potential witnesses and should be dealt with as such. We contact them first by phone, and with the hot ones, we conduct follow-ups. Interviews are tape-recorded, where we can get permission. I want you keeping good notes." He glanced at Shoswitz.

"Okay? Questions?" Shoswitz said, "Let's go."

ELEVEN

At seven-fifteen that Monday evening, beneath a heavy blanket of cloud that accelerated the early summer dusk, Daphne let herself into the Adler Mansion using Owen's master key. She closed and locked the door behind her. If she were to go undetected in her efforts, then she knew she must key in the security code within the next thirty seconds to prevent a silent alarm from sounding.

The Mansion, corporate headquarters for Adler's global business, occupied a large corner lot in the old part of town. Adler Incorporated owned the rest of the buildings on this block as well, all nestled under towering trees, but the Mansion was special for its Victorian grandeur and charm. Three full stories and a converted basement, four chimneys, eight fireplaces, mustard-colored siding with white shutters and white trim, ornately carved fascia, a glorious series of roofs aimed to the heavens and topped with lightning rods like exclamation points.

She had decided to break the law.

In her mind the choice was quite clear. Warrants need more than suspicions in order to be issued, and suspicion and curiosity were all she had. Children were dying; there was no time for lengthy debate with judges and prosecutors.

Added to this was a nagging doubt that Howard Taplin intended to cooperate fully and provide her with *all* the files concerning the New Leaf contamination. Intuition? A psychologist's instincts? During the meeting on Adler's boat, she had witnessed his cool resistance to the topic of New Leaf. It was clearly not something that he wanted discussed or investigated. *Why?* she wondered. The meeting had taken place late Friday afternoon. The Monday business day had now passed without any mention, any offer of the files to the police. She believed that to officially request the files — for a second time — was likely to get them shredded. Regardless of Adler's permission to be here, she felt that if she were caught in the act, if Taplin knew how serious she was about investigating New Leaf, that any and all files pertaining to the previous contamination would start disappearing quickly. And quite possibly, forever.

More important, the threats. Under no circumstances could she allow herself to be discovered, her identity revealed — the involvement of the police found out. The possibility of a disgruntled employee remained at the top of their suspect list. Word would travel fast within the company: *The police raided our files last night.* The faxed threats made it abundantly clear that police interference came at the price of more lives. If she made a mess of this, there would be more killing.

She searched for the security device on the wall of the pantry, through the swinging door now to her right — where Adler had told her to look. She pushed through but found it too dark to see well, and with activity in a few of the other nearby Adler buildings, she decided against turning on a light. The warnings against police involvement kept her anonymity of foremost importance.

Nonetheless, she took that risk. She wanted a look at the files alone, by herself, without the editorial screen of Howard Taplin's watchful eye. The fact that Adler Foods had been involved in a contamination incident several years before offered Daphne Matthews, forensic psychologist, the possibility of a real and potent motivation. And whereas a large percentage of crimes against persons were seemingly committed *without* an identifiable motivation, judging by the use of language in the blackmail threats, she believed this crime different.

Fifteen thousand . . . sixteen thousand . . . she counted off as she waved her hand in large arcs on the wall desperately searching for the security device while her eyes continued to adjust slowly to the darkness. *There!* Behind the door, a mahogany valance enclosing it. She pulled the cover open. A red light at the bottom flashed ominously. Her middle finger sought out the raised bump on the number 5 key, she entered the code, and the red light stopped blinking, replaced by green. She entered the security number a second time, rearming the device as Adler had advised her, ensuring both her privacy and that the building would not be broken into while she was downstairs in the files.

She had only been here a few times, always in the day, always when the building bustled with activity. She found the near-total silence, the slight hum of ventilation, somewhat haunting. It was a big place, and the old wooden floors complained underfoot and a big grandfather clock in reception tolled out the seconds sounding like someone chipping ice. Living alone for as long as she had, she felt accustomed to solitude, but the unfamiliarity of her surroundings coupled with the clandestine nature of her mission here instilled in her a sense of foreboding, as if someone might be hiding around the next corner.

"Hello?" she called out tentatively, in case she was wrong about being alone. Judging that she was in fact all by herself in this museum of a place — every piece of trim, every piece of furniture restored or reproduced to match the original era — she returned into the back hall and stood at the top of the curving back staircase that led down into the converted basement. She hesitated only briefly before taking the plunge and descending step by cautious step into an increasing darkness. Adler had described the layout of this sublevel secretarial pool to her, and the location of the file room, but it did not make voyaging down into the darkness, the unknown, any easier.

She wanted those files. But more than anything, she wished now that she had not come alone.

The drumming in her chest increased with each stair step, her breathing quickened to sharp gasps. She nervously fingered the two keys like worry beads and twisted the starched ribbon that bound them.

In the faint red glow of a pair of lighted exit signs, Daphne saw that the secretarial pool housed five computer workstations isolated from each other by office baffles. There was a string of clocks high on the wall displaying the proper time in Rome, London, New York, Denver, Seattle, and Tokyo. A pair of erasable-pen board calendars hung on the same wall, cluttered with lines, arrows, and notations. The file room, marked *Private*, was to Daphne's right. The second key opened this door.

She had prepared herself for a vast room containing row after row of gunmetal-gray filing cabinets. Instead, it was a simply appointed, small office space containing a pair of large-screen computer workstations, constantly running, that occupied a narrow counter space; two copiers; a color laser printer, and a pair of color scanners. On the left wall hung a shelving system that housed a dozen in-boxes, all labeled. The wall to her right held more shelving and two large green plastic garbage cans labeled *B+W Recycle* and *Color Recycle*. Below the computers were several drawers containing optical disks in plastic jewel boxes. They resembled small CDs and were numbered 1 through 131, with plenty of empty slots yet to be filled.

The room was windowless. Daphne switched on the overhead lights, pushed the door partly shut, and sat down at the right-hand terminal. The two computer terminals appeared to be identical. Both the keyboards and monitors bore the boldly printed name *EDIFIS* — Electronic Digital Filing System. Adler had cautioned that many of the more confidential categories were security protected, and had provided her with a credit card–size plastic pass bearing a magnetic strip that, once read, gained her the highest level of access. She pushed the proper function key for security clearance and ran the card through a slot on the right of the keyboard.

She was inside.

She quickly navigated through a series of menus to an alphabetized index that was organized into four separate databases: (C)ategory, (S)ubject, (D)ate, and (A)uthor. The indexing system felt familiar, like one used by the public library downtown. She moved deeper into the increasingly specific indexes. *EDIFIS* was a paperless filing system that called up the images

119

of the scanned documents. The index, whether by general category or specific title, referenced one of the numbered optical disks; an (a), in parentheses indicated that an archived hard copy existed off-site.

"Insurance" listed seventeen subheadings. She scrolled through them slowly. Several listings caught her eye, among them *Executive Protection Package* and another, *Catastrophic,* with additional subcategories branched beneath it.

> *Catastrophic*
> Act of God
> Criminal
> Environmental Disaster
> Health

The word *Criminal* caught her eye. She selected this, was prompted to insert the proper optical disk, and having done so was faced with yet another menu. Several case histories were listed, including one called Policy & Coverage with an (a) indicating an archived copy. She selected this option and was subsequently presented with a scanned image of the actual policy: "Page 1 of 17," it read in the bottom corner. She selected a computer icon that resembled a magnifying glass, and the document enlarged, becoming more readable. The opening pages dedicated great verbiage to defining criminal activity both within and without Adler Foods — what legally constituted it and what did not. She was no attorney, and this was an attorney's world to be sure, but extortion and blackmail, if certified by law enforcement (whatever "certified" meant) appeared to be fully covered — up to and including a ransom sum of five million dollars.

The number swam around lazily in her head: *five million dollars.*

Third paragraph, page 4: *Consumer Product Tampering.* She swallowed dryly and glanced around the room to make sure she was still alone. Gooseflesh ran up her left side and across her chest and down into her stomach, which fluttered nervously.

A long definition, followed by more legalese. It seemed to say that all costs of advertising, development, distribution, promotion, production, and publicity to reintroduce any discontinued product line that was pulled as a direct result of internal or external criminal activity — "see above" — were to be *paid in full* up to and including the sum of eighty million dollars.

She gasped aloud and reread this number: *eighty million dollars.* Under *Criminal Attack,* Adler Foods was to be compensated in order to return its goods to the marketplace. It occurred to her how it might be possible to misuse this reimbursement in order to redesign, repackage, and reintroduce a product or an entire line, with the insurance company footing the bill. It would require convincing the police a crime had taken place, and it would require paperwork from police files supporting this. Such paperwork existed already, no doubt, thanks to her enlisting the help of Lou Boldt, and the company had already issued one recall of Mom's Chicken Soup, which Taplin had claimed would cost the company a quarter-million dollars. But according to this document, it would not cost the company at all. So why had Taplin lied about the cost to the company?

A hollow, sinking feeling stole into her. Her mouth went dry; her palms grew sticky. She loosened her scarf. It did not help.

She backed up in the indexes. She touched *N,* in the general index and found an entry for *New Leaf Foods,* the original company name that Adler had operated under until his reorganization several years before. She found the appropriate disk and inserted it into the machine, hit the ENTER key, and was faced now with yet another index. She browsed a variety of categories, astounded by the wealth of information and how easily available and accessed it was.

She browsed New Leaf's legal documents and used a hypertext SEARCH function to locate all documents containing the word *contamination.* She took another ten minutes to narrow the result of this search down to several business letters and memos sent between New Leaf and the Washington State Health Department. All of these documents were shown in the index to have archived hard copies.

The first of these letters documented a phone call from the State Health Department alerting New Leaf to a possible contamination of their soup products. This and all subsequent correspondence was handled by Howard Taplin who, judging by the tone, had been cooperative but denied any wrongdoing on the part of Adler Foods. A product recall had been issued.

The dates of the correspondence were filed chronologically. In the middle of the electronic stack, Daphne discovered a copy of a State Health lab report that showed a technical analysis of New Leaf's Free Range Chicken Soup. The details of Slater Lowry's death did not escape Daphne's attention. The psychologist in her suddenly had not only a possible motivation, but a convincing similarity between the two crimes.

She anxiously hurried forward in the correspondence searching for further explanations. Memo after memo blurred past. Too many to read thoroughly, but she scanned them all. She resorted to the FIND function, searching first for "chicken" and, faced with dozens of documents, changed the search string to "poultry," which produced only six hits. She viewed the documents individually, reading each one carefully. On the third document she read the name: *Longview Farms.*

A rural route address was listed in Sasquaw,

123

Washington. She wrote this down, including the phone number, and continued to speed-read the rest of the documents. Lawsuits and countersuits had been filed. State Heath had charged Longview Farms with the contamination, clearing New Leaf.

Her eye caught the slight uphill angle of a typed word, *salmonella.* She zoomed in on the image.

Daphne would realize later that had the lab report not been scanned into the computer, had the image not been placed on a large screen that allowed her to zoom in with the magnifying glass icon, she might have missed this and the other changes that appeared to have been made. One of these changes was the date — *September 15* — which appeared slightly askew, imperceptibly misregistered on the line with the rest of the typewritten data. Over the next fifteen minutes she scrutinized this document, studying all the vital information and discovering what appeared to be five separate changes. Six or seven, possibly. At last she leaned back in the chair studying the screen and released a huge sigh that she had unknowingly been containing. It seemed possible that this lab report had been altered. Why? And by whom? And what did it mean?

Two thoughts occupied her. She wanted a hard copy to show Boldt and others — perhaps even Owen Adler. She wanted a look at the archived copy to study its condition and, if possible, to run it by the second floor for lab tests. The New Leaf salmonella contamination gained weight in her mind as having some bearing on the present blackmailing of Adler Foods. Excitement surged through her. Right or wrong, she had to prove this to herself.

With the document on the screen, she selected the PRINT icon, but a message returned to check the printer. She had not thought to switch it on. She did so, but the switch did nothing. The machine was not responding.

She traced the printer's power cord back to the wall socket, discovering a device unfamiliar to her. It appeared to be an AC power outlet that operated off a key: a metal box with a single keyhole that physically locked the printer's plug inside the device and prevented any power reaching that plug without the right key. She tried the key Adler had given her, but it didn't fit. Had he simply forgotten to give her this, or had he not wanted her gaining a hard copy without first asking?

She snapped her head toward the door, left ajar, believing she heard something. On the far wall of the secretarial pool, a red light blinked twice. She squinted and studied the box from a distance: It was a security keypad identical to the one she had used upstairs, this one located next to one of the downstairs exit doors.

She was familiar enough with security devices to know that this red blinking signal rep-

125

resented an entry by window or door somewhere in the building.

Someone was inside. Someone with a key.

A moment later the yellow blinking light turned green. This person had keyed in the proper code and reset the security.

She returned her attention to the computer screen. Whoever it was, she didn't want the person finding her and seeing the New Leaf lab report on the screen. With the printer message still on the screen she attempted to close the file, but the screen responded with a second overlapping message that she had requested to print the document and that the printer wasn't responding: "Verify printer operation," the dialogue box told her. She selected CANCEL, but this only removed the second dialogue box. It did not clear the printing error. The lab report remained on the screen staring back at her.

How long did she have until she was discovered? As if to answer this, the tiny strip of light at the bottom of the door blinked, as whoever had entered the building had used the upstairs switch. Someone was headed downstairs.

The screen-saver graphic patterns at work on the other terminal were designed to protect a monitor from "burning in" by keeping images moving on the screen, and were timed to take over the screen after a designated period of inactivity at the keyboard. Daphne had no way of knowing what amount of time had been selected for the screen-savers to take over, but she realized immediately that one possible way to mislead whoever was now heading downstairs was to allow the screen-saver to kick in. It would hide whatever document lay beneath it, and she could not close the lab report because of the printer error interrupt. She could keep trying to close it, but to do so would involve the keyboard and would further delay the screen-savers. Furthermore, she realized that even if the screen-saver kicked in, a single keystroke afterward would eliminate the screen-saver and return the lab report to the monitor, giving away her snooping. Worst of all, this screen-saver idea required her to do nothing — to sit back and be careful not to touch any key, awaiting a screen-saver that might not appear in time.

She took her hands off the keys and began softly encouraging the screen-saver to hide her efforts, while glancing repeatedly toward the door and the view of the secretarial pool. It occurred to her to lock the file room door in order to buy herself time, but she decided against it, believing this would require its own explanation and might raise the curiosity of whoever was approaching.

The lab report lingered on her screen. The screen of the terminal nearest the door continued to splash shooting stars at her. She knew that the "time out" interval for screen-saver software could be one minute, five minutes, or even ten or twenty minutes. She had no way of knowing what it might be on these terminals. If the intruder was just a security guard, she decided she had nothing to worry about. It was doubtful a security guard would pay any attention to what was on the screen. If it was an employee, however, it presented her a far greater problem. Such a person could be counted on to see and identify the document that a stranger had called up from the files.

The lab report continued to glare at her. No matter how strongly she willed it to vanish, it remained on the screen. "You piece of shit!" she hissed, tempted to put her foot through the monitor.

But the psychologist took over. Hoping to buy time for the screen-saver to engage, she leapt up from her chair and swung open the door, crying out as she unexpectedly collided and tangled with a man. She broke loose, shoved away, and looked into the face of Kenny Fowler.

"Woh!" he said, adjusting his suit jacket. "You?" he inquired, glancing furtively toward the file room door. "We got an alert that some-one had entered —"

"Owen gave me his key. He didn't want to attract attention."

"His key?" Fowler asked. "The files? I thought Howard —"

"I didn't want to bother Mr. Taplin."

He nodded, but he did not appear convinced. Again, he craned his neck toward the file room door. "You weren't on this evening's log," he explained. "No one was authorized for the Mansion. With all this trouble . . . We've cracked down on authorization. Your entry raised the curiosity of my guards."

She cast him an intentionally suspicious look. It sounded to her as if he were making this up. She didn't know what to believe.

"I was in the area," he clarified for her, knowing what she must be thinking. "I took the call." He tugged on his shirt cuff. He was nervous, she decided.

"You headed straight downstairs," she pointed out, remembering she had not turned on any lights, had not given any indication of her whereabouts.

"The security system is a good one," he said.

She took that to mean that he had known someone had penetrated the file room. Was he protecting the building or protecting access to the files?

"You need help with the file system?" he asked, attempting to ease his way around her in order to get a better look at the file room.

"I can manage." Kenny Fowler would report whatever he saw to Howard Taplin. She was certain of that. The two seemed to work in concert. "Anything on any of the employees?" she asked, knowing that by agreement with Owen Adler, Boldt had assigned the in-house side of the investigation to Fowler. This eliminated any police presence at Adler Foods or their suppliers and the chance they might alert the blackmailer to the bigger picture.

"We're working on it," he replied, taking yet another step forward. "So, he's giving you keys now?" He sounded almost jealous.

They looked at each other suspiciously. She felt both combative and defensive. If the lab report were still on the screen, then he was going to see it, because she fully understood now that Fowler was going into the file room with or without her blessing. Maybe because he felt it was part of his job. Maybe because he was curious. Maybe because Howard Taplin had told him to. He had known someone was in the file room even before he had got here. It made sense for security to be protective of the company files, and she knew Fowler to be a thorough man. Maybe that was all it was.

She did not want to believe that Howard Taplin would invent a crime in order to obtain insurance money that might allow the redesign of the entire Adler product line. Why go to such lengths? It made no sense unless the underlying economic strength of the company was a mirage. Were they in financial trouble? Had Owen hidden this from her? But no matter what, she felt she could not dismiss it without further investigation. The form she had seen on that screen implied tampering with evidence in an earlier contamination. She wanted answers.

And for the time being she wanted them kept all to herself.

Fowler stepped past her and pushed through the door. She glanced in time to see that both screens showed the shooting stars of screen-saver software. For now, she was safe.

Fowler slid into the seat in front of the first screen — the terminal she had not been using — touched the keyboard, and the screen cleared, showing the opening menu. "You haven't gotten very far," he said. "Maybe I can help."

"I don't think so." Her attention remained riveted on the keyboard to his right. If he touched one of those keys, if he bumped the mouse, the screen-saver would vanish, replaced by the altered New Leaf lab report.

"What was it you wanted?" he asked, blazing through a series of menus. "Security has its own files terminal," he said, answering her astonished look at how fluent he seemed to be.

"Some privacy," she answered, annoying him. "Thanks, but no thanks, Kenny."

"What? What is it? What do you mean 'privacy'? We're on the same team here, remember. What — I'm not one of *you* because I left the force for better pay? What — that's a crime?"

"Just some privacy is all."

"I know what you people think of me."

"That's absurd."

"Is it?" he asked. "You think I copped out — no pun intended. Took the bucks instead of the responsibility. Well fuck you."

"Kenny, I *don't* think that. I've got no grudge against your decision."

"The others do. You know I'm right."

"All I want is a look at some of these files."

"I'll help you. That's what I'm saying: I'll help. I know the system."

As distracted as she was by the proximity of the adjacent keyboard, and Fowler's tendency to animate, she found it hard to concentrate. At last she gave in, hoping to be rid of him, requesting a look at the employee records of all college-educated males with access to the Mom's Chicken Soup production facility. It seemed like a legitimate request to her, though a second too late she realized it crossed over into Fowler's domain — the very area of his half of the investigation. But he did not protest the request. He typed furiously, and quite competently, and within a minute or so called up the respective files.

"Can I get a hard copy of those?" she asked, hoping to trick him into turning on the printer for her.

Tapping the locking device, Fowler answered immediately, "Not with this box, you can't." He felt under the lip of the counter, searching out a key. She had not thought to do this, and felt angry at herself and frustrated that she actually might need Fowler after all. "If I know Suzie . . . ," he said, abandoning his search and heading into the secretarial pool.

She heard, but did not see him open a drawer in the other room. He called out to her, "The trouble with corporate security is that it's only as smart as your employees."

As he appeared in the doorway, his pager sounded. The key to the printer dangled from a small key chain, held out like a carrot in front of her. She wanted to snatch it away from him. "I gotta answer a page," he said, catching her eye. He glanced at the key, then back to Daphne.

He tossed her the key.

The key flew through the air toward her on a flight path headed straight for the keyboard to the second terminal. If she missed it, it would hit the keys and reveal the lab report hidden behind the screen-saver. She took quick measure and swiped the air, attempting the catch, and miraculously snagged the key just inches above the keyboard. But her elbow thumped against the computer mouse poised alongside the keyboard and the screen came to life, the altered lab report glaring back at her.

The sound of Fowler's voice electrified her: She was caught. Then she realized he was not talking to her, but was on the phone in other room.

Glancing between Fowler's back and the computer screen, she shoved the key into the printer's security box and twisted it. The printer's amber power light flashed, the machine hummed, and the computer screen blinked.

A new message appeared. Daphne did not read the message. All she saw were the words:

CANCEL THIS PRINT JOB
Yes   No
?

She zipped the mouse into place and clicked "Yes." The printer error message vanished from the screen. She pulled down the file menu.

Fowler said, "Okay," and hung up the phone.

Her heart in her throat, Fowler now approaching, Daphne clicked the mouse through a series of steps: *File . . . Close . . . Menu . . . Main . . .* her full attention on the screen, and the task before her.

The lab report left the screen, replaced by the main menu.

Kenny Fowler stepped through the door.

"Pretty easy, once you get the hang of it," she said. Her face felt burning hot. Her fingers were trembling. Would he notice? "Thanks," she said, trying to get rid of him.

"You okay here?" he asked. "I gotta look into something."

"Fine."

"Key goes in the center drawer, second desk over." He added, "I'm going to have to do something about that."

"No problem," she said, but her voice broke, and he looked at her strangely. He glanced over at the two screens, and she thought that he must have wondered why she was not sitting at the first terminal. But he did not say anything.

Kenny Fowler instructed her, "Use the same security code when you leave." He turned and headed up the stairs.

A few minutes later, with the file room door locked tightly, enclosing her, the first pages of the State Health Department lab report for New Leaf Foods slid out onto the printer's plastic tray.

Daphne wasted no time in folding them and slipping them into her purse.

TWELVE

At seven o'clock Tuesday morning, Daphne faxed Owen Adler at his home with the words, "The eighteenth step; eight o'clock," knowing he would recognize the shadowed heart that she drew on all her notes. One of the benefits of intimacy, she thought, is that shared experiences need only reference, not explanation. They had visited the locks on their first date.

At eight o'clock, beneath a canopy of steel-wool clouds and chilled by a temperature too cool to possibly be June, Daphne parked her Honda on the north side of the locks. Here, where the darkened waters of Lake Union spilled into the estuary of Puget Sound, the U.S. Army Corps of Engineers had built a set of locks to account for and correct the difference in elevations between the two bodies of water, overcoming what previously had been a minor set of waterfalls.

Daphne hurried through the verdant park, barely taking notice of the sweep of green lawn and the colorful beds of annuals, the dogs out on their morning constitutional with owners in tow, continuing past the refurbished administration buildings that offered postcards and

136

maps in the lobby.

Inside the lock, a thirty-foot ketch by the name of *Heather* was being eased lower as the water beneath it was evacuated at the far gates. Line was fed down as overhead the lock attendants kept the craft secure, while a handsome young couple monitored the bumpers and tracked the descent. Daphne crossed, at a brisk gait, the narrow footbridge with its chain handrails, not noticing that she turned the heads of several of the male attendants who then eyed one another with lustful expressions. She continued past the fixed floodgates, following signs to the fish ladder. Below, to her right, silver streaks sliced through the turbulent green water like knife blades in bright light, followed by an explosion of white foam as the salmon leapt and tumbled three feet out of the water, a cascade of brilliance before crashing back to the surface and disappearing.

She descended the stairs past various platforms of the fish ladder, turned and entered the bunkerlike cement viewing station where a prerecorded female voice said through thin speakers, "This is the eighteenth step."

Owen Adler, dressed in a dark blue business suit and wearing a pink shirt with French cuffs, stood alone before the viewing glass, where an enormous salmon slowly waved its tail and maintained a stationary hold in the strong current. The narrator's voice droned on overhead, but Daphne tuned it out. She approached him and they kissed, not as lovers, but as acquaintances. This bothered her.

"Not followed?" she asked.

"No. Not that I could tell. You?"

"No."

"So," he said. "It's good to see you. How did it go last night? Did you get in all right?"

"Fowler found me out." She explained her interruption in the file room. "I have to ask you a few things," she said, "that are not easy to ask, but they need answering. They need honest answering. And if the answers aren't what I hope they will be, then I want you to know that I would sooner leave the case, even leave the department than betray your confidence. I don't know how you find it, but it's hard for me, Owen, to be divided between work and you this way."

"Divided? Aren't we working together? Perhaps you should ask those questions," he said, revealing his concern.

She nodded, glancing briefly at the lumbering salmon, nearly three feet long, whose journey had carried it from the ocean to this fish ladder and soon beyond into the waters of Lake Union — a long, arduous journey.

She said, "The company is insured to the tune of eighty million dollars in the event of product tampering. How stable is the company financially? Is there any chance that anyone around you might have created this incident in order to win enough insurance money to redesign or remarket your product line?"

To her relief, the shock and astonishment that froze his features confirmed to her that he had never heard of, had never considered such a possibility. He finally managed to say, "Is it that much? Eighty?"

"Is that your answer?"

"Financial stability? We're an international corporation now, Daphne. We have assets and liabilities that are managed and juggled and manipulated to please those who issue us our credit. It's unprofitable to make too much profit, so you leverage your profits for more credit to expand your business and you go deeper in debt. It's a huge wheel. My job is to keep the wheel moving, for it's movement that sustains growth and therefore an ever-increasing asset base. At any one time we're seriously in debt, if that's what you're asking. But the product line is both well designed and marketed, and I, for one, can't see any reason to change that. And to go to such lengths to change it is absurd."

"If you wanted to redesign the line, could you afford to?"

"Right now? Is that what you're asking? We're moving into Europe. At this very moment our resources would be a little slim."

"Has anyone made such a suggestion?"

"Within the company? We're always getting those kinds of suggestions! Listen, we *invented* a market niche: the low-fat, organic ingredient — wholesome soups, frozen dinners, desserts.

For a while we existed there in a vacuum; we owned that niche. Not so anymore; we're under attack from every major out there. There's always someone within our ranks who thinks we've got the wrong look or that we're missing a major play that could be accomplished by a few subtle changes. I encourage that kind of independent thinking. There are some who want a more unified labeling to our products, others who understand the success of our diversity. Inventing a new look for our cans. You name it, I have heard about it." He studied her. "You're suggesting that, meeting my resistance, someone may have gone to this kind of extreme to see their ideas through to fruition. I don't believe that for a second. Absolutely not. We've lost market share, sure we have; this push into Europe has strained our pocketbooks, no question; but resort to something like this? Forget it!"

Another large salmon entered at the left of the window and swam forward, crowding out the one that was resting and sending it out of view, off to the nineteenth step. They watched it, the narrator's voice going on about breeding grounds.

"Tell me about Longview Farms," she said, facing the Plexiglas viewing window, but alert for any other early-morning visitors. The tourists wouldn't get here until midmorning, and if it rained, maybe not at all.

"That's going back," he said. "Did you dig

140

up that name in the files?"

She did not answer. She saw how scarred and beat-up this latest fish seemed to be, and thought that the sea was a much more hostile environment than she had envisioned it. The jaws of the big fish opened rhythmically, followed by a fanning of the gills.

"A supplier back in our New Leaf days. A family venture. Poultry farm. Good people to work with. Good product."

"Tainted product."

He nodded. "You're speaking of the salmonella contamination," he stated. "So you *were* able to find that, were you? That's what you wanted, right?" he asked reproachfully. "Honestly, that surprised me at the time. Mark Meriweather produced good birds, ran a solid operation. That's why I used him in the first place."

"That was also chicken soup, Owen. And that's the kind of coincidence that cannot be ignored. A company put out of business — bankrupted — by a series of lawsuits directly connected to your former company.

"Owen, I need an absolute point-blank answer . . ." She waited and then asked, "Are you aware that the State Health lab report that blamed the Longview Farms poultry for the salmonella contamination may have been altered?"

"Come again?"

"Altered. Forged. Changed."

The blank expression on Adler's face was all the convincing she needed. She felt the knot that had formed in the center of her chest loosen as a drip of perspiration skidded coolly down her ribs, sending a chill down her side. She told herself that he did not know anything about this. His lips moved, but no sound came out.

"I don't have proof," she said. "Not yet." She stepped closer to him. "But if someone at State Health altered that report in order to frame Longview Farms, then we have some serious motivation that may help to explain or even identify your blackmailer." She added, "Even if there was only the perception that Longview Farms was unjustly accused, it could be enough to set someone off."

"That was four, maybe five years ago."

"Part of the thrill of revenge is in the plotting, the planning. Strangely enough, the execution of the plan is often a letdown. It's one of the reasons the individual will stretch it out, given half a chance. Revenge-motivated crimes are unpredictable that way."

A young couple entered, hand in hand. Daphne studied the transparencies of the varieties of fish that might be seen in the viewing window. The woman said to her, "Pretty neat, isn't it?" Daphne mugged a smile and waited the full five minutes until the couple left. Alone again, she approached Adler.

She said, "I need access to the New Leaf

142

archives — the hard copies of what I saw on the computers at the Mansion. I need the original of that lab report."

"What about getting it from State Health?"

"If someone at State Health altered the file, I'd rather know that before paying them a visit. We may get some arrests out of this, and if we do, we may get some answers."

The big salmon grew active as smaller fish crowded the tank. After a few minutes they settled down, their mouths moving as if talking, as if mocking Daphne Matthews and Owen Adler, she thought.

"Can you get me in?" she asked.

"Hmm?" Adler was lost in thought.

"Without a lot of hassle."

"Of course I can."

"Without Howard Taplin knowing," she clarified.

"But you don't think —"

"Don't ask," she interrupted. "It's part of my *job* to be suspicious. Not that I always like it."

"I suppose it ruined Meriweather, something like that. Busted him, probably. What about the wife?" he asked. "Where did she end up in all of this?"

Daphne hesitated a second, reluctant to answer, but then decided that honesty was a two-way street and that she owed him hers. "At the top of my list," she said.

The salmon turned viciously and bit one of

its smaller cousins. The water clouded with an explosion of activity, and when it cleared again the big salmon was all alone and the bench at the viewing station was empty.

THIRTEEN

At eight-thirty Daphne arrived at the Public Safety Building flush with excitement over her discovery of the State Health lab report. She grabbed Boldt firmly by the arm, and without another word dragged him into her office, kicking the door shut behind them. Standing close to him, she searched his eyes and said, "Five years ago New Leaf Foods was accused by State Health of selling contaminated chicken soup. Lab tests placed the blame with a poultry company called Longview Farms out in Sasquaw." She passed him the photocopies of one and then a second newspaper report she had gleaned from a computer service since her meeting with Adler. "Longview Farms went bankrupt and folded as a result of lawsuits brought against it." As he shifted to the second article, she narrated for him: "Its owner, Mark Meriweather, went off Snoqualmie Pass in his Ford pickup. The fatality was ruled accidental — but what if it was suicide?"

Boldt looked up. "Are we supposed to believe they're coincidences? Chicken soup? A *suicide?*"

"Especially when you add in this." She handed

145

him the laser-printed copy of the State Health lab report. She explained what it was, and informed him of her suspicions that it may have been altered.

"A copy won't prove that."

"I know that. I'm working on it." She searched his eyes again and said: "You like this, don't you?"

"Very much." Boldt's mind was racing. "If they went bankrupt, then tracking down whoever once worked there may be tough."

"I put Meriweather's widow on the top of my list. Loses her husband, their income. She sours and hires someone to threaten Owen."

"Do we have her?"

"No. I ran her through DMV. No current operator's license, no current vehicle registration, I thought I'd ask LaMoia to try his contacts at State Tax — see if we can find a paper trail."

A knock on her door was followed by the head of one of the civilian staff. "Sergeant, we're holding a call from Gaynes for you. Says it's urgent."

The call was placed from Nulridge Hospital. Hearing Boldt answer the call, detective Bobbie Gaynes said in a frightened voice, "Sergeant, I've got two more."

Nulridge Hospital was the kind of small community hospital that was unlikely to survive health care reform. It had not been remodeled in years, though it felt clean and well kept.

Gaynes explained that via a credit card payment, she had traced one of the Foodland receipts to a woman who had purchased Adler soup on the same day as the Lowrys. The woman's husband and child had recently been admitted with what she described as "the stomach bug," but the symptoms — severe diarrhea, headaches, and mental confusion — matched those of Slater Lowry.

Boldt spent the next forty minutes attempting to convince the supervising intern to test for cholera — this, while also avoiding any direct mention of a product tampering. The doctor, refusing to be told his job by a gumshoe, remained hostile and distant until Boldt connected him with Dr. Brian Mann, after which point his attitude changed completely.

The senior Kowalski was responding well to fluids but his teenage daughter, already weakened from a two-year battle with bulimia, was listed as serious.

There was seemingly nothing to gain from visiting the two patients, but Boldt stopped in on the father. The man was lethargic and untalkative, but he was alive, which put him well ahead of Slater Lowry.

The daughter was unconscious, her medication being changed as Boldt arrived. The doctor caught up to Boldt in the hall, apologized for his earlier attitude, and thanked him, adding, "At least we know the enemy now," the irony of which was not lost on the detective.

At eleven-thirty that night the anonymous State Health van pulled in front of the Kowalski home. Once again Boldt ushered the field agents inside the home and stood by as an exhausting search so familiar to him from the Lowrys', began anew.

At 12:45 A.M., summoned back to the office, Boldt met up with Daphne, whose frantic behavior unnerved him as she explained, "Longview Farms has long since defaulted on their property taxes, but from what I can tell, it hasn't changed hands."

"It's vacant?"

"It's worth looking into, but it's well outside of our jurisdiction."

"And the widow?"

"I'm working on it. LaMoia got the property information, but he doesn't have anything on Meriweather's wife or the Longview business. What I want is an employee roster."

"That sounds like a better shot than driving a two-hour round-trip out to a vacant farm. You stay on the widow Meriweather, I'll ask a local uniform to check out the farm."

Boldt contacted one Sheriff Turner Bramm, within whose jurisdiction Longview Farms was located. He sounded like a smoker, and maybe a drinker, too.

"I don't appreciate being woke up at three in the morning."

"It's urgent," Boldt informed him.

"It always is. I'm not on call tonight, Sergeant."

"I know that, Sheriff. But this can't be entrusted to anyone but you. I need this done. I need it done right. And I need it done now. It's an active homicide investigation with a repeat offender at large."

"I got me deputies for the graveyard shift. What the fuck do you suppose they're there for?"

"I'm not KCP," Boldt reminded him. Bad blood existed between King County police and some of the local law enforcement of the smaller municipalities within King County. It stemmed from a budget-driven decision that required payment for KCP's services or the establishment of an independent police force.

"Don't give a shit you are or you aren't," Sheriff Bramm said. "You got any errand-running need done this time of night, then my deputies do it. Period," he said. He hung up.

Boldt called him right back.

"You're pissing me off," Bramm said answering, without waiting to find out who had called him.

"You get your butt out of bed and over to Longview Farms or you'll be answering to Klapman," Boldt warned, referring to the state attorney general.

"I'm trembling all over." The line went dead. When Boldt called back for a third time, the line rang endlessly: Bramm had unplugged his phone.

Lacking any jurisdictional authority in the area, Boldt returned a call to the sheriff's office and politely solicited the cooperation and assistance of one of Bramm's wet-behind-the-ears deputies. He wanted the local buzz on Longview Farms and he wanted this deputy personally to inspect the premises, getting the names of anyone and everyone currently or formerly associated with the property and the business conducted there. He tried to impress upon this deputy the urgency of his request. He needed this done immediately, not tomorrow or the next day.

"Sure," the man replied listlessly. Boldt hung up the phone, anything but convinced.

Some days his own people were his worst enemies.

When Boldt arrived at work the following morning, he was briefed by Shoswitz on an agreement reached with State Health. Should the Kowalski illnesses become the focus of media attention, the statements to the press would be that the symptoms were consistent with *E. coli* contamination. The early symptoms were in fact similar, which precluded the necessity to lie outright, and the city had been through a bad spread of *E. coli* the summer before, lessening the alarm caused by any such statement.

The first telephone call Boldt made was to Sheriff Turner Bramm, from whom he had received no report.

The phone was answered by the same gruff, raspy voice. Boldt reintroduced himself and asked for an update on Longview Farms.

Bramm informed him impatiently, "Listen, Tommy did a drive-by last night, didn't see nothin'. Gone sick with a summer cold now, so I'm what you might call shorthanded, Sergeant. I got me a grand theft auto and the DEA telling me I got a crack house operating in my village. You hear me? A crack house out here in the goddamn nowheres. You think I'm running errands for you city boys, keep on dreaming. And as for waking me up last night —"

"A drive-by?" Boldt interrupted. "A drive-by is all?"

"More than you shoulda got. More than you gonna get. You hearing me?"

"A grand theft auto?" Boldt inquired, perplexed. "I'm talking about murder one. A repeat offender at large. I'm trying to stop a killer, Sheriff," he said through his teeth, managing a modicum of control in his voice, "a killer who may or may not have a connection to a residence in your jurisdiction. I need someone to knock on that door and ask some questions, and if you're not up to it, then I'm going over your head and getting permission to send one of my own people out there and do it. Is that

151

registering with you? I'm not looking to make you any trouble, but I will in a heartbeat if you're going to go on playing southern cracker with me."

"Southern cra—"

"Final warning," Boldt said, interrupting loudly, and drawing Shoswitz's curiosity, which focused onto him. Boldt was not one to lose his temper. "Either you knock on that door and ask questions or one of my people does."

"I am *not* inviting you out here," the sheriff made clear.

"It's going to mean trouble for you," Boldt warned in an ominous voice that rang with authority.

Silence on the other end. It lasted so long that Boldt finally said, "Sheriff?" thinking he had been hung up on again.

"Give me your phone number," the sheriff said. "I'll call you right back."

"Ten minutes, Sheriff. Then I move without you."

"Give me your fucking phone number!" the man hollered into the receiver.

When the sheriff called back ten minutes later, Boldt couldn't help but wonder if he'd taken a drink of something, his mood had changed so noticeably. "You coulda told me who you were," the sheriff said. He claimed to have made a few phone calls.

"I did," Boldt reminded.

"No. I mean who you *were*," the sheriff at-

152

tempted to clarify. "Fuck it. It doesn't matter. You need a hand, you got one. I didn't know, that's all. You've got my respect, Boldt, that's all I'm trying to say. I didn't know it was you. Get it?"

"Maybe not," Boldt admitted, thinking that the man probably had him confused with someone else, but appreciating the change of tone and not wishing to challenge it. "But if you'll help, then that's fine."

"I'll head right over there. Right away while the coffee's still warm, right? Check the neighbors first, huh? Maybe the postman?"

And a good cop to boot. Surprise. "Sounds good," Boldt said.

"Be back to you by noon. That okay with you?"

"Just right," Boldt answered. "The sooner the better."

FOURTEEN

The wind blew swiftly from the southwest, changing the way the air smelled — or perhaps, Daphne told herself, it was just that she had not been out to Whidbey Island for a long time. She had driven here. After work on a Wednesday, no less . . . She felt irresponsible for having agreed so quickly and spontaneously. But Owen had that effect on her. He and Corky had arrived via his yacht, making it virtually impossible for him to have been followed. The home belonged to a friend of his. It was a split-level modern in the school of Frank Lloyd Wright — flagstone and glass, cut into a carpet of green lawn that spilled down to the shoreline.

The beach was steeply inclined and consisted entirely of fist-size smooth rocks. Huge cedar logs had been rolled up and deposited by storm tides, creating an obstacle course that Corky used for hiding places.

"We keep saying we can't do this, and yet here we are again," she observed.

"It's only for the one night, and besides, Corky insisted," Owen Adler explained. "She wants to invite you to her party, and there are some things a father cannot say no to, regardless of the so-called rules." He added, "Not my rules, anyway."

"Precautions, not rules."

"Truthfully, I think she's more excited about Monty the Clown than the party."

"Who?"

"It's an ice-cream bar with a gimmick, is all. The kids love it." He sounded like a marketing executive.

"Do you want to talk about the investigation?"

"No. It's what I came to get away from."

"Fair enough."

"In the morning if it's necessary."

"It's not," she said.

The water shimmered and she could make out several sailboats in the distance motoring with the sails down. But it was the lawn and the woods that called her, having grown up in riding boots.

She said, "The way you're keeping track of Corky, the way you're always watching her, always attentive to her needs — that's part of you . . . who you are. You do that for me, too."

"Not enough."

"Yes. It *is* enough — that's what I'm saying. It's a quality in you. It's not something I measure or keep track of — I don't think of it like that."

In a self-deprecating tone he said, "I *don't* always pay attention. I leave you in the lurch. I get thinking, and suddenly I realize I've left you out of my thoughts — and that's a criminal offense in any relationship — father/daughter, lovers, it doesn't matter. It's a selfishness, and I'm often guilty of it. I know it's the kind of thing that eventually destroys relationships —"

"You're doing it again," she warned him.

"Am I?"

"You're trying to give me a way out. Mark the exits. But I'm not going, Owen. I'm here. Like it or not, I'm in this."

"I like it. And you're right — that's exactly what I was doing." He hesitated, and allowed privately, "That's what you give me."

"What?" she encouraged — this was the great puzzle for her.

"Insight." He pointed out a flight of birds in the distance. "You call me on my games. You see what I'm up to when I'm not even aware of it."

"That doesn't sound so good," she admitted. "I don't want to be a psychologist, I want to be a companion."

"But it *is* good. I need both, I think. You're not afraid of me — you can't believe how many people act afraid of me. I hate it. It happens so much, so often, and it affects me — and it's terrible."

She collected her thoughts.

"You're nervous," he observed.

"A little uncomfortable," she admitted. "The thing is: This is your private time. Your family time — you and Corky. It feels different than

156

when we're at the house."

"It *is* different."

"Like I'm intruding."

"Not at all. You know that."

"Maybe I don't." She added quickly, "And I'm *not* fishing." She attempted to clarify. "I have a hard time knowing what's going on inside of you."

They skirted one of the large timbers, and then another. Corky slipped over a log and ducked low, out of sight. Owen Adler said, "We'll pretend we don't see her, okay? Act surprised."

"Right."

The child erupted with a "Boo!" coming to her feet and waving her arms, then threw herself into hysterics at their reactions and buried her face in her father's stomach and laughed to that point where she was forcing it. Owen pushed her off, teased her, and sent her on ahead of them.

When they were alone again he admitted, "I hide, too — just like that."

She allowed him time to think about this. "Have you always hidden?"

"No." This seemed to encourage him.

"The result of something recent or something old?"

"Both maybe. As a child I hid — physically hid from my father. He had a short fuse. He drank too much on the weekends and he'd want to 'play' with me," he said, drawing the

157

quotes in the air, "which amounted to playing too hard. Wrestling. Some punching. He hurt me often enough that I learned to hide. There was a place in the woods. I would stay there. But truthfully, I'm not sure it's that as much as when Connie died," he said, referring to his sister. "We were best friends. And she was the last of my family."

He went quiet for a time after that, interrupting the silence with, "I'm willing to work on any of this if it means the difference between losing you and keeping you."

"It's *me* who needs the work, Owen."

Corky hid again, but she gave up impatiently and chased something imaginary down the beach of rocks.

"I'm afraid to commit fully to this," Daphne admitted. "I see you tiring of me, leaving me, and that keeps me an arm's length away most of the time. It happened to my parents — they never divorced, which is *worse*. They just grew bored with each other. Bored and old and despondent. I don't want to bore you."

"Of course you'll bore me. And I'll bore you, too. But that doesn't have to be the permanent state of things." He said softly, "Corky drives me crazy sometimes. So what? If we're ready for that stuff, we're okay. If we're wearing blinders, we're in trouble." He added, "Are you worried we'll end up like your parents?"

"I see it around me all the time: happily married boredom. I am *not* charming and entertaining every second of my life."

"And *I* am?"

"Honestly?" she asked. "Yes. I'm never bored with you. That's a big part of it."

They walked for a while longer, Corky up ahead chasing the birds off the logs and running after them. His throat sounded constricted as he said, "I think maybe I've created an *image* of me rather than risk showing you the terrified boy who's actually inside here."

"I don't want to bore you," she confessed.

They caught hands, and they walked until the water turned gray and the wind slowed to a calm.

He said, "If this is going to happen, the work is ahead of us, not behind us."

"Agreed."

"And you're prepared for that?" he asked.

"Probably not. But I want it."

"You know what we're saying?" he challenged.

She did know. She squeezed his hand. He held hers tighter.

"I'm terrified," he admitted.

"Me too," she answered.

"Uncle Owen?" Corky wore a pale yellow nightgown. She had always called him this, though Owen had confessed to Daphne that he hoped to hear the *D* word one of these days.

"Yes, Love?"

159

Corky was half-Peruvian, previously Owen's niece, and now his legally adopted daughter. Owen's sister and her husband had met an eighteen-wheeler in the passing lane of I-84 five miles outside of Bliss, Idaho. "My sister died in Bliss," Owen had said. The driver of the truck, who had started his run in Chicago, was discovered to have been pumped full of amphetamines. But apparently not enough. He had fallen asleep at the wheel with a trailer of washing machines driving him through the guardrail in time to find Corky's parents passing an RV. His brother-in-law had left no clue to his past in Peru, claiming once while quite drunk that his family had been butchered because of politics, but never saying anything more. Adler, his sister's closest friend and confidant, had put up a fight to keep Corky when it had been discovered no legal guardian had been named, no will left. He had won by taking the case to the Idaho Supreme Court, and had adopted the girl on her sixth birthday.

"I'm going to bed now," the girl said.

"Not without a hug you're not."

The terrace stones were still warm from an afternoon in the sun and felt wonderful on Daphne's bare feet. The pool would be warm, too, and she had an urge to take her clothes off and go for a swim.

Corky tiptoed over to Owen and gave him a warm hug and kiss. Somewhat nervously, she asked Daphne to tuck her in, which Daphne took as a great honor.

"Do you like it here?" Corky asked her as they reached the child's room.

"I like being with you and your dad."

"I mean here — this house."

"It's a nice house."

"I like it because Owen's different."

"Different?"

Daphne stood by as Corky brushed her teeth and washed her face. She was a little adult, the way she tended to herself. Then the child dove into bed, pulled up the covers, and said, "At home he's tired, isn't he, Daffy?"

She felt a lump in her throat as she answered, "Yes, Cork, he's very tired. He works very hard."

"I can tell because he doesn't play with me as much."

"But he loves you as much."

"I don't like it when he's tired."

"No."

She gathered up all her courage and asked, "Are you coming to my birthday party?"

"If you invite me, I will."

"I'm inviting you now."

"In that case, I would love to come. Thank you."

"Promise?"

"As close to a promise as I can."

"Monty the Clown is coming," she informed her as an added enticement.

"Well, then! How can I resist?"

161

Corky liked that; she squinted and blushed. Daphne stroked the child's hair, wondering if she would ever have any children of her own, wondering if she had the strength and courage for it. The hair felt soft, her skin smooth and creamy.

Daphne returned to the patio, and without a word, began to undress.

"Things are looking up," Owen said.

Looking him over, she said, "Yes they are, aren't they?" She enjoyed that her body had such an effect on him. She carefully laid her blouse and pants and bra over the chair. By the time she stepped out of her underwear, the air felt chilly to her, and gooseflesh raced over her skin.

She ran across the lawn to the pool, hesitated at the pool's edge, and dove in. The sensation was astonishing. For a moment there was no outside world, no poisonings, no job to return to in the morning.

He caught her from behind, and she spun around and wrapped her legs around him, and they hugged tightly. "I feel like we're hiding from the parents," she said. Owen felt very strongly about limiting Corky's exposure to the physical side of their relationship. Daphne was a friend, not a lover, and though she understood this, she questioned both its sincerity and her own position in Owen's life.

He met eyes with her and asked, "Do we do it?"

162

Her throat caught and her eyes stung. This question had nothing to do with his arousal, which was substantial at the moment. It had to do with permanence and commitment. With promises, both kept and broken. Heartache and joy. A lifetime together. The question seemed to have escaped him spontaneously, and she worried he might be flooded with regret. He rarely spoke spontaneously. She allowed him time to retract the question, but he made no attempt to do so. His hands held her firmly on her hips.

He had his own way about doing things. He had nibbled around the edges of proposal several times, testing the water. And she had been conveniently noncommittal, believing that that was what *he* wanted of her — and seeing the fallacy of this, always in hindsight, tonight she braved to be honest. She held her breath. Their buoyancy seemed to rely on her answer. For a moment, all the world was perfectly still despite the electrifying shrill of the chorus of summer insects.

They never took their eyes off of each other, and neither blinked.

Daphne nodded and said softly, "Yes, we do it."

"Good," he said. The moment felt awkward to her. He looked as frightened as she felt.

It was done. She was engaged, she realized.

She did not squeal and hug him. She did not kiss him. It was not the way Owen Adler

163

sealed a deal, and she wanted this deal consummated. Her left hand grabbing for the pool's edge, her legs still locked around his waist, she pulled from his careful grip and leaned far away from him, precariously off-balance, and quickly extended her hand to him. He saw it and grinned. With both of their heads beginning to sink in the water, with both of them laughing and their eyes, like alligators', barely breaking the surface, their right hands found each other, and they sealed a life together with a handshake.

She let go her left hand, and together they sank, holding hands, bubbles rising from their laughter, her legs still entwined around him. She thought that happiness was like this pool of warm water, that the water enveloped them both, and that to be submerged in this kind of shared happiness, even for a moment, made all the other moments insignificant.

And as they broke their hold and exploded to the surface, grabbing for air, she was glad for the water and the darkness, for together they combined to mask her tears.

FIFTEEN

"Ain't no skin off my neck," the man with a bad limp said. The freight elevator clanged loudly to a stop and he slid a steel-mesh accordion grate out of the way. Oblivious to his own impairment, he towed his left foot behind him like an unwilling child; the sole dragging on the warehouse cement sounded like fingernails on a blackboard. Daphne fought off the chills. "Mr. Taplin 'posed to be here," he stated firmly.

"He's coming," she lied. "Besides, Mr. *Adler*," she emphasized, "said it was all right. You want me to get Mr. Adler on the phone?"

"No need for that," the guard said. They rode the rickety freight elevator three stories up. "Mr. Taplin 'posed to be here," he repeated, unlocking and throwing open the heavy door for her. She had to get in and out of here quickly and without being found out. In her mind, someone had altered the State Health lab report, and she intended to find out who, and *without* their knowledge. It was an enormous room, partially lit by an east-facing row of towering, fogged safety-glass windows that reminded Daphne of her gymnasium locker-room

165

door in junior high. This being the top floor of the warehouse, the ceiling was vaulted, the ridge twenty or more feet overhead. Rain fell on the roof noisily, like pebbles on sheet metal; the air smelled heavily of paper and ink and mold — stale, like an old attic, but metallic, like the inside of a refrigerator. She heard the groaning of some machinery that she identified with the odor in the dry air, made aware of the environmental controls that sought to preserve the room's contents. This was confirmed when the guard explained, "Gotta keep the door shut because of the dehumidifier." Adding, "You want me to tell Mr. Taplin you're already up here when he comes?"

"No," she said. "Let's surprise him. I won't tell if you don't tell."

"Mr. Taplin don't like no surprises." He flicked on the lights and pulled the door closed with an authority that made Daphne flinch.

Alone in here, the room felt about the size of a football field. Row after row of steel shelving, about half of which was stacked high with cardboard boxes — all carefully labeled.

The boxes were ordered chronologically, and arranged alphabetically within the year. New Leaf Foods, being the original company name, was likely to be among the first archived material. The very first boxes she encountered were labeled *NLF: A–D; NLF: E–G;* on and on — twelve boxes for the first year, 1985.

166

At the far end of the enormous room, in aisle 3, she discovered a specially designed rolling ladder — part ladder, part scaffolding — containing a battery-operated platform lift with locking wheels. She moved it down to 1985, locked the wheels, and climbed up, unsure where to begin: *C*, for Contamination; *S*, for State Health; *L*, for Longview Farms? She could spend hours in 1985 alone, and looking down the row of years, she saw more boxes labeled *NLF* in 1986 as well. She would need extended hours alone in this room. Should she jump ahead to 1986, figuring that this contamination occurred near the end of what was New Leaf Foods, and the start of Adler? She remembered the date, September 25, but not the year.

Ten minutes later she stumbled onto a set of files labeled *Corporate Security*, and a light went off in her head: by job definition, Kenny Fowler would have been involved in any possible contamination investigation. It seemed like a legitimate place to start. She pulled the box off the shelf, balancing it on the mechanical lift when she stood. She thumbed quickly through the material, heart beating strongly, a tingling on the back of her neck.

CONFIDENTIAL
RE: Salmonella contamination

CONFIDENTIAL
RE: Salmonella

All signed by Fowler. The mother lode! Fowler's investigation of the contamination might provide leads or insights. It seemed exactly what she was after.

An electronic *pop* went through her system like a gunshot as the freight elevator engaged. She jerked slightly, and felt the box going over, only it was too late: The file box was midair before she reached out to grab for it. As she did, she knocked the file she was reading off as well. The box tipped fully over and spilled its contents. Her Corporate Security file went airborne as well. The uncountable sheets of paperwork floated down and blanketed the cement floor.

The elevator hummed.

She panicked, slipped, and fell, catching a hand on the top rung and dangling from the mechanical loader. She kicked out and hooked a foot around the rail and hauled herself back aboard the ladder, tearing the armpit out of her jacket in the process.

The elevator continued its noisy ascent and she hoped that it might stop at the floor below. But it did not. It continued up. And this was the floor's only room.

It seemed impossible that so many papers could have been inside a single box. They littered an enormous area below her. She scrambled down the ladder, collected the papers in big, sweeping, armfuls, attempting both to find the Fowler letters and get the edges of the piles straight enough to fit back into the box, which she quickly uprighted and began to fill. Paying no mind to order or classification, she crammed the pages into manila folders and stuffed them into the box. She spotted a Fowler memo and separated it from the others. Then another. And a third. But only one marked *Confidential* — those she wanted so desperately. Scoop . . . Stack . . . Stuff . . . she went dizzy with the task. Papers were sideways, upside-down, dirty, folded, wrinkled — wrecked! Crawling on hands and knees, she made herself dusty, working her way around the large loader, scooping under it, looking everywhere for the adventurous piece of paper that had managed to travel great distances in free fall.

Bang! the freight elevator stopped. Daphne briefly quit what she was doing and listened. The sound of the metal grate coming open. It was definitely on this floor!

Furiously, she returned to her task, abandoning making any edges straight, and instead, cramming the paperwork into the box as if it were a trash can. She thought she had them all. She thought that was it. She forced the flimsy top back on, banging all four corners and crushing one.

Footsteps!

169

There was no time to climb the ladder, to return the box to its proper place. Instead, she shoved it into a vacant spot on the bottom shelf, freed the locked wheels, and *ran* the ladder down the aisle. She failed to look behind her, to where she had left the Fowler papers she had set aside — on top of a box in the shelves opposite 1985.

A key in the door. No voices . . . It wasn't the talkative guard; it was either Taplin or some other Adler employee.

Think!

She negotiated the huge rig around the corner to aisle 2, locked the wheels, and scrambled up the loader's ladder, yanking the first box onto the platform and opening it, while attempting to contain her frantic breathing. The box was dated 1988. It appeared to be engineering specs and floor plan blueprints. She would have to think of something fast if she were to explain her interest in this.

The door pushed open, grabbing Daphne's attention.

Boldt stepped inside and shut the door hastily. "We've got to hurry," he said anxiously. "Owen Adler saved our butts. He called downtown in a panic. You evidently tripped a security device. Taplin and Fowler are *both* on their way over."

Only then did she take notice of the box with the flashing light behind the door. She hurried over to it, keyed in the same number she had used at the Mansion, and the code

170

took. "Damn it!" she said.

"We're out of here," Boldt said.

She understood that determined look of his. As she ran back toward 1985 and the New Leaf files, she said, "You believe me, don't you?"

Following her, Boldt said, "About Longview being part of this? Yes. And I'd just as soon no one be wise to that except Adler himself. I think we want to contain this thing as much as possible. Let's get out of here."

In her excitement she had forgotten about the letters she had set aside, and began searching the box she had stuffed impatiently, missing sight of them entirely.

Boldt rattled the keys attracting her attention. "I've got to get these back to Frankie."

"Frankie?"

"We're on a first-name basis. He's big on cop shows. He promised to keep our visit quiet, but only if I got his keys back to him."

Pop! The elevator could be heard descending.

Boldt snapped his head in that direction. "Let's go!"

"The lab report!" Daphne said, running down the aisle. "Help me with this."

"No time," he objected.

"Help me!" she leaned her weight into the loader and heaved. She glared at him. Together, they wrestled the loader around the corner and raced it down the aisle, the hum of the descending elevator pressing them on.

"I think we should leave it," Boldt said nervously. "Technically, we should have a warrant."

"We have Owen's approval," she reminded him, scrambling up the ladder to a line of boxes marked *NLF-Legal*.

"Even so," Boldt said.

The boxes were alphabetized, and Daphne was forced to make a choice *C* for Contamination? *L* for Lawsuit? *S* for State Health? She chose *S–Z*, tearing the lid off the box and searching its contents.

The hum of the elevator grew distant. It was nearly down.

"Leave it," Boldt encouraged.

"No way." She clicked her index finger along the file tabs, and there it was: *State Health*. She yanked the entire file, returned the box, and skipped steps coming down the ladder.

The elevator stopped. Its opening grate echoed up the shaft, and *pop!* it began its ascent.

"Give me the keys," Daphne demanded of him. She snared them in one quick swipe. "Get this back around the corner and then get out of here. Meet you at the bottom of the stairs."

Without further explanation Daphne ran out of the room, crossed the hall, pushed through the exit door, and descended the stairs two at a time, determined to keep Taplin from knowing about her search of the files.

This being a three-story building, she had only the one floor — the second — to pass

172

the keys. The elevator opened from either side, and she knew from her ride up that after entering it, the passengers stood facing *away* from the gate that accessed the room to the Adler archives.

She cracked open the door to the second-floor hallway and peered out. The elevator was just reaching this level. At first she saw the backs of three heads: Frankie, the security guard, Taplin, and Fowler. Now their shoulders. The elevator climbed. Pressed against the wall, she hurried toward them.

The elevator was moving too fast to offer her more than one attempt. She closed the distance. Fifteen feet . . . Ten . . . Five . . .

Their waists. The backs of their legs. The elevator was dead even with the second floor. It continued to climb.

Daphne reached the stationary floor gate, diamonds of accordion steel. By contrast, the elevator's gate was slanted slats of wood. In order to pass the keys into the elevator, Daphne would have to negotiate both patterns at once. Her plan was to toss them inside and duck out of sight, at which point Frankie could claim he dropped them.

The floor of the elevator ascended past her ankles.

She held the keys, debating when to throw them. Started to, but stopped. Lifted her arm.

Frankie turned and looked right into her eyes. He must have sensed her, for his attention fell immediately to her hand — the keys — and without thinking, she lunged her arm through the steel grate attempting to pass them.

For Daphne, all motion slowed.

"Hell of a rain," Frankie said to Taplin's bald spot, taking a step back, his fingers twitching behind him for the outstretched keys. "Give me them!" this hand seemed to say. But as the elevator continued its steady rise, the pass became impossible, and worse, Daphne suddenly realized her arm was in too far: the bottom lip of the elevator could take off her hand at the wrist like a paper cutter.

Taplin's bald spot moved, as he swung his head to speak to Frankie.

Daphne ducked from sight, her arm high overhead, the steel lip of the elevator heading for her forearm like a butcher's cleaver. Her watch caught on the diamond steel gate, trapping her hand. Inches to go!

She tossed the keys, jerked her hand hard, and broke her watchband.

The keys splashed to the floor of the elevator.

Daphne flattened onto the floor.

Something thumped softly onto her back. Her watch. Frankie had kicked it out of the elevator while bending to retrieve his keys.

"Man, but I'm clumsy," she heard Frankie say, his voice rising with the elevator. "Damn near *lost* these."

"Doesn't matter," Taplin said. "I've got my key with me."

All for nothing! Daphne realized, heading back to the stairs and descending quickly. Boldt had the file, and she was anxious to see what it contained.

When she reached her car she leafed through the file quickly, nervously, eyes alert for the document that had become so familiar to her. Buried in the middle, she found it: the State Health lab report — and by the look of it, this was no copy.

SIXTEEN

The hours passed slowly while they awaited the initial results of the lab tests on the State Health document. The interviews with the Foodland customers dragged out, and those reports Boldt did receive suggested to him that too much time had passed. People simply did not remember much about grocery shopping.

Several calls placed to Sheriff Turner Bramm went unanswered and unreturned, infuriating Boldt. As Boldt's shift came to an end, replaced by DeAngelo's squad, there was a good deal of mumbling about what Boldt was really up to. Danielson had cleared a hit-and-run and they had leads in a liquor store assault, but it was clear to all from looking at the Book that most of Boldt's squad was, admittedly or not, detailed to whatever consumed Sergeant Boldt. Danielson was running a one-man show; Lou Boldt, in effect, was running a small task force.

On Friday morning, with the discovery of three hospitalizations in Portland that matched the symptoms of cholera-395, Boldt flew down for an eleven o'clock meeting with the Portland Police Department. At the same time, because the crime had now crossed state lines, the local field office of the FBI was alerted, and two Special Agents attended this meeting. Fortunately for Boldt and the investigation, he knew both agents personally and there was a good deal of mutual respect between them.

In an act of cooperation, the FBI field office deferred to Boldt's request for advice and assistance but not intervention. For the time being, the Bureau agreed to stay on the sidelines, offering its services but not its leadership. The SPD would continue to run the investigation with the PPD and the FBI as silent partners. The FBI's Hoover Building lab was made available, and Boldt passed along Daphne's request that the Bureau's behavioral psychiatrist, Dr. Richard Clements, contribute to a psychological profile. This was met with enthusiasm.

By four o'clock that Friday afternoon, some of the energy and urgency of the Tin Man investigation had begun to dissipate because of general inactivity and a lack of leads. Shoswitz settled back into his normal routine and left for home with the shift change. Lou Boldt did not.

Once again he telephoned the office first and then the residence of Sasquaw's sheriff, Turner Bramm. On the sixth ring the man's wife answered. Boldt had a brief conversation and hung up. He felt as if the wind had been knocked out of him.

Detective John LaMoia entered Boldt's office cubicle saying, "Narc, narc, anybody home?

Feel like a pizza?"

LaMoia, in his late thirties, was a twelve-year SPD veteran, and had spent six years on Boldt's homicide squad. He stood six feet one with curly brown hair, a mustache, and had a drawn face, high cheekbones, and large brown eyes. He wore pressed blue jeans that carried a heavy crease down the center of both pant legs; he worked out and had a reputation for being a womanizer. Everyone liked LaMoia — from the meter readers to Captain Rankin. He brought humor and sparkle with him, and he effortlessly crossed the line between the uniforms and the detectives.

"Sarge?" LaMoia was one of the more observant detectives.

"He never came home last night," Boldt mumbled.

"Who's that?"

Boldt said, "I'll pull the car around. You call KCP and let them know we're heading out to Sasquaw. If they've got somebody in the area, we may want backup."

"Backup?" LaMoia asked curiously.

But Boldt did not answer him. He was already off across the fifth floor at an all-out run.

By the time Boldt found the farm, it was dusk. They had become lost twice, and LaMoia had demanded they drive through a McDonald's. Using the cell phone, Boldt obtained a telephone warrant from deputy prosecuting attorney Michael Striker and district judge Myron Banks, giving him authority to search the premises. His mouth full of hamburger, LaMoia said, "You're starting to worry me, Sarge."

Boldt answered, "I'd double-check my piece if I were you." LaMoia tended to his weapon immediately.

A group of farm buildings spread out below the county road, barely visible in a determined starlight.

LaMoia switched on a flashlight, aimed it directly at Boldt, and said, "You should have eaten something. You look like shit."

"I sent a local sheriff here to nose around," Boldt explained. "He hasn't been seen since."

LaMoia switched off the light. In the silence they could hear the hum of the overhead power line.

The two hung their shields around their necks on thin black strings, and LaMoia crossed himself, and no one made any jokes. Boldt thought of Miles and that if he never saw him again, there would be no way to explain the reason a cop had kicked in a door in the middle of nowhere; and then he thought of Sheriff Turner Bramm's wife — the fear he had heard in her voice — and he opened his car door and headed toward the farmhouse.

The two men walked in silence, their city shoes juicy in the mud but neither complaining. They walked to the Powder River gate and

LaMoia opened it, quietly closing it again behind them. There were no lights on in the house, though it didn't mean anything: The driveway showed signs of recent use. A mercury light filled the distance between the house and outbuildings with a garish glare that seemed brighter than Arizona sunshine. With the shades up, there would be plenty of light inside with which to see. They were sitting ducks out here.

Boldt threw a hand signal at LaMoia indicating the dark side of the house, and the detective squatted and slid off into shadow where only the owls could see him. Deafened by the pulsing in his ears, Boldt slowed his advance, buying LaMoia a few needed seconds and forcing himself to think this through once again. A missing sheriff. A deserted farmhouse. His two-year-old son waiting at home. He withdrew the weapon from his holster, engaged the recoil and the safety, and gripped the stock between both hands. A bead of sweat trickled down his chin. His mouth was dry. So maybe Liz was right about a desk job. So what? There was nothing to do about it now. His police vest was in the trunk; he should have thought to put it on.

He walked faster now, his system charged with adrenaline, cutting quickly across the brilliantly lit farmyard and reaching the door to the farmhouse, a building in total disrepair. The white paint was coming off like sunburned skin, the windows were gray with grime, and the brown-bristle welcome mat had disintegrated at the center, leaving a frayed rope-weave underpinning.

Boldt held his breath to allow him to hear the slightest sound, then knocked loudly, paused, and knocked again. The wind blew high in the cedars and the mercury light hummed, sounding like a huge bug. Boldt peered through the gray glass at the inside of a cluttered kitchen. Although clearly well used, this was the back door. He circled the house, locating another door and knowing LaMoia would be keeping him in sight.

He knocked. Waited. Nothing.

A wave of the hand brought LaMoia out of the dark. They checked the ground floor thoroughly, and found it tightly locked up. "We could kick it," LaMoia suggested. "Not without a dammed good reason," Boldt clarified. "Not outside our jurisdiction." Boldt turned around and faced the five outbuildings. A series of muddy tire ruts led into the compound, some of them made recently.

"Try them first?" LaMoia inquired.

"Yup," Boldt said.

They crossed the farmyard to the first building.

LaMoia pushed open a huge steel door that ran on rollers. Boldt switched on the flashlight and scanned the interior. A long, narrow corridor faced them, hundreds of tiny wire cages stacked floor-to-ceiling on either side of the wide aisle. It smelled dusty. There were white, yellow, and brown feathers everywhere. Boldt experienced a similar nausea familiar to some homicide crime scenes. "You feel it?" he hissed hoarsely, his throat dry.

LaMoia nodded gravely. He pulled the door shut again. "Maybe we should call in that backup."

But they did not. They walked side by side silently through a patch of weeds that invaded Boldt's socks, prickling him. The air smelled sour and then suddenly sweet. They stopped in front of the second building, a modified Quonset hut.

"You okay?" LaMoia asked.

"No."

"Open it?"

"Go ahead."

The door squeaked on its hinges. Boldt painted the inside with the harsh beam of the flashlight. More of the same: hundreds of poultry cages; several rows of high-intensity lights hung from the ceiling.

Studying the coop, LaMoia said, "This must be the laying coop. They use the lights to trick the birds into producing more."

"Feels kind of like a ghost town," Boldt said.

"I know what you mean." They moved on.

By its outward appearance, the third structure suggested a different use — a tool shed or equipment barn. As they neared its double-door entrance, Boldt stuck out his arm and blocked

LaMoia before he stepped on the disturbance in the mud: activity, boot prints, and a series of tire tracks.

"Pretty recent," Boldt said, observing their clarity. The summer rains of the past week would have softened the impressions.

They avoided the disturbed area, cutting around the side of the structure, Boldt leading them with the light. He was already thinking ahead to lab crews and photographers, plaster casts of the boot and tire impressions. *Go with your instincts,* he had told the students in the lecture hall. His own told him that Daphne was right about a connection between Longview Farms and the Adler threats. He had nothing more than a sour spot in his gut and a few unexplained tire tracks upon which to make this bet. But if challenged, he was prepared to bet it all.

There was no entrance on the side, but at the far end they found a locked door and a reinforced glass window that had been spray-painted from the inside. They teamed up, Boldt training the flashlight under the crack in the door and LaMoia searching out irregularities in the hasty paint job, his face pressed to the glass. "To the right. More . . . ," he directed. "There!" he said. It took several blows with a length of scrap iron to punch a hole in the reinforced glass.

As they stepped inside, Boldt asked, "Do you know that smell?"

"A nose like yours, you oughta be in perfume."

"Smell it?"

"I do know that smell," LaMoia admitted. "That's paint."

"That's right."

The building was hot and stuffy. It had a cement slab floor with large drains and an overhead conveyor mechanism with metal hooks.

LaMoia said knowingly, "This is where they butchered them."

"Yup." Boldt walked a bit faster, approaching the sheriff's car.

"Gloves," he said. They both snapped on pairs of latex gloves. The flashlight caught the windshield and mirrors and bounced light around the cavernous structure in sparks and flashes. The words *Sasquaw Sheriff's Department* wrapped around a gold logo of Justitia — Lady Justice — on the driver's door. The vehicle was locked. Boldt shined the light into the backseat: no body. "Force the trunk," he instructed. LaMoia searched out his scrap-metal pry bar while Boldt fully circled the vehicle, ending up at the trunk.

Boldt said, "Clean. Too clean for all this mud. He wiped it down." His heart pounded painfully in his chest. Dead. He had sent Sheriff Turner Bramm here, had berated him until he accepted the job. He felt that he, and he alone, was responsible for whatever had happened here.

184

"Maybe he just parked it here so it wouldn't be seen," LaMoia said, reading his thoughts, working the pry bar. "The sheriff, I'm talking about. Maybe he and some farm girl are shacked up in the house, doing the business."

"Is that all you ever think of?" Boldt said a little too harshly.

LaMoia did not answer. He caught the lip well, put his weight behind the effort, and popped the trunk.

"No body," LaMoia said, relieved.

"No vest, either. And there's a shotgun clip on the dash. Empty. And no police radio," he said. "Torn right out from under the dash."

"We gonna kick it now?" LaMoia asked of the farmhouse.

"You bet we are," Boldt replied. The flashlight strayed to the cement floor and caught a blend of yellow, blue, and red spray paint, edged by a hard line where a drop cloth had been. LaMoia went down on one knee. He sniffed the paint closely. "There's the source of the smell."

Boldt followed the paint with the light. It formed a large empty rectangle on the cement floor.

"Spray-painted a car," LaMoia said.

"A truck," Boldt corrected. "With these three colors."

LaMoia put his shoulder into it for a third time, and the kitchen door came open.

The air smelled of food gone bad and windows left shut. The kitchen was small and tidy, dishes drying in a rack and dry, fresh fruit in a bowl — slightly withered. A door immediately in front of them, perhaps leading to the basement, was padlocked shut with new hardware. Using hand signals, Boldt indicated for LaMoia to search the first floor. He, Boldt, would take the upstairs.

The sergeant passed through a musty-smelling living room and climbed a flight of creaky stairs.

"Police," he warned. "We have a warrant to search these premises."

He continued his ascent, flashlight in his left hand, his right hand hovering cautiously near the stock of his weapon. Below him something moved. LaMoia slinked silently past, disappearing into a different room. The unusually white light of the farmyard mercury lamp played against the downstairs walls. Boldt ascended, unknowingly holding his breath.

The staircase led up the center of the house, leaving rooms ahead of him and to either side. "Police," he called out again, though with less authority. He passed through a pocket of foul odor and stopped dead still, his neck and arms alive with goose bumps. He knew that odor, and he identified its source as the room to his right.

His senses warned him again that this was indeed the home of the Tin Man. The closer he drew to that door, the greater his appre-

186

hension. "Police," he repeated, his weapon already in hand. "I'm coming in." Not wanting to make a target of himself, he shut off the flashlight and pocketed it.

He gently rotated the bedroom doorknob and toed the door open cautiously, greeted by a darkened room.

"Police," he repeated yet again, reaching for the light switch.

An empty room.

The room had been recently lived in. He smelled dirty laundry mixed with that same odor of spray paint. Once again he was struck by the incredible neatness of the room. That neatness troubled him: an ordered mind, compulsively neat. He was afraid, despite his training. He wanted out of here.

A noise, like a tiny bell. He knew that sound: hangers banging together. *Ding!* they rang again. The closet was on the far side of the bureau. Someone was inside that closet. A sudden scratching on the ceiling caused him to jerk his weapon overhead, and he almost fired. Rats or bats, he realized.

As he turned to call for LaMoia, a rustling sound came from the closet, preempting him.

He leapt forward and yanked the closet door open.

The hangers rang again. A cat leapt off the shelf and onto Boldt's shoulder, so quickly that Boldt went down with the contact.

Empty. The closet, the other rooms — by

the last of which LaMoia had joined him.

"Nothing," the detective said.

"There's that smell in the hall," Boldt said, leading LaMoia back to the top of the stairs. Any homicide cop knew that smell.

They both spotted the laundry chute at the same time. "That would be the basement," LaMoia said.

"The padlock," Boldt reminded him, and the look they shared silenced them as they hurried back down the stairs and into the kitchen.

Using a butter knife that he broke twice in the process, LaMoia removed the hinge pins to the basement door before Boldt had thought how to deal with the padlock. The door came open backward, and LaMoia tore away the lock, doorjamb and all, and deposited it in a crash to the floor. It was dark inside, and it smelled of death.

LaMoia reached for the light switch. Boldt caught his arm, shook his head no, electing the flashlight instead, wanting control over the environment.

Darkness closed in around them as they descended the steep stairs. Boldt's flashlight beam directed his attention. A washer and dryer. A soapstone sink. A laundry line. A pottery kiln. Otherwise, it was black down here — the windows boarded up and painted shut.

They moved slowly through the laundry room and into another musty-smelling room formed of concrete-and-rock walls, a room stacked high with secondhand furniture and rusted gardening equipment. Rocking chairs, baby's toys, pine dressers, clothes inside clear vinyl hanging bags, mattresses, and headboards. It smelled faintly of mothballs and cat urine. A hard box of white light framed the edges of a crude door leading into another room. The closer they drew to this door, the more pungent the feculent odors.

Boldt drew a box with his finger. He and LaMoia carefully searched the door frame with their gloved hands. LaMoia said, "Got it," and pointed to a delicate stretch of monofilament that crossed the gap in the door frame just above the rusted hinge. The trip wire was not entirely taut. LaMoia peered inside. "Ceiling balloons," he announced. "It's rigged for arson."

"We back out slowly, John. *Now!* And we keep our eyes open. There may be others."

Meo-ow . . .

It came from behind them, drawn by the fetid odors of early decomposition. It came hungry, and it wanted through that door. Both cops understood the threat it represented without a word between them. Boldt stooped and said, "Here, kitty," as LaMoia groaned, "Oh, shit!" maneuvering to box it between them. "Good kitty," Boldt tried.

It stopped and stared up at them — a mangy cat with a curiously distant look in its eye. It meowed yet again and LaMoia, creeping up on it, said to Boldt, "Blind it." It shied away from both, and Boldt could feel the tension set into its hind legs as it hunkered down prepared to spring.

"Ready?" Boldt asked, the flashlight held tightly in his sweaty hand.

"Ready," LaMoia echoed.

"Go!" Boldt aimed the beam of the light as he would the bead on a barrel, directly into its eyes. It froze. LaMoia took one long stride, hands outstretched, and the cat sprang through them like a bar of wet soap.

Fast little silent footsteps. Before either man could react, the wooden door creaked open as the kitty nosed and nudged it. LaMoia dove and snagged the cat, but his shoulder brushed the door and threw it fully open.

Sheriff Turner Bramm hung suspended by his wrists from an overhead pipe. His uniform seemed moth-eaten with holes where his captor had burned him with cigarettes. His shoes were off and his ankles wired to his thighs so that the full weight of him fell to the wire wrapped like bleeding bracelets around his wrists. His death mask was one of pure horror, frozen in a wretched spasm of agony.

There was a workbench, its surface clean and neat. Boxes stood beneath it.

A string of as many as twenty balloons — all sagging, filled with gasoline — was suspended in rows from the ceiling. As the detonator took, in an extreme slow motion, bright orange-and-blue flames chased through the string of balloons, running like water down a hill.

LaMoia was already up, clutching the cat, sprinting for the storm cellar door only feet behind Boldt. LaMoia shouted something, but it seemed slowed down to Boldt and he didn't understand.

Boldt felt the strong wind in his face as he followed LaMoia up the concrete steps on hands and knees, wildly racing for survival. The igniting of the balloons drew air from every crack and crevice, creating a choir of singing voices.

The force of the subsequent explosion propelled Boldt out of the storm cellar as if he had been shot from a cannon, followed a fraction of a second later by a tunnel of yellow flame that curled to the sky like a crooked finger.

Boldt scrambled to safety, unaware his jacket was afire until LaMoia tackled him and threw him upside-down into the mud.

The house went up like kindling, a bonfire of epic proportions.

The volunteer fire department arrived in time to declare it a complete loss and to take several pictures. For the time being, Boldt and LaMoia identified themselves only as passersby, keeping their occupations silent. There was no mention of a body in the basement, and the fire remained far too hot for its discovery. The sergeant and detective lingered nearby, protective of their crime scene. Fire marshals were due on the scene early morning. At 1 A.M., Boldt telephoned Bernie Lofgrin of the police lab, awakening him at home. By the time the fire cooled, sometime around sunrise, Boldt wanted an ID crew available to sift the ashes. Lofgrin complained about jurisdiction and that he was still owed the jazz tapes Boldt had promised. Boldt said he would take care of both, and even though Lofgrin knew there was little or nothing Boldt could do about the jurisdictional conflict, he agreed to have a crew available.

SEVENTEEN

A man was following her — she was convinced of it. She would have to lose him or miss the emergency meeting. She was already late. Monday mornings were always a nightmare.

The meeting had been hastily arranged by Fowler and was to be held at a neutral site. They were all to arrive within a few minutes of one another — Boldt, Fowler, Adler, Taplin, and Matthews — all having used different modes of transportation, or at the very least, different entrances to the Seattle Center. The idea was to make it impossible for one man — following any one of them — to connect them to this meeting. A pair of Fowler's undercover security people were to keep Adler under constant surveillance while watching for someone keeping him under surveillance. If such a person were identified, a police patrol, under the direction of Phil Shoswitz, was prepared to detain him or her.

If Adler was free of any surveillance, then the meeting would go ahead as planned.

But now it was Matthews, not Adler, who was being followed, or so she believed, and there were no contingencies for this.

At first it had just been a sixth sense, a bout of intuition, a *feeling* as if one too many buttons were undone and every male on the street had his eyes on her. Or maybe her wraparound skirt was not fully wrapped. Only she was not wearing a wraparound skirt today, but a pair of forest-green denim jeans, and the oversize white button-down oxford was properly buttoned right up to her collarbone, with the shirt collar flipped up to help hide the scar that had been the gift of a psychopath some years before.

The Westlake Center was just down the hill now. She had been assigned the monorail. She debated taking a quick detour through Eddie Bauer, a chance to waste a few extra minutes — she was always early to everything — and maybe even a chance to ditch or identify whoever was back there. She could not be sure she was right about this.

In the back of Daphne's mind always lingered the possibility of retaliation, of becoming a target of one of the criminals she had helped to convict. As the department's forensic psychologist, she saw more of the witness chair than many of her colleagues did, testifying ninety-nine times out of a hundred that the suspect was legally sane and therefore able to stand trial. Such testimony carried long-range implications: If and when the suspect was subsequently convicted and sentenced, the sentencing time for a suspect deemed mentally healthy was specified as hard time instead of the more gentle "hospital time" given to those identified with psychological problems. For those serving the time, a big difference indeed. To make matters worse, she knew that the cases involving her services were for criminals with unstable personalities. Or perhaps, she thought, her being followed had to do with her current efforts — the break-ins at the Mansion and the archives. The Tin Man himself, or at least the New Leaf contamination.

She did not get a good look at him, and that worried her all the more because he was good. If there *was* someone back there, he remained well back, and seemed to always anticipate her inquiries. The very first time she turned, she had seen a reaction in a man about a block in back of her; but the next time she looked, he had stopped nonchalantly, turned, and walked away from her, quickly rounding a corner. Twice more, sensing his presence again, she stopped cold and turned around abruptly. But both times she failed to identify any pursuer. Even so, the feeling, once inside her, did not go away; and she was taking no chances.

She passed over the Eddie Bauer idea, deciding instead to make her move once inside the Westlake Center, which was the departure point for the monorail. The tourist crowds were large this morning — there were two conventions in town, a greeting card sales conference and a water sports equipment show — and Fifth Avenue teemed with coffee-carrying, camera-

195

laden, T-shirt-clad enthusiasts, a swarming hive of Middle America in search of retail therapy.

The Westlake Center was just what such people were looking for: a minimall that included some impressive anchors as well as decidedly upmarket outlets for everything from jelly beans to three-hundred-dollar fountain pens. It had size without losing its substance. It catered to the gold cards, leaving the Discover set to find their thrills out on the streets amid the homeless and Seattle's unpredictable weather.

Daphne headed straight to Fireworks, not only because she enjoyed the often bizarre merchandise, but also because of its central location and floor-to-ceiling glass walls that enabled her to keep a close watch on both the escalators and the people emerging from the building's only elevator.

She declined the assistance of an eighteen-year-old windup Barbie doll whose exposed cleavage was enough to keep any warm-blooded male shopping for hours, and confined herself to the front shelves that provided her the perfect location for her vigil.

She had the monorail timed perfectly. In five minutes she would head two floors upstairs, buy her ticket, and board.

After her first few minutes of observation, she began to doubt herself. She saw no one who even vaguely reminded her of that man whom she had seen duck around the street corner. She, of all people, knew the power of imagination, the power of the mind, and she, too, knew the dangers of paranoia. She could not allow herself to be convinced of anything without solid proof. She could tolerate suspicion, but only for so long. Just as she nearly had herself convinced that this was nothing but delusion, she saw him.

How he had reached the Westlake's Metro level she had no idea, but there he was below her — at least the back of him; she had yet to see his face. But the clothes looked familiar, as did the general height and size of him. And he had that bloodhound body language about him — attentive to the crowd around him but not the stores. Maybe he had taken a bus and entered through the Metro tunnel; she had been watching the street-level entrances. But what sense did that make? How could he be following her if he rode a bus to get here? Was there more than one man involved? She willed him to come closer, to turn around and face her, but he continued away from her, and as she glanced at her wristwatch she saw that she had run out of time: Less than two minutes until the monorail's arrival.

There was no decision to make — she was expected at this meeting. She left the store, dodging a final attack by the bouncing Barbie who nearly caught up to her at the door. Her attention remained almost entirely on the man who circulated on the floor below her. She gripped the handrail and moved slowly toward the ascending escalators. He wore a khaki windbreaker, blue jeans, and boat shoes, but so did half the males in Seattle this time of year. He wasn't alone in this look, even in the Westlake — and again she found herself mired in self-doubt. Another man perhaps, not the one she had seen earlier.

As she took her attention off him to board the escalator, she suddenly felt his eyes find her. She strained to lean over the escalator and look down — to confirm this — but in those few spent seconds he was gone. Try as she did, she could not locate him.

With this man in sight she had felt okay, but now that she had lost him, her paranoia returned and she punched her way rudely up the stairs of the moving escalator, as if running from someone she could not see. *Get hold of yourself,* she cautioned internally, knowing the dangers of such behavior — fear fed on fear and could run out of control in situations like this. But she felt him back there, like her brother chasing her as a child, like her drunken uncle chasing her around her bedroom, reaching out for her — and she could not help but experience the terror of being caught. Wild with this fear, she charged out of the escalator, took the corner, and ran to the next and final escalator up, knowing somewhere within her — but not realizing — that the more she ran, the more attention she drew to herself. The easier a target.

As she entered the ticket line for the monorail

with her heart in her throat, she knew she wasn't thinking clearly. She bought a round-trip, impatiently checking over her shoulder, and then moved on to join the waiting crowd. The monorail surged around the bend and slowed for its arrival. Her agitation increased with each passing minute. The two train cars pulled to a stop and a handful of passengers disembarked. A moment later she and the others crossed the steel catwalk into the train and took seats. No one in a khaki windbreaker, she realized to great relief. The sliding doors clapped shut, and she exhausted a huge sigh. She moved forward to the lead car where there was more room, instinctively distancing herself.

But the doors, previously shut, hissed open admitting three latecomers, including a man in a khaki windbreaker whose back was already to Daphne by the time she realized these others had boarded. When she spotted that jacket, she nearly let out a small scream, but muzzled herself and faked a sneeze to cover. She could not allow herself this kind of fear. She knew that once a cop allowed him- or herself this kind of paranoia, it was difficult if not impossible to stop it. You saw the faces of killers you had helped to convict in every crowd, on every street. You imagined where no imagination should be allowed. She felt through her purse at her side to the small police-issue handgun it contained.

She collected her strength, stood, and walked

back to this other car, her full attention on the khaki windbreaker. She passed the circular bench, took a handhold on an overhead rail, and turned to face him. She stared at him until he finally looked up. He was a small man, midforties, with a tiny scar by his left eye. With boyish curiosity he said, "Hi."

"Do you know me?" she asked, not knowing where the words came from, not recognizing him.

"I think I'd like to," he said.

"Why are you following me?" she asked.

He looked around nervously at the people around them, all of whom Daphne was using intentionally. Confront, intimidate. He could not do anything to her here. "What?" he replied. If he was acting, he was quite good.

"Go away," she said, "or I'll have you arrested." She took one step away and then added as an afterthought, "If you know anything about me, you know I'm capable of delivering on that."

"Listen —" he said. But she would not give him any chance at an explanation. The worst possible thing she could do, she had just done, responding to emotion rather than logic. If he was for real, she should have played him out, should have arranged to have *him* followed, to turn the tables on him, to get something out of it. Instead she had felt the need to prove herself, and had blown whatever advantage she might have had over him. She handled this all

200

wrong. She knew all this, and yet she felt satisfied as she sat back down, because it had taken nerve to do what she had done — and right then she had needed proof of that nerve. Now she did not, but now it was too late.

The monorail came to a stop after its brief trip to the Seattle Center. She wandered the Center for longer than she had intended, keeping an eye on this man who, paying her no mind whatsoever, headed straight to a crafts show, confusing her all the more.

With this confusion charging her system, she headed toward the crafts fair at a full run. *To hell with the meeting.* She would follow him. She would call in backup and stay with him.

But he was gone. She spent ten minutes searching the grounds, the rides, a few of the displays. He had disappeared again, as quickly as he had at the Westlake.

Or maybe, she thought, glancing around quickly he was once again watching her, only this time more cautiously. This time vowing to make no mistakes.

The felt board outside the Seattle Center's planetarium was the kind used in hotel lobbies for seminar announcements. It read, NEXT SHOW: 12 NOON, with a listing of the planetarium's regular summer schedule in a smaller white press type below.

The center was mobbed with families overcome by the interactive science exhibits, pro-

201

viding the exact cover that Boldt had hoped for in calling the meeting here. Boldt discreetly showed his badge and gave his name to a security guard who stood sentry by the planetarium's door, and getting the nod, let himself in. Taplin and Fowler were already waiting.

Boldt had to convince Adler to pay the extortion money. He expected the man to flat-out refuse.

The room was a twenty-foot-diameter circular enclosure, its perimeter entirely surrounded by a padded couch. In its center was a large, fixed desktop covered with an abundance of gray-metal projection gear that looked to Boldt as if it were straight off the set of *Buck Rogers.* The room had only one entrance and it was sound-proofed, the two qualities that when combined with its extremely busy public setting made it the perfect location for a covert meeting.

Boldt had seen the real show a few months ago while here to meet a snitch who had whispered right over the words of the college-age woman with her red-light pointer narrating "a voyage into the night sky." Pretty good show at that — terrific for the under-twelves. Miles would need a few years before he could get anything out of it.

"You look a little whipped," Fowler said, coming over to him. Taplin, an open briefcase next to him, was focused on a stack of papers on his lap. "You're supposed to sleep every week or so, whether you need it or not," Fowler quipped.

"Glad to be out of it?" Boldt asked.

"*Am* I out of it? I feel like you're keeping me out of it," he complained.

"I didn't mean it like that. I meant the department."

"Hang on," Fowler said, pressing his finger into his left ear. Only then did Boldt notice a tiny, flesh-colored wire running from his shirt collar. "The boss is here." Fowler had his people in the area, and as a result felt in control. It bothered Boldt, who was accustomed to running things.

The padded door opened and Adler entered.

Howard Taplin put the paperwork aside and stood. He appeared to have lost another five pounds, emaciated by stress and fatigue.

Adler crossed the room and shook hands with Boldt. "You look about like I feel," he said sympathetically.

"I'm not sure how to take that."

"Here comes trouble," Fowler announced. "And way off schedule, I might add."

Daphne entered, looking frayed. Fowler locked the door behind her.

"If you've got problems with your watch," Fowler said nastily, "we'll get you another."

"I was delayed," Daphne said.

"It was supposed to be ten-minute intervals," Fowler reminded her. "You were due here *before* Boldt."

"I was delayed," she repeated, glancing at Boldt, who sensed immediately that something was terribly wrong.

"Let's get started," Taplin complained irritably. "We have a lot of ground to cover." He handed both Boldt and Matthews a photocopy of a fax. "This is the first of the two faxes we received."

"Two?" Boldt asked, reading.

YOU BROKE THE RULES.
YOU HAVE ONLY YOURSELF TO BLAME.
I SAID NO COPS AND I MEANT IT.

Fowler said, "I've got a staff of fifteen in a two-shift rotation. Three of the guys wore badges before this. We've got experience, we've got the best gear. Basically, I think what Mr. Taplin is thinking is that we should take over. We can't risk any more killings."

"You're trying to fire me?" Boldt asked Taplin.

Daphne asked disbelievingly, "Owen?"

Admonishing Fowler, Adler said, "We're here to discuss this. No decisions have been made."

"You can't fire the police," Boldt explained angrily. He did not want to be forced into telling them about the murder of Sheriff Bramm. Longview Farms had once had direct links to Adler's former company, though Boldt was waiting for the lab report on the State Health document before informing any of these three. "If we need to take additional precautions to prevent leaks, we will."

"It goes well beyond that," Taplin protested. "You're going to have to shut down your side of this investigation — whatever that entails — and turn it over to us. Mr. Fowler has been handling the details of our side of this investigation, and has not involved the police once to my knowledge — so the leak certainly did not come from our side."

Adler complained to his counsel, "Let's dispense with this partisan attitude, Tap. I don't like it one bit."

Boldt saw no way around exposing the murder of Sheriff Bramm. It was the only way to settle this. "We're investigating the homicide of a law enforcement officer who may have been a victim of your blackmailer. The murder occurred at Longview Farms sometime early last night."

Adler, Fowler, and Taplin all shared expressions of shock. No one spoke until Boldt broke the silence.

"I want to remind you that the evidence collected from the poisonings suggests an Adler Foods employee. But this murder is now being investigated as well. Although we have no *evidence* yet to corroborate this, we have to consider the possibility that a former Longview employee, or someone hired by one of the Meriweather family, is currently on your payroll and is perpetrating these crimes. The point being that he killed a police officer whom we asked to look around the farm for us — and that is what this fax is in reference to."

"Why weren't we informed of this?" Taplin complained.

"We just were," Adler interjected, losing his patience with his attorney. His eyes betrayed his anger with the man.

"What about your side of this?" Boldt asked Fowler. "Have you gotten anywhere with possible employees, past or present? Why haven't I seen any reports?"

"I've got all that for you," Fowler said defensively. Pointing to the attorney, he explained, "Mr. Taplin was just going over it. Nothing looks very good, I gotta tell you. I was focusing on guys — okay? And then you throw this curveball that it's a girl we're after — that Foodland video — and there I am starting all over. It takes time to do this without attracting attention. You know that." Fowler asked, "What about the Longview investigation?"

"Matthews is continuing to look into the possibility of a Longview connection," Boldt replied.

Fowler glanced over at Daphne and nodded. "If you need my help . . ." he offered.

"Thanks."

Adler instructed, "Let's show them the other fax, Howard." Boldt noted the harsh tone of voice and the use of Taplin's proper first name instead of the nickname Tap. The tension between these two was palpable.

"*Another* fax?" Daphne questioned. "A *second* fax on the same day?" she attempted to clarify.

Fowler shifted restlessly. "You're seeing 'em in the order we did."

Boldt read:

MOM'S HOME RECIPE:
$100,000 IN PAC-WEST #435-98-8332
BY FRIDAY, OR HUNDREDS WILL DIE.

"Sent to the same fax machine?" Boldt asked. Adler confirmed with a disappointed nod.

Boldt asked Fowler, "What about caller-ID? I take it you got a number?"

"A pay phone in the U district. By the time we reached it, whoever sent this — he? she? — was long gone."

"We should have been informed, Kenny," Boldt chastised, furious to have been excluded. "That's what we have patrol cars for."

"You didn't notify the police? Why wasn't he notified?" Adler inquired. He was doing a fair job of keeping his cool, but he seemed right on the edge of losing it.

"It was a matter of reaction time," Fowler explained. "I make the phone call . . . Boldt notifies dispatch . . . Dispatch notifies the radio cars . . . I've *been* there, sir." He grimaced. Boldt got the feeling Kenny Fowler did not appreciate calling anyone sir. "The fastest, *most efficient* way of handling this," he said, playing

207

to Adler's priorities, "was to jump right on it and handle it ourselves."

"Well it failed — how's that for efficient? Next time," Adler corrected, "the police will be notified immediately. Are we all in agreement on that?"

Fowler flushed with embarrassment; he did not like reprimands, either. Boldt felt the meeting falling apart. All three men seemed ready to go at one another's throats.

Boldt asked Daphne, "What have we got?"

"It uses the same language — this threat to kill hundreds. It has to be taken seriously." Boldt knew her well enough to sense something troubling her, but he was not going to push, given their present company.

"What bothers me," Adler said, "is that it seems such a chance to take just to *send* these faxes — so why send two? Why not combine them?"

"Maybe," Fowler theorized, "the extortion is what has been planned all along, and it just took pushing him over the top to trigger the demand." He put Daphne on the spot by asking, "Were the poisonings the setup? First, prove his power, then move in for the real hit — the extortion?"

Daphne chose her words carefully. Glancing quickly to Boldt and then back to Fowler, she repeated, "The extortion threat must be taken seriously. This opening line is another reference to Mom's Soup, which fits his earlier style. I think he means business. My advice, if that's what you're asking for, is to pay the ransom demand."

Taplin said, "Out of the question. We will *not* give in to acts of terrorism." To Adler he said sternly, "We have to draw a line in the sand somewhere."

Boldt hurried to interrupt. He asked Fowler, "What about the bank account?"

"We haven't done an end run on you concerning this bank account, if that's what you're asking. Sure, I could find out the particulars of the account through my contacts, but I lack the kind of access you enjoy at these corporations, so I'm leaving it to you."

Boldt did not believe any of this. Adler and his company had more than enough banking contacts to end-run the police. He assumed Fowler was already looking into it and simply wanted to avoid the legal problems of admitting it. Boldt saw the incredible opportunity this extortion presented to the investigation, realizing the importance of convincing Adler to reach into his pockets and play the game. He realized the current indecisiveness between Taplin and Adler could be made to work to his advantage, and he believed Adler would listen more closely to Daphne than anyone in this room. Meeting eyes with her, he asked, "How do we interpret this?"

She stared at him briefly and answered, "It's his first serious mistake. He has allowed greed to cloud his agenda. I disagree with Mr. Fowler: I don't believe he had this in mind all along. I would say this came as an afterthought. Perhaps faced with a violation of his demands, he realized he had one of two choices: kill hundreds or turn up the heat. I think he has elected the latter. And in doing so, I think what we learn from this is that he is indeed reluctant to deliver on this more serious threat of mass killings. Either he doesn't have the means to do so, or he's lacking in will. My interpretation is that he blinked. We should take quick advantage of it. If he's greedy enough, we can use that against him."

Taplin insisted, "We are *not* going to pay. This company will *not* be held hostage. Besides, we very well may have cut him off at the knees by changing the glues — which admittedly we have you to thank for, Sergeant. The product codes on the Portland contaminations were all for cans produced prior to the glue change. To date, we have seen no contaminated cans *post* glue change. This extortion attempt is nothing but an act of desperation. He's out of bullets."

Daphne said, "We don't know that. He could easily have a stockpile of soup — a hundred cans or more — in which case the new glue means nothing. The other thing of interest is this bank account — an established bank account. He's not asking for a paper bag filled with cash, for a dead drop in the bus terminal.

This bank account indicates premeditation — a professionalism that *must* be taken seriously. The demands have continually escalated. Are we seriously willing to challenge this person? I would warn against taking such an action at this point in time. Pay the ransom. Play him out. The FBI would tell you the same thing."

Taplin stood rigidly tall and said in a cocky, defiant voice: "And if we pay, what happens if this is just the tip of the iceberg?"

"It often is," she answered. "I don't have to explain to you that these product-tampering extortions can continue for *years*. I'm sure you've researched your position. The H.J. Heinz baby food case in England went on for over two years. Thirty thousand British pounds were paid out before they caught the man."

"I'm familiar with the case," Taplin conceded. "It is *exactly* what we want to avoid." Toying with his three-hundred-dollar fountain pen, the attorney said, "At some point enough's enough."

"This is not that time," Boldt cautioned, turning his plea to Adler. "If anything, it's just the opposite: This is when to play along." He met eyes with Taplin and then Adler. "You are both men who clearly understand opportunity. You don't have your kind of success without knowing when to play and when to fold. This isn't just another threat," he said, indicating the fax, "it's an invitation. He's handing us a real-world link to himself. It's *exactly* what we've been lacking: a way to lure him in. Forget the glue and the soup and the bacteria. He's requesting currency, which by definition *moves*. You move it into the account and he has to move it back out. And when he does, we're waiting. It's *that* simple."

"He can —"

"Wire it?" Boldt interrupted, cutting off Taplin before he constructed a compelling argument. "He probably *thinks* he can. But we'll follow it. This is the computer age — he can't do *anything* with that money without our knowing about it. Look, he has made himself vulnerable. This is our first decent chance at him. Don't take that away from us." To Adler he said excitedly, hurriedly, "If you *don't* pay him, all we're likely to have is more killings — that's what he's promised us. If you pay, we have a trail to follow."

Taplin complained, "If you give in to a demand like this and the press gets hold of it, you're seen as weak. These people never stop coming after you. Never. It's over."

Adler appeared to be deep in concentration. Boldt elected silence. Adler met eyes with Boldt, and he seemed to be searching for the right answer. The sergeant said, "If you give me the choice, I'd rather follow a money trail than a string of Slater Lowrys."

Adler checked his watch, turned to Taplin, and said, "You know who comes to a place like this — a planetarium? Kids. Kids like my Corky, like your Peter and Emily. Kids like

212

Slater Emerson Lowry. What if we push this guy over the top? What if there are a couple hundred Slater Lowrys that we're directly accountable for? How do we live with something like that?"

Taplin's expression was sullen. "I don't have an answer for that, Owen."

"I do," Adler said. He said, "Kenny?"

"Boldt's right," Fowler answered. To Taplin he said, "I understand where you're coming from with this. We *do* open ourselves up to all sorts of nightmares — but they are financial nightmares, not human ones. It's just like Boldt says: He's giving us the chance to switch tracks. Money instead of lives. I think we jump on that kind of opportunity."

"So do I," Adler agreed.

Taplin, a look of resignation overcoming him, shuffled papers into his briefcase and snapped it shut, refusing to meet eyes with Boldt. "I'll arrange the necessary deposits."

"We should start small," Fowler said, directing this to Daphne. "Half maybe. Make him keep the communication coming."

"I can support that," she agreed.

"I'll speak to the bank," Boldt said. He thanked Adler, adding: "It's the right decision."

Adler rocked on his heels and said, "We'll see."

EIGHTEEN

Boldt's hopes rode on a meeting he had set up with Pac-West Bank. Perhaps in setting up this bank account — which for good reason was presumed to be a dummy — the Tin Man had inadvertently left them a clue to his or her identity. It was for this reason that Boldt invited Daphne along: to look for psychological clues in the facts of a bank account application.

As agreed, they all left the Seattle Center separately. Boldt met Daphne at her houseboat, where they shared a pot of tea and planned the bank meeting.

Boldt filled her in on the burning of Longview Farms. "I can hear it in your voice that you blame yourself for sending him there. You can't do that, Lou. We need you at a hundred percent."

"Something bothered you about the second fax."

"You're changing the subject. The subject is Lou Boldt."

"What was it?" he asked, refusing her.

"It was a little thing: no placing of blame. *All* the others made a point of putting the blame back onto Owen. Not this latest one."

"And that's significant?"

"The assumption of responsibility is *extremely* significant, yes. He or she doesn't want to assume responsibility for these poisonings. They are Owen's fault. As long as they remain Owen's fault, they can continue. Strangely enough, the day they stop being Owen's fault, we're in trouble. The guilt for these deaths could unravel him. We don't want that to happen."

"And you think this fax indicates that it has already happened." He made it a statement.

She did not want to commit herself. She blew on the tea and looked out her window at Lake Union and a pair of windsurfers, like butterflies on the surface.

"I think that receiving two faxes on the same day, with one of them significantly different from all the others, may just be enough to attract the interest of Dr. Richard Clements. And if it does only that, then we're all better off. He's the best, Lou. We could use him."

"There's something else," he said noticing that look of hers.

"Which one of us is the psychologist?"

"Is that an answer?"

"I've changed my mind about the wife. She certainly didn't kill Sheriff Bramm. And from the way you describe it, that wasn't the work of a hired gun. That was someone extremely angry. A male."

"Yes."

"You knew that," she stated.

"Yes."

"Someone with a personal stake."

"Absolutely."

She moved restlessly on the stool. "Chances are when he killed the sheriff, he was symbolizing on Owen. It shows us the kind of anger we're dealing with. It shows us how volatile he is. He wants to see him dead, Lou. He'll stay with this until he does — or until we catch him." She looked away, not wanting to show him her eyes.

"Maybe the bank can help us," Boldt said. "Razor's going to join us."

"That should be interesting."

Prosecuting Attorney Michael Striker was of average height, but he looked small because he had a small head and a small mouth. He might have had his ears pinned as a child, but they were fanning back out in middle age, bent like leaves stretching for the sun. People called him "Razor" because his voice sounded like someone humming into wax paper wrapped around a comb. At the end of his right arm he carried a metal claw that served as his hand. As a barroom stunt, Razor would stack matchsticks into four-inch-tall wooden chimneys using only his prosthesis. When he was nervous it chattered involuntarily, sounding like an eggbeater hitting the side of the bowl.

The support of the prosecuting attorney was

critical to any investigation. A PA did not run an investigation, but he steered it in the necessary legal directions that winning convictions required. The lead detective — the "primary" — and the PA formed a team that was sometimes comfortable, sometimes not. Most warrant affidavits went through the PA or were hot-rodded directly to a judge with the PA's approval. Being around Michael Striker when he was nervous took some getting used to, as did adjusting to his volatile temper, but Boldt enjoyed the man. He was among the top five PAs in King County, and some people had him picked for a Superior Court appointment within the year.

Boldt, Matthews, and Striker were escorted to an elevator and shown up to the sixth floor, where a set of fake trees and the faint twinge of disinfectant welcomed them to an executive wing.

Lucille Guillard, a cream-skinned black woman in her late twenties with a glorious French accent, an exceptionally long neck, and penetrating black eyes, wore a blue linen suit and white blouse combo that could have been stolen from Liz's closet. An overriding confidence permeated a smile that was at once both expressive but controlled. She shook hands all around, offered them seats, and got right down to business. An assistant delivered three photocopies of the computerized account information.

"A woman!" Daphne was the first to notice.

217

Boldt felt as if the wind had been knocked out of him. The Shop-Alert video had suggested the involvement of a woman, but the torture-homicide of Sheriff Turner Bramm had convinced him that he was after a man.

"No such address," Striker declared. "I've got a cousin who lives in the fifty-nine-hundred block on the even-numbered side. There's a park across the street from him. There's no such number as 5908." To Guillard he said sharply, "Do you people ever check these things?"

Guillard bristled. "I am *not* New Accounts," she clarified, as if it were a banking disease.

"Well, let's see the original application. We're a little rushed." Striker's prosthesis began chattering.

"We're okay, Razor," Boldt said, trying to calm him.

Guillard reread her copy of the computerized sheet. "This account was opened last week. That means that the original application would be destroyed by now."

"Destroyed?" Striker inquired, leaning forward in his seat. "What the hell do you mean, 'destroyed'?"

"Razor," Boldt said. He could feel the man about to explode.

She complained, "Pac-West is a paperless workplace. We're all E-mail and voice mailboxes around here. Not that I like it. The bottom line for you guys is that the original application would have been scanned and downloaded to the mainframe in San Francisco five working days after the account opened. I can get you a facsimile of that original — the quality is exceptional — but not the original itself, I'm afraid."

"Fucking bean counters," Striker complained. "You can't develop latent prints off a copy, lady. You know what we're up against here? A facsimile? You think a *facsimile* is going to help the sergeant?"

Boldt said, "It was a long shot anyway, Mikey. This is hardly Ms. Guillard's fault. We had expected a bogus address, a bogus name."

"I would doubt that," Guillard said. To Striker she said sternly, "The applications *are* checked out."

Striker objected. "You want to know what you're looking at here? Ten to one this name belongs to a recently deceased female. The false identity gives this person a Social Security number that matches the name just *in case* your bank actually does run a check — which I still doubt. Federal agencies have taken steps for years to automate and cross-reference their obit databases in order to prevent what we call mortuary fraud, but, like banks, they are a bunch of bureaucrats, and they move about as fast as slugs and are about as intelligent —"

Daphne interrupted. "She would need a current mailing address, wouldn't she? For the statements?"

"Absolutely. If more than two statements are returned to us, we suspend the account immediately." For Boldt, Guillard's French accent turned her words into whipped cream.

"But that means she has *two months* before you close the account," Daphne pointed out.

Striker said, "That's what I'm telling you: slow as slugs." His right hand sounded like a fence gate in a strong wind.

"If this address is fraudulent, as Mr. Striker is suggesting, we will cancel the account today."

"No," Boldt cautioned. "You mustn't do that."

Guillard eyed him curiously, confused.

Daphne explained, "If an exception can be made, we would prefer the account remain open."

"I don't understand," Guillard complained.

"Of course you don't!" Striker hollered. "Jesus!"

Boldt grabbed Striker by the arm and led him into the hall, shutting the office door. "Enough, Razor!"

"I'm sorry, Lou." His metal claw ticked loudly. "You can see what she is: a foreigner, a minority, a woman — that's a quota position, for Christ's sake."

"She's an executive vice president, Razor. One of twelve. You're way out of line here." Striker was breathing heavily. He nodded.

"Things have been shitty for me at home, Lou. You're probably right."

"Why don't you talk to Legal — see if we can't get any documentation on this account without jumping through the hoops. And be *professional* about it, Razor. We *need* these people."

"Yeah."

"Okay?"

"Apologize for me." Striker headed to the elevator without another word.

Boldt returned to the office and apologized profusely to Ms. Guillard. He said, "It's personal problems."

"We all have them," Guillard replied understandingly. "Still, I am glad he is gone." She allowed a warm smile. Her eyes met the two of them. "This is something serious, is it not?"

"For the moment I'm afraid you'll have to go mostly on faith." He hesitated and then informed her, "I'm with Homicide. Mr. Striker is a prosecuting attorney. And Ms. Matthews is the police department's forensic psychologist. We're after a person who is committing particularly heinous crimes."

"And this is the person you're after? This Sheila Danforth?"

"Possibly," Boldt conditioned. "We don't know that for certain."

She appeared more than a little overwhelmed. In her smooth French accent, Guillard said, "Very well. How may I help you?"

"The application was made in person?" Boldt asked hopefully.

Checking the printout, Guillard said, "No. By mail."

"Mail?" Daphne asked.

"It is done all the time. Nothing unusual there."

"Avoid the cameras," Daphne said to Boldt.

"Exactly," he answered, then inquired of Guillard, "and the opening deposit?"

She located a code on the document and used her computer terminal to look it up. "Postal money order."

Daphne said, "Difficult if not impossible to trace. She thought of everything."

"And this number?" Boldt asked, leaning over her desk and pointing it out to Guillard. "A credit card?" If it was a credit card, the charges could be traced — just the kind of paper trail he was hoping for.

"No. It begins with the digit eight. That is an ATM card," she replied.

"She ordered an ATM card?" Boldt said uneasily.

"By now she has it," Guillard informed him. "Our latest marketing campaign. Have you not seen the advertisements? We guarantee an ATM debit card within two business days of opening a new account. No usage fees, no service fee for the first six months. Our competitors take several weeks to issue the cards, and most charge a variety of fees."

"Two days?" Daphne questioned.

"Two days if you pick it up at a branch

office. That is part of the marketing, you see. It provides our customer service representatives an opportunity to cross-sell. It has been an enormously successful campaign."

Boldt knew that unlike retail outlets, bank video surveillance systems worked on continuous twenty-four-hour loops, erasing the last twenty-four hours as they went — stopped and reviewed only in the event of a security problem. The timing of the application, the pickup of the ATM card, and the threat sent to Adler all ensured the establishment of an anonymous bank account, and a way to get at the funds that seemed to the layman nearly impossible to stop. "There have to be thousands of ATMs," Boldt let slip.

"What is it?" Guillard asked.

Boldt rushed his words. "We'll need a full accounting of the ATM card activity and the card's personal identification number." He added quickly, "Do we know if the PIN was generated by your computers or selected by the customer?"

She referenced her computer terminal, typing the request.

An ATM card seemed to Boldt an ingenious method of collecting the ransom, because they would have so little time to locate and prevent the withdrawals. And with this thought came a sickening feeling in his stomach that boiled up into his throat and forced him to excuse himself and seek out the bathroom.

When he returned to Guillard's office, he felt no better and he knew by Daphne's troubled expression that he must have been very pale. He lost more of his color when Guillard informed him that she did not have the PIN information immediately available.

"It's time," Boldt said.

Daphne understood immediately. She said to the woman, "Ms. Guillard, we need to tell you something in the strictest of confidence. When we asked to see an account executive, that eventuality was made perfectly clear, so obviously you are a person to be trusted or your name would not have come up. Before we go any further, however, you should know that by coming into our confidence you are, by default, committing to what may be a long-term assignment, possibly with a great deal of hours involved. Long days. Long hours. There's no way to know —"

"But that's how it looks," Boldt said. "If you would prefer — for *any* reason — for us to work with someone else at the bank, now is the time to say so. You should think about this carefully."

"You're with Homicide," she directed to Boldt. He nodded. "And you're a psychologist dealing with the criminal mind."

"That's one aspect of my work, yes," Daphne conceded. She felt like telling her, I try to keep the burnouts from eating their barrels, I try to keep the marriages from falling apart, and I try to help the junkies and alcoholics to save their badges. She continued: "Right now I'm trying to piece together a possible profile of whom we are after."

"I will help you," said the French woman. West Indies perhaps, Boldt thought.

"You're sure?" he checked one last time. "This isn't 'Murder, She Wrote.' This can get ugly." Daphne nodded. Briefly, it seemed to him that none of them was breathing.

"I want to help. It is either a ransom or an embezzlement or a suicide. Am I correct?"

"Or maybe all three," Daphne said.

"May I?" he asked, indicating the door. He didn't want anyone to overhear what it was he had to say.

Lucille Guillard's face registered shock, concern, and terror. She hung her head and then looked at him with impassioned eyes and said, "She's going to get her ransom through the ATMs."

"Unless we use the ATMs to catch her," Boldt proposed.

The woman's eyes began to track behind her thinking. She did not look too convinced.

"Can we do that?" he asked.

Daphne asked, "Can she withdraw enough money for this to make sense?"

"She has one thousand dollars in her opening balance. That does not qualify her as a Personal Banking Customer. Mind you, with this ransom

225

demand of one hundred thousand dollars on deposit, she will qualify for Personal Banking. PBCs have a user-defined daily ATM ceiling. The card is really a debit card. Withdrawals are made against the account balance."

"Withdrawn from the same machine?" Boldt asked.

"The same machine, yes. The same transaction, no. Do you see the difference? The physical limit of any one transaction at an ATM is four hundred dollars. That's all, four hundred. That is not something we can override, but is imposed by the manufacturer of the machine for a variety of security reasons. So: per transaction, a total of four hundred. But the number of concurrent transactions is dependent entirely on the imposed ceiling, or the account balance, depending on the type of account."

"So it *is* possible — technically possible — to get at the ransom through the ATMs," Boldt verified.

"If the account is structured properly, quite possible. Yes. Thousands a day, I suppose, if the customer set it up that way. The highest daily ceiling that I'm aware of is ten thousand dollars. That was requested by a rug merchant who uses the card for international buying. In his case, however, he uses the machines infrequently. It's used more as a cash advance card."

"And tracking the individual. Is *that* possible?"

"It is quite complicated, the ATM network.

226

Do you know anything about it?"

"I'm afraid not," Boldt said. Daphne shook her head.

"We can tell you where withdrawals have been made. Yes? But *real-time tracking* poses significantly greater problems. If she stays within the Pac-West ATM network, perhaps we can identify fixed locations. But if she accesses our network from another network's machines, then the request is handled by the regional switching station here in Seattle — NetLinQ. By the time we see the request, you would have no more than a few seconds in which to react."

"A few seconds," Boldt echoed, crushed by the news. "Sounds like we'd have to have a person watching every ATM. How many are there?"

"Pac-West operates three hundred and seventy in the state. Roughly half of those are concentrated in an area within an hour's drive of the city, including downtown. The number of machines handled by NetLinQ?" she asked, opening a drawer and referencing a file. She frowned, and Boldt felt it coming. "NetLinQ handles over twelve hundred machines between Seattle and Everett. Roughly five new locations are being added every two weeks."

An army, Boldt was thinking. Twelve hundred surveillance operatives? At the peak of the Green River Killer investigation, one hundred and forty law enforcement personnel had been involved. It made his team of four look pretty

227

damn small. It made his stomach burn.

He popped two Maalox.

"Some of our ATMs are equipped with cameras. Maybe that would help you. Still cameras and video. It depends."

"How many?" Boldt asked hopefully.

"More than half, I believe. And more in the metropolitan areas than in the country. And we are installing cameras at more than three a week. It is a top priority for us."

Half? It wasn't enough.

Daphne, sensing his despondency, suggested a meeting with whoever was in charge of NetLinQ.

"That would be Ted Perch," Guillard said. "He is not the easiest man to deal with. Especially for a woman. You understand?"

"Then I think I'll pass," Daphne said. She told Boldt, "I'll be at the office, then home."

Guillard said delicately, "I will call and see if he will see us."

"Let me explain something, Sergeant. It was *sergeant*, wasn't it?" Perch delivered Boldt's rank as if it were one of the lower life forms, as if he deserved much better. "We have always cooperated with law enforcement in the past, and we're happy to be of whatever assistance we can be. But" — and Boldt had heard the word coming — "if we interrupted the network for every extortion, for every threat, for every counterfeit card operation, we might as well go fishing instead. Clear?"

Boldt had said nothing of the case he was on.

Perch reminded him of a man who played racquet sports. He had fast eyes that preferred Lucille Guillard's hem length to Boldt's cool exterior, brown hair that was washed too often, and an athletic bag snugged up to his desk where everybody could see it. The office was unexceptional except for a pair of watercolors of the San Juans, and an unspectacular view of I-5 and a marina on Lake Union that almost counted as a water view.

Perch had telephoned Shoswitz in order to verify Boldt's identity. He called Lucille Guillard "Lucy," and he said it a little too smugly, as if she considered him an intimate friend, which she clearly did not.

From what Guillard had told him, Boldt's real-time tracking could only be accomplished through a coordinated effort between Pac-West and NetLinQ.

"This is not your everyday extortion," Boldt said.

"I've worked with Freddie Guccianno a couple times," Perch admitted.

"Freddie's not working this case." Boldt said.

"Freddie's good people."

Boldt hated that expression.

"What is important, Ted," Lucille Guillard said smoothly, "is that the bank and the switching station come up with a real-time environment that makes it possible for Sergeant Boldt to track certain withdrawals."

"I understand that, Lucy. But what I'm trying to point out — to *both* of you — is that real-time monitoring just isn't possible across the entire network. No such software exists — not that I know of. It's just not something we're set up to do. What? What, Lucy? Why are you looking that way at me?"

"It is something you *must* do. At the moment, Sergeant Boldt is asking politely. None of us, the police, the bank, wants to initiate legal steps. The idea is that we cooperate."

Ted Perch looked a little hurt. She knew more than he did, and he did not like that. And if he tried to look up her skirt one more time, Boldt was going to say something about it.

He nodded slowly at her, made a sucking sound in his teeth, and directed himself to Boldt. "The way the system works is this, Sergeant. The account in question is with Pac-West. Clear? If a Pac-West ATM is used to access this account, as I'm sure Lucy explained to you, then that request goes directly to their server. Several verifications are made almost instantaneously, the server okays the withdrawal and instructs the ATM to dispense the cash. Whambam, thank you, ma'am. But in the case of a Pac-West customer using say a First Interstate ATM, that's where we come in. First, the PIN — the personal identification number

— is encrypted by the machine, so as it travels along these phone lines, no one can grab it. Next, the account number and a BIN number — the bank identification number — are routed directly on to the First Interstate server in California, which recognizes that the BIN number is not theirs, and they then route the request back to us. Our computers reroute the new request according to the BIN number — in this case, to Pac-West. Pac-West confirms the account information and approves the withdrawal, routing the approval and an individual authorization code, through us, back to First Interstate, which then instructs the ATM to dispense the cash. In some cases, the request may pass through a national switch first, and then be routed to us, back to the national switch, back to the bank in question. At any rate, this entire process I've just described takes three-point-two seconds. There are four-point-one million credit and debit cards in use in the Northwest alone — and eighty million in the U.S. And to give you an idea of volume, of usage, of the number of hits we receive: ATMs in Washington and Oregon alone process one *billion* dollars a month. That works out to somewhere around twenty million dollars a day during the short week — *fifty* million dollars a day Friday, Saturday, and Sunday. That's four hundred thousand hits per day! And you want us not only to pull an individual hit on this system, but pull it *real-time?* Are you be-

231

ginning to see my problem?"

His intention had been to mow Boldt down with the facts and figures, and he did just that. Four hundred thousand withdrawals a day. The number fifty million rang in his head.

"Have we met before?" Perch asked, as if Boldt had just walked through the door.

"No."

"You look damn familiar to me. Do you play racquetball?"

"Piano. Jazz piano."

"A club! Am I right?"

"The Big Joke."

"Exactly. I *knew* I'd seen you before." To Lucille Guillard he said, "He's good." To Boldt he said, "You're *very* good. Happy hour. Right?"

Boldt thanked him and pointed out that he had to drop the piano when a case like this came along.

"A case like what? You're not Fraud, are you, Sergeant? Not unless you just transferred. I *know* the guys from Fraud, believe me."

"Homicide," Boldt said.

It was a word that hit most people sideways, and Ted Perch was no exception. He actually jerked his head back as if he'd been struck. "The big leagues," he said.

"Just another division."

"What is this thing? Blackmail? No, extortion — right?"

"Right."

"Bet someone's dead," Perch guessed, "or what would you be doing here?"

"Someone's dead," Boldt confirmed. "Maybe others if we don't hurry."

"If people's lives are at stake, that's different."

"We *need* your help," Lucille Guillard said earnestly. "The problem is that by the time a real-time system identifies a hit, Sergeant Boldt has about ten seconds — or less — to apprehend this person."

Boldt added, "And that's not enough. Not even close."

"Slow down the entire system?" Perch queried. "(A) It's not possible — not that I know of, and (B) I would be hanged. If the system goes down for five minutes, it makes the news these days. People have gotten *used* to ATMs. They expect them to work. Twenty-million a *day*, don't forget."

"Does it have to be the whole system? Couldn't we isolate just these requests?" Boldt asked.

"It doesn't work like that. Sometimes there are two, three, even four ATMs installed right alongside one another. What's this person going to think when his transaction takes forever and the guy next to him receives service as usual? Let me tell you something: People have built-in clocks when it comes to ATMs. They *know* how long a transaction is supposed to take. The average transaction takes twelve seconds. You stretch it to forty and a guy like this, someone jerking the system around, is going to notice. Plain and simple. He's gone."

Boldt was glad that Perch had the gender wrong.

Guillard said, "But if the whole network were to slow down. Or at least every request in the city. What then, Ted? So it makes the papers for a couple of days?"

Boldt agreed. "Oddly enough, that kind of publicity might help us. Might convince him it's a regional problem."

"Help you, maybe. It'd get me fired. I can tell you that. But it's all moot anyway. I've never heard of such a thing. You can't just slow down the network by flipping some switch."

"That is what I told the sergeant. But I was hoping you might know more than I do." She hit Perch right where he lived. He *wanted* to know more than she did, and he didn't see the trap she had laid for him.

"We have some software techs. I could ask them."

"Our people are looking into it, too," she said, adding a sense of competition.

"I'll need permission from the nationals," Perch said, already a step ahead. "There would be some serious explaining to do."

"We're long on people capable of serious explanations. That shouldn't be a problem," Boldt offered.

Perch suggested, "Let me circle the wagons.

How soon you need this?"

Lucille Guillard recrossed her legs and Perch didn't even notice.

That was when Boldt knew he had him.

NINETEEN

Someone *was* watching her.

Daphne had studied enough paranoids, had worked with some, and knew the symptoms well. Symptoms she now displayed: a heightened nervousness, the constant checking over her shoulder, insomnia, loss of appetite, the suspicious pauses to stop and listen. But it was an *energy* and she understood energy. An energy focused on her, and if she were imagining this, then she intended to compliment her imagination, because this was like nothing she had ever experienced.

Back there somewhere? Over there? she wasn't sure. It seemed at times to be all around her. At others to be in a specific place — yet when she checked: no one. It made her skin crawl, this feeling. And it wasn't just while out on a run, which was where she was at the moment. It was in the bedroom, in the car — she felt it when undressing even in the bathroom, which is where she changed clothes. The rest of her houseboat made her feel naked before she took off a thing. This filled her with a nauseating fear, a sense of violation she had not known.

236

Was that the same car? she wondered. It looked awfully familiar. Had it been parked across from the dock entrance to the houseboats? What was it, Japanese? Detroit/Japanese? She wished she were better with cars. It was the same *color,* she thought. Same size. Dark blue. Small. Non-descript. *Just the kind of car one would use for surveillance!* Just the kind of paranoid thinking that could get you in big trouble. "Conspiracy vision" — there were all sorts of slang terms for it. "Oliver Stone disease," she had once heard it called; and that one had made her laugh. No longer.

She broke with her regular Tuesday evening running route and turned right up Galer and right again onto Eastlake, a procedure similar to the consecutive four right-hand turns used to spot moving surveillance when in a vehicle. She glanced over her shoulder. *Watch it!* a voice cried out inside of her. That was symptom number one.

She ran another quarter mile, and literally leapt into the air when a blue car overtook her from behind. A different blue car, she realized quickly enough. Upset with herself, she turned around, cutting short the run. It was dusk. It would be dark by the time she got back, and whereas normally her run would take place after work and therefore under the streetlights, tonight the idea bothered her. It cut her run nearly in half, but she could make up the difference tomorrow.

Daphne ran hard, working up a good sweat, pushing herself to go a little harder today since she had cut it short. Her gymnasium-gray tank top was soaked dark below her breasts and down her back. Her hair stuck to her neck, and her white wristband was damp from sponging her brow.

Typically, she used her runs as meditations — a quiet break devoted to nothingness, to thinking as little as possible. She waved to a walker, thankful for a familiar face, and the woman waved back at her with a broad smile. Although they had never formally met, she knew all about this woman — the houseboat community was like that. The woman was an M.D. who volunteered her time at a local clinic for the poor; her husband was a former minister turned author. They lived in a small houseboat, though it was one of the more charming ones — with very few pretensions. And they waved at you when out for a walk.

A scruffy dog crossed the road lazily, either not seeing or not caring about a sleek black cat that sat atop a shingled mailbox house at the end of pier 11.

She walked the last hundred yards, peeked into her mailbox for the second time today, and headed down the dock.

Halfway down the long dock her skin crawled, and she blamed it on a light breeze off the lake and the slight chill it induced.

Whether attributable to caution or paranoia,

she took inventory of her houseboat as she approached. It was tiny, less than eight hundred square feet, but with the proportions that created an illusion of a house twice its size. From behind her came the constant drone of traffic from the interstate, distant but intrusive — it seemed so much closer at this moment. Edges and corners seemed sharper. Her motion seemed to slow, despite the quickness of her heartbeat. This increased awareness had come all of its own, and yet Daphne Matthews the psychologist knew better: Something had triggered this — nothing came all of its own. The cop she worked with in a survivors clinic described similar sensations moments before a firefight. But Boldt would talk instinct, Daphne would talk reflex. She had caught something out of place perhaps: a sound, a smell, an image; she fell victim to this stimulus, misinterpreted or not.

The air smelled of charcoal. She heard a seaplane taking off in the distance, and, much closer the nauseating laugh track of a television show.

Her face felt hot from the run, her skin itched. Her mind worked furiously trying to sort things out.

At the same time, she began an internal dialogue, chastising herself for being such a paranoid. *What a baby!* She also wrestled with the internal voices of several friends, Lou Boldt among them, who had once attempted to talk her out of buying a houseboat. The investment had silenced her critics — the place was worth a fortune now, and her timing couldn't have been better. But it was an isolated location, and tonight in particular it felt just a little too removed.

Get in the house! she told herself. She bent to retrieve the key that she had tied to her shoelace. *Get in the house,* her mind repeated more loudly.

She unlocked the door, leaving it slightly ajar until she got the light on, and hurried to the nearest lamp, on the entrance table along with her purse. Inside the purse was her gun. This thought did not escape her. The light flashed brightly and died — the bulb had blown.

She felt a gust of wind at her back. The front door thumped shut of its own accord. Startled, she leapt over to it, and swiveled the dead bolt, locking it. Issuing darkness. Nothing — not even the pitch black — was going to convince her to open that door again. *Safe!* She inched carefully forward, the picture of the downstairs emblazoned in her mind: directly ahead, the living room, a center post in the middle of the room, a small sofa and end table, a rocker, the wood stove; to her right, the narrow ladder ascending to the tiny bedroom and its balcony; to her left, the small galley demarcated by a blue tile countertop with two ash stools looking across the Jenn-Air range; around the galley, the head to the left — and opposite this, a small hall flanked by two closets

240

and the back door directly ahead.

Her eyes beginning to adjust, she reached out and found the arm of the rocking chair. Good, she knew exactly where she was. Some light off the lake found its way through the window behind the sofa, though not enough to help: the room oozed with a gray, ghostly paste. She inched ahead and slightly to her left and brushed up against the rough wood of the room's central support post. Small waves lapped against the pier, sounding like an animal licking the floats. The refrigerator hummed loudly. The lamp she sought remained a few feet to her right and then directly ahead: its fuzzy image loomed before her.

She crossed the room. Just as she reached the lamp, she heard a board squeak. It came from the back of the house, past the galley by the head. She reminded herself that the houseboat was always making such noises. On any other night, she might not have noticed a squeak. But that particular sound was as individual, as distinct, as the voice of a friend. A year or so ago rain had leaked in under the back door and had warped the floorboards. When stepped on, one of the wide pine planks, and only one, chirped like a bird — the sound she had just heard.

With her thumb on the lamp switch and her voice caught somewhere between "Hello?" and a scream, she froze. *It must have been something else,* a voice inside her reasoned.

It's nothing! Right?

But the voice warned: *A person has to step on that board for it to make that sound.*

Her heart hurt in the center of her chest. Her ears burned. *I'm overtrained,* she thought, as a dozen instructions from her police training flooded her head noisily. *Paranoid is all.* Each idea separate and individual, she processed them differently, sorting out contradictions as best she could.

Get out of the building. Call someone! Seek help.

Turn on the light and see . . . It's nothing.

Go for the gun, then turn on the light.

Her gun was in her purse, and her purse was on the table by the front door.

Indecision plagued her. She despised herself for just *sitting* there — a policewoman frozen in fear.

She crouched, held her breath, and switched on the lamp. She didn't look toward the source of that noise first, she looked toward her purse.

She processed more information: A few steps to get there; a few added milliseconds to flick the safety off and load one into the chamber. From the moment she made her move, to having a functional weapon in hand, perhaps five seconds. *An eternity if someone is inside this house. A lifetime?*

A good cop could not afford indecision. And if that was the only measure of a good cop, then she was not a good cop. Indecision had provided her with a four-inch scar across her throat. She *hated* that scar, not only for its appearance, but because she wore it like a flag. Indecision.

At this point, all she wanted was to prove herself wrong: That squeak had been nothing. She wanted a hot shower, a warmed-up dinner, and a glass of Pine Ridge on the deck. After that, a good book, with every door and window locked tight. Tomorrow, a security system, courtesy of Kenny Fowler. Her feet felt nailed to the pine planks.

The light, which had been on perhaps two seconds, went out. She grabbed for it and threw the switch. Nothing!

Silence! she thought. Not even the refrigerator was running. The power was out!

The board squeaked again.

She moved fast: two quick, bounding steps. She planted her forehead smack into the center post and went down hard and fast. Head swimming. Nauseated and dizzy. She imagined dinosaurs in a tar pit struggling to get out, sinking deeper. Black and gooey. She didn't know how much time had passed, if any. She struggled to her feet and clawed her way over to the gun.

She announced in a slurred voice, "I'm armed. I have a weapon! Go away now!" Training. Arms sagging with the weight of the gun, her head swimming. "Go away now," she mumbled. She fell to one knee and struggled back up to standing, feeling a thousand pounds heavier. Her head complained with the slightest movement. She inched her way forward, her right toe feeling in front of her. "Go away now," she repeated in an unconvincing voice that sounded to her like someone else talking.

Her left hand searched out the flashlight that she kept in the kitchen drawer with the knives. She plunged her hand inside the drawer. "Shit!" she said as she caught a knife blade on the tip of her finger and yanked her hand out quickly, instinctively delivering the cut to her lips and sucking on it.

She switched on the flashlight, its beam a white tunnel splashing a large circle on the walls. But her vision was all wrong.

Sweating heavily, heart beating furiously, she staggered uncertainly out of the galley and pivoted left, bracing for a shot. No one.

Slowly, she lowered the intense beam of light until it illuminated the warped plank responsible for the bird chirps. She gasped as she saw beads of water catching the light like jewels. This was not her imagination. Someone was inside.

Assess the situation! She had a 50 percent chance. The intruder could be to her left, hiding in the head, or to her right, down the small hall, about to go out the back door. She hadn't *heard* the back door open or close, and although it wasn't a terribly noisy door — might have been opened and closed without her knowledge, the intruder gone — she didn't believe this.

Think! But she could not.

"I'm armed," she repeated, this time more strongly, her strength returning.

She leapt ahead, spun completely around, and slapped her back into the corner — the head now to her right, the back door nearly straight in front of her. No silhouette. She shined the flashlight there. No one.

Hiding in one of the closets? Or is he gone? Did he get out without me hearing?

She summoned her courage, maintaining a firm but awkward grip jointly on both the gun and flashlight. She spun to her right, first aiming into the head — *nothing!* — and then, in self-defense, spinning fully around and covering the closets. The quick motions drove her to the edge of vomiting.

The intruder made contact from behind — pushed her hard. She screamed loudly as she lost her balance.

Her furtive glance into the head had been too quick. *He must have been standing in the tub,* she realized, as she struck the opposing wall face-first. She heard two heavy steps, the back door come open, and then two more footsteps. In her mind's eye she could see the intruder leaping to the next platform, the adjacent house, then, no doubt, the next after that, and the next. Too fast to be stopped. In the shadows, too dark to be seen.

She clambered back to her feet and surged

forward and out the back door, handling the gun with great care. She knew she had lost him, but her training and her nerves required her to determine the area was clear. She made no attempt to try to follow or catch up. Her intention was self-defense. The area *was* clear: There was enough ambient light here to see. She reentered the house, shut and locked the back door, and hurried to the front door, which was still locked.

She found the flashlight, shook it several times, but it did not respond. Dark.

Trembling, her heart now running away from her — slipping into shock — she came around the corner, found a chair that offered her back against a solid wall, her eyes on the front door, the back door down the short hall to her right, and she dragged the phone toward her by its cord.

Twenty minutes later she unlocked the door for Boldt as she heard him running down the dock.

Shining a flashlight on her, he said, "Jesus!"

Daphne said, "The fuse box is inside the closet by the back door. I wasn't about to go back there."

A moment later Boldt called out, "Do you have enough coats?"

It made her laugh. Made her feel better. So did the light coming on.

The refrigerator growled back into operation.

A digital clock on the microwave blinked CLOCK at her.

Boldt came around the corner wearing her faux leopard-skin hat. "Salvation Army time, if you ask me." Daphne laughed. It hurt her head. He noticed her wince. "Gotta get you some pictures taken," he said, meaning X rays.

"I'd rather have a glass of wine."

He poured her one. He said, "I'm not going to harp on it, but I do think you should have that looked at."

"Maybe later, okay?"

"It's your call."

"You must make a nice husband," she said. She did not mean anything more than to give out a compliment, but the comment made Boldt uncomfortable anyway. It made him think of Liz and Miles at home, where he had left them with barely any explanation. It made him think of Owen Adler. Then he looked at her forehead again and said, "Did he get anything?"

"Haven't looked," she said. She locked eyes with him and stated, "It isn't your standard breaking and entering."

"Not when they pick a cop's house, it isn't."

"I don't mean like that." She tried the wine. It tasted good. She drank some more.

"Then how do you mean it?"

"I'm being followed — stalked — I don't know . . . Someone's out there." Another sip. "That someone was in here, I'm sure of it."

He did not argue; he did not question. He

247

went to work. For Boldt it was sometimes the only thing he knew.

Boldt conducted a thorough search of the house. Daphne was a compulsively neat person, so he assumed it would not be difficult to spot a burglar's handiwork. The bedroom was tidy; the galley, he had already seen. He checked the bathroom — the head — and the back hall and closets. Daphne sat all the while, a bag of ice pressed against her forehead, the wine in the glass getting lower.

His second time through the house, gloves on, he opened drawers, checked shelves and closets. He had not done any robbery/burglary work in years, but it came to him naturally: He had searched too many homicide crime scenes to count.

The third time through the residence, he concentrated on minutiae — looking for smudges on the glass of doors and windows, crawling hands and knees across floors, alert for everything from bodily discharge to spilled change or a receipt — or even pet hair (Daphne did not own a pet). If she were being stalked by a parolee, it meant one kind of danger; if it was someone attracted to her looks, another entirely. For reasons that went mostly unexplained, Washington State and the greater Seattle area in particular attracted more than an average share of what the papers called "psychos." Daphne and her colleagues used different terms. But to Boldt it all boiled down to the same thing: sick people, often violent, often targeting women; and when they snapped, their crimes were among the most heinous.

It was during this third inspection that Boldt discovered the charred electrical outlet in the head and the small drops of water next to the sink. Without telling her, he checked the toilet thoroughly, as well as the shower/tub stall in case the stalker had used these. Masturbation was often the last step prior to the acting out of whatever violent act was planned.

When Boldt had completed his search, he pulled up a chair alongside Daphne's and said, "Why don't you tell me about it?"

She chuckled nervously. "You sound like me: That's how I often get a therapy session going."

He waited her out. He knew she had to be terribly afraid no matter what exterior she presented. After a difficult silence she encouraged him, "Why don't you go first? Please."

"Your visitor knew your schedule well enough to enter while you were on your run." She looked good — too good — in the tight jog bra/halter top and shorts, but he said nothing. They could deal with what she could do defensively later; a baggy T-shirt and running pants was a place to start. "You cut your run short," he said.

This comment snapped her head toward him. "How did you know that?" she asked incredulously.

"To put it bluntly? If he had meant to harm

you, to assault you, then I think he would have tried. We both know that you can hear a person approaching. Right? He was already in the bathroom. Where are you going to head after a run?" he asked rhetorically. "So all he had to do was wait. You're not going to carry a weapon with you on the way to the shower. But he wanted out. See? That's why after your description I thought it was a burglary. Maybe a well-planned one. It would fit with your feeling of being watched. He determines your schedule, times your run, and breaks in after a few days of sizing you up. But you surprise him by cutting your run short. When you open the front door, he freezes. Then he decides to get the hell out of there."

"The door moved," she interrupted, remembering. "The front door."

"Moved closed," he told her.

"Yes. But how —"

"In a place this small and relatively tight, when one door opens, it moves air. It moves doors, or a curtain in a window."

"I think I knew that instinctively; when it moved, I was scared. I locked it immediately."

"He was trying to get out, but he looked back — his eyes were more adjusted than yours —"

"There's a night-light in the head."

"There you go. He looks back — he's left something next to the sink. He doesn't want you to find it.

"He didn't move after that. He stood very still, just inside the back door, which explains the small puddle of water. If you had come looking, he would have been out of there in a flash. But if he could pull it off, whatever he had left was worth going back for. I think we can be quite sure of that."

"But I didn't come looking. I tried to find a light that worked."

"Exactly. And so he seized the opportunity. He stepped back into the house and you heard him."

"I hate this guy." She crossed her arms, fighting a chill.

"As you tried to find a light, the intruder crossed back into the bathroom."

"I heard the floorboard."

"Exactly."

"And I turned on the light."

"You can imagine his panic. But he's a fast thinker. There's a basket of bobby pins and whatnot on the bathroom counter. He's wearing gloves. We know he's wearing gloves because he takes the bobby pin, spreads it, reaches *around* the corner into the hall, and puts the bobby pin into the live wall socket. He's lucky. This is a small house and he shorts out all the downstairs outlets, including the light you turned on. The place goes dark again. Again, he makes for the door."

"I hear him and I run." She felt suddenly colder. Perhaps it was not the sweat. Boldt's

251

descriptions enabled her to visualize this intruder. She felt violated. She felt lucky to be sitting here drinking wine.

"But he hears you smack into that beam, fall over the chair. He hesitates — just an instant — unsure what to do. You're too fast for him. Suddenly you've got a gun. It's doubtful he has one. The law views breaking and entering *without* a weapon so much more leniently. But in any case, he didn't come here to be shot, or to shoot you. Things are definitely looking bad. And now here you come, shouting your warnings, as you said you did, and he's in trouble — a cornered rat . . . and all that. But the point is —" He caught himself. "Are you okay?"

"You're a little too good at this," she said. "It wasn't *you*, was it?" She forced a smile but winced with the pain it caused her.

"Well, you know the rest."

She stood out of her chair and faced Boldt, arms crossed.

He knew that same look in Liz. "Need a hug?"

She nodded.

He wrapped his big arms around her and pulled her tightly to him unreservedly, unashamed, unconnected to their past and that evening when they had done this without clothes. She did not want to cry. She returned the hug, and buried her face. Her hair smelled like sweat. A boat motored slowly across the lake. She thanked him.

He said softly, "Why don't you point me toward a newspaper? You get yourself showered and dressed. Let's get you settled. Okay?"

"I'd like that. But I hate to take your time."

"After that, we need to talk some more." She nodded. "Do you want to report this? Officially, I mean? I don't want to discourage that. You have every right —"

"No, Lou. No thanks. I've been there. You're asking, do I want to stay up until two in the morning? Do I want to answer a hundred questions I'd rather not? Do I want to make a huge scene, all in order to never catch this guy? I don't think so."

"Still, it's not right of me to discourage you."

"I can do that all by myself."

"You're sure?"

"Absolutely. I'm a big girl now. But if you would stay. Have you eaten?"

"We eat early. Miles," he explained.

"Right."

"I'd like to use the phone if it's all right."

She nodded. She went upstairs and he heard her undressing and he thought maybe he should go. But he did not. A few minutes later she descended the ladder stairs with an unavoidable amount of leg showing, and headed straight to the shower without comment.

Boldt sat with her as she ate warmed-up leftovers and drank another glass of wine.

She glanced up at him occasionally and smiled

through her eyes while chewing. "I feel kind of silly," she said. "You sure you won't have something?"

"Tell me, if you're ready. I'd like to hear."

She set her fork down, took some more wine, and nodded. He saw that she was going to have a bruise on her forehead, though maybe not too bad, and if she kept up the ice as she was, the lump might not be there in the morning. Sitting this close to her, both on stools at the galley's food bar, he could see the dozens of flecks of gold and red in her otherwise brown eyes — magical sparks that seemed to increase in candlepower with her enthusiasm. She had a ferocious amount of energy, of reserve power that at times seemed boundless. She stepped him through her experience leading up to the monorail ride. It took Boldt some getting used to that the planetarium meeting had taken place only yesterday; if he had been told a week, he might have believed it. She also described how she had lost the man in the crafts fair. She told him about the blue car she had seen what seemed like one too many times. And then she confessed her general state of paranoia over the last few days. "I don't know that a man can understand it," she said. "Women come to *feel* when they are being gawked at. It is something society condones: men undressing women with their eyes. Call it a zipless fuck. Whatever the term, when you're on the receiving end from the age of twelve or thirteen on, you develop a real sense for it — at least I have. The thing of it is, I feel as if the person *can* see what's underneath the clothing. Does that make sense? I feel violated. More than once I've felt like just ripping my shirt open and getting it over with. The fifth floor is *the worst.* Present company excluded, I find cops the worst — and I'm surrounded by them. But the point is, I *know* when someone like Michael Striker is looking down my blouse.

"And that's the way I have felt for the last three or four days. Just like that. As if someone has a pair of binoculars trained on me. As if someone is in the room with me when I'm undressing — when I'm in the shower — *all* the time. Like I'm being stalked. That's the only way I know how to explain it. Someone back there. Someone creepy. Someone all over me, like an oil you can't wash off.

"And then the car, and yesterday morning, and now this . . . I know it looks like a burglary, Lou. Especially from a male point of view. But I don't think so. I can't tell you what. I can't tell you why. I wish to hell I could tell you who, but someone's out there and he's got my name written all over him" — her voice cracked — "and I want it over with." Her eyes were pooled. She pushed her plate away, her appetite ruined.

Boldt felt responsible. In a strange way he even felt responsible for what was happening to her.

"I know I haven't got a shred of proof," she said, reading his thoughts.

"You confronted the guy on the monorail?"

"Yes."

"And what did your feelings tell you then?"

"I'd like to tell you that I felt as if I were looking into the eyes of Jack the Ripper — because I've seen those eyes before; I know that look, and there *is* often a look. But truthfully, there wasn't in this one. He seemed embarrassed, put on the spot. Weird thing is, for a moment there I even felt as if I knew him, as if we'd met. But that's the thing about a stalker, you see — about the good ones, the Ted Bundys — they know how to project that air of safety. Old friends. Good buddies. Hop in the back of my van and I'll rope and murder you. I'll tear your liver out and eat it for dinner, good friend."

"You know what Shoswitz would ask?" Boldt said.

"Am I overworked? Under stress? Sure. I know. And if it wasn't me, I'd be sent to me for a little chat to see what's up. But it *is* me. And I *am* under stress, and I am overworked. But no, I honestly believe it has nothing to do with that. Good enough?"

"For me it is."

Daphne said, "Probably not for him, I know. But it's you I care about anyway."

Boldt asked, "Do we talk about what neither of us is comfortable talking about? That this

256

may be related to your New Leaf work?"

"I want another glass of wine, but if I have one I'm likely to start belly dancing in the living room, or maybe I'll just pass out. Ever carried a woman up a ladder?"

"I'll leave you on the couch," he said, standing and bringing the bottle of wine over for her. "Anesthesia. You're allowed this once in a while." He poured.

"It really sucks that I'm not allowed to see Owen."

"I feel real sorry for you," he said sarcastically.

"Jealous?"

"Maybe I am just a little."

Her eyes warmed, those flecks sparkled, and she was about to say something but she caught herself. He wanted to hear it, but he knew it was better that he did not. He felt no confusion about his emotions or desires, but that did not mean he could not love this woman just a little more than was acceptable — not as long as he kept it to himself. And maybe she kept it to herself, too.

He reminded: "You first sensed this three or four days ago, you said. To both of us, that feels more like a week. Do you remember back three or four days ago? Can you separate it out?"

"We're going to talk about it," she said, their exchanges suddenly quicker.

"Yes," he affirmed, "we are."

257

"You think it's connected to my work on New Leaf?"

"I think it *may* be. I think it's worth exploring."

She ran her hand through her hair in a nervous manner. "Someone knows what I'm up to and doesn't like it. Is that it? Is that how it goes?"

"Several people know what you're up to. Many more may suspect it. Maybe that guard at the archives said something. Maybe Kenny or Taplin saw you pass those keys, but hasn't said anything. Maybe there's an employee who figured it out."

"An employee involved in the original fraud."

"It's serious stuff what you're suggesting. People would have positions to protect —"

"Do not bring Owen into this!"

"I didn't say anything," he protested. He waited a second and said what he had to say, what had been on his mind for several days now: "*Was* Adler in on it? Has he said anything to you?"

She gasped, and the warmth in her eyes froze over. She stiffened and nearly spit at him, "Some things need not be asked!" She averted her eyes and said, "Do you think I would keep something like that from you? How can you possibly think that?"

"I think it would put you in a difficult position. You wouldn't indict him without some damn good proof — not if you're human. And maybe you'd look elsewhere for the proof, if

258

things got a little too warm where you were looking. And maybe — just maybe is all — you would ask him at some point and he would say that he'd rather you didn't, and what then? Where does that leave you?"

She softened some. "Well, it hasn't happened like that."

"It's Longview Farms I'm focused on," he confessed. "The New Leaf situation is of interest to me only insofar as that if it proves true — that State Health or someone at New Leaf deliberately altered records to throw blame onto Longview — then there's all sorts of places I can run with that. We've talked about it. And what happened out there yesterday bears it out, I think. And maybe — just maybe — whoever was involved in document tampering at either State Health or New Leaf, if anyone, is also involved in this present situation. Crime makes strange bedfellows — we both know that."

"More than one person?"

"There's a woman involved. We've all but confirmed that. Is she alone in this? Is she working with a boyfriend? A lover?"

"The sheriff," said the psychologist.

"I just don't think a woman would have done that. Not what I saw."

"Those burns," she said. He nodded. "His genitals?"

"No."

"His face?"

"Yes."

259

She considered this. "The face? I don't like that. Not for a woman, I'd have to agree. You may be right. Where the hell does that leave us?"

"I can put someone on you," he offered, changing the subject. "Watch for someone watching."

She said sarcastically, "With the dozens of people at your disposal you have to spare. Who do you have in mind, Sergeant?"

"Or maybe Fowler could. If you asked Adler —"

"He'd do it," she finished for him. "Is that what you think? You're probably right," she admitted. "But they're rent-a-cops for the most part. If there is someone watching me — and mind you, I hate that idea — and we scare him or her off, then we've lost whatever we had."

"But on the other hand," he countered, "if they caught the person and we could have a little chat, we might be light-years ahead."

"Point taken," she said. "I could fax Owen and ask."

He offered her an expression that said, "I would if I were you."

"And meanwhile, Sergeant?"

"We tear into Longview Farms. Physically, we already have: The lab is busy on a dozen fronts. But I mean historically. We find the wife. We find the people who worked there. We chat up the neighbors, the meat inspectors,

260

the UPS driver. Anyone and everyone. My bet is that that's where we're going to find our boy."

"Boy?"

He mocked, "You get this feeling when you're a homicide dick."

"And New Leaf?"

"Yes. I think we keep going . . . *you* keep going. If you're up to it. We want that connection, if it's there. From where I'm sitting, we want whatever the hell we can come up with."

"The sheriff," she said, coming back to Boldt's nightmare. "Police involvement."

"He warned us, and I blew it."

"You didn't blow anything."

He gave her a look. Enough was enough. He knew what he knew. "You okay?" he asked, coming off the stool.

"Fine. Get out of here," she teased.

"You sure?"

"Go."

He leaned over and kissed her on the cheek. She blew him one back.

She stopped him when he reached the door. "Just one thing, Sergeant."

He turned to her.

"You might want to take that hat off before someone sees you."

He felt up there, realizing he had been wearing it — looking stupid — for the better part of two hours. "Jesus," he said, throwing it at the rocking chair. "You could have said something."

"Yes, I could have," she admitted, laughing, and wincing with the pain.

TWENTY

On Wednesday morning, two weeks since Daphne had involved him in the case, Boldt was in the midst of dealing with the first ATM withdrawal when LaMoia arrived and made his announcement. This first hit had come at eleven-thirty the night before: Twelve hundred dollars had been withdrawn in three consecutive transactions. The nearest surveillance personnel had been eleven blocks away. By the time this undercover cop reached the first ATM, a second machine was hit, this time another ten blocks away. The dance had continued for ninety minutes, at the end of which thirty-six hundred dollars had been withdrawn, the police never anywhere near a transaction. It was an embarrassing display of Boldt's lack of manpower; Shoswitz was chewed out by Captain Rankin, and in turn spoke his mind to Boldt: They would have to do better . . .

Boldt thought one answer might be the ATM card's PIN number. Lucille Guillard, the Pac-West bank executive, had informed him that the PIN number had indeed been requested by the account holder. People requested specific numbers because they were easier to remember;

263

and they were easier to remember because they held some significance to the account holder.

Therefore, Boldt reasoned, this number — 8165 — held some significance to the killer. It was a piece of evidence that Boldt intended to follow.

Data processing was presently searching these four digits against phone numbers, driver's licenses, vehicle registration numbers, Social Security numbers, other credit card PINs, active credit card account numbers, and bank account numbers. He even went so far as to request a list from the Washington State Department of Revenue for all individuals born on August 1, 1965, or January 8, 1965. The Postal Service was to provide the names of any individuals owning post office box number 8165. He used the tax assessor's office to generate the names of residents at any addresses that included 8165. Somehow this number meant something to the killer, and Boldt was pursuing every possibility.

LaMoia charged through the security door that accessed the fifth floor's Homicide unit, looked around quickly, and shouted to Boldt, "I found a witness!"

Boldt led him around the corner and into the privacy of a tiny interrogation room that smelled like sweat and cigarettes. When LaMoia became excited, his brown eyes grew large, his face thinned, and his voice cracked.

"Okay, so here's the thing. I'm doing an

264

interview, right? I mean typical WASP house-
wife: Volvo. Hardwood floors. You know the
type. And when I introduce myself at the door,
she kind of sags, right? Like she's seen cops
before. Maybe too often. I'm thinking her
husband's a drunk, or a gambler, or is a regular
at Vice. Or maybe he's using or dealing or
something, and she's worried sick. We get talking about Foodland — because she's one of
the ones shopping — one of the ones on the
list of thirty-four — and she's noticeably upset,
right? And she is a *major* strikeout. I mean,
before I can ask her the question, this one is
already shaking her head at me and glancing
toward the door. You know the kind? She wants
me gone. I'm thinking maybe the husband is
expected home early. Then I'm thinking maybe
it's *her* — maybe she's getting some on the
side. What do I know? But she's a mess. And
then I hear the back door, and the mother
practically does an *Exorcist* thing with her neck
— like an owl — trying to cop a look into
the kitchen, but I beat her to it, right? and
who do I see but *her?*"

"*Her?*" Boldt inquired.

"Our vidqueen, Miss Foodland. The one with
the floppy hat and the pierced ears."

"*Her?*" Boldt repeated, excited now.

"You're thinking there's no way I could make
her considering we hardly got a look at her
in that video — but what I'm telling you: You
know me, right? *I know women.* What can I

265

say? We've all watched that video how many times? And this MacNamara girl had the *exact* same moves. Right down to the way she turned her head when she saw her mother talking to me. And another thing: She *knew* I was a cop. You know what I'm saying? You can feel it. She knew — and she wasn't sticking around to small talk."

"Did you interview her?"

"Hell no. A minor. The mother seeming the protective type, figured you'd want to maybe try for a warrant. See if we could turn up the clothes we saw in the video."

"We'd never get a warrant," Boldt said.

The detective reached into his coat pocket and pulled out a sheet of paper. "Striker took care of it. Said because she's a minor and we'd never get a look at her record without someone like him requesting it."

"Her *record?* A minor?" Boldt asked.

"She's a klepto. Seven arrests for shoplifting in the last six months. And I mean *klepto!* Drugstores, department stores, hardware stores — you name it. Big-ticket items. Stuff it's damn near impossible to get out of a store without getting caught. So maybe it's a game for her."

"But if she's a kleptomaniac —" Boldt began.

"Then chances are she was lifting, not putting poisoned soup onto the shelves."

"Which means she's not our suspect. But she may have *seen* him. The timing is right,

266

after all. There's only a seven-second envelope during which *someone* put those five cans of soup onto the shelf."

"When can we interview her?"

"Do we know that the girl will be home?"

"She's on a juvenile home-release program. Summer school and not much more. Comes home from school and stays put. At least, she's supposed to. That Foodland tape is time-stamped. Holly was a bad girl; she wasn't supposed to be in that store."

Boldt explained, "If she's been picked up for shoplifting this many times, a quiet chat in her mother's living room is not going to get us anywhere."

"You're probably right," LaMoia agreed.

"What I'd like to do is hit the house hard. A really thorough search — something to shake her up. Something she hasn't seen. And I want her watching. I want her there. Then we bring her up here to the box and let Razor read her the gospel. Then I chat her up and hopefully she sits up and flies straight. And if she doesn't, we book her on violation of home release; we print her and strip-search her and toss her into a jumpsuit and let her spend the night in the juvenile pen. Then," Boldt said, "we go at her again."

"You're certainly in a charitable mood," LaMoia replied.

Within the hour, Boldt sat down with one

Mildred MacNamara, mother of their possible witness.

Boldt held up the large, clear plastic bags containing her daughter's clothing, and if the mother had herself been a detective assigned to the fifth floor, she might have also noticed that the various labeling of the bags lacked a case number — this because the Adler blackmail was still not in the Book, was still in many bureaucratic ways an unofficial case. "This hat and jacket were found in your daughter's wardrobe."

"Why aren't we on the juvenile floor?" she asked.

"Because I'm Homicide, and I'm running this case. And your daughter is a possible suspect."

"Dear Lord . . ." She broke down. Boldt slid a box of tissue in front of her. "What about her attorney?"

"As lead detective, I'm in a pretty unique position, Ms. MacNamara. What I say goes — pretty much, anyway. Which means that if I say Holly walks out of here with no charges, then that's what happens."

"I don't understand."

"I need to talk to your daughter, as an adult, on her own. Have you ever known an attorney to simplify a situation? Think about that: They may help you, but they *always* complicate matters. In matters of juvenile crime, there are so many gray areas right now — legalistically — that if we bring in the attorneys, we're both going to be here for a month of Sundays, and chances are I'm going to be *required* to charge your daughter just in order to speak to her. I don't want that; Holly doesn't want another charge on her pink sheet, and I have a hard time believing you would either."

"Of course not! But how — ?"

"Holly violated the terms of her most recent sentencing. We have *proof* of that. And as I've read it, that was pretty much a last shot for her." The woman confirmed this with a nod. "So basically all I have to do is charge her and eventually I'll get my interview with her. But, cards out on the table, I can't wait until 'eventually.'

"So what I'm asking for is written permission from you for me and some of my colleagues to ask her a few questions. It isn't much, from your side of this — I *know* that. All I can do, as a parent, is give you my word that if there's any way to avoid charging her, then that's the way it'll work out. But there are no guarantees," he added reluctantly. Honesty came at a price.

There was no need to tell her that the search of her daughter's belongings — an exhaustive one — had offered no proof of any connection to Pac-West Bank or an ATM account. The search had, however, uncovered a hidden stash of stolen goods from CDs to jewelry — the knowledge of which Boldt kept to himself, to be used as a crushing blow should he need it. This single lack of discovery seemed to support

269

LaMoia's theory that Holly MacNamara had been in that aisle within seconds of the drop having taken place, but was not herself responsible.

"May I call my husband?"

Boldt told her she could do whatever she pleased, but repeated to her what he had told Betty Lowry two weeks earlier, that the husband might overreact, and if so, Holly's chances for clemency were lost.

"I don't know . . . ," she gasped, and broke into tears again. Boldt found room to really hate himself. He waited her out, and when he saw the faintest of nods, slid the minor's consent form in front of her and asked her to press hard. "It's in triplicate," he said, "like everything else around here," hoping to win back a smile, but admitting to himself — correctly, as it turned out — that there was little hope of this.

"I don't like you, Sergeant. And if you've lied to me, if you've tricked me," she said pushing the form toward him, "then you're no better than the people you go after."

Boldt took the form and hurried from the room.

Holly MacNamara sat quietly with Daphne on the other side of the cigarette-scarred table in interrogation room A. Boldt and LaMoia faced them, and everyone sat in uncomfortable straight-back metal chairs. The large plastic bags containing the hat and the dark coat with the hidden pockets sewn into its hem were in full view, like a Thanksgiving turkey.

Boldt switched on the tape recorder, named those present, and stated the time and date.

Striker joined them a few minutes late, his prosthesis clicking nervously, and Boldt added his name to the tape, too.

Holly MacNamara met Boldt with a steely-eyed determination that he hoped Miles would never adopt. Too hard for her young age, too brooding, too suspicious, and far too self-confident given her present situation. She had dark eyebrows, high cheekbones, and long, dark hair. She had some acne that she hid with cosmetics, and her bottom teeth held a retainer. A child in a grown-up's game. She wore silver studs in her ears, and was quite confused when Boldt opened the discussion by asking her to remove them.

It didn't help Boldt to connect her to the woman in the video, but it served to disarm her and set her slightly off-balance, which was extremely important to the interviews.

Boldt said, "On the twenty-first of June, during your house detention, in-store security cameras captured you at the Foodland supermarket over on Broadway. You were dressed in clothes similar to these," he said pointing to the bags, "and your behavior suggested you were trying to avoid these same security cameras."

"So?" Holly MacNamara asked.

Daphne, who would play the role of friend for this interrogation, advised her, "You don't have to answer anything you don't want to, but it's best just to go ahead and answer the easy stuff."

"Maybe you were shopping with your mother," LaMoia suggested, giving her a way around the implication of criminal activity. "You were in the soup aisle, do you remember that?"

"I don't remember."

"Try to remember, Holly," Daphne encouraged.

"Soup?" she asked. "I don't think so."

Boldt nodded to LaMoia, who turned on the Sony Trinitron and ran the video that Shop-Alert had dubbed for them. They watched it together: Holly watching the screen, the police watching Holly. When it was just at the point where she crashed into a cart being pushed by a man or a woman — it remained impossible to tell — LaMoia stopped the tape.

"Holly?" Boldt asked.

Maintaining her suspicions of all of them, she glanced toward Daphne, who nodded gently.

Boldt clarified: "We don't want a made-up story from you, we want and need the *truth*."

Striker's hand ticked several times as he told her, "If you cooperate, there will be no charges against you stemming from this discussion. It's like immunity. You know what that is; I don't have to explain immunity to you. Whatever

272

you tell us is off the record, and just between us. But Sergeant Boldt is right: We need the truth. You should also know that we're prepared to play tough if that's the way you want it."

Boldt said, "You saw something just now that made you remember."

"The thing of it was," she began in a flurry of words. "Like maybe I'd taken some Better-Veggie — the drink, you know? Like maybe I was thinking about *buying* some of that."

Boldt conveyed his doubts with a single penetrating look.

"So maybe I wasn't going to buy it," she admitted. "I wasn't. I'd lifted three cans. And I'd lifted some fruit salad, and something else — I don't remember. Like there I am, pretty loaded up, and I'm thinking about some V-8, which is the same aisle as the soup, but it's a hard grab because of that overhead eye, and then there's this guy —" She caught herself and stopped.

Boldt felt the hairs on the back of his neck go erect. *Go on!* he wanted to scream. *What guy?!*

As if hearing him, she met eyes with him and said, "This guy came out of nowhere. I hit his cart — really *hit* it, you know? And this look he gave me — right through me, you know? Like he knew *everything,* and I'm in his way. Like he's a lifter, too, or else a security guy. And I'm thinking I'm busted, but all he wants is me out of the way. And

273

like I'm gone. But I look back, you know, and what's he do? He drops a couple cans out of his coat into his cart, walks a few feet, and puts them on the shelf! So like I'm thinking, Oh, shit, there *is* a security guy nearby. He's dumping his stash. And if he's dumping his stash then I'm sure as hell dumping mine." She winced, taking them all in, clearly fearing she had gone too far.

"It's all right, Holly," Boldt assuaged her. "You're' doing fine."

"Doing real well," Striker echoed.

Daphne asked, "Do you remember anything at all about this man?" *Start general; work specific.* It had been several weeks — how much could they expect?

"You mean like what he looked like?" she asked nervously. "No way."

"His clothes," LaMoia suggested. "You say he dumped his stash out of a coat?" The streetwise LaMoia used her language, making it sound as if it were his own.

"A raincoat. It's *summer*," she reminded them. "You only lift when it's raining, 'cause like where are you going to stash it when it's hot out?"

LaMoia said, "A raincoat."

She nodded. Boldt wrote it down. *It's a start.*

"What *kind* of raincoat? Hip? Conservative? Khaki? Black?" the detective asked.

"Green maybe. Long. Like those guys in

274

westerns. You know?"

Young kids made some of the best witnesses. The girls recalled clothing down to the buttons — male and female. The boys remembered a girl's face and her body shape.

"A green greatcoat," LaMoia repeated.

"A greatcoat, yeah. I didn't see his face."

"A hat?" LaMoia asked. There had been a glimpse of this individual in the video, though it blurred in freeze-frame.

"Yeah. Baseball cap, I think. Kinda like mine."

"How 'bout his shoes?" LaMoia tried.

"Boots," she spurted out. "Not shoes."

The way it flew out of her, Boldt trusted this. "Boots," he repeated, making note of it.

"Cowboy boots," she said. "And blue jeans!" she announced proudly, somewhat surprised with herself.

"Like mine?" LaMoia asked, showing off his Tony Lamas and his pressed blue jeans.

"No. They were worn jeans," she said. "Like, frayed at the bottom, you know? And brown cowboy boots. Muddy maybe. I'm pretty sure they were brown. Maybe they were work boots. Hiking boots. I don't remember."

Mud, Boldt thought, recalling how thick the mud was at Longview Farms. He caught Daphne looking at him, her eyes flashing with a heightened energy — she believed the witness; she thought they had a live one.

LaMoia asked, "Jewelry? Tattoos? Scars? A

limp? Anything distinguishing?"

"The boots," she repeated proudly. "I sort of remember the boots."

"Did he say anything to you? Did he speak to you?"

"No way. But that look he gave me was heavy. Like he was going to kill me for running into his cart."

"Did you see him again, anytime after that?" Daphne asked.

Holly MacNamara shook her head.

"Take your time," LaMoia encouraged.

"In line, maybe," she said to the detective. "The checkout line. He was buying something." She said definitively, "You always buy something."

"Do you remember what he was buying?" Boldt asked.

"I'm sure!" she said sarcastically. "I don't even remember *if* I saw him in line," she admitted. "I was in a hurry. I just wanted the hell out of there."

Boldt leaned to Daphne and whispered, "Get her started on the employee photos — Adler, Foodland, Shop-Alert. Then mug shots." Data processing had compiled DMV photographs of the Foodland employees. The other companies had their own, for security reasons.

The video, Boldt thought. Was one of the Shop-Alert security cameras aimed down the line of cash registers?

What was that guy's name? Don? Dave? Ron?

★ ★ ★

Gus at Shop-Alert, the Redmond-based security company that handled Foodland, greeted Boldt as if he were an old friend. He escorted him quickly to the back room and the plethora of electronic equipment. "The minute I got your call, I started running the data looking for the guy you described. Been at it for the better part of an hour. He's good, Lieutenant. Very good." He triggered a key, and a screen-saving pattern left the monitor, replaced by the shadowy black-and-white flickering image of a tall man wearing a Mariners baseball cap and a greatcoat. "This is about all we have of him. And if you watch him closely," he said, allowing the image to advance in a broken, mechanical movement, "you see he's using the person at the register in front of him as a shield from the camera. See? He moves right along with this heavy woman — so the camera doesn't catch much sight of him. He knows what he's doing. Like I said: He's very good."

Two aisles behind the suspect, Boldt caught sight of Holly MacNamara, though she too was screening herself from the camera.

"What about his face?"

"We never see it. I've tried some enhancement. I tried some of the other time sequences, but we hardly ever see him. He *knows* this system well. Too well."

"An employee?" Boldt let slip, his mind whirring.

"Or a regular," Gus hypothesized. "Or a guy

277

who's studied the hell out of it. Done his homework."

Boldt wrote down the exact time that was electronically stamped into the lower corner of the screen. "Register six," he noticed.

"Six, seven, and eight are Foodland's express lanes," Gus confirmed. "Shoplifters like express lanes."

Using this time stamp, Boldt hoped it might be possible to cross-check the register tapes and identify the exact items made during this particular purchase.

When he returned to the Public Safety Building, he assigned Bobbie Gaynes the task, and two hours later she entered his office cubicle announcing that with the help of Lee Hyundai, she had found the cash register receipt in question. She handed him an enlarged photocopy, grainy from the enlargement, the computerized lettering angular and spotty but still legible. It listed four items purchased at Foodland's register 6.

Of the four items, listed as CANDY and ICECRM, three were preceded by a four-letter producer code that Boldt had long since come to recognize: ADFD — Adler Foods.

"Adler candy bars," he whispered under his breath.

"Maybe he intended to *eat* them, Sergeant," Gaynes said optimistically. "We don't know for certain what he has in mind for them."

"Yes, we do," Boldt replied ominously. "I'm afraid we do."

278

TWENTY-ONE

At five o'clock Thursday, July 12, Bernie Lofgrin poked his head into Daphne's office waving a plastic bag containing the State Health document. "You win the Kewpie doll, Matthews. This report is one legal-size piece of bullshit." He looked more closely at her, "What did you do to yourself?"

"A box fell off my closet shelf and got me."

"That was a heavy box," he said.

She caught sight of a man just over Lofgrin's shoulder and asked, "Can I help you, Chris?" She was asking Danielson, who seemed to be loitering within earshot.

Danielson fumbled with his words, claiming to be reading the bulletin board just outside Daphne's office, but to her the excuse fell short. She waved Lofgrin inside and asked him to shut the door.

"I've got a better idea," the ecstatic Lofgrin said. "You come down to my office and I'll show you my etchings." He winked, which with his magnified eyeballs felt to her a little bit like a camera's flash going off.

A few minutes later, Lofgrin eased his office door shut. Through the large window the lab was mostly empty of workers at this hour. The office was its usual mess. "Like what I've done with the place?" he asked, as Daphne moved two stacks of papers in order to win a seat. "You mind?" He put on a jazz tape and set the volume low. "Helps me think," he said, grinning widely. Lofgrin had a contagious enthusiasm when he was happy. And he was happy whenever the lab results gave him conclusive findings — which filled Daphne with optimism.

"It has been altered?" she repeated.

"A lousy job. A bunch of amateurs. They used Wite-Out and typed over it. At least someone was smart enough to use the same typewriter to make the changes — but the carriage alignment of those changes ran fractionally on an incline, just as you spotted."

Lofgrin explained, "The Wite-Out was old, and at one time it probably approximated the paper color quite well. It was an enamel and therefore bonded well to the document's pulp and fiber content, rendering it virtually impossible to remove using solvents without risking the unintentional destruction of the primary surface, thereby losing indentations caused by prior impact — a typewriter keystroke, for instance." His eyes moved like overinflated beach balls in a light wind. "Our interest, of course, was archaeological in nature: What lay beneath the Wite-Out that was so important to cover up? The cities of Troy, if you will."

"Okay," she said.

"Wite-Out is, of course, opaque. I'm afraid that our efforts to use illumination to develop a print-through were a failure." He handed her one of the lab's efforts: a heavy sheet of photographic paper. The bulk of the document text was fuzzy, for it had been photographed *through* the existing paper of the document by shooting strong light at it while negative film was placed underneath it. The spaces where the changes in the text had been made appeared as black strokes, revealing nothing of what words had once existed beneath the Wite-Out.

"The way we got to it," Lofgrin explained enthusiastically, "was by using a long-wave light technique commonly used in the detection of counterfeit currency. The enamel is porous, of course — opaque only in the light of certain frequencies. What we did was analogous to taking an X ray, where the enamel Wite-Out is the skin, and the words beneath it the bone, if you will. And we developed this," he said, offering her yet another sheet from his file folder.

She had rarely experienced one of Lofgrin's detailed explanations in person — his "sermons," as LaMoia called them. But she knew that such explanations were to be expected. The lab man never, *never* simply handed an officer the final results. He put on his jazz, leaned back in his chair, and he talked. He detailed each and every step of his arduous journey so that the peace officer would understand just what a superhuman job had been done.

This latest document was a negative, indeed reminding her of an X ray, but in the spaces where earlier there had been just one word, now there were two, typed one on top of the other, creating in all but one space a mishmash of hieroglyphics impossible for her to decipher.

"Not exactly readable," Lofgrin admitted, "but the first, and perhaps most important, step to discovering what someone did not want read." He leaned back in his chair, and it squeaked as he gently rocked himself, the rhythm conflicting with that of the sax music. "The typewriter used a ten-character-per-inch Courier typeface. A few years back we would have located a similar typewriter and typed over the top letters using a white ribbon in order to remove them. But computer graphics enhances and speeds up that process considerably. Amy Chu spent the better part of the afternoon drawing out the top layer of typed letters." He handed her yet another sheet — this one computer-printed. "And this is what you get." In each of the areas where changes had taken place, now only flecks of characters remained, looking a little like chinese characters, or, in a few cases, worse: like paint splatters. "Not the easiest thing to read," Lofgrin confessed. "And that's because the letters often overlapped significantly, so when you took out the stem to the letter *t,* you might also erase the letter *i* beneath it. But if you think about it, there are only two characters — a number and a letter — that are interchangeable on the standard typewriter keyboard." He allowed her to think about it only briefly before he answered for her. "Not even zero and *O,* capital or lowercase, duplicate one another."

Daphne answered like the good student: "The number *one* and the lowercase letter *l.*"

"Gold star, Matthews!" he chirped. "Which means all other letters and numbers essentially leave their own fingerprint, if you will, whether a serif or a loop, a dot or a stem." He stopped rocking. "Computer scanning technology gave us something called OCR — optical character recognition — software. The computer knows all these individual characteristics of each letter for each typeface, and using logarithms is able to predict within an error factor of only a few percent what letter is on the page. You scan a document, and it's a graphic. You run OCR on that graphic and it's converted into a text format that can then be manipulated. Bottom line," he said, "we ran OCR on this jumble of flecks and spots and asked it to guess what it was we were looking at." He held the final sheet in his hand, but he would not pass it to her. "It took Amy seventeen passes with the OCR, because even for the computer there just wasn't enough there to work with, and its error rate was atrocious. But here you go: all the names, the date, the information they tried to hide." He said proudly, "The *truth* they tried to hide."

The document was indeed restored to its original form.

Lofgrin said, "You put me on the stand, and I'll say the same thing to the jury or judge." *Heaven help us*, Daphne thought.

She ran her finger down the form, comparing the altered document to the one she now held, her curiosity driving a trickle of perspiration down her ribs. And there was the box she had most wanted to see.

FIELD INSPECTOR: *Walter Hammond*

Alongside was Hammond's legible signature that for the past several years had been covered by Wite-Out. More shocking to her was the cause of the contamination, listed not as *salmonella*, as it had been on the altered document, but as *staphylococcus*. Knowing exactly where her eyes were on the page, Lofgrin said, "Staph is a *contact* infection, passed from human to human. An entirely different animal from salmonella."

It all but confirmed her suspicions: Longview Farms had been improperly accused of a contamination for which it was not responsible.

Walter "Roy" Hammond lived in what Daphne's friend Sharon called a "die-slow com-

284

munity." Pontasset Point called itself a "progressive community" and consisted of doublewides with postage-stamp lawns that someone else mowed. There was a community center, a shuffleboard court, three tennis courts, and a pool — all next to the Hospice, a shabby-looking halfway house nursing home that probably struggled to meet the state minimums.

Hammond wore ceramic teeth, a pair of pink Miracle Ears, and carried a lifetime of french fries and short-order cooking like a backup parachute at his belt line. Apparently if he dropped something, he left it there, indicated by the existence on his nut-brown carpet of a wide variety of pens, candy wrappers, and two spoons that would have to wait until his "girl" came to clean. The TV, which was the size of a refrigerator and which fully blocked one of the room's only two windows, ran loudly, even after Daphne asked that they turn it off.

"You wouldn't be carrying no tape recorder, would you?" The man had steely blue eyes the color of deep ice and big stubby hands with wrinkled, age-spotted skin, his fingernails chewed grotesquely short.

"No tape recorder," she answered.

"Is this what you'd call 'off the record?' "

"It can be," she allowed, her heart beating more quickly. Why did he want that?

"I think that be best, lady," he said.

"Fine. Off the record, then."

"What exactly is it you want?"

Daphne sized up her opponent and played him against himself. "What is it you think I want, Mr. Hammond?"

"Call me Roy. Everyone else does." He liked her looks — there was no missing that glint in his eyes, and it disgusted her. She wished she had worn a jacket. "No clue," he answered.

"None?"

"You teasing me?"

"Up until four years ago, you worked as a field inspector for the State Health Department."

"Matter of record."

"Does the name Longview Farms mean anything to you?"

His swollen neck moved as he swallowed dryly, failing in his attempt to portray a man bored with her line of questioning. "Every place I inspected on a regular basis means something to me, lady. Part of my route, you understand. Part of what I did for a living. What exactly was it 'bout Longview you had a question 'bout?"

"Exactly this." She handed him two photocopies — before and after.

Again the boa constrictor in his neck moved and he blinked repeatedly — both signs to her of an increasing anxiety. He switched off the television and adjusted both hearing aids, one of which screamed a high pitch while he toyed with it. His white, scaly tongue worked at

286

his crusty lips, but his mouth remained bone-dry.

"Is there a question to go along with this?" he asked.

"Why the difference between the two?"

He considered this for a moment, his eyes darting between Daphne and the two documents. "Don't know where you got this one," he said of the document as it had existed before the changes. "But this one here," he said, shaking the salmonella document, "is dated later and therefore's the one the department would go by. But honestly, lady, I don't work there no more, and I think you're asking the wrong guy."

"The *original* document," she emphasized, "lists you as the field inspector." She added, "In the later one, the name's been changed."

"You know," he said, his face reddening and his nostrils flaring, "I *do* remember this one."

"Terrific," she said flatly, letting him sense her distrust.

"Once upon a time we had a good department, lady. Then they started making us hire all the different colors — the United States government did — and things went straight downhill."

"And women," Daphne pointed out.

"Girls, too. Yeah, that's right. Not that I got anything against girls."

"But you do when it comes to 'different colors.' "

"Ain't none of them smart is the thing. I

287

got no tolerance for people with their hand in Uncle Sam's pocket. You know? They're just plain stupid. Take Jake Jefferson, okay? You're asking about the Longview, okay? Well it was that Jefferson who got things wrong in the first place, and made the rest of us have to work to fix it."

"A lab report?"

"Got everything wrong he did, and then refused to admit it. Nothing worse than a nigger who thinks he's right."

"I don't care for your language, Mr. Hammond."

"Well pardon fucking me," he said angrily. "It's a free country, lady, in case you was off smoking pot while the rest of us was defending it. Just my luck to get the Flying Nun. You know there's a Mariners game on the TV that I'd rather be watching, if we're all through here." He heaved himself out of his soft throne with great difficulty and shuffled over to pour himself a double Wild Turkey with two cubes of ice. The cushion where he had been sitting remained dished in a deep crater. He mumbled a steady stream of unintelligible dialogue with himself.

Daphne looked toward the door to make sure it was close by, and she kept a very close eye on Roy Hammond as he opened and closed some kitchen drawers. "Why did your name get changed on that report?"

"Why?" he asked, his back turned, and she

could sense him vamping for time. He returned to his La-Z-Boy swivel recliner and drank an enormous amount of the liquor without batting an eye. He toyed with it, clinking the rapidly melting ice cubes against the glass.

She added, "The man whose name replaced yours, a Mr. Patrick Shawnesea, does apparently not live in this state any longer. That makes it difficult for us to locate him for an interview."

"Harder than you think, lady. Pat Shawnesea is long dead. Lung cancer, and he never smoked a single cigarette in his life. Radon, I heard it was. Living atop a hot spot. Makes sense: The wife died of woman problems two years and change before Pat. Cut everything off her and outta her and she still up and died on him."

She thought that maybe Shawnesea's death explained the change of date on the document, for it had been backdated eleven days, and that had been bothering her the whole way out here. Why backdate a document? Unless you need a window of time in which Pat Shawnesea was still working, so that the only person who could answer important questions was certain not to be available. She had a few nuggets of what she wanted, though the mother lode still avoided her. "Let me see if I have this right," she said, slouching her shoulders forward involuntarily because of this man's insistence on fixing his eyes on her chest. "Shawnesea took this case over from you eleven days *before* your initial investigation began. He decided the illnesses had been caused by salmonella, not staphylococcus, which was the finding of your investigation."

"Let me explain something —"

"Please do," she interrupted.

"They wasn't *my* findings, the way you say — they was Jefferson's. He's the one done the tests, okay? And as for Pat, I don't remember exactly what he had to do with any of this."

"But it's his name on this second document — the *altered* document."

"I understand that, lady, but it don't necessarily mean it makes sense, now does it?"

"But you knew Mark Meriweather."

"Sure I did."

"And Mr. Shawnesea?"

"What do you mean?"

"He knew Mr. Meriweather, too? He inspected Longview, too?"

"Well, he must have, now mustn't he?"

"I thought you said Longview was part of your —"

"We picked up each other's slack."

"But did you investigate this New Leaf contamination or Mr. Shawnesea? I remind you that your signature is clearly visible on the original document."

"I did." The man looked confused. "How many years that been? There one of them statues of elimination on this thing or what?"

In another interview, Daphne might have cracked a smile, but Hammond disgusted her, and she immediately felt tempted to lie. What the general public failed to understand — to their loss, she thought — was that there existed no code of ethics or other formality instructing or limiting law enforcement officers to speak the truth, except while under oath. No place was this more evident than in the Box — the interrogation room, where police officers commonly invented any truth that helped their cause, and their cause was to put criminals away. The best liars were the best interrogators, and Daphne Matthews was considered close to the top. The only real difference she could see between an interrogation and an interview was the location of the discussion. What Hammond did not know was that she was out of her jurisdiction and had made no formal application to conduct this interview with King County police, meaning that everything either of them said was off the record from the moment she first opened her mouth to speak. Meaning also that she could tell as many lies as she wanted, and could act on anything Hammond told her, but could use none of the interview itself in a court of law. These thoughts circulated through her conscious mind before she answered untruthfully, "I believe the statute of limitations has expired on the Longview contamination. I don't believe there's any way we can prosecute anyone for what happened to this document. But to be honest, I don't really care: It's the truth I want, Mr. Hammond. A man may go to jail for a very, very long time if we can't find the real truth about Longview." There was a joke that lived on the fifth floor that she heard circulate year in and year out: What's a Chinese court deputy say to those in the courtroom at the start of every trial? "All lies."

"That boy, Harry," he said.

"Yes, Harry," she repeated, her heart backfiring.

"A real troublemaker, Harry was. Got it in his head all wrong and wouldn't have it any other way. Disappeared as fast as he arrived. Called me a liar to my face. Stood there looking me in the eye and called me a liar."

"What did you say his last name was?" she asked quickly, hoping to trick it out of him.

"I *didn't* say. I got no idea. Seeing people around a place and knowing them is two different things, lady. I regularly inspected seven dairies, five bird operations, a rabbit farm, a goat cheese outfit, and eleven food manufacturers. More, some years. People like Mark Meriweather, I had a business knowing. But his hired hands? Some drifter who thought he was God's gift to chickens? Hang it up!"

And yet by this very statement, Hammond revealed he knew more about Harry than he had first let on.

"I understood that he was college educated," she tested.

"Was going to take over for Hank Russell

292

when Hank stepped aside. Sure — that was the story anyway. Mark spent too much time and too much money on that boy, you ask me, treating him the way he did. Just a no-good drifter, and Mark goes treating him like a son. He mixed the boy up is what he done. Went to jail or something, I heard."

She carefully wrote down: *Jail?*

"Mr. Russell was part-time, was he?"

"Hank Russell? He ran that place, lady. Was foreman for half a dozen years. Damn fine operation, too."

She pretended to check some papers. "I don't show any record of a Henry Russell."

"What kind of record? Taxes, I'll bet." He laughed and had to wipe his chin afterward. "Pay Uncle Sam? Not Hank Russell. My guess is that he worked it out with Meriweather, just like when he was over to Dover's Butter-Breast before that. Roof over his head, some food, some cash under the table — that's Hank for you. Part of the family."

"I'm confused about something." She held up one document, then the other. "Was it a staph or salmonella outbreak?"

Hammond's eyes were glassy from the booze, of which he took another long swallow as he stewed on this. Boiled was more like it, she thought. His Adam's apple bobbed as if food were going through the boa. His left hand gripped the arm of the chair in a choke hold. She felt him on the verge of opening up to her. When his throat cleared he said, "I got nothing to say to you, lady. Take it somewhere else, why don't you?"

"It's just that —"

He interrupted her with a bone-numbing delivery that drove his face scarlet and overfilled a blue vein in his long, pale forehead to where it jumped right off his face. "I said take it somewhere else! Get outta here. You get outta here now, 'fore I make you *pay* for that comment!" She was up and out of her chair, struggling with her briefcase.

"I don't want to talk no more," he said. He turned his back on her, snatched his nearly empty drink from the side table, and headed back for the tall bottle that awaited him.

She was out of there in a matter of seconds, in her car, and down the road. Exhausted, and still tense from the encounter, she drove until the phone cooperated and placed three calls — one of them downtown, one to the owner of Dover's ButterBreast turkey farm, and the third to a tiny farm up the road toward Sammamish. After telling the farm's owner that she worked for Publishers Clearing House, he claimed that Hank Russell was out in his trailer "watching the game, I think."

She disconnected the phone, placing it on the seat beside her, and drew in a deep breath. She shifted gears, took a curve suicidally fast, and whispered under her breath the punch line to that joke — "All lies" — a wry smile twisting up the edges of her lips, where her color had finally returned.

"Where's your jacket?"

"Pardon me?"

Hank Russell was short and solid. He looked like a fifty-five-year-old rodeo rider — jeans, dusty cowboy boots, and an azure blue work shirt with a western yoke and snap pockets. He had a silver belt buckle the size of a salad plate, and when he turned around to silence the television with a remote, she saw that on the back of his brown leather belt it read simply HANK, in big embossed letters. His twangy voice sounded like tires on gravel: "Them Publishing House Clearance folks got them blazers like I seen on the tube. You ain't one of 'em, are you?"

"No, sir." She liked his smile immediately.

"You lied to me, young lady."

"Yes, sir, I did."

"You're too damn pretty to be a tax lady, and it's too damn late at night. Tell me you're not a tax lady. God help me!"

"I'm not a tax lady."

His relief was genuine. "Some unknown relative of mine died? You look more like an attorney than a tax lady."

"I'm not an attorney either," she told him. "I'm a policewoman, Mr. Russell. I think Harry may be in trouble."

"Harry Caulfield? Again? Well, Jez-us!" he

295

swung the screen door open wide. "Come in. Come in!" He zapped the TV this time killing the picture as well. She thought of cowboys and six-guns; and now they used remotes. "How about some lemon pie?" he asked with a twinkle in his green eyes. "Made it myself. It's the best damn pie you've ever ate."

She and Boldt wandered his small backyard, side by side, the sergeant stopping every now and then to pick up one of the brightly colored plastic toys that were scattered about everywhere.

"Last name of Caulfield," she said. "Harry Caulfield. Wandered onto the farm at seventeen. Wouldn't talk about his past. Not to anyone. Worked hard, learned fast. Everyone treated him like family. The owner, Meriweather, made him earn his high school equivalency if he wanted to stay on at Longview. Sent him on to college after that. Paid for everything for the boy."

"Here?" Boldt asked, briefly pausing in their slow stroll.

She nodded. "That's how the foreman remembers it. The university. Studied sciences, he said."

"Like microbiology?"

"Could be," she agreed. "It would help him with the poultry business — the diseases, the doctoring."

"It's him."

"Worked back at the farm summers and on breaks. Evidently loved the work. Named a bunch of the hens. Really took to it."

"And came down hard."

"Russell says someone got paid. Said there was a break-in about a week before State Health shut them down, but that nothing was taken, and they blamed it on some kids and paid no attention. Never reported it."

"Someone doctored their birds," Boldt speculated.

She nodded. "Set them up. They never saw it coming. About the time the infection spread, the State Health inspector, Hammond, shows up and shuts them down that very day. It happened real fast. Too fast for Hank Russell; that's how he claims he knew it was rigged. The farm was ordered to destroy the birds, and the boy was there, back from college. Meriweather wasn't himself. His wife got into the booze. The people who got sick threatened lawsuits. He was going to lose it all, and worse: He and the boy both knew it. Russell says Meriweather wasn't sleeping, couldn't think clearly. He refused to poison the birds, so instead they butchered them — *all* of them. All in one day. Over a thousand birds. By hand. The boy, too — Harry. Russell says he's never had a day like that in his life. Ankle-deep in blood, covered in it. 'A mountain of headless birds,' he said. And another pile of just the heads. And Mark Meriweather and Harry Caulfield crying the whole time, crying for sixteen hours while they slaughtered those birds and put an end to the farm." The psychologist in her said, "They should have never involved the boy."

Boldt stopped and rocked his head back toward the moon, and his voice cracked as he tried to say something to her but stopped himself. When he did manage to speak, he said, "I don't know that I can go on being a parent." He picked up another piece of plastic — it looked like a bridge — and stacked it with the others. Maybe they combined to make a fort or a house, she could not tell which.

"The lawsuits did come, and on an icy fall night Meriweather drove himself off Snoqualmie Pass for the insurance money. The wife ended up committed; the way Russell described it, it sounded like wet brain. Ownership of the farm was never worked out. Meriweather owned it outright, and the wife was still living. So it just rotted away, according to Russell."

"And our friend Harry?"

"Wouldn't speak after Meriweather died. Nearly starved himself to death by not eating. Russell said he was hospitalized for a while, and that when he got out, he came to Russell with a plan to prove they had been framed."

Boldt sat down into one of the midget swing-set seats and stretched his legs out. The swing set was bright blue in the moonlight, with a yellow wrapping like wide ribbon. Daphne took the swing next to him, but was afraid their combined weight might break the set, so she stood up and held the chains, feeling awkward.

"But Russell didn't want any of that," Boldt guessed.

"Hank Russell is what you might call the original honest outlaw. He's simply not in the system. Doesn't drive. Doesn't pay taxes, I don't think. But he knows livestock, and he seems to have been around every kind there is, if you believe him."

"And you do."

"I do."

"So Harry launches his own crusade against Owen Adler."

"No," she corrected. "This is several years ago when Harry gets this idea."

"I don't get it," Boldt said, looking over at her.

"Russell's story stops there. He heard the boy had gotten into some trouble, but never knew what it was."

"Jail?"

"Hammond mentioned jail. I didn't call in a request because I wasn't sure about using the radio."

"You did exactly right." This pulled Boldt out of the swing and to his feet. "So we check Corrections."

"The kid's a mess, Lou."

"The kid is killing people, Daffy. You want me to feel sorry for him?"

She did not answer.

"Maybe I can see it," he said. "Maybe some-day even come to understand it on some level. But I'll never condone it. I'll never forgive him for Slater Lowry."

"It's not him doing this."

"Don't start with me."

"It's not, Lou."

"Yes it is, Daffy. He *is* the one doing this. Don't kid yourself. You *found* him, Daffy: You identified him. You did it! You should feel proud about that."

"Well, I don't," she said, following him toward their cars.

Boldt, too, elected not to use the radios, to take no chance whatsoever that the name Harry Caulfield might be overheard by an eavesdropping reporter. Instead, he and Daphne returned separately to the fifth floor and immediately sought the man's prior convictions and outstanding warrants through Boldt's computer terminal. The search for H. Caulfield produced a single hit.

"Harold Emerson Caulfield," Boldt read to her from the screen. "Twenty-eight years old. A narco bust. Arrested and convicted four years ago for possession of two kilos of cocaine. Paroled four months ago. Home address — get this! — Sasquaw, Washington." He looked up at her excitedly and confirmed, "That's our guy." He took her by the arm, pulled her down to him, and kissed her quickly on the lips. Their faces just inches apart, hers alive with excitement, there was a brief moment in which he felt confused, but he let go of her arm in time to allow the sensation to pass. She smiled and laughed somewhat nervously. "Well!" she said, letting out a huge sigh.

"Come on!" he encouraged, tugging on her hand. "Let's pull the file."

They hurried across the floor in brisk elongated strides that neared an all-out run — which, at that early hour of the morning, caught the attention of the few members of Pasquini's squad who were at their desks. "Where's the fire?" one of the men called out. Another answered, "In their pants!" And laughter erupted all around. Boldt knew it probably looked that way — running off together to find an empty room — and this once, he did not care. The discovery of Caulfield made him feel drunk.

There was only one elevator in use this time of night, and it was a long time coming, so Daphne suggested the stairs. They raced each other down, in the middle of which she called out to him: "I want to run this by Clements if it's all right with you."

"Is he here?"

"Arrived this afternoon. There's a meeting called for tomorrow. Any objections?"

"None at all."

"It will help with his profile."

"No objections," he repeated, winded already. They reached the basement floor and started first at a walk, and then broke into a run simultaneously. All police of the rank detective or higher possessed keys to the three file rooms, and Boldt used his to open first the door, and then the interior chain-link gate. This basement room was nicknamed "the Boneyard," and contained the files for all cleared cases three to seven years in the past. Twice a year the oldest of these files were removed to a permanent graveyard for police files in a warehouse off Marginal Way.

There were thousands of files contained in row after row of gray-metal racks, all color-coded with the same system used by doctors and dentists. The lighting was dreary, the files thumbworn, and the organization miserable. But the colored stickers, marked by alphabetical reference, made it easy to find C-A-U-.

Boldt had to pry one file from the next, they were crammed in so tightly. Daphne lent a hand, opening a space between files so that Boldt could read the case number and name.

He made one pass, then another. He glanced down at her — she was standing on her toes to reach this shelf — and said, "I don't see it."

"You hold," she instructed, and they switched jobs. She became somewhat frantic on the fourth pass. "It *has* to be here."

"It isn't."

"Misspelled maybe."

Boldt checked the tattered ledger by the door,

302

leafing through the scrawled listings of what files had been signed out, and by whom. It was an archaic system where half the entries were illegible. "Not here," he called out.

At Daphne's frustrated insistence, together they spent another ten minutes leafing through all the files beginning with the letters *Ca* and found no file for Harry Caulfield, at the end of which Daphne was out of breath. She blew on her bangs to move them off her forehead, but the hair was stuck there and she brushed it out of the way.

They stood in an uncomfortable silence staring at the towering wall of smudged and ragged files, both of them seething with anger. The room seemed the size of a football field to Boldt, and the records on Caulfield could have been misfiled.

"Someone took it," Boldt finally said, voicing what he knew she too was thinking.

She looked up at him, so frustrated that her eyes were brimmed with tears, and she said in a tense and raspy voice, "What do you want to bet that whatever went on with Longview Farms reached further than State Health?"

"I'm not a betting man," replied Lou Boldt.

TWENTY-TWO

"It's no secret that some of you consider this voodoo," the renowned forensic psychiatrist and FBI special agent Dr. Richard Clements said in a deep-throated voice that filled Homicide's situation room. Thirty minutes into the evening shift, LaMoia and Gaynes were already on ATM watch, as were a total of eight other police officers.

Boldt, Shoswitz, Rankin, and Daphne Matthews were all in attendance for SPD. They were joined by two plainclothes detectives from the King County police, a homicide lieutenant and two detectives from the Portland Police Department, the Special Agent in Charge of the FBI's Seattle field office, and two FBI public information officers.

Dr. Clements looked a little green under the artificial lights. He wore a plain gray suit, white shirt with a loud, abstract tie, and black wing tips. He had long gray hair, wild over the ears, and steely dark eyes, and looked like someone who ran a museum for a private foundation. He never blinked. Wearing half-glasses, he read from a dog-eared folder, and made notes with a black mechanical pencil as he went.

Prior to the start of this meeting, he had complained to Boldt that he would rather be back in Virginia mowing his lawn and drinking a sloe gin fizz. This, Boldt assumed, was his attempt to give a romantic impression of himself. Boldt knew all about Dr. Richard Clements.

Dr. Clements had interviewed the most vicious mass murderers and serial murderers in confinement in the United States as well as several overseas countries, including the former Soviet Union, and had compiled a psychological overview of these killers that later led to the now commonplace practice of criminal profiling. For four of the Reagan years, he had been adviser to the Secret Service, analyzing both real and perceived threats to the president's life. According to rumor, on three occasions he had accurately predicted where to find the would-be assassins just days before the attempts.

He had come to work with Daphne Matthews as an adviser while serving as a special agent on the FBI's Behavioral Science Unit during the Seattle Police Department's attempt to apprehend the Cross Killer. An eccentric, he was the stuff of legend in law enforcement — the Einstein of the criminal mind. He lectured at Yale and Johns Hopkins regularly, and had authored several books including a textbook in use in nearly every criminology course in the country. It was said that extensive scars, barely visible above his shirt collar but more obvious at the cuff of his left sleeve, covered most of

305

his upper torso and had been given to him by Mad Dog, a Swedish inmate who had nearly devoured the man before guards saved him. There were other stories about Dr. Clements — some even about these same scars — that Boldt had heard over the years, some of them flattering, some not. Until today, he had not believed them. Now, looking at this creature, he was not so quick to rule anything out. In appearance, Dr. Clements had been around mass murderers for too long: He was wide-eyed and given to explosive bursts of animation followed by eerie stretches of silence and contemplation that one dare not interrupt.

"Perhaps this science is part voodoo. Sometimes the profiles help, sometimes not. What I am going to tell you about this man — oh yes, a *man* — is intended merely as a reference point, a fallback that hopefully, may help guide you toward a better understanding of this individual, or even possibly predict his future behavior." He addressed Captain Rankin, a big burly man of Irish coloring. "My job is part science, part invention. But like you, I take it seriously, and I ask only that you give me serious consideration and your undivided attention.

"First, a point of business: At my suggestion, Sergeant Boldt has instructed Adler Foods to begin a quiet recall and subsequent destruction of all its candy bars. As you may know, an individual believed to be our suspect has been identified as having purchased several such

306

candy bars, and it is my contention that he intends to poison them. This is a substitution recall only — that is, all such products currently on the shelf will be replaced with fresh product, and random testing will be conducted on recalled product. In this way we do not violate the demands, but we serve the public interest. Now, as to the larger issue.

"The individual in question goes by the name of Harry Caulfield. He is single, twenty-eight years old. Despite a possible residence at Longview Farms, I believe he has recently lived within a two-mile radius of the Broadway Foodland supermarket. He may be cohabitating, though I doubt it — a loner is more likely. He is or was recently employed in a blue-collar job or jobs that involve manual labor. This employment may have temporarily included Adler Foods or association with Adler Foods, though it is my contention he was never on the payroll.

"I can see, Captain Rankin, that you are skeptical of my assessment." Rankin shifted uneasily in his chair. "I can explain some of this. The first two faxes that Mr. Owen Adler received some months ago were pasteups, not computer faxes like the more recent threats. Your lab identified the source publications for these pasteups as including typography from both *Playboy* and *Penthouse* as well as a local shopping giveaway. The two skin magazines help us define his demography; the giveaway helps narrow his current or former place of residence, because the publication does not enjoy wide circulation. He also clipped both *Sports Illustrated* and a national blue-collar rag called *Heartland* — these identified by our Hoover lab — which further narrows his demographics and suggests the likelihood of manual labor. We don't dream this stuff up." He smirked.

"But who is he?" he continued. "He is a loner. A possible insomniac. The actions he is taking are his — that is, he is not some hired gun, but instead his own man. He may or may not have a background in" — he held up his fingers — "microbiology, animal husbandry, electronics, or food production. He believes his cause righteous, and as far as we are concerned, that makes him extremely dangerous and he is to be taken at his word. He believes he is doing what he has to: punishing Adler Foods, or Owen Adler himself, for some grievous wrong committed in the past.

"Technically, clinically," he went on, "he is assumed to be a paranoid schizophrenic. He is really two people, if you will — the evil person committing these crimes and the voice he hears both encouraging him and warning him of the severity of his actions. There is a voice of reason within him, hence his ability to organize and seemingly remain one step ahead. Although schizophrenic, he's not crazy in the way you think of him," he addressed to Rankin. "Not organically. He's disturbed certainly, but

308

there is a vast difference. No drooler, this man. He is to be taken seriously. He is to be feared. If he says two weeks, then two weeks it is. If he says he'll kill a hundred, then it shall be no less."

Clements scanned the room and continued. "He does not believe he can be caught. You snicker, Captain, but it is the truth. He believes himself smarter than all of you — all of us *combined*. I promise you that he monitors the media closely for signs of his success or failure. Your ability so far to disguise his acts is to be commended. As I understand it, you were concerned about the proliferation of copycat crimes — a legitimate concern. But worse, this is a man who will try to outdo his own head-lines."

Rankin, still not convinced, asked, "Where does the extortion fit in? The extortion demands?"

"It's a complex issue," Clements answered. "It appears he has a grand scheme, a grand design in mind, perhaps from the beginning. Three phases: a warning phase, an attack phase, a final phase, if you will. I believe we have moved into the attack phase. He has not seen the results he had hoped for, but he was prepared for this all along. He has shifted from the larger demands that even to him must have seemed unlikely for him to win, to the more specific monetary gains of these extortion demands."

"And the final phase?" one of the Portland cops asked reluctantly.

"Phase three is to deliver on his promise to kill hundreds, I would assume. Do not doubt it. It is not inconceivable that he has devised a plan in advance to accomplish this in the event of his arrest." As an aside he said, "With an individual as seemingly capable as this, *nothing* is inconceivable." He allowed another wry smile, and his glassy, unflinching eyes sparkled in the harsh light. Dr. Richard Clements was enjoying himself.

TWENTY-THREE

That same Thursday night, LaMoia pulled up in front of Boldt's house knowing the sergeant was expecting him. Still tucking in his shirt, Boldt came out the door with his coat slung over his arm. A cloud of moths fluttered overhead, surrounding the porch light. Another group enveloped a street lamp above the car.

LaMoia met him on the porch and handed Boldt a scrawled note containing an address that was surprisingly close. Over by Greenlake on Seventy-fourth, it was a neighborhood Boldt remembered well from another case, and one he would have just as soon forgotten.

"Dixie?"

"On his way. His people will meet him there."

"Razor?"

"Left your cellular number with him." LaMoia handed Boldt his cell phone and Boldt absentmindedly slipped it into his coat pocket. He patted his side; his gun was there. "It's a tough break, Sarge."

Boldt double-checked the front door. The two men hurried to the waiting car. "Who called it in?" Boldt asked.

"Who else would land this kind of *black hole?*

Hollywood, Sarge," he said, answering Boldt's blank expression. "Danielson." A second later from inside the car, LaMoia shouted, "You coming?"

Boldt stood frozen with his hand on the door. Daphne had mentioned Danielson's eavesdropping. Boldt did not like it.

"Sarge?"

Boldt climbed inside.

"You okay?"

"Step on it," ordered the man who liked to drive under thirty at all times.

The house was a two-story shake, closely situated to its neighbors on both sides. The street rose up a hill, and so LaMoia cut the wheels into the curb and let the car settle back. A set of cement steps carried Boldt up to some wooden steps that led to a landing and to the front door where Danielson sat on the stoop. Bernie Lofgrin and his ID crew remained below for the moment, waiting to be summoned.

The ME's chuck wagon arrived next — an unmarked, lime-green van. A color green no one could possibly like. Usually reserved for cadavers, but sometimes used to transport the field technicians. Boldt saw the scene they were creating, and told LaMoia tersely to spread out some of the vehicles to try to lessen the attention drawn to the scene. "We want this done as quietly as possible. If the neighbors do get involved, no one answers any questions.

And I mean *no one.*"

"Got it," LaMoia answered. He saw to it and returned to join Boldt as he was preparing to enter.

Boldt and LaMoia donned latex gloves.

Boldt tried the front door, but it was locked. He signaled Bernie Lofgrin, and a few minutes later one of Lofgrin's assistants had used a speed key on the back door.

Boldt motioned for LaMoia to go first. The young detective pushed open the door, leaned his head inside, and called out, "Honey, I'm home."

Boldt felt a depressing weight in the air. It was not the smell of vomit that triggered it — he smeared some Vicks under his nose and took care of that, and he passed the tube to LaMoia, who did the same. The weight was the result of a sense of failure that would not let go of him. Four more lives. Four more Slater Lowrys.

Uncharacteristically philosophical, Boldt said to LaMoia, "Death touches us all, but murder affects people permanently. Twenty years later the average guy will have forgotten some of the ones who died, but not the ones who were murdered."

"I'm sure that's right," LaMoia said, unsure how to answer.

"If it would do any good to swear to you that these are the last we're going to see, I would."

"If you had those kinds of powers, you'd be wearing a turban, not a badge."

The table was set for four — but it looked like breakfast, not dinner. It looked as if someone had reset the table ready for a morning that never came. The stove top was clear and there were dishes inside the dishwasher that would be analyzed by the lab.

The two bathrooms, downstairs and upstairs, were ugly. People had been real sick, and in the end no one had taken the time to clean up. Boldt could imagine them awakening with bad stomachs — first the kids, then the parents. Two to six hours after the meal, Dixie had told him. And as the reaction worsened, the parents would have become scared, would have discussed the idea of the hospital. Guts wrenching. Children screaming from the pain in their abdomens. He could not imagine that kind of fear — that moment when one of them realized they *all* had it — whatever it was. Projectile vomiting. Diarrhea. Slamming headaches. The father or mother running for the car. Thinking about 911, but deciding they could make it themselves . . .

But they did not make it.

On the very top of the tin-can recycle bag in the pantry, Boldt found two crushed cans of Adler's Homestyle Hash. Evidence for Lofgrin's ID crew that would follow into here shortly.

Here was a crime scene that seemed bound

to hit the press. The deaths of an entire family could not be contained. Boldt was already working on a believable story that Dixie and State Health could feed the media. The family was believed to have eaten out at a restaurant, as yet unidentified. "The symptoms observed in the deceased do not conflict with those found in other *E. coli* contaminations." At face value, the truth. The only way he could see of keeping the real truth from the public in order to protect it from even more such poisonings. The Seattle community was numb enough from earlier *E. coli* contaminations to accept the explanation. He could not buy forever with such a story, but a few days — a week if he were lucky.

The girls' bedroom — he could see that they shared the room — devastated him. A Raggedy Ann doll sitting in a low wicker chair. It was the way the bed linen was folded back — a mother helping her child out of bed. But they were out of bed. Dixie's office had them in black plastic bags, zippered down the middle. Their breakfast table was set, but within a few minutes, breakfast would be in plastic, too.

Boldt had tried to help an injured sparrow once as a child, but it had struggled in his hand, and he had broken its neck and it had died. He remembered holding it outstretched in his open palms and tossing it into the air, encouraging it to fly. Picking it up and tossing it, until his mother, weeping, caught up to him and stopped him.

Though she had tried to convince him otherwise, he had killed it trying to help — and this was how he felt now as he sank down to the floor of this small pink room and pushed the door shut in a vain attempt to make his peace.

Striker arrived late, looking and smelling a little drunk. Waving his pager at Boldt, he slurred, "Fucking thing's a piece of shit."

"It's him," Boldt said, indicating the house.

"Mr. Caulfield's work?"

"Right."

Striker said, "For what it's worth, I think all women are shit."

"Another Adler product. Hash this time." Boldt realized he was not getting through.

"They yank your chain. They mess with your brain."

"A family of four. All four *died*, Razor."

Striker's prosthesis clicked violently. "Died?" He was only half there.

"All four. Waited too long before going to the emergency room. The mother did okay for a while, but they lost her. They say grief, maybe. They say it can do that."

"The wrong people always die," Striker complained. "You know what I'm saying?"

"No," Boldt answered honestly.

"Well, fuck you," Striker said. He passed Boldt, intentionally bumping him with his shoulder, and went inside the house. Boldt waited fifteen minutes under a low, overcast sky that threatened rain. A gang of uniformed patrolmen held back the reporters and cameramen. He heard the words *E. coli* on the tongues of the spectators. So far, so good, Boldt thought, growing accustomed to the lies, and hating himself for it.

"Stinks in there," Striker said on his return. "Same old, same old."

"We need a mug shot or file photo of Caulfield. Department of Corrections should have one."

"You don't need me for that."

"It would be easier. I want everything they have on Caulfield, and I'd rather they don't connect the request directly with me or the fifth floor. Your office makes those requests all the time."

"I'll have it for you by morning." Striker made a note. It was the first sign of sobriety.

"Been hoisting a few, Razor?"

"Hey, I'm not on call. Shit, Elaine's never home. Why not?"

"Just don't go picking any fights." Striker had a reputation for challenging thirty-year-olds to one-handed fights — and winning. And sometimes there was no challenge. Just an explosion, and Striker was on someone.

"Well, there he is," he said, noticing Danielson glaring at Boldt from the parked car. "That warrant must have done the trick, huh?"

"Which warrant?" Boldt asked. "Holly Mac-Namara?"

"The klepto? Hell no. I mean *his*. Danielson's. The W-2s on Longview Farms. I had to bitch and scream to get you those. Fucking tax boys have assholes as tight as squirrels'."

Boldt did his best to hide his shock. He looked away, as if still interested in the house. "The W-2s," he repeated.

"Right. Going after the Longview employees. That's how you got Caulfield's name. Right? And all thanks to yours truly. And Danielson, too, maybe — or was he just your go-boy on that?" He poked Boldt a little too hard with his metal claw. "You can thank me. I won't complain."

"Yeah, thanks, Razor." Boldt's words barely left his mouth.

"You don't have to sound so overjoyed," Striker stabbed sarcastically.

"No. I appreciate it. Really." Boldt said, sounding stronger, his attention focused across the lawn on Danielson's profile. "The Longview tax records," he repeated.

"Damn straight. *You* ought to try going up against the tax boys sometimes. It ain't all fun and games, believe me."

Boldt had LaMoia drive him downtown. He left the car before it came to a full stop and hurried to the door with the detective shouting loudly from behind him, "Wait up!"

Boldt was not waiting. He took the stairs two at a time, descending into the basement. He had his key out for the Boneyard before

318

reaching the door. Through the door, then the chain-link gate. He found the light switch without looking.

Several long strides down the second aisle, around the corner to the shelf so familiar to him. C-A-U-

And there it was: the arrest file for Harold Emerson Caulfield. Exactly where it belonged.

TWENTY-FOUR

Armed with a variety of mug shots, including those of Harry Caulfield that had been given to her by Boldt, Daphne approached Holly MacNamara the following Friday morning before the young woman left for summer school.

Holly was dressed in blue jeans, a white T-shirt, and black running shoes. The mother continually tried to push herself on them, and to prevent her from interfering, Daphne and the young woman sought privacy in Holly's bedroom. The walls were covered with posters of grunge bands. The bed was on the floor, and the room smelled of incense.

"You see what I live with?" she asked Daphne.

"Mothers can be harsh," Daphne agreed.

"Yeah?"

"My mother was a real jerk when I was in high school. She thought I was going to get pregnant and become a junkie."

"You?"

"Me," she answered. She placed the first series of mug shots in front of the girl, withholding Caulfield's for the third or fourth group. She wanted to get her acquainted with the process before risking their prize. But more than that, she wanted to help this young woman if possible.

Holly MacNamara studied them all carefully, picked one of them up, placed it down, and shook her head. "Not here," she said.

"The thing is," Daphne told her, "the more time I spent at home, the worse it was, because it seemed like everything I did was wrong. My mother wanted me to be her cute little girl. She couldn't handle that I had breasts and my period, and that I was curious to find out what drinking beer was like." None of this reflected her high school years in the least, but she had studied the Holly MacNamaras and she thought she knew the general situation well enough to establish a rapport.

"Talk to me."

"Same with you?"

"Absolutely."

Daphne laid out another set of four mug shots. "How about these?" she asked.

Holly was not looking at the photographs, but at Daphne instead. "The thing is, she never lets up. And all I want is for her to chill and give me some *space*. You know? She doesn't have a clue who I am."

"Maybe a clue," Daphne said, "but not much of one."

"Exactly."

Daphne indicated the photos for a second time, and Holly studied them carefully — perhaps more carefully, Daphne hoped, than had they not had this conversation.

"No, I don't think so," Holly said.

"Make sure."

"No. Definitely not."

Daphne picked up these, but waited before placing down the next, for the photo of Harry Caulfield was among these. She said, "I volunteer at the Shelter —"

"The place for runaways?"

"Yes. A close friend of mine is the spokesperson, and I put in about eight hours a week there — evenings mostly. Have you ever considered volunteer work?"

"Me?"

"I know it's not the same as hanging out at the mall, as hanging out with your friends. But the girls are about your age — closer to your age than mine, that's for sure — and more than anything, they need contact with people, they need to find a base, to get themselves centered again. Volunteers do everything from serve meals to change beds to just sit around talking. What I was thinking — you're kind of in a bad scene here. Your sentencing requires you to stay home, but this is where a lot of your problems seem to stem from. What if I could convince the judge to allow you to spend some time volunteering at the Shelter? Maybe the same hours I'm there — at least at first. Would you have any interest in that?"

"I could try it."

"Is that a yes?"

Holly studied Daphne's face. "Yeah, that's a yes."

"Good," Daphne said, grinning.

She laid out the next series of mug shots. First one, then the second, then Harry Caulfield, then a fourth. "What about these?" She watched the girl's face carefully, as Holly's eyes moved progressively down the row. When she reached Caulfield, her eyes widened and she bit her lip. Then, without saying anything, she looked at the fourth in the line.

"Let me ask you something," Holly Mac-Namara said. Daphne nodded. "If I *did* recognize this guy — not that I'm saying I do — then I become involved, right? I become a snitch." Her voice changed, driven by anger. "You know how much trouble I've gotten in because someone ratted on me? Do you know what that feels like? And now you expect me to rat on some guy? Do you see anything wrong with this picture?"

"I'm going to tell you something that I'm not allowed to tell you. I'm going to tell you because I trust you *never* to repeat it. If you were to repeat it, you could get me in some serious shit — maybe even cost me my job — it's *that* secret. I don't know you well, Holly, but I like you — and this is one time I had better be a good judge of character." She hesitated, to allow this to sink in. "I know what you're saying about snitching. I think I understand where you're coming from. And I can see how it would be hard for you. Especially if you were turning in a shoplifter. Shoplifting is nothing to be proud of, Holly, but I can see how that would be difficult for you. But the person we're after is not a shoplifter." Caulfield stared back at her from the mug shot. He was clean-shaven, dark eyes, with an average face of average looks. He was Mr. Anybody. He might have been a waiter, or an attorney, or a cop. Dark hair, a firm jaw line, and strong eyes. He was a multiple murderer, and he seemed to be looking right at Daphne with an expression of smug contempt and hatred. *I hate you all,* his eyes said.

Daphne continued, "The man we're after is no shoplifter. He killed a boy young enough to be your little brother. He killed a family of four — two little girls and their parents. He's put other people in the hospital. He has threatened much worse, and we take those threats very seriously. We believe time may be running out — and we need to know if we're after the right person or not. We have a suspect, but no one that we know of has seen him but you. If you are able to identify him, then we know where to focus our investigation. We just may stop him in time." She pointed back to the line of mug shots. "Do you see him, Holly? Is he any of these men?"

Without any indecision, Holly MacNamara reached down and picked up the photograph of Harry Caulfield. "This is the man I saw at Foodland."

Bernie Lofgrin's magnified eyeballs looked fake, like a pair of joke glasses won at the ringtoss at an amusement park. His office was crowded with stacks of reading material and reports vying for chair seats and rising like teetering skyscrapers from the office floor. A cup of steaming coffee sat by the phone and he waved a Bic pen in the air as if it were a baton.

Boldt set the jazz tapes down on the man's cluttered desk, moved a stack of printed matter, and took a seat across from him.

"Well, I'll be damned," Lofgrin said, holding the cassettes close to his face so he could read the titles that Boldt had written on them. "Uh-huh," he muttered and repeated with each new discovery, quite pleased. "You're a man of your word," he said. Peering more closely, he added enthusiastically, " 'Jumping Off a Clef!' Chet Baker! And Red Rodney, too! Terrific." Lofgrin liked the trumpet.

"An added bonus for my tardiness," Boldt said.

"You mind?" Lofgrin got up, shut the office door and put the trumpet tape into a boom box and turned it on, setting the volume low. For Boldt the jazz improved his mood immediately, and he was glad it was as familiar to him as it was, because it did not distract him, stealing his attention the way unfamiliar music did.

"We checked out all three ATMs last night. No latents. No evidence whatsoever."

While Boldt had been investigating the poisoning of the Mishnov family, three ATMs had been hit for another twenty-eight hundred dollars. Again, Boldt's surveillance team had been nowhere near the ATM locations hit. Bernie Lofgrin's forensic sciences squad had dusted for prints and inspected the sites for any other evidence.

Lofgrin said, "One thing bothers me . . . We've seen four ATMs hit, right? And according to ATM security people, some fifty percent of the machines are equipped with optical surveillance — cameras. So is this extortionist of yours just lucky or what?"

"It bothers me, too, Bernie."

"It gives you the feeling someone's got a hand in your back pocket — know what I mean?"

"I know *exactly* what you mean. I've got some ideas."

"I get the hint. We've got other things to discuss."

"The Longview Farms evidence," Boldt reminded as Lofgrin sat back down.

"We focused on that basement room, as you asked. Worked closely with the fire marshal, Peter Kramer, and also Fergus in their lab because a total burn is really its own science.

326

And there is a lot of work yet to go, I'm afraid, some of which we've shipped off to Washington, thanks to your agreement with the Bureau boys. There just isn't a hell of a lot left after a fire like that. Where we got lucky is that the workbench under which all these boxes were stored was topped with sheet metal. The weight of the collapsing building, combined with the limited protection of this layer of sheet metal, compressed the contents of some of the boxes, and there just wasn't enough oxygen for it all to burn. So we have small clusters of flaky carbon, kind of like the layers of French Pastry — extremely fragile, sensitive still to oxygen, and yet basically intact. We shipped a lot of this off to the Bureau because we want to get it right, and evidence this volatile only allows you one shot. Exposed to air, it literally turns to dust before you can work with it."

"How long?"

"The Bureau is thorough. They can, and have, taken weeks to get back to us. I'd say two weeks is average. We've asked for a rush, but everyone does, so I doubt it means much. They do know about the case, though, and that helps. My guess is that it will get some kind of priority, which may mean a week or ten days if we're lucky."

"We don't have ten days."

"I understand," Lofgrin said sympathetically. "I'm just being up-front with you. It's out of my hands."

"So we wait?"

"For the real detail work, we do. The specifics that may turn this thing on its ear. Oh, check this riff!" He leaned back. A pair of trumpets soared on an unpredictable harmony and fluttered to a gentle landing. Lofgrin sighed, as if he had just finished a good meal. "What we have for you is not the best news," the lab man said, sitting forward again. "The boxes beneath that workbench contained varying sizes of thin sheets of paper. Printed matter. Color, probably."

"Labels," the detective said.

"Yeah, labels, I'm thinking. But who knows? Could be *any* printed matter — church programs, political flyers. We didn't get a good look at any of them because of the decomposition during oxidation, and that's what we're hoping for by sending them out: some kind of positive identification for you to work with."

Boldt took notes despite the knowledge that Bernie Lofgrin would provide him with a copy of the preliminary report. Lab reports were overly technical and therefore difficult to interpret.

"As far as you're concerned, the most disturbing news was the detection of strychnine."

Boldt shouted involuntarily. "What?"

"In a basement we expect the presence of rodent poisons — anti-coagulants, mostly. But strychnine has no business being down there, especially in the proximity of the workbench, which is where we detected it. We picked up

328

traces in some of the ash samples — parts per million, mind you; trace amounts is all — but there was definitely strychnine in and around that area."

"Cholera?"

"If it was there, the bacteria were sterilized by the fire. We're pretty damn sure that what remained of the electrical gear we found could have fit the parameters of a light box of the kind Dr. Mann described to you, and we've detected abundant amounts of melted polymers, plastics specific to the manufacture of petri dishes."

"So it *was* a home lab," Boldt stated.

Lofgrin nodded. "Sure could be." His eyeballs seemed to be on springs.

"Why strychnine?" Boldt asked himself quietly, though Lofgrin answered.

"Jim Jones's Kool-Aid jamboree," Lofgrin reminded. "The Guyana massacre. The Sudafed case here. The Tylenol tamperings. Poison of choice for tampering." He explained, "Tasteless, odorless, easily blended."

"A mass poisoning?" Boldt questioned, reminded of the faxed threats.

"With cholera," Lofgrin said, "if it's identified and treated properly, the patient stands a good chance of recovery. Not so with strychnine. It's extremely fast — a few minutes is all. There's your primary difference."

"A few minutes," Boldt repeated, reminded of Caulfield's threat to kill hundreds.

Lofgrin's phone rang. He turned down the music, answered the phone, grunted, and placed it back in the receiver.

"Matthews," he informed Boldt. "She says she's got some good news for you."

"It's about time someone did."

"Do we dare release the mug shot to the press?" Boldt asked, buoyed by MacNamara's positive identification.

Daphne told him, "I think not. If he sees his own photo on the news, two things are going to happen: One, he's going to go underground — we lose any chance of catching him at the ATMs; two, he'll feel betrayed and may attempt to deliver on his larger threat. Let me run this by Clements. He'll have an opinion for us."

Boldt mentioned the strychnine, and they discussed possible psychological motives for a more deadly poison, and again she deferred to Dr. Clements. Leaving her, Boldt made himself a copy of the face and left the original with one of the civilian office workers, asking that it be photocopied and made available to all patrol personnel. A Be On Lookout was issued — Caulfield would be detained and brought downtown if spotted.

Boldt spent the afternoon distributing copies to the ATM surveillance team, moving between the various locations where his people were in position. They had a face now, and Boldt considered it their first decent break.

Kenny Fowler lived in a deluxe apartment managed by Inn At The Market, with maid and room service. He seemed both proud and embarrassed by it as he showed Boldt inside. Located directly above Campagne Restaurant, the corner view looked out over the red neon sign — PUBLIC MARKET CENTER — and across Elliott Bay and the slowly moving lights of Seattle's commercial shipping traffic. The first room encountered housed a wet bar, two couches, a pair of overstuffed chairs, a coffee table, and a small dining table. Off of this was a studio kitchen, a single bedroom with a water view, and a luxurious bath that Boldt knew Liz would kill for.

Boldt needed a favor, and he did not enjoy coming to Kenny Fowler with his hand out. He did not feel he could trust Fowler fully, for although they both wanted to see an end to the tampering, Fowler wanted credit, no doubt motivated by a corporate hierarchy that encouraged competition. He was also likely to want something in return for Boldt's request, and Boldt could not be sure he could, or would, grant any such request.

Facing the picture window, Fowler said, "Must be something important to bring the mountain to Mohammed." Then he continued his nervous orbit of the room, pouring himself a gin and tonic and joining Boldt in the sitting area.

331

"I need your help," Boldt announced, once Fowler's back was to him. It caught the security man by surprise, and he left his glass at the bar and returned to his seat without it.

"I'm listening."

"One of my people is exhibiting some peculiar behavior. I need a background check, maybe some surveillance, and I don't want to involve Internal Affairs."

Fowler nodded. "Puts you in a bad position."

"He's on my squad, Kenny. It's Chris Danielson."

"Danielson? Are you saying you think he's involved in this somehow? Have you spoken to him?"

"Not yet. I want this background check first."

"What exactly has he done?"

"I need your help, Kenny. Maybe we should leave it at that."

"Everything?"

"Everything you can get without it getting back to him that you're interested." The discussion made Boldt feel ugly and dirty at the same time. He knew this was not the way it was supposed to be done, and yet it seemed to him the most efficient use of manpower and time.

"You think Chris Danielson is maybe drilling these soup cans?" Fowler became crimson, beside himself with confusion.

"No, I don't. But I'm a little short of explanations of how the extortionist is never near the ATMs we're watching."

"Fucking A! Danielson's giving out your surveillance information?"

"I don't know what he's doing, but I want his dirty laundry if he's got any. It's that simple."

Fowler took some notes, saying aloud, "Finances. Travel. Big-ticket purchases." He glanced up at Boldt, then returned his attention to the notepad. "Family background, maybe."

"*Full* background check. College record, all of it, as much as you can give me."

Fowler had that deer-in-the-headlights look about him.

"What?" Boldt asked.

Fowler nodded. "Am I to assume this conversation never took place? That I found out about Danielson poking around and decided to sit on him? 'Cause I can do that for you if you like. I got a shitty memory, Lou. That's the truth."

"It won't come to that. Let's hope it's all a big dead end."

"But if it does?"

"If it does . . . I don't want any lies."

"You sure?" Fowler tested. "It could mean your badge if it comes to that. You realize that, don't you? I'm telling you, I got a bad memory."

"Save it for when you need it. I'll make note of this meeting so that at least you're covered. My idea. My responsibility."

"Whatever."

This felt like criminal behavior to Boldt, and he blamed the sensation in part on Fowler and his dramatics, because the man had a wormy quality to him. Technically, within certain parameters surveillance was not an illegal act, but the background check was, and both men knew it. The truth was that people in Fowler's position were paid under the table for such background checks all the time. Boldt knew there was no new ground being broken.

"I'm not comfortable asking you, Kenny. I've got to be up-front about that."

"I'm here, Lou. I'm part of this. I know how the department feels about the Kenny Fowlers of this world."

"It's not that."

"Of course it is. I steal a lot of your best people away from you. I offered you once, Lou, and you know that offer's always open. Starting pay would be *twice* where you are with your three stripes —"

"I know —" Boldt cut him off. He had no use for another Fowler recruitment pitch. "Thanks."

"Listen," the man said honestly, "I shade a lot of the laws. There's a reason police drive black-and-whites, you know. 'Kay? So, I live in the gray. So what? And I live better than any of you guys. And maybe there's just a touch of resentment there. No triplicate forms. No bullshit. We do our job and we collect big paychecks for our services. And maybe our job takes us a little outside the code. So what? Civil libertarians screwed the code up years ago, anyway. Am I right? 'Kay? Fucking sandbaggers have more rights than a badge does any day. So the system is set up to favor guys like Kenny Fowler. And now you need me. And I'm not going to bullshit you: It feels good, Lou. This is a day I'll remember. But maybe not for the reasons you think. This just settles some of my own shit."

Boldt had feared this exact lecture, having to sit there and eat crow while Fowler gloated. And if he knew the man, the quid pro quo was right around the next corner.

His piano, time with Miles, the lecturing, and now stepping outside the system he held dear despite his frustrations with it. Little pieces of Boldt's life were slipping away. And the little pieces added up to the whole, and it terrified him where this might be headed. He worked on a pair of Maalox.

"It's expensive, what you're asking," Fowler said, reading Boldt's mind, "although it's Adler's money, and he wants this thing wrapped up — obviously — so what the fuck? We can do it."

"I can't help you there, Kenny. You know the way it is."

"I'm not talking about money, Lou. You know what I'm saying."

"I was hoping maybe Adler wasn't the only one who wanted to see this thing wrapped,"

Boldt tested. Fowler offered a wooden smile, and Boldt felt his bowels stir.

"Sure. Sure," he said. He carefully measured his words. "We would like to be part of the extortion surveillance, Lou. Adler, Taplin, me — we don't like you guys being the only ones looking out for Mr. Adler's money. You know how it is. We have access to some super technologies. Stuff that there's no way you guys have. We can tie all your operatives together, restrict access, use GPS location devices — Adler's pretty much given me a blank check these last couple years. We've got the latest shit, Lou."

"My hands are tied, Kenny, you know that. we don't include privates in our surveillance work. It just doesn't happen."

"That's bullshit, Lou. Come on! Who you talking to? It's *me*, Kenny. Shoswitz eats out of your hand — you've been all but running that department for years. You get what you ask for."

"That's not true."

"It *is* true. All I'm asking is to protect my client's interests. 'Kay? To be kept up to speed. To help out. You include us in the surveillance, I can throw maybe ten guys your way. I can loan you guys access to my dispatch center. There's any number of ways I could help out. You've gotta see that. You can't tell me you got enough guys on this. Hell, you guys are still using open-channel radios — tell me you aren't. I'm *decades* ahead of you on this. All our shit is digital, fully restricted, and encoded; we can help in a big way — I'm telling you!"

Boldt suddenly understood the pitch. He felt stupid that he had missed it at first. "You're *already* watching the ATMs, aren't you?" Boldt inquired rhetorically. "Just the Pac-West machines, or others as well? You're trying to avoid possible charges later by making yourself included. Am I reading this right?"

"Lou . . ."

"How many machines, Kenny? What kind of access to the system do you have?"

Fowler would not look at Boldt. He rose, crossed the room, and finished pouring that drink for himself. To the mirror behind the wet bar, he said, "A list would do, Lou. Just the list of the ATMs you people are covering. No reason to have two guys playing second base. 'Kay? Spread out the team. I know you won't let a private in on the surveillance. I accept that. But me and my people — my resources — can help out. We can cover the areas that you're not. 'Kay? You see that, don't you? Is that *wrong?* Or is that cooperation? Coordination? I *want* to help, and no one, including you, will fucking let me. What kind of fucking ass-backwards sense does that make? Am I talking nonsense here? Tell me. Am I?" The drink was mixed and he carried it over to his chair and sat down carefully so as not to spill it, because he had poured it tall. "My guys are good, Lou — you know some of them as well as I do. They were *your* guys not long ago: Hal Fredricks, Jonny Chi, Mac Mackensie — quality guys. With me and my guys working some of the ATMs, you get more coverage. Isn't that what you want?" He met eyes with Boldt. "How about this? You supply me with a list of the ATMs, your guys are watching. Just the list, Lou. That's all. So we don't overlap." He sipped the gin while Boldt considered the deal. "You keep me current on that list and I'll give you Danielson's deepest, darkest secrets." He waited. "How 'bout it?"

Boldt attempted to gain some air. The apartment, despite its substantial size, despite its stunning view, suddenly felt claustrophobic to him. He weighed his choices: If he wanted the book on Danielson, Fowler could have it for him nearly overnight. Was it so stupid to avoid duplicating surveillance of the ATMs? He clarified, "I need the background work on Danielson done quickly. I need the surveillance conducted without his or anyone else's knowledge. No slipups. No risks that could jeopardize that."

"I understand, Lou. I understand."

"Fredricks, Chi, Mackensie — he'd recognize any of them."

Somewhat angrily Fowler said, "I can run a surveillance, friend. Would you be asking if I couldn't? What the hell do you think we did in Major Crimes, eat pizza all day and talk sports?" It was a stab at the Fraud division,

338

but Boldt let it pass.

The sergeant asked, "Matthews was going to ask you for some help?"

"Got her place wired up good and tight. Nice stuff. She won't be having any more prowlers." He added in a bellicose fashion, "We take care of our people. Someone has a problem, we fix it. That's what we're here for. It's a lot simpler than wearing that badge of yours, believe me."

Boldt's cell phone rang, and for a moment he did not know the sound was coming from his own pocket.

"I think that's you," Fowler encouraged him.

Boldt, feeling self-conscious, was not terribly comfortable with the device, and he thought that Fowler probably sensed this as he turned it on. His awkwardness seemed to lend weight to Fowler's claim of technical superiority, and this bothered the sergeant.

He spoke in blunt, terse acknowledgments. Grunts. As he did, Fowler's phone rang, though the security man did not move. He watched Boldt intently, allowing an unseen answering machine to take the call. Boldt shut off the phone and said, "You want some involvement?" He was already out of his chair. "We've got an ATM hit going down."

There was no hope of catching the extortionist during this first withdrawal; but if this night were like the others, there would be a second hit. Boldt wanted to be there.

He was on the phone with Lucille Guillard at Pac-West Bank by the time he ran the red light on First Avenue. Fowler secured his seat belt. They ran another light heading north toward Queen Anne and Ballard. The first withdrawal had been made in the U district; Lucille Guillard was playing percentages, believing a cluster of four banks on North Forty-fifth Street presented the next closest target. "How many people do you have in the field?" Fowler asked. The blue light of the dash-mounted police bubble played off his face, doing cruel things to his looks.

"We have three roamers. KCP has loaned us another five — they're at fixed locations."

"Eight people?" Fowler gasped. "Eight fucking people to cover every ATM in the city? You're fucking kidding me?" Fowler confessed, "I have four stationaries. They are each within a two-block distance of three or more separate ATM locations. I have another four people on unmarked patrol, but with very definite territories. All told, I figure I've got somewhere around thirty-five of the fifty most active ATMs in the city covered. But I bet you're covering some of the same ones."

Boldt withheld comment. Fowler was organized, well financed, and obviously had a reserve of manpower on which to draw. For someone in Boldt's position, it was discouraging.

340

The second ATM hit occurred at position 33, according to the police dispatcher whose constant running commentary and absurdly calm instructions could be heard from beneath the dash. On the off-chance that a savvy reporter had figured a way to eavesdrop on this or any of the other secure radio frequencies, the surveillance team was utilizing these reference numbers. Fowler spread it open on his lap. He studied it a moment and said, "North Forty-fifth Street."

Boldt turned right, passing the *Waiting for the Interurban* sculpture, and Fowler said, "Nice system. Nice and private. I like it. Do you pretty much stick with this, or mix it up?"

"We're going to start mixing it up," Boldt informed him.

"This is all I need, Lou. You give me this map and at least we won't be stepping on each other's toes."

"Hang on!" Boldt interrupted, recognizing Adrian Walcott's voice as he announced his location as North Forty-fifth and Latona.

Boldt put his foot down hard and blew past traffic. He turned left on Stoneway, ran two lights while sounding his horn, and skidded the back end of the car through a yellow light at Forty-fifth, as Fowler pointed right.

Walcott announced in a harried voice: "I'm stuck in traffic."

Fowler said to Boldt, "Friday night. Forty-fifth street — it's a good place to disappear

341

in a hurry if you have to. A good place to lose the cops."

The maximum amount of time Boldt could hope for was fifteen to twenty seconds per transaction. He estimated that this time was about up, confirmed when the dispatcher's voice said, "Transaction is complete. Repeat: Transaction is complete."

"I'm going on foot," announced an anxious-voiced Walcott. "Passing Meridian."

Three blocks to go, thought Boldt.

"Are you there?" Lucille Guillard asked over the cell phone.

"Right here."

"That's twelve hundred. We could still see more."

From beneath the dash, a winded Adrian Walcott announced, "I'm at position thirty-three. There's no one using the machines."

Boldt pulled over, slammed the car into Park, taking the key, and cut through the stalled westbound lane of traffic. Car horns sounded. Fowler cut to the right, increasing the distance between them.

Face after face of what were mostly young college students streamed past. Seeing his intensity, these kid strangers looked away uneasily. He encountered no six-foot male wearing a greatcoat. He caught up to Walcott, who, sweating, shook his head and cursed.

Fowler said eagerly to Boldt, "Let's stay with this."

Dodging traffic, the two men ran back to the waiting car.

Boldt grabbed the police radio handset. He was willing to play a gamble. "Cover the banks to the south. And let's make sure our patrols are aware of the Be On Lookout for that mug shot."

Dispatch acknowledged.

"What about the north?" Fowler asked. "Do you want my people —"

"South," Boldt insisted. "The density of the ATMs favors the city."

"That's a hell of a chance to take," Fowler objected.

Boldt rudely handed him the cell phone. "Tell your people to cover south of the bridge: Broadway and east of I-5. I'll keep our people west of the interstate." He was, in effect, giving in to exactly what Fowler had suggested. The security man looked a little stunned, but he made the call quickly before Boldt changed his mind.

The radio began to sparkle with the new deployment. Boldt headed toward the university. As he drove past the ramp to I-5, Fowler, coming off his call, queried, "Where the fuck are we going?"

"Back to square one."

"Why?"

"Exactly," Boldt said, swerving to miss two kids on mountain bikes who had disre-

343

garded a crossing light.

He came around the block and parked in front of the Meany Tower Hotel at Eleventh Avenue NE, because this offered him immediate access to the U district — and the ability to block the most predictable route the extortionist would take back to I-5, the entrances to which were only two blocks away.

Fowler scratched at a stain on his pants. Boldt explained softly, so as not to cover the dispatcher's voice, "If I'm this person, I want it as crowded as possible, as confusing as possible. Friday night, this is where you come. A couple of the malls, maybe — but they've got cameras everywhere. I hit the 'Ave.,' then I go out Forty-fifth — it's close, it's quick and easy. I head back to the U because it offers me everything I'm looking for and it worked the first time I was there."

"I don't know," Fowler disagreed.

"Broadway — where your people are — is my backup choice. Again, lots of weekend activity — a difficult area to police, and only a few —"

He was interrupted by the dispatcher's bizarrely calm monotone. "Position four-one. All field operatives: Position four-one is active. Repeat: active."

Checking the map, an excited Fowler said, "It's a Pac-West. It's right around the fucking corner."

Boldt stuffed a radio earphone into his ear

344

and was already out of the car and on the run.

"Ten seconds active," the dispatcher announced.

The average ATM access time, from keying in the PIN to the ATM card being returned to the account holder, ran eighteen seconds.

"No operatives in the immediate vicinity," the dispatcher announced into Boldt's ear. Boldt had neglected to make his own position known and, therefore, dispatch remained unaware of his presence.

Ten thousand . . . Eleven thousand . . . he counted in his head.

Natalie Smith, normally assigned to SPD's Sex Crimes, checked in. She had been crossing Montlake Bridge when the hit was announced. Now she was on her way back, a minute away. An eternity.

Fourteen thousand . . . Fifteen thousand . . .

"Transaction complete," dispatch announced.

Boldt turned right, took an immediate left through a parking lot, and broke around the corner. The blue-and-green Pac-West Bank sign hung over the sidewalk, twenty yards ahead.

Boldt said, "Six feet tall, maybe wearing a greatcoat." He signaled Fowler across the street. Boldt took this side, moving quickly toward the sign and the entrance to Pac-West Kwik-Cash. The sidewalk was mobbed. He searched for Caulfield's face in the crowd. The effect of the kids flowing past him was dizzying.

He reached the Pac-West sign. Through the

glass window, he saw three ATMs side by side. One was in use by a young redheaded woman, a short woman — not a six-foot-tall Harry Caulfield. Boldt tugged on the door. It was locked. A small sign indicated how to use one's cash or credit card to gain entrance. Boldt slid a cash card into the slot and the door opened.

She glanced quickly at him, but displaying none of the fear or concern he might have expected of a guilty party.

"Someone just left." He interrupted her transaction, showing her his badge.

She squinted. "That girl?"

"A girl?" Boldt questioned, recalling the account application.

"Weird chick — she was wearing a motorcycle helmet." She nodded toward the door. "Just left," she said, echoing him. "Just now."

Back out on the sidewalk, in a teeming horde of college students, Boldt searched left . . . right . . .

He saw the glossy dome of a motorcycle helmet on the opposite side of the street, heading away from Fowler's position.

Not wanting to shout, not wanting to alert the woman, he signaled Fowler, making a motion around his head, attempting to indicate a helmet, and he pointed down the street.

Fowler saw her.

Boldt crossed the street, just as Natalie Smith's tires yipped to a stop in heavy traffic. A horn sounded. The helmet turned. "Sergeant?" Smith

346

yelled loudly from her car.

The helmet broke down an alley at a run, Fowler sprinting to catch up.

Boldt pushed through the melee of teeming students and headed down the adjacent alley. Suddenly overcome with the stench of urine, he jumped over a pair of legs at the last second and turned to see a man sleeping next to a bottle.

The helmeted figure blurred past the intersection with another alley, heading to Boldt's left.

Another blur — Fowler in pursuit.

Boldt ran fast and reached the corner, which he rounded in time to see Fowler's back turn down an alley parallel to his.

He rounded this next corner as well, and when he came to the end of the alley, he faced another street teeming with hundreds of students.

Kenny Fowler was doubled over, winded, clutching the knees of his pants.

He gasped to Boldt, "I lost her."

Boldt searched the crowds for another half hour. He issued a Be On Lookout for a motorcycle with a black helmet and female rider. Frustrated and out of his element, a failed Lou Boldt returned to where he had last left Fowler, but the man was gone. Back at the car he found a business card on the seat where the surveillance map had been. The map now belonged to Kenny Fowler.

With this one agreement, Boldt effectively doubled his surveillance manpower — and yet he did not feel right about it. He did not feel entirely right about Fowler, something he attributed to Fowler's having left the department to seek his fortune. Or maybe it was just the man: unceremoniously direct and brusque.

He flipped the business card over where Fowler had written: *Thanks, partner.*

He pocketed it, and drove straight to the Big Joke.

TWENTY-FIVE

A late-night talk show was playing on the television in the living room as Bear Berenson unlocked three locks and admitted Boldt to his upstairs apartment.

"Kill the fatted calf," Berenson said, admitting his friend and locking the door behind him. Whenever he heard a lock turn, Boldt felt he was somehow failing in his job.

"Liz is pregnant."

"Do I congratulate you or offer my sympathies?"

"Miles gets a sibling," Boldt said, elated.

"Congratulations."

"Thank you."

As usual, the place was as a mess. Berenson lived the quintessential bachelor's existence: He termed it *magical realism,* because lately he was reading Latin American writers. Boldt called it hedonism, enhanced by a generous consumption of marijuana — hence the magic.

Bear stood just under six feet. He was stocky, with dark Arabic features and intense brown eyes — often bloodshot. He owned the Big Joke, the bar, restaurant, and comedy club immediately below them where Boldt often performed during happy hour.

"I thought I'd find you downstairs."

"The stand-up is awful. I booked the wrong act."

"Place is pretty full."

"No accounting for the taste of the public."

Berenson punched the remote, killing the television. "Went channel surfing instead. You know what I think? All this information superhighway shit? Bunch of crap. Even with thirty channels, there's nothing on. I mean I have a hard time believing that, but it's true. Crap to the right of me. Crap to the left of me. Five hundred channels? Give me a fucking break. Five hundred times zero is still zero."

They sat down. Bear rolled a joint. The policeman in Boldt felt tempted to ask him not to, but not tonight.

"I'm kind of at wit's end," Boldt said seriously.

Bear nodded.

They were the kind of friends where Boldt felt no need for apologies or approval. They had been — and continued to be — there for each other through, as Bear called it, "the good, the bad, and the ugly."

"I'm right back into it: solid work. Leaving Liz and Miles and you and others in the lurch. In to the point I can't get out. Buried in it, along with a few victims."

"Do you want out?"

"I need out — there's a difference."

"For me? It's this damn club." The IRS had shut down the club and seized much of it property about a year earlier, and Bear had stood up and fought them and had won. Now he had the place back, though at times he complained about it. "Are we talking about freedom or escape?"

"Breathing room. To be away from death more than my three weeks a year. Three weeks I never take. I love this work — that's the thing."

He lit the joint. "So do you hate it, or do you love it?"

"I'm exhausted. I say stupid things when I'm exhausted."

"You say stupid things all the time." He grinned, pleased with himself, and smoked more of the joint. He stubbed it out gently in the ashtray, holding his breath for an interminable amount of time. When he exhaled, surprisingly little smoke escaped.

Boldt said, "I think I've got a bad apple."

"One of your own squad?"

Boldt nodded.

"That hurts."

Another nod. "A guy I like."

"And what do you do about it?"

"I hide the truth from him. I sit back and watch." Boldt informed him, "Someone broke into Daffy's. Maybe following her."

"This guy of yours?"

"He's moved to the top of my list."

"He's got good taste if he's after Daffy."
Then Berenson added, "Just kidding."

"What do you do if you suspect a bartender is robbing your till?" Boldt asked.

"I watch him. I lay a trap for him."

"And does it work?"

"Sometimes. Sure. It's a funny thing with the people who cheat. They get numb to it, you know? They talk themselves into things. If it's petty stuff, if I just want to *stop* it, I confront the person. If it's the bigger shit, I lay a fucking minefield and blow a leg off. Like this," he said. He turned the television back on and switched channels. The screen showed a black-and-white image of inside the club — an area immediately behind the bar, including a close look at the cash register and several of the stools. He said, "No one knows it's there."

"Are you so sure?"

"It's funny you should say that. Some people obviously *feel* the thing, you know? Look right at it. They can't *see* it — it's behind a beer mirror — but they *feel* it. That third-eye thing. Yet after a while they stop looking. Numb, just like the thieving bartenders." He said, "Maybe you're just numb, Lou. Maybe you're looking into the mirror a little too hard."

"Maybe you're stoned."

"No maybe about it. I'm roasted." He waited a minute and asked, "What's your excuse?"

"I'm thinking."

352

"So that's what that is. I always wondered what that looked like."

Shoswitz had ordered Boldt to take the weekend off. The city and department had rules about consecutive hours on the job — rules constantly broken, but easily enforced if someone like Shoswitz felt the necessity to do so. Nevertheless, Boldt spent the early morning at the kitchen table doing paperwork.

"There's a Mercedes out front, and I think it's for you," Elizabeth Boldt announced from where she stood, parting the front curtains. "Who is coming by unannounced at eight-thirty on a Saturday morning? And me, looking like this!"

Boldt had been up for the last hour tending to Miles and working at the kitchen table with a baby spoon in one hand and a pencil in the other. He had had four hours' sleep, and felt it.

Liz wore a white satin robe tied tightly around her waist, open in a long V of bare skin at the chest, stretching from her neck to her navel, and black Chinese flats for slippers that lent a further touch of elegance. Her dark hair was pulled tightly off her sleepy face, held back by a turquoise rubber band, and she had silver studs in her ears. "I think you look fantastic," he told her, handing her her first cup of coffee and stealing a look for himself. "Oh shit."

Boldt seldom cursed, and this caught his wife's attention.

"Lou?"

"It's Adler." Hurrying toward the front door to open it, Boldt defensively apologized, "I did not schedule this."

"I'm gone," his wife said, beating a hasty retreat.

Miles caught a glimpse of his mother and complained for her attention as she dashed into the bedroom, all satin and skin. "Not now, sweetie," she told the child, although this communication only added to the child's longing.

Boldt yanked open the door, said, "Inside," and closed it just as quickly so that Adler never broke his stride. "*What* are you doing here?"

His eyes bloodshot, his skin an unhealthy gray, Adler wore a wrinkled aquamarine polo shirt, stone-washed blue jeans, and leather deck shoes with leather ties. His arms were hairy. His watch was gold. He needed a shave. "I'm folding the company," he declared. "I thought that you should be told before the press conference."

Boldt felt like throttling the man on the spot, but maintained his composure.

Boldt offered him coffee and Adler accepted. Too nervous to sit down, Adler faked a smile at Miles and paced the small kitchen, toying with whatever he found on the counter. Mumbling, he said, "It's all over the news — this family dying — although they're claiming it's *believed* to be *E. coli*. It's not *E. coli*, right?"

"The first thing you have to do is settle

354

down," Boldt advised sternly. "I know that's easier said than done."

"I thought you wanted us to pull our product."

"Have you eaten anything?"

"Eaten? Are you kidding? What would you recommend — some *soup* maybe?"

"Have you slept?"

Adler's eyes flashed anger. "This isn't about *me*. This is about that poor family. It's about Tap and I trying to stay in the market, because once you leave — especially in a situation like this — it's damn near impossible to get back market shares. It's about greed, Sergeant. And ego — trying to hold on to something we fought hard for. And it's *over*."

"And are you going to kill yourself?"

That stopped Adler from fiddling. He looked over at Boldt, who said, "Because that's the second half of the demands."

"I don't know what I'm going to do."

"Hello?" It was Liz. She who had apparently dived into a pair of jeans and a T-shirt. Barefoot. A hint of lipstick, nothing more. She introduced herself to Adler — reintroduced, as it turned out, for he recognized her immediately as being connected to the bank. Liz's bank had partially financed Adler's move into the European marketplace, something she had never told her husband because she took client confidentiality at face value. Wisely, having taken one look at the man, she made no attempt at small talk.

355

She said, "Why don't I take over duties here?" pointing to her son, whose arms were begging for her.

Boldt led Adler back into the front room. Liz stopped Adler on his way by and gently took the serrated bread knife from him. He seemed embarrassed to be holding it, as if he did not know how it had gotten there. Boldt guided him onto the couch and placed his coffee down for him.

Sounding on the edge of tears, Adler said, "No more deaths."

Boldt had no intention of babying a man like Owen Adler. Adopting a business-as-usual tone of voice, he said, "If you intend on shutting down your business, there's little I can do to stop you. But I would caution you against it. And although I strongly objected to keeping product on the shelves during the initial contaminations, I don't see any way around it right now."

Boldt understood then that he had no choice but to take Adler into his confidence, and though he would have rather checked with Daphne before doing so, he could not allow Adler to risk the lives of hundreds by panicking. "We know who the killer is."

Adler, too stunned to get a word out, cocked his head at an unusual angle and glared at him.

"His name is Harold Caulfield. He worked for Mark Meriweather at Longview Farms."

"But why wasn't I — ?"

Boldt interrupted, "We think he blames you for the Longview salmonella contamination. He wants to see you bankrupt and dead, just like Mark Meriweather. Daphne is the one running with this, but I have to tell you that it was *my* decision not to inform you or your company. We have evidence that the State Health department altered at least one lab report crucial to the placement of responsibility for the New Leaf salmonella contamination. It seemed to me unlikely that a state government employee would take such an action without an incentive. The who, when, and what of that incentive remains in question."

This news clearly struck a blow to Adler. Looking ill again, he sank back into the couch, too dumbfounded to speak. Boldt continued: "In the short amount of time I've known you, you've struck me as being straightforward. So that's what I'm being with you. Whether you're an honest man . . . I can't say. But whatever you or your people may have done to Mark Meriweather, it's insignificant when compared with the lives of Slater Lowry and the Mishnovs. If you or one of your people was behind that altered State Health report," Boldt said. "I need to know right now."

"I have no idea what you're talking about."

People could lie, and Boldt, in his role as a homicide cop, had sat across from some of the best of them and could often spot them. But

357

to his knowledge, a person could not intentionally make himself pale, much less pale to the point that the skin seemed green and the lips looked like those of a cadaver. He believed Adler.

"I won't pretend we're close to apprehending this man, but we are *closer*, and if you shut down your company now, there's no predicting his response. We believe that the ATM surveillance offers us the fastest, most predictable way to apprehend Caulfield. Even if he is using a runner, which remains a strong possibility, that ransom money is our way back to Caulfield. Shutting down your company, pulling your product, is likely to have an adverse effect on him. Change his agenda — take his attention off the money and put it back on the mass poisoning. At the moment, he seems reluctant to deliver on his larger threat, and I for one have no intention of testing his resolve, of pushing him over the top."

"I want to know everything there is to know about this Longview Farms incident," Adler said too calmly. He appeared to be in shock. "What exactly do you know, Sergeant?"

"We *believe* the contamination was not salmonella, but staphylococcus. Staph is most commonly transmitted by physical contact, which suggests maybe one of your workers forgot to wear his gloves. Your product went out on the shelves and people got sick."

"Good God!" he gasped.

"We *believe* there was a cover-up to keep New Leaf in the clear, and that it involved altering documents to place the responsibility on bad poultry at Longview Farms."

"This is why Daphne wanted access to our files."

"Yes it is." Boldt added, "Your cooperation, your confidence is crucial to the success of this investigation. As difficult as it may be, you need to continue on as if you knew none of this. At the same time, your cooperation in proceeding with the investigation — helping Daphne get what she needs — would be a welcome asset."

The man nodded slowly, his eyes in a fixed stare at someplace over Boldt's shoulder. "Are you telling me that these killings . . . all of this suffering, is the result of some misconceived attempt six years ago to keep us out of trouble?"

Boldt nodded. They saw it often enough in homicide. "The biggest crimes are often committed trying to hide the smaller ones."

On Sunday morning he and Liz and Miles drove up to the lake because Liz asked him to, and he had no desire to fight her as well. Another member of their family was on the way, and yet the very family this child would soon join seemed fragmented and in a fragile condition. The lake cabin always helped: No phone; no radio. A game of Scrabble maybe, some chores, some reading. A fire if the evening

359

was cool enough. A swim if he was brave enough to endure the coldness of the lake water.

But Boldt did not sleep, and somewhere in the night he strayed out into the darkness in a plaid bathrobe with worn elbows. After a commune with the flat blackness of the lake's starlit surface, he migrated toward the car, where he had left his briefcase and his papers. When Liz rose to a cold bed at four in the morning and found him by a small fire going through his papers, she said nothing — though he knew he had ruined their stay. At dawn he did swim and it chilled him to his bones, and Liz was there with a towel when he came out.

She was quiet on the drive back; Miles was noisy. They had to leave by six in order to make work on time, and they beat most of the bad traffic. After forty minutes of following license plates and sitting tall so that his visor blocked the morning sun, Boldt reached for the radio knob in order to catch the start of "Morning Edition." Liz reached out and stopped him.

"I try not to involve myself in your cases," she said quietly, not looking at him. "Even cases like this — the ones that seem to kill you — because there is so little I can do, so little I know that might help, and I believe it important that at least one of us be rooted in some kind of reality to help the other find ground."

He could think of nothing to say to that.

360

An eighteen-wheeler passed them. He noticed that it was a poultry truck and this serendipity did not elude him. The chickens were stacked in ventilated, crowded cages; some feathers escaped and, caught in the slipstream, were carried along behind the trailer like a bridal train.

"I think I may be able to help," she offered, "but I'm afraid to, because in a way it violates the parameters of this relationship — and that frightens me. When I am crazy at the bank, you are my anchor, and I would like to think that the same is true for you, and I fear that if I become involved, even in the smallest, most insignificant way, that in effect that sets us adrift, that joins the two of us but separates us from any tie back to reality. Does this make any sense?"

"Sure." But he knew he did not sound convinced.

"I am a *banker,* love. As in ATM machines, accounts, withdrawals, loans. Now does it make sense?"

He did not answer.

"You have explained this case to me — at last some of it, the ATM part — and yet you never asked my advice. The one area I know something about, and you didn't ask."

"I didn't think —"

"No, you didn't," she interrupted, in order to make her own point. "And I didn't know if it was because you didn't *want* my input, didn't want to cross that line we keep so delicately stretched between us, or because it never occurred to you to ask."

Boldt did not like car discussions, and his wife knew it. He had to wonder why she had waited until now to start this conversation. They had just spent twenty-four hours in the solitude and quiet of the lake, and she waits for the morning commute that affords no eye contact, no real contact at all, to launch into this.

"You're upset," she said.

"The timing is all."

"Car talk."

"Right."

"But it's easier sometimes for me. Can you see that? For all the reasons you don't like it, it makes it easier for me. I can avoid those hard looks of yours even though I feel them."

"I never mean to exclude you from anything," he apologized.

"I know that. You do it, but I know you don't mean to."

"And I can use all the help I can get."

"That's all I needed to hear," she said, and she reached for the radio knob. This time, Boldt stopped her.

"Are you going to tell me?"

"I need to make some phone calls, research a few things. But I didn't want to put the time into it, I didn't want to do it, if it was something that might cause us problems. We have enough of those."

Boldt took his eyes off the road briefly and

met hers. He went back to the dotted lines and the turn signals, but that look of hers hung like a transparency through which he saw all else. She was as terrified of their future as he was, and for some inexplicable reason, he found this comforting.

He slid his hand down onto the seat and inched it over and found hers, and they rode down into the city's sparkling skyline hand in hand, Miles grunting and fidgeting from his car seat. Part of Boldt wished he could just keep on driving.

It was clear from looking at her that Daphne Matthews had not taken the weekend off. "I spent most of Saturday and all of Sunday and Sunday night with Dr. Clements, going over the profile. He's upset about those two faxes coming in on the same day and the lack of any attempt to place blame in the extortionist's demand."

"So you were right about that," he reminded her, trying to cheer her up. But it was not the opinion of Dr. Richard Clements that was troubling her, it was the fax she handed to Boldt.

"This just came in," she told him.

HAVING A CRAVING FOR SWEETS?
MOTHER WARNED THAT CANDY IS BAD.
BUT YOU DO NOT LISTEN, DO YOU?
YOU WILL WISH YOU HAD.

363

Boldt reread the message several times, though there was no need to do so. She pointed out that in this fax the placement of blame had returned, and she did so in a forceful way that carried a subtext that she failed to explain to him.

"Caulfield bought those candy bars at Foodland for a reason," he said. He had sensed this from the moment of discovery, but had hoped differently.

"They substituted all their candy products," she reminded, though she gave away her own fears in the tight knitting of her brow and the way she entwined her hands in a squirming knot. "He told me about your conversation."

"You've *seen* him?" Boldt protested.

"No, not in the flesh. But we call each other, both of us from pay phones — it's really a perfect arrangement," she snapped sarcastically. "Don't worry, Sergeant," she said caustically, annoyed with him, "we're taking all necessary precautions." She added, "And let me say that I consider my private phone calls my own damn business."

"I respect that."

"I certainly hope so." She was clearly miffed. Her exhaustion hung over her face like a veil. "He's incredibly angry over the possible cover-up. He offered to help get any paperwork we need, but I told him that we were more likely to subpoena what we're after from here on out, so that we kept it admissible. I can see you're worried, but let me tell you something: Owen Adler can handle any amount of stress and keep a poker face through any dealings. We don't have to worry about him, Lou. He's not going to give any secrets away."

"I know this must be hard on you," he offered.

"It's hard on *all* of us. But thank you. Yes, it is." She still was angry, though less so perhaps. With him, or with the situation — he was not certain.

He placed the fax down onto his desk. "I would hope that we've learned enough from his earlier threats to issue a second recall immediately. Threat or no threat. Freeze all sales at the retail level and try to trade out product again. Restock the shelves overnight and hope that Harry Caulfield doesn't hear about it."

She agreed that he should fax Adler with the request immediately.

"You know what really ticks me off?" Boldt said. "Another couple of days, the new soup labels will be ready to go. And now he goes switching products on us. And more curious to me — is he just lucky, or does he know which ATM machines we've got under surveillance?" On his desk were field reports for the ATM hits that had occurred both Saturday and Sunday nights. A combined amount of forty-two hundred dollars had been withdrawn. No agent had been within ten blocks of the ATM machines chosen for the hits. He did not tell her that Fowler now had a copy of the sur-

365

veillance map and that they had effectively doubled their team, because to include her was to involve her — and if it went up in flames, he did not want her part of it. Boldt said, "He's got over ten grand already."

"Not bad for less than a week of work."

"A little more than my take-home." He won a slight grin from her, though it did not qualify as a smile. "So we wait for him to kill someone?" he asked. He reminded himself that Adler had offered to pull all their product and that he, Boldt, had talked him out of it. He reminded himself of the lab's discovery of strychnine in the Longview ashes, Bernie Lofgrin's reference to the Jim Jones tragedy, and his reasons for convincing Adler not to panic. But it was Lou Boldt who now felt in a state of panic.

"Call Clements," he told her, passing her the phone. "Ask his opinion about pulling the candy bars immediately instead of waiting until tonight. And see what he would think about putting out the recall on the news — about warning the public about this."

She looked as terrified as he felt. She dialed the number from memory to the room, and was put through. They talked for the better part of five minutes in the middle of which she shook her head at Boldt — Clements was advising against violating the conditions of the threats. She hung up and said, "He's taking Caulfield at his word. But it's still your call."

He tasted biting sarcasm on the tip of his

tongue, but kept it in. He kept in his fear as well, as best he could. Over the next few hours the clock hands actually seemed to slow down, and it seemed incredible to him that these were the same minutes by which he lived his life. They seemed hardly related at all. He willed his phone not to ring, and yet heard the endless ringing of the phones around him in a way he had never before experienced. There was rarely a moment of silence on this floor. There always seemed to be someone talking, a phone ringing, a door shutting, a shout, a reprimand, a curse. He wanted to yell for them all to shut up. Each time a phone purred, he thought it signaled the end of a life. And many of these calls did, even though they had nothing to do with the work of Harry Caulfield. The business of Homicide went right on without Lou Boldt. The teenagers, the lovers, the drownings — all required investigation. Pasquini's squad was up to their waists in new cases.

But the department's only *black hole* belonged solely to Lou Boldt, and the fax staring back at him was a signpost of what lay around the next curve — and Boldt had no desire to get there. He mentally backpedaled, knowing full well it was as useless as swimming from a waterfall.

At a few minutes past six o'clock, Owen Adler instituted the second secret recall of all Go-Bars and Mocha-Lattè Peanut Crunches, a costly, time-consuming effort that Boldt feared would prove too late. To date, as far as Boldt could tell, Caulfield had only sent a threatening fax once the contaminated product was in someone's hands. He could envision the man as he stood around and watched, as he inspected the shelves periodically to see if his prize had been taken.

LaMoia brought Boldt some Thai takeout before heading out on ATM surveillance duty. He offered it to both Daphne and Boldt, but neither touched the food. Boldt had not eaten all day — a day that dragged interminably into evening.

When phone calls did come, Boldt answered them tersely, prepared for the worst: more cholera, more illness, more people clinging to their lives. He answered them rudely, hung up quickly, and he found it difficult, if not impossible, to get any work done.

BUT YOU DO NOT LISTEN, DO YOU? YOU WILL WISH YOU HAD.

He thought many times of his conversation with Adler, of his efforts to convince him to allow the product to remain on the shelves. Even with the support of Dr. Richard Clements, he could only see this now as a huge mistake.

He prepared himself for nearly every eventuality — except the one that finally came. He noted the time of the call — 7:22 — out of habit. And out of habit he checked for his weapon, for his identification wallet, and for the keys to his car.

There were two boys dead — still up in their tree house, he was told by the 911 dispatcher. Not cholera. No chance for emergency rooms or resuscitation. Without any pathology report, without a lab test or a professional opinion of any sort, Boldt knew both the murder weapon and the cause of death.

A chocolate candy bar. And strychnine.

TWENTY-SIX

The bodies had been discovered in Wedgewood, in the backyard tree house of a home in the thirty-one-hundred block of Northeast Eighty-first Street. The hysterical mother explained to the 911 dispatcher that the boys had not responded to her summons to come inside. "They're just sitting up there!" she had sobbed over the phone. "Just sitting there." Because it was a death by suspicious causes, the 911 call was first relayed to Wedgewood authorities, then mistakenly to King County police, and finally, because of an astute switchboard operator, to Boldt's office phone.

Boldt arrived reluctantly, not wanting to get out of his car. As in one of his recurring dreams, he had a longing to turn back the clock to that moment immediately before the incident and to be there to save these victims.

The evening sun worked unmercifully to blister the tree house's Cape Cod–gray paint. An old wooden ladder with initials carved into the stock stretched up into the darkened hole above. The tree house itself was not like the ones Boldt remembered from his own childhood. It appeared more the product of a catalogue purchase.

He elected not to speak with the hysterical mother, but headed directly to the crime scene instead. There would be time later for talking. Too much of it, as far as Boldt was concerned.

A uniformed officer stood at his side, and she knew better than to say anything. Boldt had a reputation as a loner at homicide crime scenes — and every uniform was aware of it. Dixie was on his way, as were Bernie Lofgrin and his ID crew. It was all being done as quietly as possible, though this time there was sure to be press, and this time there could be no stretching the facts to include *E. coli* contamination. Certainly Caulfield knew that the press and the police *had* to be involved — and this, above all else, terrified Boldt the most: Caulfield no longer cared; something inside him had changed.

Facing the press would not require the public information officer to make any mention of Adler Foods, or, for the time being, the candy bars that Boldt felt certain to find in the tree house above him. The press would be told that the case was an active homicide and was under investigation. No more, no less.

He looked up the long stretch of ladder once again, up into that dark mouth in the floor of the Erector Set tree house. She handed him a flashlight without a word, and he reminded himself to get her name later and to thank her for her professionalism. A few more cops arrived in the backyard, but seeing Boldt at work, they left immediately and kept others out. Only Boldt and his uniformed sidekick remained.

He climbed the ladder slowly, not wanting to see the first true homicide crime scene this case had presented him. Again, there were no witnesses to the actual crime, and again Lou Boldt would have little to go on.

Boldt recalled explicitly his promise to Slater Lowry's mother that the boy would be back to finish his model of the Space Shuttle. There would be no such lies to tell this woman inside this house. She had been up this ladder first.

One of the boys had made for the hatch, for the ladder, but had come up short. He was facedown, his arms outstretched as if reaching for a ball. The other was curled into the fetal position in the corner wearing a death mask of pure horror, as if in the middle of a scream.

It was a small room. It was going to be hard on all the technicians.

The weakened flashlight beam illuminated a pink plastic squirt gun, sandwich wrappers, and comic books. A deck of cards. The small white skull and part of the spine of a mouse kept as a game trophy. A Stephen King paperback on the room's only shelf, its pages curled. There was a candle on the shelf as well, its wax puddled at its base. A baseball, with a tangle of autographs. A poster of dinosaurs and another entitled "The Marine Life of Puget Sound."

Boldt could imagine them talking up here.

The laughter, quiet now.

The first candy bar he saw was half-eaten. In bold, excited letters, the wrapper read ironically: *NEW! Good for You!* It was an Adler Foods granola-and-caramel Go-Bar. Poisoned.

Boldt recalled the grainy image of Caulfield at the Foodland checkout counter. He recalled the register tape listing three candy bars and some kind of ice cream. He recalled his diligence in convincing Adler to keep the shelves stocked.

He apologized to the boys, and he caught himself dragging his sleeve across his eyes, and could feel that uniform down there looking up at him, wondering what he was doing.

"Get out of here!" he shouted down at her. And she hurried away before he could stop her, before he could apologize to her as well.

He wondered what had become of him, and turning back to these two fallen victims, whatever became of a child's departed soul.

TWENTY-SEVEN

"Come up the park steps to the guest house. No lights. I'll meet you there."

Click. Daphne hung up the phone, checked the clock: twelve midnight. Owen had risked a call. That alone told her enough about his state of mind; the palpable fear in his voice told her more than she wanted to know. She jumped up off the stool, quickly buttoned her jeans, and left her project on the counter. It was the affidavit requesting the New Leaf bank records that she had meticulously reviewed with Striker over the phone. In order to mark where she had left off, she pointed the lead of the pencil to the word *intractable*.

Leaving the houseboat, she took special care to arm the alarm system, locked up, and hurried to her car.

Made somewhat frantic by that tone of voice of his, she drove around the lake, crossed at the Fremont Bridge, and took Leary and Market out to Shilshole Marina, entering the park and winding her way up the series of switchbacks until she reached the picnic ground on the left. She parked deep into the area, and it was not until she climbed out into the darkness, the traffic below whining eerily, that she became aware of her isolation. She took her bearings, allowing herself a quick pang of fear — the woods were dark and she was still far below the estate. Her fears were only partially alleviated by the presence of her handgun. She had never seen a handgun as any kind of solution. Had there been any choice, she would have gladly entered through Adler's front gate. But Adler could not be seen having any contact with the police — the threats were adamant in that regard — and so she felt obliged to approach the estate from the back side, as he had asked of her. And to do so secretively, without being seen.

She had been on several long walks with Owen during which they had descended through the forest trail to this same picnic area, and farther down to where the same road looped back around and lower again to the condominiums that lived uncomfortably, like unwanted in-laws, on the shore's edge bordering the marina. She had never hiked it in darkness, never by herself — had never climbed the trail's precipitous steps, but only descended.

Her key chain carried a strong penlight, and despite Owen's instructions to the contrary, she felt tempted to use it. She always carried her small handbag with her because of the weapon and identification it contained. It usually hung at her side suspended by a thin strap. But it was also capable of being secured to a belt,

European-style, which was how she presently carried it.

This, the park's steepest and longest stretch of steps, had not been maintained since the city park system, citing budget constraints and angry over Adler's challenge of a right-of-way across his property, had abandoned its maintenance several years before. For his part, Owen claimed they had closed the stairs after settling a lawsuit out of court. The result of this abandoned maintenance was an impossibly steep and dangerous set of rotting railroad ties engulfed by untold species of junglelike plants. At a few of the more treacherous switchbacks, the route offered an occasional steel-pipe handrail, though they were not to be trusted. She entered the trail and began the arduous climb, finding more light than she had expected. The going was slow, and she stopped repeatedly to catch her breath and contain her frantic heartbeat. Halfway up, she wished she had made other arrangements.

It was during her third rest break that she at first sensed, and then heard, movement deep within the woods, realizing to her considerable alarm that she was not alone.

"Hello?" she called out reflexively, then chastised herself for doing so. Despite her suspicions over the past two weeks, she still failed to think like a victim. Ever a cop, never a victim. Within seconds of her outcry, she began moving again, aware that an object at rest offered an easy target. It occurred to her that it was faster to descend than continue to climb, but the sound had come from below and to her left — on the trail itself, and not very far back.

She moved quietly, her ears alert, telling herself that a deer, a dog, even a squirrel might cause such sounds. She stopped again, and there it was: but this time above her and to her right, nearly the opposite direction as before.

Struggling against the idea, she convinced herself that someone, not something, was out there, and he or she knew that she was on this trail.

The psychologist in her realized that fear could be dissipated only by acceptance, not challenge. To challenge fear was to succumb to paranoia and terror, both of which she had experienced in the last several weeks. She focused on turning off all thought and allowing the fear to rise in her chest. There was no choice but to take this back route. Tempted to cry out, she channeled this release into her legs and bounded up the trail at an all-out sprint. On the run, she reached into her purse, removed the handgun, and with the touch of a finger ensured that the safety was engaged. She welcomed the weapon defensively — a scare tactic if needed.

Finding her pace, she moved fluidly, following the steep switchbacks. Her eyes now fully adjusted, she kept watch for a place to duck off the trail and hide, deciding it would be foolish to lead a possible pursuer to Owen's guest cottage. She had three strong candidates for who was back there: first — and the most likely, it seemed — a reporter; second, whoever had been following her; third, Harry Caulfield. But it was a possible combination that charged her with energy: Had it been Harry Caulfield following her and watching her?

Her foot punched through rotten timber and she fell hard, looking out at a short, level stretch of trail connecting to another set of steps. Hearing her pursuer even closer, she ducked into the woods. She was quite near the top, as little as forty yards to go, the surrounding terrain quite steep, the trail wedged between a V of rock and offering the only clear way up.

She hid herself against a cedar tree and muted her keys as she sought them from her pocket, interested solely in the penlight attached to them.

Below and to her right, her pursuer approached up the trail, not twenty yards back. She visualized the area through which she had just passed, settling her nerves with deep breaths and planning her actions like a hunter in a blind.

The next thing she heard was ragged breathing and the rapid approach of footsteps. And then complete and total silence — the drumming of blood in her ears. Her hands shook, belying her self-confidence. Again, she trained her fear into the center of her chest, allowing it a physical presence in her like some kind of demon, and her hands steadied.

How close was he?

No sooner had this thought entered her mind than the looming shape of a man appeared within a few feet of her, stealthily moving up the trail. He, too, appeared on edge — he had lost track of her.

She sprang with incredible force and speed, driving her heel into the side of his knee, her right shoulder into his left, and propelled him to the trail's dirt floor. In this same steady motion she delivered her words loudly and with great authority: "Police! I am armed. *Do not move!*" The flashlight came on brightly under her direction and found him facedown. His hands were empty of any weapon, instead clutching that painful knee. He moved his arms slowly for her, like the wings of an awakening bird.

"Easy," he announced. "I'm on your side."

She knew the voice, though she could not place it. The light followed his motions. "Mackensie?" Formerly *Detective* Mackensie of Major Crimes. Recruited by — "Mac?" she asked again, though it was clearly he. She staggered back a step and made her weapon ready and returned it to her purse. "*Why* are you following me?"

"*Following* you?" Mackensie inquired, adding his own emphasis, working his knee carefully and sitting up. "Don't compliment yourself."

Trying his knee again, he said, "Jesus, Matthews, you coulda broke it."

"What are you —"

"What am *I?* What are *you* doing here? I'm perimeter patrol. Kenny's got one of us on all four sides of the estate. You're lucky it wasn't Dumbo you tried that on — he'da broke your collarbone and then some."

"Patrol?"

"He is the *boss,* Matthews. The CEO. Hell, he doesn't even know we're out here. But here we are." He stood up and brushed himself off. "What's left of us," he said sarcastically. "In case you haven't been paying attention, there's a wacko out there drilling holes in his soup cans. It's our job to make sure he doesn't try to drill a hole in the boss. *Comprendo?*"

"Kill Owen?"

"It's one of his stated aims, right? Or are you going to try and throw some psychobabble shit at me that says this boy is going to play by the rules? Don't do that, okay? Not with me. Play Dr. Ruth with someone else."

Mac Mackensie was so much the opposite of what she had expected that she felt momentarily speechless. Fowler had stolen him away from the department less than a year before for a huge salary, a company car, and six weeks' paid vacation. Mackensie was a good cop — or had been. He was a prime example of the brain drain being effected on SPD by the private firms.

380

"What exactly *are* you doing here?" he asked in a lower voice, touching her hand and convincing her to extinguish the flashlight. "I mean I know you two . . . you know . . . but I thought . . . I was under the impression that . . ."

"It's not *that*," she fired back at him, realizing that sex was the only possibility in Mackensie's perverted mind. "It's an emergency," she explained. "He wouldn't say what. And if you make a crack about *that*, I'll snap your other knee."

"If you tell *anyone* about this," he warned, defending his manhood, testing his knee and finding it sound, "I'll make some serious trouble for you, Matthews. And that's no shit."

"Go lift your leg on a tree, Mackensie. I'm terrified." She added, "Do not follow me any farther!" and broke off at a run.

As she approached the summit, she wondered why she had failed to consider the possibility of an attack on Owen, why this had not come up in her discussions with Clements. Had it been kept from her because of her personal connection to Adler? She moved faster, her imagination explaining the reason for Owen's call. Had there been an attack? She ran now. Was that why Mackensie was patrolling the woods? The thought of losing Owen terrified her. And this fear of losing him seemed to further define her feelings, to illustrate to her just how committed to him she was. Since the

381

start of their relationship, she had taken on more work, hiding. Afraid to get too close. Her volunteer work at the Shelter, her contact with her girlfriends had suffered as well. She thought about him all the time, and she ran from those thoughts. But now she ran toward him, terrified by the thought of a world without him.

She swung open the cottage door and spotted his distinctive silhouette against the blank pane of a darkened window, hurried across the room, and threw herself into his arms. "Thank God," she said.

He held to her tightly and said how nothing was worth their separation, how worried he was about losing her — and she laughed that they could be thinking the same thoughts. Perhaps, she thought, she finally knew love.

After several minutes of holding each other, they settled into a comforting stillness and a satisfying warmth. Later they untangled themselves, and she said self-consciously, "You didn't call me for this."

"It's nice," he admitted.

"Then what?"

"He called me." He stated this so matter-of-factly that Daphne nearly missed the content. She studied his face in the ambient light from the main house that penetrated the large window. "I wasn't sure what to do."

"Called you?" Although she had clearly heard his words, the professional in her vied for time, attempting to fit this behavior into something she understood.

"I answered the phone and there was this silence on the other end. It's funny, because I normally would have hung right up — wrong number, prank call, one of Corky's friends too bashful to speak, a phone solicitation. But I didn't hang up. Somehow, I knew. Don't ask me how."

She studied his face to measure his state of mind. How far could she dig? He seemed rattled, but okay. This was her chance to hear the truth. His mind would betray him; his memory less clear. Embellishments, omissions. She faced these with all witnesses.

Adler said, " 'It's me', he said, 'the one you're after. The faxes.' And I couldn't speak. I froze. I've been in dozens, maybe hundreds, of complex negotiations and I've never frozen like that." His next words came out with difficulty. "He said that I took everything he loved away from him, that I had ruined everything, that I had lied and cheated long enough. He told me that I could stop it. And that if I failed to, he would take everything away from me. He said something like, 'How simple it is for you to stop it. And yet you won't, will you? And you know why, don't you? We both know why —' " Adler's voice caught and he looked away. In doing so, his face was blanketed in shadow and she could not make out his features, only the top of his head, which he hung in shame.

"Owen?"

"He called me a coward — which I am, of course —"

"That's absurd and you know it."

"He asked if I had heard the late news. He said, 'It can get much worse. It *will* get much worse. Time is running out — you know that, don't you? Tic, tic, tic, tic, tic.' He made noises like a clock. He said, 'It will be too late to stop it.' And he hung up. Strange thing is — I never said one word. He might have been talking to a baby-sitter, for all he knew."

A cold, penetrating chill started at the back of her scalp. "Are you sure?" she asked.

"Never a word."

She grabbed on to his shirt, slid off the couch, and pulled him to the floor with her. "Daffy!" he protested, but she quieted him with a "Shh!" and led him crawling across the floor and into the windowless bathroom. She pushed the door shut, locked it, and turned on a pale night-light that colored the white walls cream. Her clothes were damp from the exhausting climb up the trail.

"What are you doing?" he asked tenderly, grinning, amused with her, fingering a lock of her hair that hung in her eyes.

She glanced at him hotly, afraid, fumbled through her small purse, and pulled up the antenna on the cellular phone. She questioned, "How did he know it was you on the phone, Owen?" She keyed in the phone number too hastily and made a mistake, forcing her to cancel

384

several digits and reenter them. Angrily she asked, *"How did he know?"*

Adler's mouth slacked open.

"Did you come by the tunnel?" she asked. Again, he failed to answer.

Adler had purchased two water-view estates on Loyal and had connected them into one. The former landowner, product of the paranoia of the early sixties, had installed a bomb shelter in his backyard, at great expense, with an underground tunnel connecting it to the main house. Owen now used the bomb shelter as a wine cellar, and had also connected the guest house to it via a tunnel so that guests could share access to the fine wines and, more important, avoid the miserable rains when going back and forth between the two houses. It was a gimmick, and used rarely because Owen Adler rarely entertained overnight guests with his busy schedule. Still he loved showing off both the tunnel and his extensive wine collection, and he used the tunnel whenever possible — even in nice weather. "Did you —"

"Yes, the tunnel," he managed to say.

Boldt was not home. She apologized to Liz for calling late, hung up, and called Boldt's pager number, keying in her cellular phone number when the recording asked for it. For two minutes she and Owen Adler sat shoulder to shoulder in an awkward silence on the bathroom's tile floor.

Her cellular phone chirped, and she answered

385

it instantly. "It's me," she told Boldt. "I'm at Owen's. He was here, Lou — Caulfield — he may *still* be here."

"What?" Adler exclaimed.

"Right!" she said into the phone. "We're in the guest house. We'll wait."

"Corky!" Adler said, thinking of his daughter. He came to his feet, but Daphne caught hold of his shirt.

She disconnected the call. Still holding him back, she told her lover, "I'll go."

Adler's face contorted. "Here?"

She spoke rapidly. "He *knew* it was you on the phone, Owen. You said so yourself." She waited briefly for this to register, but Adler was a mass of confusion. She said impatiently, "He knew because he was *looking* — he was *watching* you."

Adler sprang for the door, but Daphne blocked him with a straight arm and ordered him to lock the doors behind her. "It's *you* he wants. I'm going for Corky."

"To hell with that," he said, shoving her aside abruptly. He threw open the door and ran for the tunnel.

Daphne followed, but failed to catch him. The concrete tunnel consisted of two long subterranean passages that met outside the wine cellar's vaultlike steel door. The passage to the main house was noticeably older, its lights more widely spaced and therefore darker.

When she did catch up to him, he was in

Corky's room, his arms wrapped around his eleven-year-old, who was caught halfway between waking and dreaming.

Corky wrestled loose of her father's constraints, jumped out of bed, and assaulted Daphne, leaping into her arms, "Daffy!" she exclaimed, using Boldt's nickname for her that followed her everywhere.

Carrying the heavy child, who hung from her neck awkwardly, Daphne edged to the windows and pulled the drapes. Seeing this, Adler helped her, and the darkened room became darker still.

"What now?" he asked her, helping Corky off her.

"You stay *right here*," Daphne said defiantly. "I'll get the lights and lock up."

This time Adler nodded.

"Are you cooking breakfast?" Corky asked her. This was the euphemism they used when Daphne spent the night.

"No, not tonight," Daphne answered. She met eyes with Owen. His eyes were filled with tears.

Boldt understood immediately the difficulty he faced. If he descended on Adler's estate with ten patrol cars and the entire late-shift ID unit, and if the estate were being watched, the involvement of the police would be rather obvious. On the other hand, if the Tin Man were somewhere on the property and Boldt passed up an opportunity to contain him and apprehend him, then he was throwing away innocent lives.

He checked his watch: His squad's shift had ended at midnight, forty-five minutes ago.

He reached LaMoia at home, and ten minutes later, Bobbie Gaynes at her apartment. He tried Danielson's apartment, failed to reach the man, and had the dispatcher page the detective, hoping for a call back on the cellular. He called in five patrol cars, each with two uniforms, and deployed them roughly around the perimeter of Adler's estate — not an easy task given the terrain and layout of the Loyal area. One officer from each team was to stay with the car, the other to make ready to work his or her way toward the main house, if requested.

He roused Shoswitz and prosecuting attorney Michael Striker and informed them of the developments. It was during his conversation with Shoswitz that he learned that two different ATMs had been hit that night and yet another three thousand dollars withdrawn.

Boldt arrived at Adler's nine-thousand-square-foot home ahead of either of his detectives. He pulled Daphne aside and the two talked over Boldt's plan for several minutes. "It's pretty low-profile at the moment," Boldt explained. "In case things change and we need it, Shoswitz is arranging for KOMO's traffic chopper for air surveillance." The news radio chopper — its services often lent to SPD — would also carry a SWAT sharpshooter, but Boldt left that part out. Daphne abhorred the entire approach of SWAT — shoot first, talk later.

He was shown to Adler's sumptuous office, which was hidden behind a moving bookshelf. The decor reminded Boldt of an English manor home. The office window faced out to the water and the precipitous terrain leading down to Daphne's unseen car parked far below in Golden Gardens Park. "The only point of view into this office," Boldt observed, "would be from the lawn or one of those trees."

They looked out at the broken teeth of the jagged horizon. In private, Daphne told Boldt about her encounter with Mackensie in those very woods, and Boldt weighed what to do about it. As Gaynes and LaMoia arrived separately, but nearly at the same moment, Boldt was on the phone to Fowler. The security man dodged any direct answer about the estate's surveillance and said he would look into it. Boldt, furious, advised that he look into it quickly. "We're going into those woods with our safeties off," Boldt explained. "You had better get your people out of there."

By the time a nervous and perspiring Boldt had quickly briefed his two detectives, Kenny Fowler called back. "There's no one currently deployed," Fowler told him. "But we have a slight problem on this end — might be technical.

Might not be. We can't seem to raise Mackensie."

With Daphne's help, they searched the house thoroughly, checking every possible hiding place, and then locked it up tightly and armed the security system. Outside, LaMoia took the high ground, assigned to check the gardens and shrubs and landscape. The three of them used secured police-frequency radios that connected them to one another and with the perimeter patrol personnel, who were put on an armed-and-dangerous alert. Boldt and Bobbie Gaynes took the hillside, while Daphne patrolled the home's interior.

They started down the steep hillside trail together but quickly separated, because it became obvious that the only trees offering a view of Adler's office were perched near the very top of the incline. Boldt went left, Gaynes right.

He checked behind him frequently, watching for the beam of her flashlight as it swept the trees and ground cover. From training, he mentally divided the area into a number of grids and approached his search as he would a homicide crime scene. Methodically, he moved from grid to grid, patiently alert for some sign of recent activity.

He found just such a sign about twenty yards into the thicket — deep enough that when he turned, he could no longer see the light from the efforts of Bobbie Gaynes. The stems of a large plant were crushed, and a few feet farther along he noticed a skid mark where a boot or shoe had recently kicked a rut into the fallen brown pine needles. Beyond this, he encountered yet another swath of broken twigs through a thicket. It smelled moldy deep in the woods; it smelled of decomposition and too much moisture and not enough sunlight. Boldt used the radio to softly announce that he had picked up signs to follow. He advised Gaynes to return to the main trail and descend slowly, alert for indications of where the man may have departed from it. LaMoia was to stand guard at the top of the trail in case they flushed the suspect.

Boldt moved slowly now, painfully aware of the easy target he offered by carrying a lit flashlight. Within a few yards his trail ended at the trunk of an extremely climbable tree. The bark was scarred pale where a clambering shoe had scraped it clean. Boldt shined the light up the tightly spaced branches. Considering himself too big and too clumsy for such acrobatics, Boldt nonetheless snapped his weapon in tightly, stuffed the light into his coat pocket so that it aimed up, illuminating his ascent route, and began to climb.

He did not have to climb far. Fifteen feet up, he got his first look at the house. He could see LaMoia pacing impatiently at the top of the trail steps near the guest house. He climbed up higher and discovered a large, heavy branch that ran nearly level and probably offered a fairly comfortable perch. The flashlight revealed that here the dark tree bark was excessively shredded yellow. Someone had spent some time here. He did not climb up onto the branch, for he wanted to leave it for ID, who were waiting for a call while parked only a few blocks away. But there seemed to him little question as to the quality of the unobstructed view this offered of Adler's home office.

He aimed the light back down to the ground, with a little voice calling to him never to look down, and experienced a brief sensation of vertigo. But it was as he was planning his descent through the branches that his eye caught the flash of something bright. Suddenly his planned route meant nothing to him. He descended out of the tree as effortlessly as would a chimpanzee.

From above they had looked like yellow pine needles, and yet unnatural and misplaced. Boldt counted three of them — not pine needles at all. Each chewed to a pulp on both ends — discarded as the Tin Man had sat patiently up in this tree biding his time, waiting to place his call. Toothpicks. Three of them. Freshly chewed — damp to the touch at one end, dry on the other.

The radio spit static and the urgent voice of Bobbie Gaynes said, "Sergeant, I need you down here. I'm about thirty yards lower than where we split up. I'm waving my light."

Boldt covered his own flashlight and saw the beam from hers reflected in limbs of the trees.

392

"I've got you." He took note of his surroundings so he could find this same spot again. He contacted Bernie Lofgrin's ID crew and told them to come onto the property and to wait with LaMoia at the top of the trail. LaMoia copied.

Boldt contacted Daphne and asked her to relay to prosecuting attorney Michael Striker that they needed an immediate access to the calling logs of all the area cellular phone companies. If it had been Caulfield in that tree, and if he had made the phone call from up there, then it had to be from a cellular phone. If Caulfield had a cell phone, then he had an account; if he had an account, he had a mailing address. Striker was to contact Boldt the moment he located a record of any such call.

The park trail was rough going at a run. Boldt punched through a railroad tie, crashed, and recovered himself, but not without winning some bruises to show for it.

Gaynes was fifteen yards off the trail into the woods, in an area that seemed to Boldt nearly directly beneath the observation tree. As Boldt approached, she asked, "Did you have dinner?"

"No."

"Well, you're lucky. I just left mine in a bush over there."

Boldt did not think of Gaynes as having a tender stomach. He reached her. He could smell the metallic bite of fresh blood in the air well before he saw the body. She lowered her light onto Mackensie's corpse. The branch that had been used to cave in his face was lying a few yards from the twisted wreck of a body, and Boldt thought that the man might have survived that blow had his hands not been cleaved from his arms at the wrist with something incredibly sharp. But there they lay — at the ends of his arms looking like a pair of deerskin gloves. Mac Mackensie, knocked unconscious by that branch, had bled to death, his face now the color of a bedsheet.

A few minutes later when LaMoia arrived, he said to Gaynes, "Come on, help me. I think we should give him a hand."

At three in the morning, Boldt drove Daphne down to where she had parked her car in the picnic area.

"You're awfully quiet," he said.

Daphne nodded.

"You're just tired," he tried. "It's late."

"I'm wide awake," she answered. She could not think how to explain what she felt to another person; she barely understood it herself. As a psychologist, she wanted to be strong and able to quickly overcome such pain — to adapt. But as a woman, a human being, she ached not for Mac Mackensie, but selfishly, for herself. Then she thought that Lou Boldt, of all people, would understand. "Five minutes either way," she whispered hoarsely, her voice giving her away.

Boldt pulled the car next to her Honda and left it running. "And it would have been you," he said.

She nodded, and she felt the choking sensation in her throat, she felt the tears, and she hated herself for this reaction. She leaned forward and Boldt put his big hand on her back and rubbed her there, and it comforted her. "That was too damn close for me," she said, sobbing now. "And it's *me* I care about, not Mac Mackensie — can you believe that? And you know how he went out? He went out being a jerk. A real goddamn prick. And that's the last thing he ever was — a jerk. A real jerk. Listen to me!"

He continued to rub her back, and when his hand reached her neck, she felt the tension spill out of her and she found her self-control again. "Sorry," she said.

"Whenever a cop — someone I know — goes down, my first sensation is gratitude. Glad it wasn't me. My turn. I always felt guilty about that — until now. I've never talked about it with anyone, never shared that part of me. Not even with Liz. My *second* thought is for the deceased — it's not that I don't care; but my *first* reaction is a huge sense of relief. I dodged another one — something along those lines."

"I was there," she said softly. "I heard someone in the woods. First to my left, then below me, then later to my right. I heard *two* people, not one. *He* was there. For all I know he was coming for me when Mackensie caught up to me. For all I know he was *right there*." She looked over at him then with surprise in her eyes. "For all I know it's been him following me all along."

"Or Mackensie for that matter," Boldt suggested.

"No," she said, "Mackensie was just doing a job. After he left me, he didn't make it far."

"He probably heard something. Wandered into the woods. Caulfield jumps up and hits a home run into the side of his face. The hands were an afterthought, I think. Maybe Mackensie tried for his piece. Maybe he grabbed for a radio or something. I think Harry used the hands to buy himself time — no time to tie him up, so he cuts them off. Something that simple. The question I have to ask is what the hell kind of knife is he carrying around?"

"You're trying to say there was nothing I could have done. You're trying to make it right."

"It wasn't you who disobeyed the signs." Boldt pointed through the windshield to where the headlights caught the parks department sign. It read: FOR YOUR OWN SAFETY, PLEASE STAY ON THE TRAIL.

Daphne parked her car down the street and across from the houseboats in a space for which she paid seventy-five dollars a month. It was a well-lighted lot, which lately made her appreciate it all the more. She turned off the car, locked it, and made the trip to the houseboat at a brisk pace. It was after three-thirty in the morning and all of her neighbors were locked up and dark.

She reached the door, unlocked and opened it, and headed directly to the home security box that she found flashing its violation, indicating her entry. She rekeyed the device, locked the front door, and turned on more lights than necessary, keeping her purse at her side while she made a full trip around every room, checking coat closets, even under the bed, and confirming to herself that she now qualified fully as a paranoid.

She convinced herself that at this hour any sane person would head straight to bed, but on this night it was not for her. She considered a bath, but not tonight. Sleep would not come for another hour or so, and to try to force it would only delay it more.

She unbuttoned and unzipped her pants, slipped off her bra without taking off her shirt, washed her hands twice in a row, and poured herself a glass of Pine Ridge.

She set down the wine, pulled out the stool, climbed up onto it, and let out a long and meaningful sigh. She was in the middle of a second sip when her heart fluttered. She felt her eyes go wide, and acting on instinct, she was suddenly off the stool, pants still unfastened, over to her purse . . . her shoes . . . the alarm . . . out the door . . . *lock it!* Feet not fully in the shoes . . . running . . . shoes flapping . . . refusing to look behind her . . . running . . . up the gangway . . . past the mailboxes . . . down the street toward her car. . . . A dog lunged from a shadow, and Daphne screamed at the top of her lungs and ran faster . . . faster. Into the parking lot . . . straight for the car . . . unlock it! Inside! Relock it! Start the engine . . . She pulled out of the lot, spinning gravel behind her tires, and fastened her seat belt on the fly. Ran a red light, horn sounding . . . Ran another . . .

She would take a hotel room. Charge it to the department, for that matter. She would not return to her own home until it was light again. She would not tell anyone if she did not find some other piece of evidence. And perhaps — she allowed herself to believe, now that she found herself in the safety of the vehicle — perhaps she remembered wrong.

But the image in her mind stung her with certainty: She had left the mechanical pencil pointing at a word. What was the word? What was it?

Intractable — she remembered!

And now that same pencil was sitting alongside her papers. Pointing nowhere. Which was not how she had left it.

And that was wrong.

398

TWENTY-EIGHT

Boldt stood before the bathroom mirror shaving when he heard Liz climb out of bed. Miles was still asleep. As he shaved, she slipped off her nightgown and pressed her warm, sleepy body against him.

"Honey?" he said cautiously.

"I *have* something for you." She reached around him, grabbed a hair band, and put her hair back. She meant business. Elizabeth did not let her hair down before sex, but put it up instead. Reaching around him, she unfastened his pants.

"I'm going to cut myself," he warned.

"Be careful," she said, teasing his chest in a way she knew he liked.

"I have something for you," she repeated. He dropped the plastic razor into the water and it splashed into the islands of shaving cream. She led him over to the counter, sat up on it, and wrapped her legs around him. "Come and get it," she said.

Later, she leaned her head back against the wall, but refused to let him go. She was sweating and her eyes looked dreamy.

She allowed them to separate then, and her

legs sank down, but she did not move until Boldt finished shaving — and then only once she had talked him into running the shower for her.

Drying her hair in the living room, a white terry-cloth robe cinched tightly around her waist, and watching her son, who was now awake, she said to Boldt, "They had a similar case in London," which won his attention.

"Who did?"

"The London authorities. A kidnapping. Ransom by ATM machine. I told you I had something for you."

"I thought you meant —"

"No," she corrected. "That was for *me*."

"Liz?"

"They paid out one hundred and eighty-five thousand pounds over a ten-month period. If your case goes on for ten months, I figured we would end up divorced, so it was in my best interest to get to the bottom of this." He moved closer to her. She smelled good. "From what I can tell, it was incredibly similar to what you're facing. The guy moved from one ATM to another, one town to another, making withdrawals, and no matter how fast the police responded, he was always long gone."

"That's us exactly," Boldt replied, anxiously awaiting whatever else she had to tell him. Elizabeth could not be rushed. She had her own timing — in everything.

"At one point, if I'm right about this, they

400

had over two *thousand* police watching ATMs. They still couldn't catch him. But there was a reason, of course: the average ATM transaction is only a matter of seconds. It's what makes it such a clever way to collect a ransom demand."

"And they found a way around that obstacle," Boldt speculated, seeing that sparkle in her eye.

"Yes, they did. A couple of brilliant computer hackers were called in. They devised something they called 'time traps' — software that slowed down the entire system."

"We talked to the switching station here about doing just that, slowing down the network, but starting from scratch they claimed it could take months."

"They're right. It *did* take months. But it has already been done. All these networks, all these systems speak the same computer language — they have to in order to interface, in order for you to make a withdrawal from an ATM in Paris on your Seattle account. So it seems to me that whatever time-trap software they came up with should be easily adapted for use here. If not, right up in Redmond we have some of the brainiest software wizards in the world; they should be able to port it for you."

"Time traps," Boldt repeated.

"You slow down the system and buy yourself time to catch this guy. Another thing that occurred to me?" she asked rhetorically. "Are you aware that some ATMs can be instructed to 'eat' ATM cards? They use it to pull the counterfeit cards and bad accounts off the market."

"We thought about that, too. But we want him to have the card. That card is how we catch him. But these time traps."

"Go," she said, anticipating his apology before he ever spoke it.

"You sure?"

"It's my idea. Go."

He grabbed his weapon and his badge wallet and literally ran to the back door. The last thing he heard from her was, "And catch the bastard! We could use a little peace around here."

Boldt exchanged a dozen phone calls with his wife, each bringing him more encouragement. At twelve noon Pacific time — evening in London — in an amazing show of technology, the time-trap software was beamed by telephone company satellites via computer modem and downloaded by technicians at Ted Perch's NetLinQ ATM switching station. The entire transfer took twenty-two minutes.

With an open phone line to London, NetLinQ technicians worked furiously to install the software, which crashed the first time on-line, freezing twelve hundred cash machines for over fifteen minutes. At 2:18 P.M., July 17, Perch authorized the activation of the software networkwide for a second time. And for seventeen minutes, it held.

The second crash involved a cluster of 120 First Interstate machines, which was later deemed something of a success. By five o'clock sharp, with 17 percent of NetLinQ's directly controlled ATMs time-trap operational, the first effort was made to place a six-second drag in the transaction time. These intervals of delay were quickly tagged WOTs — for "window of time." The six-second WOTs were placed between the customer entry of the PIN number and the appearance of the first transaction menu. Remarkably, the system held. For 279 cash machine customers, a brief but effective test pause had been created in their transaction, virtually unnoticed by any of them, but sending up a cheer at NetLinQ that was heard all the way to London.

Through a series of conversations, Boldt encouraged Perch to increase the number of machines that were time-trapped, but Perch was reluctant to risk a third crash in a single evening. "I would like to be working here tomorrow," he teased Boldt. But Boldt hounded him. By 7:22, another commercial bank's network had been added to the core group, leaving 27 percent of all ATMs in Washington State and western Oregon under the direct control of time-trap software.

Boldt spent the early evening at NetLinQ monitoring the effectiveness of the new software, and congratulating the crew for their efforts.

The ransom account had never been hit before eight o'clock in the evening, leading Boldt and others to suspect Caulfield might be holding down a day job — although Ted Perch pointed out that late evening made sense for such hits. Many banks restocked their cash machines at the close of business; if an extortionist wished to avoid being seen by bank employees, then at the very least he or she would wait until after the close of business — as late as 6 P.M. at some branches.

The NetLinQ operations room was an impressive collection of high technology and reminded Boldt of what he had seen of telephone command centers. It was nearly pitch-black, the focus of the room being three enormous flat-screen color monitors that visually mapped all ATM traffic in the NetLinQ region. The floor descended toward these screens in three tiers, each housing rows of computers, some of which were attended. The far right-hand screen showed all those ATM locations under time-trap control. After pestering from Boldt, Perch reluctantly added another six-second WOT, this time between account authorization and delivery of cash.

NetLinQ's public information office had earlier distributed a press release, announcing that due to system maintenance some "inconveniences" were to be expected. The eleven o'clock news had promised to run it.

For the sixth consecutive night, an ATM hit

occurred shortly after 8 P.M. "It's getting like clockwork," Perch said, pointing out the flashing dot on the overhead screen. Clockwork was what Boldt hoped for — the more predictable and repetitious the withdrawals were, the increased chance of apprehending a suspect.

Perch announced, "Five seconds and counting."

Boldt relayed news of the hit directly to SPD dispatch. "Location is N-sixteen. Repeat: En-one-six."

"Ten seconds," Perch tracked. He checked a computer screen. "This one is *not* under time-trap control," he warned.

Boldt could imagine one of his plainclothes detectives throwing a car in gear and speeding toward the location. But with less than five seconds to close the gap, he did not see much hope.

He needed more people. He needed more of the machines time-trapped.

"Transaction complete," Perch announce, dejected.

"Lieutenant?" Boldt barked hopefully into the telephone receiver.

Shoswitz said, "Surveillance is four blocks and closing."

Boldt felt tempted to cross his fingers. He envisioned the unmarked car running traffic lights and braking loudly to a stop. To Perch, Boldt said, "We need better communication with the field."

"Tell me about it," Perch replied, frustrated and upset.

Shoswitz said through the phone, "Nothing. Repeat: No visual contact."

Boldt relayed this to Perch, who cursed so loudly that he raised the attention of several of the NetLinQ employees.

An hour later there was a second hit, though this time on a machine not under software control. Surveillance failed to close within twelve blocks.

"We need more of the machines on the software," Boldt complained.

"Don't tell me my business, Sergeant. We can't make any more headway until morning. We have two lags in usage: nine-thirty to eleven A.M. and two to five P.M. That's as soon as we can hope to put more machines on-line."

"We need them tonight!"

"The system will crash. And if it crashes while this person is on-line, then it could look intentional. Is that what you want?" he asked heatedly.

Reluctantly, Boldt sat back and watched a third and final hit take place. And for a third and final time that night, surveillance was nowhere close.

At a few minutes before midnight, he was summoned to the hotel room where Dr. Richard Clements was staying.

Boldt arrived depressed and exhausted.

406

Shoswitz and Daphne reached the Alexis before Boldt, and all were awaiting him when he arrived.

The suite was spacious, with paper Japanese sliding doors separating the bedroom from a sitting room that included a large glass conference table, two couches, a coffee table, several freestanding lamps, a fireplace, and a wet bar. The decor was granite, glass, and steel — ultramodern — which was not to Boldt's tastes, and yet here he found it to his liking.

CNN was muted on the television in the corner — Michael Kinsley with his coat off, interviewing an author — and Clements kept the remote within reach.

Clements was dressed casually in linen pants and an Italian-designed white Egyptian cotton shirt, with black loafers and no socks. He was drinking what looked like brandy out of a snifter the size of a fishbowl, and he carried a wad of chew neatly in his upper lip, leaving a bulge there as though he were trying to stop a nosebleed. He wore half-glasses, tortoiseshell imitation that rode on the bridge of his nose precariously. He sat at the glass conference table in a black leather-and-stainless steel captain's chair, waving a two-hundred-dollar mechanical pencil in the air and punctuating his authoritative instructions.

"You sit there. And you there. No — there, please," he advised Shoswitz. "Yes, thank you.

The Armagnac is excellent, and seemingly endless, and comes highly recommended. Whatever your pleasure." He looked them over.

Daphne and Boldt declined. Shoswitz requested a Miller Lite, an order that so disgusted Clements he referred him to the wet bar's refrigerator, advising him to "use whatever's there."

Dr. Richard Clements began with a self-possessed arrogance that immediately offended all present: "Before we get into Twenty Questions, let me head off whatever possible by offering you my updated profile." He rolled the liqueur around in his mouth, and Boldt had to wonder what a mixture of Armagnac and chew tasted like when spilled across one's tongue. "It's interesting: Behavior will always tell you more than a rap sheet. I am referring, of course, to the incident in Mr. Adler's woods and the telephone call that immediately preceded it.

"It's late, so I'll try not to bore you. You are all aware of the stalking phase that a serial killer or rapist enters into prior to the attack. Any of a number of specific incidents may precede the stalking phase, including arson, the killing of house pets, voyeurism, and masturbation, but the stalking phase is unique in that it directly precedes the offense. We see it in the wild — a cat, even some packs, will stalk prior to the kill, even if the intended prey is wounded or incapacitated. Still, the stalk. What our Mr. Caulfield is doing is getting up close

408

and personal with his intended prey, Mr. Adler. The fact that he has entered this phase is warning sign enough: It is drawing to a close. We are in the last act. The stalking phase can go on for days, weeks, even months or years, and we are still at odds to know exactly what precipitates the craving for completion of the act. Boredom? Rage? Sexuality? So different in every case." He swilled more of the snifter's contents and inhaled, apparently enormously satisfied with the results. His audience was too stunned to interrupt.

"And so we know that he has begun this final coda before the finale." He waved the pencil in time to music within his head, and Boldt could see his lips close as he hummed silently along with it. "But unfortunately, we do not know the length of the piece. *Point number one*," he said strongly, "Adler — or someone in that house," he conditioned, "— is the target of his intentions."

He excused himself to the bathroom, and apparently leaving an interior door open, urinated loudly enough that all could hear.

Shoswitz said in a forced whisper, "Is the air-conditioning on, or is it just him?"

Daphne, noticeably upset, reminded in an equally soft reply, "Like it or not, he's one of the best there is."

Boldt added, "And he knows it."

"*Point number two*," Clements began anew when he returned, "he is distracted by his own

409

greed. He is withdrawing two or three thousand a day. He finds himself addicted to this easy money. He has a good thing going, so why not prolong it? All of that sounds so logical, does it not? Well, it's bullshit, plain and simple. What we have is a theoretical conflict that I must admit weighs heavily upon me. On the one side, he has clearly entered the stalking phase; this includes a verbal threat to Adler over the phone, and a use of language, a reference to certain personally historical issues, that confirms a deeply profound sense of injustice. On the other side, he is running around milking ATMs. If this were a game show, the buzzer would have sounded: wrong answer. So which is the real Mr. Harold Caulfield? And to what extent can we predict his schizophrenia, so apparent in these conflicting personalities within him? Will the real Harry Caulfield please stand up? Revenge-motivated killer, or greed-driven extortionist?" He had lost the chew while in the bathroom, for the lump below his nose was gone, and he inflated his cheeks and lips, using the cognac like mouthwash.

"*Point number three:* There's method to this madness. It appears increasingly obvious that a grievous wrong was done to person or persons with whom Mr. Caulfield had strong emotional ties, and upon whom he was otherwise financially and emotionally dependent. He appears to have a personal agenda to which he is committed, and I must say from past experience

410

that we should prepare ourselves for the un-expected. Nothing that we can imagine for Mr. Caulfield is out of the question. Kill a hundred? Why not? A thousand? Same answer. Caulfield believes he is justified in this, and that makes him especially dangerous. Drive a truck full of explosives into a barracks of marines? Why not? Blow up the World Trade Center? Same answer." He reached for the phone, and ordered another. Without asking the lieutenant, he also ordered a Miller Lite, though he pronounced it as if it were a disease. He met eyes with each of them individually and said patronizingly, "Okay, time for Twenty Questions."

Stunning them all, Shoswitz said, "Twenty minutes ago, when Captain Rankin heard of Mackensie's murder, he ordered us to pull all Adler products from the shelves by six A.M. or the start of business tomorrow."

Boldt felt the wind knocked out of him.

"Is this that bulldog I met? The one with the cheap suit and buzz cut?" Clements asked.

Boldt said, "Captain of Homicide."

"If you are asking for a prediction of the effects on our Mr. Caulfield of such a decision, I can tell you this: He won't like it. Pulling the Adler products will signal Caulfield that he has lost control of this — and control, after all, is what is and has been getting him high." The man closed his eyes and his eyelids fluttered oddly, and he said softly, "Imagine the *power* he must feel! Dictating demands to a man of

411

position like Owen Adler. Poisoning people with the medical community seemingly powerless to stop him. Withdrawing cash like it's Christmas. That carries an awesome sense of power and control." He opened his eyes, stood, and answered the door — before even Boldt with his keen sense of hearing heard any approach — and greeted the room service boy perfunctorily. A moment later he sat back down and began sloshing the liquor around his new fishbowl. "The loss of control, or even the *perception* of such a loss, will accelerate his timetable. He was unpredictable before; he is even less predictable now. I will chat-up your Captain Rankin."

Boldt decided to reveal what he had mentioned to no one. He glanced at Daphne, then met eyes with Clements, and said, "Owen Adler will pull all the product if given half an excuse. He lobbied me to do just that and I dissuaded him." Daphne looked horrified that she had not heard of this. "If he gets wind of Rankin's request, he'll bypass any of our concerns and get out. He wants out. He is staying with the game plan only because he fears making the wrong decision himself, and I convinced him that to go against the demands was the wrong decision."

"By 'get out,' I presume this to mean pull the product, not conform with the ultimate demand and commit suicide."

"That's right," Boldt agreed. "The killings

412

have weakened him. He feels directly responsible."

"Which is exactly as our Mr. Caulfield intends. Interesting."

"What I'm hearing," Shoswitz said, "is that
if Rankin bypasses us and gets to Adler, we're
going to lose this anyway."

Clements said, "I have little doubt that the
intelligent thing to do is to keep as many Adler
products on the shelf as possible. We would
also like to keep the news media at bay for
as long as possible, though we may have lost
that battle. The point being — as I think Sergeant Boldt will concur — with these ATM
withdrawals, we have our first real chance to
trap our Mr. Caulfield."

"And we are making some progress there, I
think," Boldt interjected. He told them about
the limited success of the time-trap software.

"So I suggest we advise your public information department to issue a series of no-
comments, and that we staple down the tongues
of anyone associated with this investigation. If
there are no sources, there is no story; it is
that simple. This should include our friends at
State Health, this infectious diseases lab," he
said to Boldt, and turning to Shoswitz: "And
anyone within your division who may be privy
to this." He sipped the drink. "I will work a
little while longer here, and by morning I will
hopefully be armed with enough of a profile
to convince our Captain Rankin of his inep-

titude, and the certainty of his own fall from grace should his orders be carried out. Seeing you work as a unit, I believe in you — in *all* of you — and I must confess to you now that my secondary role in coming here was to act as a kind of spy, if you will, in assessing your abilities to handle this investigation. I hope you will be pleased to know that my initial report and subsequent follow-ups have been glowing, and they will continue to be. But I should warn you that there are those looking over your shoulders, and they will pounce if given half a chance." Clements sipped more of the Cognac.

"What about Special Agents?" Boldt asked, spotting an opportunity. He addressed Shoswitz: "What if we requested the Bureau's assistance with the ATM surveillance? Fifty or even a hundred Special Agents to place in the field? Equal partners, with us drawing on what is admittedly a formidable expertise in ransom situations. This allows them in on perhaps the most critical aspect of the investigation as it now stands, perhaps defusing any later attempts to take over the investigation completely and, at the same time, seems to satisfy a great need of our own, namely a shortage of field personnel."

Shoswitz considered this.

Boldt said, "I don't mean to put you on the spot —"

"No, it's not that," Shoswitz allowed.

"Perhaps something to give some consideration to," Clements said genially. "No hurry. Sleep on it." Boldt sensed immediately that Clements approved of the suggestion and that it might help his own position in walking a line between the two agencies.

"I like it," Shoswitz admitted. "My only real concern," he directed to Clements, "is that if we let them in a little, do we give it up completely somewhere down the road? This is our town, our citizens, our investigation. We have our own political concerns. The Bureau has two faces: one is cooperation, one is complete control. Surrendering control of this investigation would not go over well, and is not what we want."

"I understand. It is one reason I like Sergeant Boldt's suggestion. Working as equals on the surveillance — and I'm sure that can be arranged, might indeed fend off any . . ." — he searched for his words — "hostile takeover." He added, "I can explore such a relationship, if you like."

Shoswitz thought a long time, checking with Boldt repeatedly by firing off hot glances in his direction. "If we catch him at an ATM, we all win," Shoswitz said. It was his way of giving his approval.

On their way down in the elevator together, Daphne and Boldt agreed to meet on her houseboat for a recap. It was not very far out of

415

the way for Boldt, and he wondered if she wanted someone to escort her inside and make sure the place was empty, and so he agreed. At one-thirty in the morning, she made a pot of herbal tea and poured them each a mugful.

She began in a tone of voice that placed Boldt on attention. "I completed my affidavit, Striker obtained a warrant, and we made an inquiry with Norwest National to obtain the checking records for New Leaf Foods." Norwest National was Liz's bank, renamed after a string of acquisitions, and this was certainly not lost on Daphne, he thought. "I want to see what checks were being written on and around the date of the altering of that State Health report, because I firmly believe someone was paid off, and maybe there's a paper trail."

"I have no objection to that. But my focus remains on Caulfield."

"It's not that," she interrupted him. "The bank told me that they had already cooperated with us, had already turned over that information to us with no warrants involved. They complained at having to do so again."

"Not me," Boldt admitted.

"Obviously not me," she agreed.

"Danielson," Boldt said, guessing. "How is it that Caulfield manages to always be where our ATM surveillance teams are not?"

"Danielson is in bed with him?"

"Do I believe it? No. Can I rule it out? Also, no. Providing he's not criminal, what

416

would motivate Chris?"

"Money?"

Boldt nodded. "An offer from the tabloids, a book deal, a movie deal — there are a lot of temptations out there for a cop these days. Different than when I was coming up."

"Chris, sell out? He's the department's number one overachiever."

Boldt hesitated before dropping his bomb, feeding Daphne's earlier suspicions. "What if Taplin was paying him for inside information? What if Taplin had promised him Fowler's job if Danielson could settle this affair without the publicity certain to surround a police arrest?"

"Which one of us is the psychologist?" she asked nervously.

"Do you like it?"

"I can see it, if that's what you're asking. Yes, it's possible. It explains a hell of a lot of what's been going on, and it fits with Taplin's defensive position. Taplin's name is in and around all of the communication on the New Leaf contamination. You want to look for someone with a lot to lose if Caulfield blew the whistle on State Health, Howard Taplin tops the list. We need Caulfield for more than these murders," she suggested.

"We need Caulfield, period." Boldt said.

TWENTY-NINE

I READ ABOUT THE TWO BOYS YOU KILLED.
AND YOUR FRIENDS WITH GUNS
SHOULD NOT WANDER THE WOODS.
YOU JUST WON'T LISTEN, WILL YOU?
I MEANT WHAT I TOLD YOU —
YOU WILL PAY.
SOONER THAN LATER.
AND MORE WILL DIE UNTIL YOU DO.
MANY MORE.

Two newspaper articles were included at the bottom of the fax — one about the boys, and one, the mysterious murder in Golden Gardens Park. Technical Services informed Boldt that the articles had been scanned into a computer and pasted into the fax, which had been transmitted electronically from a pay phone on a side street near the Kingdome. This was all supposed to mean something to Boldt, but it did not. His entire interest lay with the words at the top of this page, and the implication that Clements was right: Harry Caulfield was running out of patience. Time was almost up.

Like water seeking its own level, Boldt sought out the evidence, calling Bernie Lofgrin and complaining to him about the delay in the FBI report on the Longview Farms evidence. Lofgrin suggested he lodge the complaint with Clements; Boldt did so, and Clements promised to do what he could.

For his part, Clements believed he had convinced Captain Rankin to rescind the Adler recall that he had threatened, though the psychiatrist admitted to Boldt that Rankin was "a difficult bastard to read."

There was a lot of talk and little action. Public Information called repeatedly, frustrated by a press corps that sensed a much bigger story than two boys dying in a tree house. Boldt issued a string of denials and no-comments but could see the inevitable coming. The story was going to break, and when it did there *would* be a recall. According to Clements, if anything was certain to push Caulfield into following through on his threat of mass murder, it was this combination of events.

MANY MORE.

Boldt could not get the words out of his head. Again he waited for his phone to ring with the news of more murders. Again his mood went sour and his squad steered clear of him. Again his appetite deserted him. His bowels bled, and the Maalox did nothing more than make his breath smell like lemon creme.

He did a quick turnaround at the dinner

hour — refusing food, but swallowing down a Zantac — and prepared to join Ted Perch at NetLinQ where tonight, for the first time, Lucille Guillard's monitoring of the Pac-West ATM network had been brought on board. The time-trap software had been expanded to cover 60 percent of the NetLinQ system.

Liz was ironing a pleated skirt for the following morning.

"I owe you a champagne dinner for that software," he told her.

"Make it in Rome and you have a deal."

"Rome it is."

She laughed.

In the corner by the dryer was piled a gigantic stack of clean laundry that was his responsibility to iron, and he looked away from it because it made him feel guilty to see so much of it. In his exhausted state, it seemed to him a physical manifestation representing his total failure as a father and husband.

"If you leave, what do I tell poor Michael Striker?"

"What about Striker?" His shirt tucked in, he leaned for a kiss.

"He called when you were in the bathroom. Said he was coming by. He was checking to see that you were here, and I told him you were." She tugged at the skirt and said down to the ironing board, "My guess is that it has nothing whatsoever to do with work. He feels a lot closer to you than you do to him." She

420

looked up at him. "That's true of a lot of your friends, you know."

He knew her well enough to know when she was concealing something from him. "Liz?"

She said calmly, "I thought that he probably wanted to talk to you about whichever detective of yours is screwing Elaine."

"What!" Boldt bumped the ironing board, and the spray bottle fell to the floor. Miles, who should have been in bed two hours earlier, began pounding the floor with a spatula. Up until that moment, his father had not realized the boy was on the other side of the inverted laundry basket, although it helped to explain Liz's constant distraction, Boldt realized. This discovery that he had overlooked his son's presence for the last five minutes hit him hard. Boldt asked Liz, "Are you sure about this?" knowing that she had to be. Liz was not a gossip.

"I'm sure he's coming over." She added, "And it's kind of an odd time to talk shop. Are you telling me you really hadn't heard anything?"

"Do you know who it is?"

"No. Only that he's fifth floor and that he's on your squad. They met when whoever it is came knocking on the front door one Saturday afternoon looking for Michael's approval for a warrant — something like that. Only Michael was on the back nine and Elaine was feeling pretty mad at him for spending his weekend

421

with a golf club, and maybe she was feeling a little bit creamy as well, and anyway: She jumped your boy's bones. The way Suzie tells it, makes Elaine sound like she knows how to pick them. Evidently, your boy is a rocket in the sack. And it didn't end with the back nine either — just in case he asks. It's a near-regular thing now."

"LaMoia?"

She laughed. "That's exactly who I guessed," she admitted. "Great minds."

Boldt had often accused Liz of having the hots for LaMoia, though it had always been teasing.

"Suzie doesn't know who the mystery man is, only that it's incredibly hot sex and that Elaine claims to be in one of those self-discovery phases."

Liz had had her self-discovery a few years earlier, though they never discussed it anymore.

"Jesus. Razor will kill the guy if he finds out. Talk about having a short fuse."

"Laws of nature, love. Survival of the fittest, and all that. We have no place in this."

"Can't you talk to Elaine?"

"Me? I hardly know Elaine. And besides, Suzie promised she wouldn't tell a soul, so I'd just be getting her in trouble. If Michael says anything about it to you, you had better look surprised, buster."

"I am surprised."

"Laws of nature."

"I can't hang around for him," Boldt complained.

"Oh no you don't. You're not sticking me with him." She suggested, "Why don't you put 'himself' to bed. He's up late as it is."

Boldt spent the next twenty minutes with his son. He changed the boy's diapers — knowing they neared the day when they could do without — gave him a quick sponge bath with a warm hand towel, and had another of those limited-vocabulary conversations with him that amounted to listing quite a few nouns and the occasional verb: "Wa" meant both "water" and "wash"; "bunky" meant "bunny"; and "mama" meant that it eventually required Liz alongside to coax him to give sleep a try. They returned to the laundry room, where Liz was still ironing the same skirt. Clearly sensing a comment coming, she said, "I'm not very good with pleats." And when Boldt offered to give it a try, she kissed him on the cheek and started folding what was just coming out of the dryer.

As he ironed, watching her fold the clothes, he wondered if she felt envious of an Elaine Striker with her young lover, the fawning and attention, and the hot-blooded romance. He felt tempted to ask, but decided against it. There were some things a husband should not know.

They hadn't talked about her pregnancy in days, so he asked her about it, but she immediately changed subjects, mentioning something about a yoga class she wanted to attend, and he was reminded of his wife's superstition about pregnancy in the first trimester.

Striker pulled up out front just as Boldt held the freshly ironed skirt at his waist and asked, "What do you think?"

"You'd look better in something brown, and below the knee," Liz fired back, deadpan.

Striker's steel claw clicked like a telegraph key, and he circled the small front porch like a dog searching for a spot to lie down. "Awfully late for you," Boldt observed, trying to initiate some kind of dialogue. Watching a colleague bounce off the railing of his front porch was not great sport. He glanced at his watch, impatient to get downtown. An air force of small black bugs convened around the porch light.

Striker explained, "I didn't want you to think that I had let you down on this cellular phone thing. All three companies searched their calling logs for a call placed to Adler's home number, and all came up blank. Since we're pretty confident about how this went down — Caulfield making the call while up in that tree — I pushed hard for some results, and two of the companies actually tried the search for a second time, but they still came up dry. About an hour ago I talked to a supervisor in data control and she said their lack of record could be explained technically, but I didn't ask."

"He burned us," Boldt summarized.

"It looks like that, yes."

Striker stared, his eyes dead and distant, his prosthesis chattering like cold teeth.

Boldt asked, "So? You heading downtown?"

Striker's face contorted into an unforgiving knot.

"Razor?"

"Better than going home," Striker said.

"Problems?" Boldt asked as innocently as possible.

"She's never where she says she is, Lou. And she's smelling a little too good these days when she leaves the house. She's a little too happy. You know? And worse, her friends are doing a shitty job of covering for her. It's like everyone knows the secret but me. But eventually you figure it out."

Striker met eyes with Boldt, who saw the anger and hurt in his friend's expression and offered what he hoped was good advice. "Forgive her, Razor. In the long run, it's the only thing that works."

He said, "You've been there, right?"

"Right," Boldt confirmed. "I feel for you, buddy — I want you to know that. But at the same time, this stuff happens to all of us. And sometimes what we think is happening isn't happening at all. It's pretty easy to allow your emotions to give false reports."

"She's definitely screwing someone," he said bluntly, giving in to the anger. Chewing his upper lip, eyes downcast, he repeated, "She's

425

screwing someone — and in our bed — in *my* bed, if you can believe that shit!" He turned away. "And I don't know what the hell to do about it."

"Have you confronted her?"

Striker looked over with tears in his eyes. He was pale and his nostrils flared as he spoke. "I'll knock her head off."

"Razor . . . You want to *think* before you do anything. On second thought, maybe it's better you don't confront her," he said, backtracking. "Maybe it's better if you do some counseling together. Work this thing out with a professional. Hell, I'm no professional."

"In my own fucking bed!"

No pun intended. "Maybe it's not like that," Boldt tested. He wondered if Liz was right about the lover being one of Boldt's detectives. He hoped not. He also hoped that Striker didn't know anything about who it was, did not have a name, because where Striker might restrain himself from hitting his own wife, he would go after her lover with a vengeance. Boldt had no doubt about that. "Listen, I need you on this investigation," Boldt said honestly, selfishly. "You want to watch yourself."

"You want to talk about watching?" Striker asked, following his own skewed logic. "I can picture her, you know, in the act with him. Enjoying it. Getting off. She used to really get off, you know? Not so much anymore — pretty bored, really. I bet she gets off with him."

He grew paler. His eyes fixed on a stationary object and his lower lip trembled. Boldt could hear the bugs striking the glass bulb around the light. Down the street someone had their television too loud. He felt it weird to have this discussion with a laugh track running faintly in the background?

Striker snapped his head toward Boldt so hard that his neck cracked loudly. "What the hell did you do when you found out Liz . . . you know?"

Boldt closed his front door and led Striker down the steps, and they stood in the small front yard with insects swirling overhead and the sound of that laugh track even louder. He did not know how, but somehow people had found out about Liz's affair with a coworker. To Boldt it was ancient history now; he didn't even think of it as having to do with her. It was something that had gone wrong with them — like a disease they had shared. As far as he knew, only Liz was aware of his one-night adventure with Daphne. But Liz's distraction had gone on for several months. He said, "What I would do if I were you is start with myself. With you. Because when a relationship goes south, it's both of you. It's never — ever — a one-way street."

"Clichés?" he said, furious. "I show you my dirty laundry and you hand me a bunch of clichés?"

"I'd start with myself is all," Boldt repeated.

427

"Me? I work too hard. I know that. So what? I break the little promises, okay? I'm home late. I work weekends, or I hit the links. I'm selfish with my time: I know that. I'm away from the house too much — I know that? But not the big promises! *Okay?* Am *I* getting laid on the sly?" he asked hoarsely. "I'm not *like* that, damn it? *She's* not like that."

"Maybe it just happened, Mike. Maybe it's one of those things that just happened. I think you start by keeping your head and opening a dialogue. I think you go into that dialogue well aware that you are half the problem, and you use a counselor —"

"I am not seeing a shrink!"

"A counselor as a referee — a go-between. A therapist. A shortstop. However you want to think about it."

"I don't want to think about it. I want to catch the guy — catch them both in the act. I want to prove this one way or the other. But I don't have a clue how to go about it. You on the other hand —"

Boldt saw the trap he was being led into. "You *don't* want to do that, Razor. That's a bad idea."

"Whose side are you on?"

"You want to catch her in the act," Boldt repeated, so the man could hear his own words, so he could face the reality of it. "When? Just before? In the middle? When? Think about it."

"Shut up."

428

He was thinking about it, and Boldt thought that was good, because a guy with Striker's temper had to be discouraged from this at all costs. "Is it for you or her that you want to catch her in the act?"

Striker's one good arm was incredibly powerful, and when he shoved Boldt with it, the big man tripped on a lawn sprinkler and went down hard. "You see?" Boldt asked, sitting on the damp grass. "You want those kinds of images permanently living inside you? Worming around inside you? Do you? Because I'll tell you something? They eat their way right back out eventually. Those kinds of things will kill the relationship forever. You can't erase that stuff. It's a big mistake. If you're smart, you'll stay *as far away from that as possible*. What you want to do is talk. To listen. You want to sit her down and talk, and you've got to accept what she says — no matter what she says." He added, "No matter what, because she may be a little hateful right now. Feeling guilty. And that's where therapy comes in — because a therapist won't let you play games with each other. She'll call your number." Boldt came to his feet. Striker appeared lost. "You with me, buddy?"

Striker did not answer for a long time. "What do you care? You got things straightened out."

"Razor, I *do* care. I care a lot."

The attorney hurried to his car.

Boldt ran after him. "Mikey . . ."

"Fuck you!" He climbed inside the car.

"Mike, listen —"

But the man drove away. Boldt chased the car on foot, calling after him, but pulled up short when he saw it was a lost cause. His son's three-wheeler was crashed into an azalea bush. He fished it out and carried it around back and left it with the other stuff. He could not believe the mountain of toys this kid had.

He saw Liz through the kitchen window, holding Miles. The boy had not stayed down. She was watching him with a worried expression. He shrugged. She shrugged right back.

"I've got to get going," he reminded her when he reached the kitchen. She opened her arm and the three of them hugged. Miles touched his father's face and nearly poked him in the eye.

"I'm sorry you have to go through this stuff." she said.

"There are always a couple of blowouts on a case like this. Always happens."

"So long as it isn't you," she said, holding to him tightly. "We're lucky," she added. She did not try to look into his eyes. "What do you think? About him?"

"I wouldn't want to be on the receiving end of that."

"This could make trouble for you, couldn't it?" she asked.

"It's all right," he answered. But she knew him better than that.

"Da-da?" Miles reached out for his father. "Go-fo-wak," he slurred.

Boldt stood him on his right shoe, and the boy clung to his thick leg as if it were a tree trunk.

"Go for a walk," Boldt announced. His son stared up happily into his eyes with unrequited love, and Boldt began walking him slowly around the kitchen, his son squealing with joy.

"Don't get him too worked up," Liz reminded, well aware that with Boldt leaving, she would have to face the terror of Miles on a roll.

Boldt wanted this and only this: to be in his kitchen on a summer night with these two people; to hear squeals of joy coming from his son. To be free of the Tin Man and Michael Striker and Adler's nine-thousand-square-foot estate. To play along with a Scott Hamilton cut when no one was listening.

A few minutes later he walked out to his car, climbed inside, and drove off. As he passed the house down the street and the sound grew louder, it seemed quite obvious that the laugh track was laughing at him.

THIRTY

"But did it help?" Liz asked from across the breakfast table.

The time-trap software had failed to make a difference the night before. Boldt said positively, "We got closer than we've been. Only a couple blocks away by the time the transaction ended." He did not like bringing his work home like this, to where Liz had an active interest in a case, but he owed her whatever she wanted to hear. "I'm told there's a pretty good chance the Bureau will partner up with us, which would mean more people and better gear. If that happens, I think we stand a chance." The phone rang. Liz did not move.

Boldt recognized the smooth French accent as belonging to Lucille Guillard. "Sergeant Boldt? I have something in my hands I believe you would very much like to see. You will please come to my office?"

Boldt was in the car fifteen minutes later. He hit horrible traffic, costing him another thirty to reach downtown. He had to sign in with a receptionist and wear a badge marked VISITOR, which was new since the last time.

Guillard wore a navy-blue suit with gold but-

432

tons, and a blouse with a French collar and white silk embroidery on the cuffs that looked like waves. Her hair was straightened and pulled back into a topknot, elongating her face and enhancing her eyes. She wore pale red lipstick that contrasted with her black skin and her white teeth. She offered him coffee; he asked for tea with three aspirin.

"Funny way to drink your tea," she said. She called in a male assistant and placed their orders with him, and she went looking for aspirin. A few minutes later, when all had been delivered, she shut her door and they were alone.

The blinds were open, and the view from the Pac-West Bank tower included the Westlake Center, with a thousand shoppers swarming in and out of it like bees on the hive. The Seattle sun poured over them like golden honey. A street juggler tossing pins into the air caught Boldt's attention. From this distance the pins looked like matchsticks.

She slipped something out of a folder, leaned forward across her desk, and declared: "Here is your extortionist."

The eight-by-ten black-and-white photograph that she handed Boldt was a grainy, slightly blurred image that at first glance looked like an astronaut wearing a black space suit. He donned his reading glasses, reducing some of the blurriness. Guillard explained, "This was recorded on stop-frame videotape during last

433

night's nine P.M. withdrawal. I did not know of it then or I should have mentioned it. The camera, you see, was installed just this last weekend."

The photograph was shot through a star-shaped form of spread fingers in the foreground, and behind it, a reflective surface — a motorcycle helmet, he realized — and the high, padded shoulders of a biker's black leather jacket. No face. No identifying features. His heart sank. Out of politeness, he studied the photo for a long minute and then put his glasses away.

"This person wore gloves," she pointed out.

"Tried to cover the plastic in case there was a camera," Guillard explained, "but you can see this was done a fraction too late. Some of our cameras are triggered by card access. Others, by motion detectors. I am guessing that this was a motion detector."

Out came the glasses again as he drew the photograph close to his face. The gloved hand had triggered the autofocus of the lens, which helped to explain why all else behind it was fuzzy. Very few people could get away with wearing gloves in summer without attracting attention or, at the very least, being remembered. A biker was the one exception. The helmet hid the face effectively. It confirmed his chase in the U district — they were, quite possibly, after a woman wearing a helmet.

"Are you certain you have the right photograph?" he asked.

She showed him the entire three-photo series. By the time the second shot had been taken by the hidden camera, there was nothing to be seen, the gloved hand having effectively screened the shot entirely; but at the bottom of the frame, where it showed the date and time and listed the ATM's reference location ID, there was now also a card number identified, and it did indeed match the card belonging to the dummy account. The third photograph was nearly identical to the second, except for the time stamp, which had progressed by several seconds.

"I know it's not much," she apologized.

"More than you might think," he said, trying to make the best out of precious little.

"So it's good."

"It's very good."

She seemed hesitant as she asked timidly, "May I express something that concerns me?"

"By all means."

"It is the cameras — their location. As I said, this camera just came on-line in the last few days. Because of this, it has yet to appear on any list here at the bank. You understand? No lists. None. And before this? This person has not once made a withdrawal from any ATM that has a security camera in place. Not one. You understand? Such coincidence is not possible. I am sorry — not possible. And that means this person has a copy of our most recent

ATM security list. Those with surveillance security are indicated on this list."

Understanding this, Boldt felt the first sinking sensation in a string of many. Would Harry Caulfield have access to such information? Definitely not. But Chris Danielson? Howard Taplin? Kenny Fowler? All had access to the information.

"Who has copies of this list?"

"Yes. I wrote these down. I thought of this also. Perhaps a dozen of us here at Pac-West. I have written down their names for you. All top executives. No one below executive vice president. Also, I should think that the companies that performed the installations would of course have record. Pac-West employees working at the particular branches during installation would know — but only about that specific branch. Ted Perch at NetLinQ would have a much more comprehensive list, I would think, encompassing all the ATMs in the entire Northwest region."

Anyone, Boldt realized, in or out of the bank.

"It means something," she said. "Do you think? This is significant, I feel."

"It means something," Boldt agreed. Once again, suspicion fell onto those around him. He called Fowler, and insisted they talk.

At lunchtime Boldt met Kenny Fowler in the Pikes Place Market, amid the bustle of swarming tourists searching out "Save the Whales" T-shirts, asparagus, and fresh salmon. The two men walked slowly atop pavers engraved with names of contributors whose donations had helped restore the open-air market. The tourists wore micro athletic shorts, neon rubber sandals showing lots of long leg, and filling the air with the distinctive smell of optimism: suntan lotion. There were big bellies and bigger chests, and Kodaks and nylon web leashes on the children under six. There was real money and plastic and unwieldy ice-cream cones and the smell of fish.

"That looks pretty awful," Boldt said, noticing the blister on the end of Fowler's index finger that he kept pushing as if he might pop it.

"That's what I get for smoking a roach with the lights off," Fowler teased, amused by his own joke. Fowler walked farther on before he told him, "My people drew a blank on Danielson. No big cash purchases, no real money problems. Pays his taxes. Pays his bills. Maybe a little short on social activities. I've got some of the paperwork for you in the car."

"What about surveillance?"

"He works out at the Body Shop every day, rain or shine — not the soap store, the gym." Boldt knew the place. SPD was given special discounts there. "He lost my guys a couple of times — which is not easy to do, I might add — but both times they reported it as their fault, not some maneuver by Danielson to avoid them. Middle of the day, both times."

"Any private life?"

"About the worst thing we've got on your boy is that he's a palm greaser. Calls the 900 numbers and likes to hear it real dirty. Likes to hear them describe things *in detail*. Frankly, I think he's oversexed."

"Background?"

"Bright kid. Good middle-class family. Father is an aerospace engineer. His mother is middle management at Nordstrom. Brother died as an innocent bystander in a gas-station holdup, which is supposed to explain his being a cop."

"Supposed to?"

"You know him better than I do. The guy is driven. 'Kay? He's not doing this for some dead bro, he's doing this for Chris Danielson. He wants a suit and a secretary and a gold badge, not nickel."

"Money?"

"He wouldn't take a kick, if that's what you mean. Do you think? I don't. Too ambitious. He's not going to risk that desk and secretary for a few lousy bucks."

"He's dirty, Kenny. I don't know how, but he's dirty."

"Not from what I've found, he isn't. You were smart not to go to IA with this — woulda made you look bad." They stopped in front of a fruit stand where the produce was stacked perfectly, flawless, and in beautiful groups of rich colors. Fowler bought an apple with a five-dollar bill, so they had to wait for change. When they were walking again, wedged in a claustrophobic stream of loudly talking tourists, Fowler reminded, "Mr. ATM burned us again last night. Go figure."

Fowler was as competitive as the next guy. Boldt elected not to share any of his meeting with Guillard. An uncomfortable silence resulted.

"You missed Mac's service," Fowler criticized.

"Did I?" Boldt had not realized this.

"Lisa wanted it over with. She's lucky there weren't no kids."

Boldt waited several steps and asked, "Was Mac on patrol that night or was he following Matthews?"

Fowler missed a step, though he covered it well by pretending he had stepped in something. "A person goes asking a question like that, you'd think it's *you* running into posts in the dark, not Matthews."

"Is that your answer?"

"The way I see my job in all of this, my primary responsibility — 'kay? — is looking out for number one, which in this case is Adler. We watch him pretty much round the clock, Lou. He don't like it, so we don't tell him. Mac had the woods that night. Bad draw."

"He was in the woods. On patrol." Boldt clarified.

"You got it."

"And Danielson's clean?" Boldt repeated skeptically.

"I can hear it in your voice, you don't believe me. 'Kay. So why'd you ask me to do this for you if you're not going to believe me anyway? You're pissing me off here, Lou. What? I'm not busy enough without your laundry? Trouble with you, Lou?" he asked rhetorically. "You want everything nice and clean. Square pegs in the square holes. But it ain't like that, pal." He was building a head of steam. A vein rose in his forehead. "Order out of chaos, all that shit. I remember you." They dodged around a street musician. Boldt threw a quarter in the guitar case. Seeing this, Fowler put a dollar in and took out fifty cents in change. "You want Danielson dirty because it fits some preconceived notion of yours. You want Taplin, too, judging from our last conversation. For all the looks you give her, maybe you want your face in Matthews's pussy." Boldt stopped cold. "How the hell do I know? But it ain't that way, Lou. The square peg never fits. Danielson's *not* dirty. And it's Adler riding Matthews, not you. There's no fucking order to it, Lou. It's random — it has *always* been random. No fucking way to make things fit. *That* is your problem."

"You've got a foul mouth, Kenny."

"And a dirty mind," Fowler added. "But Danielson is still clean."

"No he's not, *pal*. You just don't like being

440

wrong. And you knew your guys screwed this up somewhere." Boldt turned and walked away. Fowler had drilled too close to the nerve. He counted to ten, and then he counted to ten again. He wanted a drink. He wanted some food. He wanted to go back and pop Fowler in the face. Or maybe he wanted Fowler to pop him. He wanted some order where none existed. He walked for three hours before returning to his car.

And he had blisters in the morning.

THIRTY-ONE

Friday morning Dr. Richard Clements left voice mail for Boldt informing him that the Seattle field office of the FBI had been in touch with the Hoover Building and that the Bureau was sending Boldt seventy-five Special Agents and providing a digital tracking and communications package. A man named Meisner wanted to speak via a conference call with Boldt and Shoswitz about logistics.

Slater Lowry had been dead three weeks.

Boldt jotted down some notes to himself while riding the elevator to the second floor. His feet hurt too much to take the stairs. Another piece of voice mail had been from Bernie Lofgrin.

He entered the lab and signaled its director from across the room. Lofgrin carefully removed a pair of goggles and caught up with the sergeant in his office. The goggles left a dark red line in the shape of a kidney bean encircling his eyes and bridging his nose. His thinning gray hair was a mess, much of it sticking straight up. He patted it down, but it jumped right up again, charged with static electricity. He looked like a cockatoo.

442

The office had been tidied, though it could not be considered neat. Boldt took a chair.

"Clements must have leaned on the Bureau," Lofgrin said as he closed the door for privacy. "At seven o'clock this morning our fax machine started humming. When the Feds issue reports, they don't mess around. With all this paperwork," he said. indicating an impressive stack of faxes on the desk, "it's no wonder it takes them a month of Sundays to get back to us."

Lofgrin settled into his seat and switched on the tape of Scott Hamilton at Radio City that Boldt had copied for him. The sergeant felt impatient, knowing full well that all indications pointed to a Bernie Lofgrin lecture.

Lofgrin cleaned his Coke-bottle eyeglasses, carefully rubbing them with a special soft cloth, and returned them to his face. He leaned forward. "Do you know what we call the volatilizing chamber on our gas chromatograph?" The process of gas chromatography involved burning — *volatilizing* — a sample and analyzing the gases emitted in order to determine the organic and chemical compounds that comprised it.

Boldt shook his head. Lofgrin's jokes were famous for falling flat.

"The ash-hole."

Lofgrin loved it; he bubbled with pleasure. Boldt felt obliged to twist a smile onto his lips, but found it impossible to maintain it. Foremost on his mind was Caulfield's threat

— as yet, that dreaded call had still not come in.

"The ash-hole uses helium injection and weighs in at nearly twice the temp of your standard arson," Lofgrin explained. Boldt had heard most of this before. He did not care about method; he wanted results. "Thirty-five hun and up. We reburn elements in the ash that weren't torched the first time around, and the gases allow us to identify all but the inert compounds."

Seeing Boldt's lack of interest, Lofgrin said, "Okay — I'm lecturing again. Sue me. Caulfield had several boxes under his workbench. We've identified them as cardboard. You and I discussed that we had some supportive evidence that three of these boxes may have contained paper products — labels, leaflets, who knows? The cardboard in those boxes is apparently from the same manufacturer — a set, if you will. Produced by Everest Forest Products up to Anacortes. Everest has clients all over the state — but I have a list," he said, digging into the pile and handing Boldt a fax. It was several pages long and listed over two hundred clients. "About seventy of those clients have their company logo printed on the boxes before final shipment. Seventeen of those seventy have zip codes here in the city." He grinned and teased, "And I bet you thought you were the only one who loves detective work."

Boldt asked anxiously, "And do we know if

444

the boxes at Longview Farms were printed or not?"

"We do not *know* anything conclusively. We're talking about the examination of *ash*, Lou. Our tests *suggest* that these boxes were the unprinted, generic variety. And that means they could have been supplied to any one of the other one hundred and thirty Everest clients."

Boldt's hopes waffled.

"The FBI techs have turned up a mixed bag. In all three boxes we show pulp fiber inconsistent with the production of the cardboard, meaning there is a high probability that all three contained paper products." Reading another of the Bureau's faxes, Lofgrin said, "In one of the boxes we find the presence of bleach and heavy metals consistent with some commercial inks — commercial printing techniques. In the other two, we show trace quantities of organics that suggest, but do not confirm, what we usually see in herbal inks —"

"Adler uses herbal inks," Boldt reminded.

"Yes. That *had* occurred to me." Lofgrin did not like being interrupted.

"Sorry," Boldt apologized.

When Lofgrin's enlarged eyes blinked, Boldt felt as if the man were waving at him. Lofgrin said, "*Knowing* that Adler uses herbal inks on his labels, we asked for a comparison, and you'll be pleased to know that the ink found in these two boxes at Longview is consistent with that used on Adler labels. We cannot differentiate

445

between say a chicken soup label and a hash label, but we can say with some degree of certainty that the labels in those two boxes could have been Adler Foods labels.

"What is of interest to us," he continued, "is that the contents of this other box — the one with the heavy metal content — have nothing whatsoever to do with the labels of Adler Foods products. Did I mention that because of a nice stratification, the Bureau lab was able to approximate paper size?"

"No."

"Well, I told you how when we exposed the contents of these boxes to oxygen, they basically disintegrated. The Bureau boys have a vacuum chamber large enough for something like this, and they were able to pull accurate measurements for us. And those measurements also support the assumption that two of the boxes were Adler labels, and one not. So, basically, of the three boxes with paper products, two conform to what we see in Adler products and one does not."

"A different company," Boldt suggested.

Lofgrin nodded. "Right. And by the size and shape, they could very well be labels from another company's product. Whether or not it is food, we can't say."

"It's food," Boldt said.

"One other element of interest to you," he said, spinning to face his computer. "And this was sent via the proverbial new information

446

superhighway — which we just happen to have been using for the past eight *years,* I might add . . . and there's a hard copy to follow by express courier . . . " He clicked through some files, explaining, "The Bureau people got a beauty of a photograph of a sample in what I'm calling the heavy metal box. While inside the vacuum chamber, no less? I wish to hell we had this kind of gear . . ." The screen went completely blank, and lines slowly drew across the screen until what looked like a piece of a jigsaw puzzle appeared. Lofgrin stepped the computer through several moves, and the piece enlarged. He said, "This is a piece of what we believe to be one of the labels in the heavy metal box. It's tiny, only a few centimeters square — a flake is all — but notice the colors."

With the next enlargement, the colors became apparent: red, yellow, and blue. Strong, primary colors.

Boldt, leaning over Lofgrin's shoulder, asked for the crime scene photographs from Longview Farms.

"Color or black-and-white?"

"Color."

It took Lofgrin a few minutes to locate the photos. When he returned to the office, he rewound the Scott Hamilton tape to his favorite ballad.

While Boldt leafed through the dozens of eight-by-tens, he grabbed the phone and tele-

447

phoned upstairs to LaMoia. "Find someone at Adler Foods who can tell us who does their label printing. Fowler was handling that for us, but I don't want to involve him."

"Don't want to involve him, or don't want him to know?" LaMoia asked.

"Both," Boldt answered. He told him he could be reached in Lofgrin's office, and hung up.

While it was on his mind, and while still leafing through the dozens of Longview crime scene photographs, Boldt said to the lab man, "I need an opinion."

"That's my middle name."

"If I take a bobby pin and insert it into an electrical outlet, and I'm wearing gloves, would there be enough heat to burn through the glove *and* get my finger?"

"This is not something you want to experiment with," Lofgrin teased, though serious. "If you're *lucky*, all you'll come away with is a burned finger. If they're thin gloves, if the curcuit is carrying a lot of amps, maybe your heart stops, too, and then you're all Dixie's."

Kenny Fowler's fingertip had been burned. He had made a joke about it to Boldt, but something he had said later in their conversation about Daphne's head injury continued to trouble Boldt.

"Here it is!" Boldt passed the photograph to the lab man.

Lofgrin's head rose slowly, his eyes suddenly the size of dinner plates. Little Orphan Lofgrin,

Boldt thought. In a hushed voice, uncommon in the confident Lofgrin, the man said, "Same colors."

He set the photograph down. It showed the cement floor of the slaughterhouse — a blend of spray paints in a rigidly straight line left by the removal of a drop cloth intended to catch the paints.

Boldt said, "Yellow, blue, and red." He held the color photograph up to the computer screen, and the colors matched nearly perfectly.

The phone rang. Boldt snatched it up first and barked his name into the receiver. LaMoia's voice said, "Grambling Printers, here in the city."

Boldt's stubby finger, with its dirty fingernail, ran down the customer list for Everest Forest Products and came to a quick stop at the end of the *G*'s: *Grambling Printers.*

"It's here," he said to LaMoia. "Get a car ready." He hung up the phone. Boldt kissed Lofgrin on the forehead. "You're a genius."

"Lou?" Lofgrin asked, scrubbing his forehead vigorously.

Boldt's voice cracked as he said, "Caulfield's threat — to kill hundreds. It's for real. The strychnine, another food company's labels, spray painting a truck — maybe a delivery truck — he's got everything in place."

"So what's the *good* news?" Lofgrin asked.

Boldt hoisted the photograph. "We've got these colors."

★ ★ ★

LaMoia drove a white Pontiac with privacy glass. The vehicle had been confiscated by SPD in a porn video bust. It had custom, wire-spoke aluminum wheels and a red velour interior, the backseat of which folded down and converted into an impressive bed. It was said to be featured in several of the videos, though only Special Ops and some attorneys had ever viewed them. This was the car that LaMoia drove regularly and had since been dubbed the Pimpmobile by his colleagues. He called it Sweetheart, as in, "Let's take Sweetheart," or "I gave Sweetheart a bubble bath and a wax today." He treated it better than he did some of his friends.

From behind the wheel, LaMoia queried Boldt. "Fowler already ran the mug shot by all the Adler printers, right?"

"In theory."

"Meaning?"

"What a guy like Fowler tells you he does, what he does, and what he gets from whatever he does are all different animals. He's got a company to protect. He's working for people."

"Kenny Fowler hosed us?"

"Kenny has some explaining to do. He's been putting his nose where it doesn't belong. My guess is that it's just competitive bullshit — trying to keep a step ahead. But if I'm right, it's ugly stuff. Dirty. The kind of stuff you can't forgive him, whatever the motivation."

LaMoia pulled the car to an abrupt stop,

450

forcing Boldt to brace himself against the fringe-covered dash. "Nice driving," Boldt said.

"Need the brakes adjusted."

The office was all cheap furniture and bowling trophies. Boldt pushed the door shut. It rubbed against the floor, requiring an extra shove. There was a skim of oil on the vinyl seats from fast-food bags. He and LaMoia remained standing.

"Does this man look familiar?" Boldt asked, passing Caulfield's mug shot to Raymond Fioné.

"Never seen him before," the man said bluntly. Fioné made it clear that he did not like cops.

"Look again," Boldt encouraged.

"My vision's fine."

"A minimum-wage job. Maybe you just haven't seen him around."

"Listen. It's true, Sergeant . . ." He searched for the name. "Blot?"

Boldt corrected his name.

"Sure — I spend nearly every waking hour with my head buried in a damn computer screen. Who doesn't these days? It's like the lead in the Roman pipes, right? Machines this smart, they're going to make us all dumb. But I sure as shit know who's on my payroll, and this guy here is *not* one of them."

"Do you run your own deliveries?"

"With the insurance what it is? Hell no."

"So maybe he trucks your product."

"Maybe he does," Fioné agreed, "so what the fuck do I care?"

451

"You care," LaMoia said.

Fioné glared.

Boldt asked, "Who delivers the Adler product for you?"

"They're a good customer of ours, Adler is. Listen, Fowler and I already did this dance. Okay? What I'm supposed to say? You want I should *lie* to you? Tell me."

"Who delivers the Adler product?"

Fioné answered, "Pacer handles *all* our shipping."

LaMoia wrote it down.

Taking a wild guess, Boldt handed the mug shot back to Fioné and said, "This man applied for a job with you." He paused. Fioné's face flushed and he would not look at either of them. "He had a prison record. He was fresh out of prison and you turned him down."

The man spoke to the desk. "He was wired. All hyped up, you know? I didn't like the guy." He braved a look at Boldt. "Is that a crime?"

"But you didn't tell Fowler that."

"He didn't ask."

LaMoia said, "You had to get rid of him, so you gave him the name of another company."

"No. Nothing like that. I got rid of him. That's all."

Boldt said, "Are Pacer's colors red, yellow, and blue?"

"No," the man answered. "Black and green, I think."

452

Boldt tried again. "One of your customers, then. A food product company uses red, yellow, and blue in their labels."

"You remember first grade, Sergeant Blot? The primary colors are in every other color," he instructed.

"Just those colors. *Only* the primary colors. Red. Yellow. Blue. One of your food accounts uses just those colors."

"Food companies are our specialty — our niche. All right? You know how many there are in this state? You know how many customers we have?" Fioné asked rhetorically, answering, "Maybe sixty or seventy. You know how often those customers change their designs, their colors, their look? You expect me to identify one of our customers by their colors? Do you know *anything* about this business?"

"Heavy metals," Boldt stated.

"My son listens to that shit," Fioné said.

LaMoia stepped closer, "Not the music, asshole. Ink."

The man looked ready to fight. "Heavy metals? Those aren't in your primary colors — those are your silvers and golds, your foils."

Boldt said, "So okay. How about a customer of yours that uses red, blue, yellow, *and* a foil? Does that clarify matters for you?"

Fioné warned, "If you're going to treat me like some ignorant asshole, you can go suck wind, far as I'm concerned, Sergeant. The door is right behind you. You got it?"

He turned back to his computer and started typing.

LaMoia checked with Boldt, who nodded, then the detective stepped forward and spun the man around in his chair. He leaned in close and said with intentional dramatics, "We're with Homicide, *asshole*. There's some guy killing people, and *your* labels are part of it, and that could drag you in deep. We need some fucking answers here. *Right now!* You *got* it?"

The man's face went scarlet. He met eyes with Boldt, and looked back at LaMoia. "I'll pull the artwork for you."

Back in the garish car, LaMoia asked, "Where to?"

"Let's say you're Caulfield. You're out on parole, and you're determined to make Adler pay. First place you apply for a job —"

"Is Adler Foods."

"But you're turned down — let's say because of your record. Next?" Boldt asked, while at the same time seeing the fallacy of keeping Caulfield's name away from Fowler and Taplin, and regretting that decision.

"You go to the source: Grambling Printers."

"But they turn you down, too. No one wants you."

"You find out who trucks the labels. You try to go to work for them, or maybe you steal a couple of boxes out of the back when the driver's in making another delivery."

"Exactly. And you put the boxes under your workbench," Boldt said. "And you go to work."

"Pacer Trucking?" LaMoia asked.

"I'll call for the address."

LaMoia and Bobbie Gaynes kept the south entrance of Pacer Trucking under surveillance while the back entrance was covered by Freddie Guccianno, back from vacation, and Don Chun, on loan to Shoswitz from Major Crimes.

Boldt and Daphne waited for Jerry Pacer in a booth at a Denny's restaurant. Daphne ordered an English muffin with cream cheese. Boldt ordered a hot dog with everything, fries, and a side of cottage cheese. Pacer arrived and took coffee with cream and sugar and made them switch to a smoking table. He had basset hound eyes and a double chin, and his hair seemed to be two different colors, indicating a rug. He was the kind of man who would be bored in the middle of an earthquake.

He handed Boldt an employment form for Harold Caulfield. Boldt recognized the residential address as a rooming house by the community college. Only a matter of blocks from the Broadway Foodland, it was within the designated area where Dr. Richard Clements had stated the killer would be found.

Pacer took one quick glance at the mug shot and pointed to it. "He's younger, but that's him." His voice sounded like a cement mixer

455

slowed down. "Are we done now? I got trucks to move."

Boldt felt both the surge of excitement and the wash of relief. He felt a knot in his throat. He felt like laughing.

She said, "You don't seem too surprised."

"In this business, lady? What do you think, I deal with college grads? I probably know more cops than you do." He added: "We done?"

"Is he on the schedule today?" Boldt asked hopefully.

"Wouldn't matter he is or he isn't. Not working for me, this kid. No calls, no nothing. Just stood me up. Happens all the time, but it still pisses me off. You figure they're in trouble when they don't even pick up the back pay. His is sitting in on my desk. So I wasn't exactly shocked and stunned to get your call. That's what I mean. I really can't help you. Is that all? Can I get back now? Please?" he added sarcastically.

"Stay," Boldt said firmly, waving the hot dog at the seat. Some mustard dripped onto the table.

Pacer sighed heavily and glared at him indignantly. Boldt realized the man had indeed spent a lot of time with police when he began answering questions without being asked. "This kid was okay. All right? So why do the cops care?"

"Did he socialize with the other drivers?" she asked.

"No. A loner. So what? I ain't much for beveraging, either."

"What kind of cat do you have?" Boldt asked. He liked throwing questions that broke a person's train of thought. Pacer had cat hairs all over the sleeves of his shirt.

The man's face twisted, and only part of his hair moved. Definitely a rug, Boldt realized. "Just a street cat is all. What's it matter?"

"What's its name?" Boldt asked between bites. He was starving.

The man shrugged. "Trix. Trixie. What the hell's my cat got to do with this?" He asked this of Daphne, who returned his shrug.

"Any inventory ever missing from Caulfield's trucks?" Boldt asked.

"Stuff gets mixed up all the time."

"But Caulfield in particular?"

"Hell, I don't know."

"Is there a way to check that?"

"We got manifests, we got paperwork up the ying yang, if that's what you're asking."

"So it could be checked," Boldt stated.

"Not by my people, it couldn't," Jerry Pacer said defensively. "Not on my nickel."

"But you would supply us the paperwork," Daphne suggested. "Without a lot of attorneys."

"No problem whatsoever."

"Do you file invoices by driver?" Boldt added.

"No way. We file by customer. Our drivers mix up the routes, because some damn insurance study showed that it reduced accidents. I gotta tell you, I think it works, but as far as administration goes, it's a real pain in the ass." He checked his watch. "You gotta understand, the place goes to shit without me this time of day. Can we speed this up any?"

Boldt pretended not to hear him. "One of your clients is Grambling Printers."

"Whatever you say."

"And is the Grambling work invoiced by Grambling customer, by specific delivery, or all grouped together?"

"Grouped. We contract out to a lot of outfits. They handle their paperwork, we handle ours."

"We want that paperwork," Boldt reiterated.

Indicating Daphne, Pacer said, "Already taken care of. Come on! Let me out of here."

Daphne tried: "One of the companies you ship for uses a logo or a name — I can't remember — of red, yellow, and blue. The three colors by themselves. Maybe some silver or gold in there."

"Hell if I know."

"Think!" Boldt said, too impatiently.

The rebuke rattled Pacer. He played with the salt shaker sliding it between his hands like a hockey puck. "I don't know. Sounds more like fruit and vegetable crates to me. Del Monte, you know? Some of the truck farmers. Eye-catching shit. Flowers maybe. We don't do no produce."

Boldt and Daphne met eyes, and Boldt started

sliding out the booth, reaching for his wallet as he went.

"What?" Pacer asked, tentatively.

Daphne offered him a business card and told him, "We need the Grambling paperwork immediately. Right now. Right away."

"I understand the word *immediately*. It's my drivers can't read, not me."

"We'll have it?"

"You'll have it."

Pacer stood, uncertain and confused. He swept a hand over his rug, ensuring it was still in place. He nodded and headed out of the restaurant at a fast pace. Boldt flagged the waitress, while stuffing the hot dog down.

"Produce," Daphne declared. "Truck farmers. He could be out there anywhere, selling spinach out of a pickup."

During the summer months, truck farmers proliferated on Washington's back roads, interstate rest areas, and downtown parking lots.

"Buy it, shoot it up with strychnine, and sell it off the back of your truck. He keeps moving, he keeps killing."

"Or deliver it to grocery stores."

"Or restaurants."

His pager sounded. Reluctantly, he reached down and shut it off, not wanting to read its tiny LCD display and whatever information was contained there. Just the sound of the device turned Boldt's stomach; it was actually *worse* than a telephone ringing.

Boldt read the code on the display. He felt the blood drain from his face, and his hands go cold.

"Lou?"

He stole Daphne's purse, rummaged through it, and removed her cellular phone. He called downtown, and the moment the dispatcher answered, he spoke his name clearly, "Boldt," though to him it sounded like somebody else talking. "Who is it?" He waited to hear the answer, then shut off the phone and handed it back to Daphne, his hand visibly shaking.

She grabbed his pager from him and read the display. "An officer down?" she said, her voice wavering. There was nothing so painful as this for any cop. "Who?"

"Striker just shot Chris Danielson in a hotel room over on Fourth."

THIRTY-TWO

Boldt had been to over a hundred such crime scenes, but with his friends and coworkers involved, this hotel room looked somehow different. Shoswitz had assigned Sergeant David Pasquini as primary in the officer-involved shooting, and Boldt tried to stay out of the man's way.

According to a uniform by the door, Danielson had gone out on a stretcher, alive but critical; Striker was in handcuffs, ranting and raving about what a lousy shot he was.

There was a good amount of blood on the bed, and two piles of clothes on chairs, with Danielson's weapon still snapped into its holster. Four shells had been discharged onto the carpet. An ID man was taking photographs of them. The air still smelled of cordite. Boldt crossed the room and glanced out the window. Downstairs on the street, a media circus was brewing.

"Where's that coffee?" Pasquini shouted after cracking open the bathroom door a few inches.

Boldt, back at the room's entrance, grabbed the green Starbucks coffee from the patrolman and delivered it himself, inching the door open

461

with his foot and not allowing Pasquini to get full hold of it.

"Okay," Pasquini said, relenting, and admitting Boldt to the tiny bathroom.

Elaine Striker, wearing a hotel towel wrapped around her middle, sat on the closed toilet. A woman officer was braced in the tub, a notepad in hand.

Boldt pushed the door shut.

Pasquini removed the lid from the coffee and handed it to the woman, who used both hands to steady the cup before taking a sip.

Elaine had mascara on her cheeks, bloodshot eyes, and a mottled chest. Her skin was freckled — a good deal of it showing — and her tousled red hair framed her face in a ring of fire. She looked up at Boldt with hollow, apologetic eyes. "It just happened," she said.

Pasquini wanted her talking to him, not Boldt. "He had a key?"

"He came in without us knowing. We were . . . busy. He must have just stood there watching." She broke down crying. Pasquini shook his head impatiently and took the cup from her as she spilled some coffee across her hands. Boldt offered her a towel. She dried off her hands, tucked herself into the towel that was wrapped around her, and looked back up at both policemen. "Chris sat up, and Mike started firing."

Boldt could see the blood in her hair. There was some on the left of her neck, too. And

462

only then did he notice the small pile of blood-stained washcloths used to clean her up.

"How many shots?" Pasquini asked.

"No idea."

"One? Ten?"

"More than one. Several. And then Chris —" She broke down again. Boldt had heard enough. He leaned in closely to her, offered some reassurance, and took her hand as she reached out to him. It took a few seconds to win his hand free again, and he left.

Using an address listed on Caulfield's employment form with Pacer Trucking, warrants were issued to search the rooming house, and that afternoon seventeen uniformed and plainclothes officers descended on Caulfield's room like a swarm of bees. A check of records confirmed that Caulfield had moved out of the hotel the day following the murder of Sheriff Turner Bramm — a date Boldt could not get out of his mind. Since that time, the room had been home to a grunge musician and his girlfriend, destroying any chance the lab techs would recover anything of use — and nothing admissible in a court of law. Boldt was reviewing the search with Shoswitz and Lofgrin when Daphne entered the lieutenant's office and said, "I can get us into Striker."

The nurses in Harborview's psych ward knew Daphne by name, and allowed them to bypass much of the red tape usually required. Even so, before being allowed into the ward that housed Michael Striker's barren hospital room, she and Boldt were required to leave behind their weapons, badges, belts, pens and pencils, and Boldt's shoelaces. This was their first indication of Striker's condition. Daphne had stretched the truth to gain them access so quickly, saying she was here for "a session" with the suspect, and explaining Boldt's presence as "some protection." After the shooting, Michael Striker had broken a patrolman's arm before jumping into traffic in an apparent act of suicide. This, she explained to Boldt, was the reason for his admission to the psych ward, and his doctor's refusal for police interrogation. A male nurse unlocked and then relocked the door behind them.

Striker had cut up his legs by running into traffic, though nothing was broken. He was under physical restraints. And Daphne informed Boldt in a whisper that he was also mildly sedated.

"Hey," Boldt said, trying to sound casual.

The room's mood was grim. In place of a real window, there was an electronic contraption mounted to the wall that emitted light and offered an incredibly lifelike pastoral view of the Canadian Rockies.

"So I can't jump out," Striker informed him from his bed. "They pay ten grand for those things. Supposed to help improve your state of mind." He grinned thinly at this. "Suppos-

464

edly, the thing even does sunrise and sunset."
He wore a blue-and-white hospital gown that
used Velcro instead of ties, to eliminate the
chance of hanging oneself. Striker had sad, lifeless eyes. He had hollow, drawn cheeks and
bulging eyes that indeed made him look a little
crazy.

"They've got so much shit in me," he said,
"that I'm basically a walking pharmacy. Check
that," he corrected. "I'm not doing much walking." He tugged at his strapped-down arms.

Daphne spoke with him for the better part
of twenty minutes, through which she remained
incredibly calm and Striker slowly began to
make some sense.

"Listen," he said, in what sounded to Boldt
like the man's familiar intolerant attorney voice,
"I was out of my gourd to do what I did.
And that includes diving for the grille of that
truck. But it's over now, and I feel *great*. Valium
is a wonderful thing."

"Can you tell us about it?" Daphne asked.

"What's to tell? The guy was fucking my
wife; so I fucked him." His cheek twitched
and he asked Boldt to scratch his neck for
him.

Boldt said, "You found him with Elaine. Is
that it, Mikey?"

"You warned me, Lou. I know that. I thought
about that right after I did it, too."

"But you followed her anyway."

"Sort of. Right."

465

"Is there something you want to tell us?" Daphne asked. Boldt felt the avoidance in the man, too, and it impressed him that Daphne seized upon it so quickly.

"Jergenson was the house dick. Remember Jergenson, Lou? I offered him a fifty, and he said how it was on the house because catching people fucking was part of his job, and he remembered me. People don't forget this," he said, indicating his prosthesis. "The one shrink I've seen made a big deal about my mitt. Talked a lot about manhood and what I tried to do to Danielson. No offense, Matthews, but the guy is full of shit."

"I'm not a shrink," she said.

Boldt was not sure if Striker even heard that. He did seem pretty stoned.

"It had a lot less to do with my mitt than it did with my dick and my heart. She tore my heart out is what she did. Especially at the end there: She wasn't trying to hide it at all. Just wave it in my face and head out the door all dolled up. Came home smelling like love. Jesus."

"So Jergenson let you in."

"Right."

"How did you know which room, Mikey?"

He looked over at the Canadian Rockies, and when he did, Daphne shot Boldt a quick look of apprehension.

"And he was . . . And you should have seen her . . . He had her on another planet. He

466

had her so far gone that I'm not sure she even recognized me. Know what I mean?"

Boldt could sense it, and he thought Daphne could as well — that was what that look had been about, though he felt at a loss as to how to get at it. This was her territory; he felt more like a spectator, and yet Striker seemed more comfortable talking to him. He did not look at Daphne at all.

"Did this man Jergenson know your wife?" she asked.

"Nah. He was a beat cop once upon a time. Spent his last years as a court guard. That's how I knew him. I'm surprised you don't remember him."

Daphne inquired, "So it wasn't he who told you where to find your wife."

Boldt asked, "Did you follow her? Was that it?"

"It's not what's important," replied the attorney authoritatively. "They were in the act. Boy, were they. And I caught the bastard, and I blew him away. What little shooting I've done in my life was done right-handed. If I hadn't had this," he said, indicating his prosthesis, "I'da hit the target."

They remained silent.

"Not easy to shoot left-handed is it, Lou? You ever done it?"

"I'm still a little confused about something, Razor," Boldt said. "When we talked out in front of my house, you said that you weren't comfortable following her. You asked me to do it for you. So did you change your mind, is that it?"

"You're missing the point," Striker repeated, avoiding an answer, attempting to use his attorney skills that were considerably dulled by the drugs coursing through him. "I had to have proof. Can you understand that? I'd been through her dirty laundry — and I don't mean that figuratively; I had asked questions and had studied her carefully for her reactions — it's my job to spot the guilty. I knew I was getting lies, and there were times she would come home and completely avoid touching me until she'd had a bath or a shower, and when you see enough of that, you no longer wonder what's going on. But I had to *know*. That's just part of who I am. I've *got* to know."

"Is there something you would like to share with us about how you identified the particular hotel?" she asked.

Boldt felt warm, and the room was not warm. Not unless that fake window was responsible. He felt anxious, because Striker was incredibly nervous, and the sergeant knew that if the claw had not been tied shut, it would have been chirping away.

"I've fucked things up for you," Striker apologized.

Boldt said, "I've always wished I could throw you a curveball, Razor, but I've seen people try it in court and I've seen you blow them

468

away, so I'd just as soon lay it right out there."

"Do it."

"Who did you hire to follow Elaine?"

Striker shook his head like a person who had a bug caught in his hair. Boldt took inventory of Daphne, who gave him a slight shake of the head, indicating for him to let Striker be. Her eyes said, Don't push.

Striker took a moment to recover. This was the first time he met eyes with Daphne, and she sensed in him a hatred of all women, and took this as normal. She offered, "I can leave the room if you like."

"No. It's not that." He looked at Boldt. "I didn't hire anyone, Lou. It wasn't like that."

"Okay, so you didn't hire anyone. After you spoke with me, did you *ask* someone else in the department to do this for you, or maybe one of the investigators in your office? Someone like that? No curveballs, Razor. I'm putting it to you straight: you *have* screwed things up for me. I need *answers*."

"I received a call."

Boldt glanced over and met eyes with Daphne as she sat forward in her chair. "A call?" Boldt asked, as calmly as he could force his voice to sound.

"I received a telephone call telling me that if I was looking for Elaine, I could find her in room four-seventeen."

"Male or female?"

"Elaine is female, Lou." This was the medication talking, and though Striker chuckled for a little too long, Boldt waited him out.

"Male," Striker answered.

"Did you recognize the voice?"

"No, I did not." He seemed a little bored, a little let down in himself for talking about this.

"But you believed him. You went there prepared to shoot a man."

"I didn't think about it. I was on autopilot." He laughed more strongly this time. "You know, I've put guys away for twenty years who tried that line on me! Talk about the tables turning!" He hesitated and said, "You're messing with my head here, Lou, because I hear what you're saying to me. You're saying someone fed me that phone call knowing damn well that I'd go and blow the guy away. Counting on me to do it. And if you don't mind, right now that's a little much for me, okay? Because I know what people think about my temper — I mean, it's no secret."

Boldt asked, "When did you receive this phone call?"

"A little after ten."

"At the office?"

"Yeah, the office."

"And is that number published?"

Striker nodded. "I see what you're getting at, Lou, but it's no good. I didn't recognize the voice. I'm being straight with you on that."

"You were set up, Razor," Boldt informed

470

the man. "Someone wanted you or Danielson or *both* of you out of the way."

"Yeah?" Striker said angrily. "Well, I couldn't care less about that. If I got that phone call again, I would go right back there and finish up what I started. I swear I would. My one and only one regret is that I *missed*. I wasn't aiming to *kill* him. A PA knows the difference between assault and murder one. But I missed, goddamn it. Four shots and I couldn't hit the damn thing. Four damn tries. Not that it was very big anyway. So much for the myth — I'm here to tell you."

At first the laughter seemed all right, though Daphne looked concerned. And then Boldt realized that the laughter would not quit, and after a minute it frightened him, because Striker had lost all control. He was crying and laughing and looking at them desperately as though he did not understand where it came from and that they should pull the plug and shut off the machine. He was laughing ten minutes later, when the male nurse kicked them out and delivered a shot of something that Daphne said would take care of it. But it did not. When they reached the car, Boldt imagined he could still hear the man's laughter, as if it had penetrated the electronic window, reverberating down to the parking lot below. Even the car door closing did not shut it out for Boldt. And he told Daphne this.

"You know what those two words are together?" she asked, placing the car in reverse. "*Man's laughter?* Combined?" she asked. "What we witnessed up there is how most of them pay for it."

Boldt combined the words in his head and spoke softly: "Manslaughter."

She said, "Michael Striker has a long road ahead of him."

He placed his hand on hers and stopped her from backing up the car. "How good is your memory?" he asked, taking his hand away.

"You know damn well that I pride myself on it."

"I forget who it was," Boldt said, "but someone told me that the bump on your forehead was from a box coming down off a shelf."

"That was Lofgrin or LaMoia or Bobbie. They were the only ones who asked." She said, "It's after seven, aren't you supposed to be over at NetLinQ? You want me to drop you?"

Boldt asked, "Why? Why did you invent the box coming down?"

"Because we agreed to keep my break-in at the houseboat between us, and trying to explain running into a post in the dark was a little much. It was a white lie, Lou. So what?" Again she asked, "You want me to drop you or not?"

"And what about Fowler? If you told the others one thing, why tell Fowler something different?"

"I've never told Fowler anything about it. I've hardly *seen* the man since then."

472

"But he's seen you," Boldt said. And her face froze. "I made him nervous with a question, and in trying to get out of it, he made reference to your hitting that post." He hesitated. "So how did he know?"

"Exactly *what* are you saying?" Her lips quivered and she crossed her arms tightly. She knew.

"When they put in your security system, they swept your house for bugs, right?"

She gasped. "Fowler's people."

Bear Berenson had told him that some people could feel the camera's presence. Boldt said, "But that feeling never went away, did it?"

She threw her head back as if to keep her tears from running. "*Why?*" She choked out.

"Longview Farms," Boldt answered.

She looked over and met eyes with Boldt and tried to speak, but nothing came out.

"I've got an idea," Boldt said.

The device looked like a small squash racquet, or an electric charcoal starter, though it worked more like one of those hand-held metal detectors used at airports. The people in Technical Services referred to it simply as Clark, for Clark Kent, he of the X-ray vision. There was said to be a flyswatter variety, and another in the form of a feather duster that came with a four-foot extension, both of which could be used without telegraphing that the room was being swept for electronic bugs. Detective Laura Battles carried Clark in her briefcase; a wire ran to her ear and would emit a beep if a bug were encountered.

Once activated, a microprocessor inside the device continuously checked for magnetic fields caused by hidden microphones, and was said to be 95 percent effective in detecting them. It was less dependable in the detection of fiber-optic cameras, the latest generation of which were smaller than a shirt button and emitted no magnetic field whatsoever. But Clark, through some advanced technology that no one had ever bothered to attempt to explain to Boldt, scored in the 67 percentile in this department as well.

Daphne, accompanied by Battles, entered through the houseboat's front door — and by agreement, already in the midst of a real estate discussion. Daphne the seller, Laura Battles the agent. They toured the houseboat room to room. Battles took detailed notes on a clipboard — the studious type.

Back in the parking lot where he had waited, she told them both, "The place is a floating sound studio. Sorry, Daphne," she apologized. Checking her notes, she informed them, "Audio in the galley, sitting area, head, bedroom, back deck, top deck, and telephone line." She hesitated, uncomfortable with this. "Fiber-optic in the bathroom, sitting room, and bedroom." Daphne sank to the gravel. Boldt tried to catch her, but she fought him off. Battles said, "Most of them these days are infrared, night-vision, sensitive."

"Everything," Daphne stated. She looked up at Boldt with eyes he had never witnessed in her. He said, "We'll want to keep them in place, I think." She sprang to her feet and began hitting Boldt ferociously. He tried to hold her off, but she was hurting him, and as Laura Battles climbed out of the car, Daphne threw her knee into the car door, turned, and threw her knee into Boldt's crotch and sent him down to the gravel. He heard her say, "Oh my God!" and then her feet took off at a run.

Laura Battles helped him up and seemed more bothered by the dent in her car door than Boldt's condition. They drove around the neighborhood for the better part of an hour and checked the houseboat twice. "I'll keep looking," Battles offered.

Boldt was due for yet another night at NetLinQ. And this time, he had an army at his disposal.

Another night spent at NetLinQ passed without success, the main problems being logistical. With so many people added to the surveillance team, and virtually overnight, tracking them and deploying them proved a technical nightmare. It left Boldt watching technicians switch wires and install sophisticated radio receivers while the extortionist walked

475

away with another $2,400 in cash.

Depressed, he left for home at two in the morning. But on the way he made a detour, after a sleep-interrupting call to Laura Battles confirmed that Daphne Matthews had not been found.

He stopped at the houseboat first.

She was not home. He pounded on both the front and back doors, and was beginning to worry, when it occurred to him to check his voice mail. No message there, either.

He finally thought to call her cellular, and she answered on the first ring.

"Where are you?" he asked.

"Room six-fourteen."

"A hotel?"

"Inn At The Market. Interesting view."

She sounded terrible. "Daffy? You okay?"

"Peachy."

"Are you with someone?"

"In a roundabout way. No one in the room with me, if that's what you mean."

"Did I wake you?" She sounded that way to him — dazed.

"Not a chance."

"Can you stand some company?"

"If you can possibly forgive me for what I did to you."

"Make yourself decent. I'm coming over there."

Room 614 was a suite with a water view. It had to cost three hundred dollars a night.

It smelled of Earl Grey tea. She did not allow him to turn on the light, though he tried twice. "No!" she insisted angrily, holding his arm the second time. He caught sight of her in the dimly lighted room, and her eyes looked cried out.

Holding his arm, she led him over to a sitting couch that fronted the huge plate-glass window. A moment later she delivered a tea to him and kept one for herself. She sat down beside him. Two people in a dark room, looking out a window.

"Nice view, huh?"

Boldt looked out across the bay, its surface in a constant shifting motion catching the moonlight, broken only by container ships awaiting a morning dock. "She arrived about an hour and a half ago. They talked awhile — actually he talked *at* her. He was angry, I think. Then he took her from behind. Right there. She leaned against that table. See that table? I don't think she liked it much," she said. "But she put up with it, which tells you something about the way he negotiates a deal. I wonder how much she goes for."

It was Fowler's apartment. She was watching Fowler's apartment, not the water. Not the boats or the moon. A set of gauze drapes was pulled, but Boldt could make out the shapes of two people, clearly a man — Fowler — and a woman. No telling her age or what she looked like.

"This is what he does in his free time when he's not watching other people." Her angry tone of voice worried him. "Buy a little piece of ass for a midnight snack. A Hostess Twinkie." In a Betty Boop voice, she said, "What? Can't sleep tonight? Dial: One-eight hundred-I-DO-FUCK."

"I'm right here," he offered.

Staring out the window, she asked, "Have you ever watched other people screw? Not movies — I mean for real. It was disgusting. It was my first time. It's really a disgusting dirty little act in many ways — especially like that, at the table like that. All the bumping and grabbing. A couple minutes is all, like alley cats. They never even kissed. Can you imagine? He just took her like a piece of meat. Like he had ordered a pizza or something. I don't think she liked it," she repeated.

"Let's get out of here," Boldt suggested.

"I'll bet you anything he watched me and Owen." She snapped her head toward him then, but looked away immediately. She said, "He didn't learn anything, judging by his own performance."

"We could get some eggs," Boldt suggested, wanting her out of here.

"She's leaving now. She's smart." Boldt saw that the woman was in fact leaving. "Two hours on the nose. Well, not exactly the nose. No matter what he paid her, it wasn't enough. Not with a man like that. I wonder what two

478

hours cost. Is it by the hour, or what?"

"What does this accomplish, Daffy?"

"If I'm watching him, then I know he's not watching me. You want to fault that logic?" She added, "I want to bring charges, Lou."

"Daffy, do whatever you have to do."

"If you're going to say something, just say it."

"We were cutting him out, Daffy. He knew it. He even said as much. You were nosing around some old skeletons, and he wanted to know what you had."

"No pun intended," she sniped sarcastically. "I'm *quite certain* that by now he knows what I *have*."

"You want to blame someone, try Taplin. You think Fowler dreamed this up? He takes orders, Daffy. He's Taplin's go-and-fetch-it."

"They probably had pizza parties and watched me take showers."

"They're in business. They're not running peep shows. If you really want to hurt them, then forget filing charges. We wait and we use this against them somehow."

"How?"

"I don't know."

"You think I can go back there and pretend I don't know?"

He waited her out.

"You're saying they've already seen all there is to see, so why not?" she questioned.

"I'm not really suggesting that. No. We make

479

an excuse. A friend needs you. Adler asks you to move in with him."

"We had to stop that because of my badge."

"We'll think of something. I'd just rather not blow the whistle yet."

Fowler's light went off. It was over.

"You're staying here tonight?" he asked.

She nodded.

"Are you going to be all right?"

Another nod. "I'm a big girl." She smirked. "Just ask him."

"I can stay."

"Go home to your family." She glanced over at him. "I'm sorry for the way I behaved. I lost it, that's all."

"Yeah. You lost it," Boldt said. And she grinned for the first time.

He kissed her. She flinched. And he left.

THIRTY-THREE

"Where were you until four in the morning?"

"You're not supposed to ask that at six-thirty."

"The question stands."

"If I told you I was in an ocean-view suite in a fancy hotel with a beautiful woman, what would you think?"

"That you're full of you-know-what."

"Good. The answer stands."

"You're hopeless." She walked around the room, and in and out of the bathroom, naked, getting herself ready. Boldt thought back to someone watching Daphne, and how she had reacted, and he thought he understood her better now that he saw his own wife being so casual with herself. And he, too, was angry, and perhaps more determined to do something about this anger.

"Wake up."

He had drifted back to sleep. "You said I shouldn't let you sleep." Adding, "It's not fair to ask of me such things." She was dressed now, but not for work.

"What day is it?"

"Suzie and I are going over to Elaine's. Mi-

481

chael is still locked up in that room with rubber walls."

Boldt realized that losing the prosecuting attorney would set back the investigation, but he pushed this thought aside. "You should be sainted."

"Taken to dinner would do."

"I haven't forgotten."

"Yes you had," she told him.

"I had," he admitted. "But now I remember. I owe you a champagne dinner."

"And you owe your son about two weeks off."

"So noted."

"He's spending too much time at day care. I'll drop him," she frowned. "But I'll pick him up early. So forget it, in case you were thinking about it." She looked at him. "You weren't thinking about it."

"I can hardly think at all."

"Sleep deprivation has that effect." She hesitated in the doorway, reluctant to leave.

"What?" he asked.

She asked tentatively, "How beautiful? And which hotel?"

He smirked.

The phone rang, and they both hesitated. "Do we have to?" she asked. Boldt answered it.

Shoswitz's voice named an address on Lakewood.

Boldt hung up.

"Honey?" she asked.

"It has happened again," Boldt mumbled.

By the time Boldt arrived at quarter to eight, the crime scene had turned into a circus. Scores of the morbidly curious, plus television and radio vans including the three nationals with satellite links, every variety of police and — never explained — two fire trucks, crowded the area so badly that Boldt was forced to park on Sierra and cut through someone's backyard. Much to his chagrin, the crime scene had been held for one man: Lou Boldt, and his arrival sparked a kind of instant celebrity that proved one of the most distasteful experiences of his career. Reporters shoved microphones at him, but he shielded his face and avoided both cameras and questions. When he finally made it inside the home, he discovered a video-cam crew from a tabloid television news show in the process of recording every aspect of the deceased — three bodies, total. The crew had set up in the living room and were waiting for him, complete with a portable light that was blindingly bright. The crime scene was contaminated, yes, but the violation of this family's privacy was what triggered Lou Boldt's explosive rage. He had the entire crew arrested for trespassing and breaking and entering.

By the time the area was finally cleared, both Dixie and his crew, and Bernie Lofgrin and his, were on hand. The three men closed the kitchen door, shutting out the chaos outside, and studied the dead.

The husband had made it to the phone, though he had apparently never dialed. Dixie attributed these extra few seconds to his body weight "and a great deal of courage." The middle-aged suburban woman appeared to have lunged for her eight-year-old girl, perhaps knocking over her chair in the process. Mother and daughter were curled tightly in each other's arms, now dead beneath the kitchen table, the mother's face locked in an expression of pure horror.

The source of the poison — Dixie guessed the cause of death as such within minutes of his preliminary examination — appeared to be a watermelon. *Lividity*, the settling of blood in the body, indicated a time of death of between eight and sixteen hours earlier; additional tests would further narrow this. There were three slices of the melon on three plates, the seeds carefully removed, the slices cut up into cubes. No one had ingested more than six cubes of melon. Dixie declared, "We've both attended a lot of deaths, Lou, but I've never witnessed anything quite like this."

It was true. The father's final effort was frozen, mocking his attempt; he was lying on the floor, arm outstretched, the phone's receiver still in his hand. The dishes were neatly stacked alongside the sink. They had eaten barbecued pork chops, corn, and a green salad.

Lofgrin said, "The news crew has already

destroyed any chance of clean evidence, but we'll go through the motions."

The similarity to the tree-house killings had reporters asking about a serial killer. Fishing still, but closer to the real story.

He needed to be alone. He passed through the kitchen and into a small sitting room where a color television aimed at a couch and a bookshelf was crowded with hardcovers and paperbacks. The name of the family was Crowley, and the neighborhood, the house, the furnishings, the appointments, put them firmly in the combined six-figure income. This was another house that Liz would have wanted, and he could not help but think of mother and daughter beneath the kitchen table, huddled against the fears and pain of death. And how glad he was that this was not Liz and Miles.

The stairs were maple and climbed quickly to a second story. He heard the whining as he reached the top, and he moved toward it cautiously, not knowing what to expect. It grew sharper and sadder as he approached, and he understood it was a dog before he opened the door. There, lying at the foot of the parents' bed, pressed into the floor, lonely eyes trained up at Boldt in complete confusion, a shepherd-collie cried plaintively. This dog, Boldt realized, was the only witness to what had happened. This dog had lost her entire family in the course of one evening's meal.

He bent down and petted it, and fought

back a seething anger.

Dr. Richard Clements commandeered Shoswitz's office. Daphne Matthews was there, as were Boldt and the lieutenant. Clements said to Boldt, "You are focusing on these truck farmers. Is that right?"

"Yes."

"That is *not* right."

"We've pulled every watermel—"

"Schmater-melon. Blah! He no longer cares about claiming authorship. It is ending. He is leading you astray, Sergeant. You mustn't be misled. I saw your work in the situation room. Stick with that — the paint, the colors, the *evidence*. This watermelon is a ruse, intended to mislead the hunt. He is the fox, let us not forget, and you are the hound," he said to Boldt, "and we must remember that the only way the fox ever wins the chase is not to outrun his pursuers, but to deceive them."

Shoswitz huffed audibly, losing patience with Clements. His agitation surfaced as small tics to the shoulders and the eyes, so that he looked like a marionette whose strings were tangled. Boldt feared he might say something to offend the doctor, and realizing the value of Clements, quirky or not, Boldt headed off any such confrontation between the two by speaking first.

"He could kill hundreds by poisoning produce."

486

"He doesn't desire to kill hundreds. What did he say on the phone?" he asked Daphne. "That Owen had killed the ones he loved."

"He wants to kill Adler. My diagnosis is that his schizophrenia has progressed to a point that whatever voice may once have vied for such a grand scheme has since been overpowered by the drive for vengeance, a far greater motivation. As Caulfield perceives it, Owen Adler owes him several long years of his life. How many have read this?" He waved a group of papers in the air, impossible to see. He explained, "It is his defense of his innocence subsequent to the trial. A thoughtful, powerful, *convincing* piece of writing. I for one believe him. He claims to have been the victim of a frame — that the drugs were not his. He supported this by an offer of proof that not one blood test administered to him had tested positive for cocaine use. He points to the police lab tests that failed to find any trace evidence *whatsoever* of the drug in his home or automobile. In his third year of medium detention, he wrote this most extraordinary appeal, but because of the state's minimum sentencing failed to be granted parole or a retrial. It is my judgment that a schism developed within him, driven perhaps by a valid injustice, as we now understand his situation. His more logical half advised him to follow the system; his disturbed half revolted, rejecting any such alliance with the very forces that had led to his demise.

487

The latter half has gained control now, I am suggesting. But there is a cunning, logical, intelligent mind at work here, and one that has been alerted to the substantial powers and abilities of his adversary. It's all over the news. He knows the clock is running. He knows what he is up against, and he has little conscious desire to be a martyr and be caught, regardless of the efforts of the subconscious."

"So he tricks us," Daphne said, following the reasoning.

"Exactly. He poisons a single melon. Off go the hounds chasing the melons, following the wrong scent, while all the while the fox has doubled back and is raiding the chicken house."

Shoswitz protested, "But we don't *know* it was only the one melon."

"Sure we do," Clements countered. "We've not had one other report. Correct? Not one other incident. And if he intended to kill hundreds using melons, this would hardly be the case." He giggled. "Don't you see how *obvious* he's being about this?"

The lieutenant bristled with the giddy pleasure Clements was taking in all of this. Any homicide cop felt the pain and suffering of the victims and their relatives — no matter how callous to the crime scenes he or she became, no matter how quick the one-liners, and how easy it was to move on to another case. The tragedy of the Crowley family had deeply affected everyone on the fifth floor, and in this way Clements was clearly a visitor.

"I'm saying it's Adler he wants. Do not be fooled by his cleverness. He will deceive you at every opportunity. I warned you of this before: You cannot put yourself in this man's mind. But *I* can, gentlemen." He acknowledged Matthews and smiled. "I can."

THIRTY-FOUR

Boldt entered NetLinQ's "war room" on Sunday night, losing faith that the ATMs might ever be used to trap Caulfield. For too many nights now he had sat in a chair and stared at the electronic map projected onto the huge screen. For too many nights he had gone home with nothing more than a headache.

Special Agent Sheila Locke was about twenty-six years old, with short brown hair, a thin pale face, and enormous eyes. She wore a blue blazer that hid her figure, and a wireless headset that covered her right ear and a foam-covered microphone that hid her generous mouth. Using the newly added FBI communications, Locke and another agent, whom Boldt knew only as Billy, were in constant touch with the nearly seventy-five men and women watching ATMs in King County. Although Boldt's tiny squad of eleven was keeping tabs on downtown ATMs, the FBI special agents and King County undercover officers had been deployed in the outlying regions, including Kirkland-Bellevue and SEATAC-Renton.

Ted Perch was chatting up Lucille Guillard, who monitored a computer terminal allowing her personal control of all Pac-West ATMs. She would also get a real-time look at the extortionist's account balance so that if a hit slipped through the screening software again, they would at least see a balance change indicating a hit.

Over seventeen hundred ATMs under NetLinQ's control were now subject to the time-trap software. In the past forty-eight hours, the system had not crashed once. Publicly, the delay was still being attributed to maintenance.

The electronic wall map was peppered with different-colored dots: Red represented cash machines not under direct surveillance, of which there seemed to be hundreds. Green, considerably fewer, depicted the ATMs under covert surveillance. No ATM had been hit twice, and the amber dots represented the machines previously hit.

It was indeed a remarkable display of technology, he realized, though it did little to buoy his mood. NetLinQ's two other enormous screens, part of the switching station's regular command center, displayed ATM traffic as blinking orange-and-green lines. These colorful lines shot across the maps like arrows, reaching hubs that represented banks' mainframes, changed color, and traveled on. There were six people from NetLinQ tracking these screens, though they were generally disregarded by the law enforcement visitors.

"Ready, Billy?" Locke asked the male dispatcher after several minutes of relative silence. Billy rolled his chair forward to a computer terminal that was positioned central to the wall maps. He adjusted his headset and tested it twice. He typed into the keyboard, checking his monitor and the maps, and spoke in a soft, even monotone: "Check seventeen." He listened, typed again, and said into the headset, "Check forty-six." Again. "Check sixty." He did this for several minutes before giving a nod to Locke.

Dispatchers, Boldt thought, were a different life-form. They needed nerves of steel and a steady monotone voice to go with them. In the middle of the most complex, chaotic, life-threatening emergency, they were paid to keep calm and direct human beings and vehicles as if they were chess pieces.

Twenty minutes of silence followed, punctuated only by the clicking of computer keys. Boldt had nodded off when he was pulled awake by the sound of a human voice.

"We have a hit! Three seconds and counting."

Where once this announcement had brought excitement, now it brought only frustration.

On the display a bright white light flashed in Earlington, indicating the hit. A digital display ran in the upper right-hand corner, counting off the passing seconds of the active ATM transaction.

Billy dispatched two of the field agents, directing one to the north of the hit, and the other directly to the ATM. Not surprisingly, given the odds, this ATM was not under direct surveillance.

Guillard called out: "It's not ours."

Perch shouted, "Ten seconds elapsed." He hawked instructions at an assistant who worked furiously at the keyboard. "Twenty seconds."

To Billy, Perch said, "Where the hell are your people?"

The dispatcher, maintaining his calm, did not reply.

Boldt watched as Perch's assistant shook his head and announced, "Transaction complete."

Boldt said, "We need more time," and cued Billy to rush the surveillance teams. A volley of calm instructions followed. Billy informed Boldt, "Surveillance nine is closing. Also fourteen."

Perch, Guillard, and Boldt all fixed their attention on the two dispatchers, motionlessly, silently. Cars racing down streets. Caulfield calmly walking away.

Billy finally looked up. "Surveillance reports no visual contact. The ATM is empty."

Perch slammed the desk violently. "I'm increasing the window of time." He added, "The system had better hold together."

The room settled into an uncomfortable but workmanlike atmosphere. For the next thirty minutes Boldt checked his watch frequently, glancing between Billy and the overhead screen.

For NetLinQ, it was business as usual. The

493

rows of technicians monitored the endless transfer of money as hundreds of transactions representing thousands of dollars raced through the NetLinQ computers.

At five minutes to nine, Guillard announced excitedly, "We have a second hit. I'm pushing the time delay to thirty-five seconds. Objections?" She had independent control of the time-trap software for her bank's ATMs.

Perch sounded apoplectic as he questioned the wisdom of such a long WOT. "Thirty-five seconds?"

Boldt glanced at him hotly.

Perch said, "Fuck it. Just do it!" he okayed.

Boldt stood to his feet as the screen changed to an enlargement of the Earlington area, showing all its streets. The small dots were now large circles with numbers inside them. Each surveillance agent carried a Global Positioning System transmitter, relaying back his or her exact real-time location, which the electronic map then displayed. A blue triangle bearing the number 6 moved steadily toward the yellow ATM on Southwest Seventh. Another blue dot numbered 4 moved north on highway 167, and another, under Billy's monotone instructions, north on the 405.

"Authorization requested."

Boldt could picture Caulfield at the ATM waiting for the cash. Would he notice the added time? Would he have heard the fabricated news stories that the entire Northwest system was

494

experiencing delays due to maintenance operations?

"Authorization approved," Perch called out, reading over Jimmy's shoulders.

Twenty seconds.

"Currency delivery in progress," Guillard announced.

The time-trap software included a routine to slow the actual delivery of the bills. This was because Perch had explained that a customer can hear the machine counting out the cash, and he believed that once the suspect heard and recognized this sound, psychologically it would be much more difficult to walk away from the machine.

Thirty seconds.

Billy said into his microphone. "I copy, six." To Boldt he said calmly, "We have visual contact." He handed Boldt a headset.

At that moment there were no sweeter words for Lou Boldt. Given all their efforts, this was the first time anyone had actually seen Caulfield. "Description?" Boldt asked.

He did not recognize the voice of field agent number 6. It belonged to one of the dozens of FBI agents who were now participating. He did not recognize the description of the suspect either, which was when his head felt faint and dizzy.

"Five foot seven or eight. Motorcycle helmet. Leather jacket."

"Repeat height," Boldt ordered. Harry Caulfield stood an even six feet.

"Five foot eight."

"Sex?"

"Female."

"Repeat."

"Definitely female. I'm looking at her backside, don't forget."

Boldt recognized the description well enough: Lucille Guillard had shown him a photograph. Disappointed it was not Caulfield himself, he settled for the accomplice.

"Orders?" Boldt heard through the headphones.

He glanced around the room. All eyes were on him.

Billy asked calmly, "Instructions, Sergeant?"

He felt cheated. He sorted through his choices as the accomplice stood waiting for her cash, and the field agent stood waiting for instructions.

"Maintain visual," Boldt said, though barely loud enough to be heard.

Perch jumped forward and complained, "But the software *worked!* You've *got* her!"

"Back off!" Boldt ordered the man. "Maintain visual," he repeated calmly to Billy, feeling himself again, his eyes glued to the electronic map.

The dispatcher repeated the command with all the energy of ordering a tuna sandwich.

"How long to throw a net around it, Billy?" Boldt inquired. The plan all along had been for one or two surveillance personnel to make

496

the bust. Patrol cars readied as backup, in case it went sour. But now, all that had changed.

Billy and Sheila Locke consulted several screens. Locke said, "Two minutes and we can have all the major routes in and out with a minimum of single-agent coverage. I can put the bird up if you want." She checked a mileage chart. "Seven minutes and we're there. That would give us backup support, although it's a dark night out there tonight."

"Do it. Tighten it up and close it down." He ignored Perch, who hovered alongside. "Maintain visual surveillance only."

"Right."

"Transaction complete," Guillard announced from her corner.

"What the hell are you doing?" Perch implored.

"I heard you the first time. Thank you," Boldt said. He had other answers, all clichés: "My job." "What they pay me to do." But he held his tongue, wondering if a civilian could be made to understand the balance of risk and assets.

Billy deployed the agents to cover on-ramps and intersections, bus stops, bike routes, and running paths. Not taking his eyes off his work, he explained to Boldt, "If she goes too far south of town too quickly, I may lose her. We're not set up for that."

"I understand," Boldt returned. "She won't go south," he predicted. Clements and a pair of FBI experts had studied the ATM hit patterns from the previous nights and had determined that the extortionist always moved toward the city and I-5 as the hits progressed. It was assumed that I-5, possibly in combination with other major highways, was seen by the extortionist as an escape route. In truth, law enforcement welcomed the use of limited-access highways.

Lucille Guillard's telephone purred softly, and she answered it. A moment later she hung up and informed Boldt, "We have a stop-motion video image of the hit." To Locke she said, "Your techs have been informed."

Locke said to Boldt, "We may be able to pull a video feed for us here."

Boldt had seen the satellite van outside in the parking lot and had wondered what it was for.

He had no chance to doubt his decision. With the suspect clearly not Caulfield, and Caulfield the only person of interest to him, he felt he had no choice but to follow the suspect, hoping she would lead them back to him. The thought crossed his mind that Caulfield had never been any part of the extortion, but he could not allow himself to give any weight to this, given his current commitment both mentally and logistically to the surveillance operation.

"The chopper is picking up the video for us," Billy told Boldt, a finger pushed to his ear. "We should have it back here in a matter of minutes." He returned to his keyboard.

Locke indicated Boldt's headphones, which the sergeant had slipped down around his neck. He pulled them back on in time to hear the same field agent describe the suspect moving northwest on foot.

"Turning left at the corner," the voice said.

Boldt caught himself holding his breath.

The agent announced in a low voice, "I'm about thirty yards back. Maintaining visual contact."

Pointing to the screen, Billy told Boldt, "We'll have another agent in play at the next intersection."

"Possible vehicle spotted," the field agent announced.

"A motorcycle?" Boldt asked him through the headset.

"Negative. A brown Datsun, Washington vehicle registration: Nine-four-five-one-one."

Billy repeated the number into his headset and told Boldt, "Your people are running the plate through DMV."

"I've got it," Locke announced, freeing Billy of this communication. A minute later she leaned into her headset and, having been instructed not to repeat such a thing aloud, wrote out for Boldt,

Vehicle registration: Cornelia Uli,
26, female, Caucasian.
Address: 517 1/2 Airport Way, Seattle.

Boldt folded the piece of paper and placed it in his pocket. Assigning this a top priority, he instructed Locke to place the residence under tight surveillance. She went about redeploying the field surveillance personnel in order to accommodate this change.

"She's getting into the vehicle," the field agent announced. "I'm on foot, I'm going to lose her."

"Likewise," said the second agent to arrive in the area.

Boldt, terrified they were about to lose her, checked with his dispatcher, who went off-mike, grinned, and said, "Don't worry, Sergeant. We've got this tighter than a gnat's ass." He pointed to the screen. "I've got five vehicles within a four-block area. Unless she beams herself up, we've got her."

The radio traffic in Boldt's headset heated up as Billy orchestrated the vehicular handoffs. No one car stayed with the target vehicle for more than six blocks or two miles of highway. On the screen, the blue triangles representing the agents' location transmitters clustered in and around an area where Billy kept manually moving a white flashing dot indicating the suspect.

The white dot left I-5. Billy announced, "Suspect is coming to a stop."

Boldt listened in on the continuous dialogue between dispatcher and field agents. He closed his eyes and tried to picture a sidewalk ATM on a not-too-busy street, the approach of a petite woman wearing a motorcycle helmet in the faint glow of the streetlights, and the swarm of police that now surrounded her and would continue to monitor her every moment. She was, as of that moment, public property. Cornelia Uli would be stripped down to her moles and birthmarks if necessary — all in due time. For the moment, under the duress of a nervous stomach, he sat back, consulting a printout listing the various field agents and assignments, and listened to his team at work under the unusual calm of the FBI dispatcher.

DISPATCH: Twenty-six . . . Give us a walk-by visual.
TWENTY-SIX: Twenty-six. Confirm. Walk-by visual.
DISPATCH: Affirmative. Walk-by, please.
TWENTY-SIX: Roger.

A few anxious seconds passed.

TWENTY-SIX: Affirmative, suspect is standing at the machine.

Boldt consulted the deployment printout. Number 26 — James Flynn — was dressed as a pizza delivery man tonight. Carrying his pizzas, he was passing the ATM, glancing briefly at the mark, never breaking stride. No wide eyes of recognition, no probing stare. Professional. Sure.

Lucille Guillard announced, "We have a hit."

A hit flashed on the wall map, surrounded by a sea of blue triangles.

Boldt instructed the dispatcher. "Can we kill the Datsun on the run?"

Billy held up a finger and talked rapidly into this mouthpiece.

DISPATCH: Tech Services mobile:
Request a car kill on the suspect's vehicle. Copy?

TECH SERVICES VAN: Car kill.
Affirmative One minute, please.

Boldt and Billy met eyes. The dispatcher looked completely relaxed.

TECH SERVICES VAN: Suspect's vehicle is parked one-and-one-half blocks north — repeat, north — of the ATM location. Looks good for a kill, Billy.

Guillard announced, "Fifteen seconds have elapsed. Twenty seconds left."

Boldt told Guillard, "Extend the time trap. Give us a few seconds longer."

Boldt asked Billy, "Can they do it in thirty seconds or less?"

"Extending to forty-five seconds," Guillard confirmed. "We should not go beyond this, Sergeant."

TECH SERVICES VAN: Thirty seconds is an affirmative. Deploy?

Billy glanced at Boldt, who hit the transmit button and said sharply, "Go!"

DISPATCH: Forty-four. Keep us alert to any change in suspect's position.
FORTY-FOUR: Roger, Dispatch. Will do.
TECH SERVICES OPERATIVE: I'm going in.

Boldt could picture the man hurrying down a quiet street to one of many parked cars. In his pocket would be an oil-filter wrench.

TECH SERVICES OPERATIVE: Dispatch? Problem. I have a couple out for a stroll. I'm aborting this pass.

Guillard counted off, "Ten seconds to go."

DISPATCH: Time's a-wasting.
TECH SERVICES OPERATIVE: Affirmative. Making another pass.

Guillard announced, "Five seconds."

DISPATCH: Five seconds until transaction is complete.
TECH SERVICES OPERATIVE: Affirmative, Dispatch. Five seconds. Making a second pass. . . .

>All clear. I'm going under
>the car.

Sheila Locke said, "Tech has live video for us. Coming on-screen."

All eyes riveted to the screen, now divided, showing two black-and-white images. On the left was a wavy telephoto image of the helmeted woman standing at the ATM. On the right of a split screen, the Tech Services man in eerie night-sight video slid under the parked Datsun and disappeared. Boldt caught himself white-knuckling the chair.

How the FBI personnel managed this live video was beyond him. But he did not question it. Tech Services in every department was famous for performing miracles.

"Transaction complete," Guillard announced.

The video followed this woman as she left the ATM and rounded the corner heading toward her car. Once a good distance away, she pulled off the helmet and shook out her hair.

>DISPATCH: Tech operative. Suspect
>on her way. Do you copy?

There was no response from the operative, whose feet could be seen on the screen sticking out from under the suspect's car.

Billy calmly reported to Boldt, "He's not responding. Must be radio interference."

The suspect was now less than a half-block

away and closing quickly. "Get him out of there!" Boldt ordered.

DISPATCH: Tech Services? Request an interrupt. Repeat: Physical interrupt requested on the car kill.
TECH SERVICES: Roger, Dispatch.

On the screen, a woman dressed casually in blue jeans and a T-shirt hurried out of the van, moving quickly down the street toward the car. She made no effort to look in the direction of the suspect, now but a few yards away and coming up the sidewalk.

As the Tech Services woman came alongside the suspect's vehicle, she flung her purse to the pavement, intentionally spilling its contents.

Boldt watched the overhead screen, hearing only the hum of the computers, Billy's soft mumble, and the endless tapping of the computer keyboards. The woman field agent threw her head under the vehicle and said something as the suspect rounded the final corner, now only two cars away. The Tech Services man scrambled out, came to his knees, and immediately began helping her to clean up the contents of her spilled purse.

Cornelia Uli approached the driver's door and encountered them both. The field agent laughed and shook her head at Uli as if embarrassed to have spilled her purse. She said something, as did the Tech Services man. The last of the

505

purse contents were collected as Uli unlocked the Datsun's trunk and set the helmet inside. She acted as casually about possessing a motorcycle helmet while driving a car as the two field agents did about collecting the items from the spilled purse. Their job completed, the field agents made no sudden moves, no panic. Together they headed down the sidewalk in the opposite direction from the van and the camera that recorded them.

The Datsun pulled away from the curb and drove off.

"Stay with her," Boldt ordered Billy. He was thinking: These next few minutes are critical.

There were two ways that Boldt could play this woman whom he considered Caulfield's accomplice, and he had already made the choice. The first, and most conservative, was to keep his distance and sit on her. Obtain the necessary warrants and tap her phone, perhaps even install video surveillance in her residence, record her every move, her every spoken word, and hope for the contact with Caulfield. The second — and the method he had elected to follow — was the more aggressive: to force a problem onto her and hope that in her moment of panic, she turned to Caulfield for help, either identifying his location, or luring him to her.

He felt powerless not being in the field with the others, and he sensed that by staying behind and coordinating the effort, he had crossed the imaginary line to desk jockey — and did not care for it one bit. Following the radio traffic in the headphones, he pictured the cars swapping responsibility for surveillance of the Datsun. He rejoiced with the others as the stream of leaking oil was spotted behind the vehicle, and he alerted Locke to open a line to U.S. West; they were going to need a listing of all pay-phone locations.

Three minutes later the Datsun pulled over, stopped dead in the middle of a strip of fast-food, quick lube, and car lots. One surveillance car pulled past and into the parking lot of a burger joint. Two others stopped fifty yards short, and divided to either side of the road.

"Billy, what's the address?" Boldt asked hurriedly.

The dispatcher checked with the field agents and reported back.

Boldt signaled Locke like a conductor, and she repeated the address to the Ma Bell supervisor she had on the line. Within seconds, her pen was moving rapidly. She tore off the piece of paper and handed it to Boldt, who scanned it quickly and passed it to Billy, asking him to put them up on the screen. A minute later, six pink stars with a *T* in the middle appeared on the electronic map.

Over the course of the next few minutes, reports streamed in that the suspect was repeatedly attempting to start her car. During this time, Sheila Locke determined the physical locations of the pay phones according to their

507

addresses: Two were behind the suspect in a McDonald's and a Burger King, respectively; one was across and up the street in a strip mall; one each in a pair of competing gas stations nearly half a mile in front of her, near the interstate; and one in a booth adjacent to a bus stop not a hundred yards ahead.

Boldt instructed the trailing Tech Services van to set up with a view of both the Datsun and this bus-stop pay phone. Three minutes later, NetLinQ's center screen showed a grainy black-and-white telephoto image of the sad-looking Datsun pulled awkwardly onto the shoulder of soft grass.

"Suspect is moving," announced a male voice in the headset.

Boldt and Billy met eyes. Billy's earlier doubt that had been present when Boldt elected to follow rather than apprehend was now gone, replaced instead by a confidence that bordered on admiration.

On the screen, the woman climbed out of the car, clearly disgusted. She looked both ways, trying to decide where to find a phone. Boldt silently urged her to head back toward the fast-food chains; he did not want her seeing the bus stop. But as if hearing him and going against his wishes, she elected to walk in the direction her car was headed.

Trying to consider every possibility, Boldt advised Locke, "Get in touch with the local bus service and find out their schedule. Any bus due at that stop in the next ten minutes we want detoured. Tell them we'll want an empty bus on standby ten blocks back. And get the chopper back here. I may want a lift." She scribbled all of this down. "And let's see how many taxi companies cover that area. We'll want our people in as the cabbies. And *no patrol cars*," he emphasized. "I don't want to see a patrol within ten blocks of that area."

For the next several minutes, Locke and Billy occupied themselves with Boldt's requests. Field agents were deployed to two area cab companies and the bus company. The regularly scheduled bus was diverted, the driver telling her passengers that an accident blocked the road ahead and thereby required a detour.

The camera followed Cornelia Uli, who was by no means a fast walker. Nervous, or perhaps just worried about her car, she continually checked over her shoulder, island-hopping from one parking lot to the next in search of a pay phone.

Overhead, Boldt heard the mechanical thunder of the helicopter.

"It's going to be the bus stop," Boldt predicted.

"Chopper's down," Locke announced.

Boldt said to her, "Tell the phone company which phone we think it's going to be and that we need a real-time report on whatever numbers she calls."

"Got it."

To Billy he said, "I want seven passengers and a driver on our bus. Mix it up. More of our people on the stops along the route, with everyone keeping a strict eye out for Caulfield. We're going to have to allow civilians onto the bus, in case Caulfield sends a go-between, so I want to make it real clear: No cowboy theatrics. We consider her armed, but any civilians are our first priority. If she calls for a stop near her place on Airport Way, that's our cue to take her. I don't want her getting inside her place before we do. Got it?" He added, "And give me someone at the bus stop now. Right away. I want to hear what's said, if at all possible."

Billy had to work quickly, though his motions conserved energy and his voice never indicated the slightest degree of excitement.

Sheila Locke turned and told the sergeant that the phone company was all set.

On the screen Boldt saw the suspect cross one final parking lot and quicken her step as she spotted a pay phone. In the distance of the same frame, a young woman approached the bus stop. Boldt asked, "Is she ours?"

Billy nodded.

Boldt thought to himself, *These people are amazing.*

He asked Locke, "Do we have an open line to the phone company?" She nodded confirmation.

The suspect stepped up to the phone and

seconds later was dialing.

Boldt sat half off his chair, his attention split between the giant television projection on the wall and the back of Sheila Locke's head.

For these few seconds, the room went absolutely silent save for the hum of the equipment, everyone hanging on this phone call.

The agent on foot arrived at the bus stop late. The suspect dialed, waited, and hung up. There was no way to tell from the camera's angle and distance if she ever spoke.

"What the hell?" Boldt let slip. Both Billy's and Boldt's attention focused on Sheila Locke, who thanked someone, asked this person to "stand by, please," and turned to tell Boldt, "It's a business number. They're searching." Boldt wished there were a way to effect a line interrupt and to listen in on whatever conversation took place, well aware of the technological ease with which such an interrupt could be accomplished. But he was equally aware that any such interrupt required warrants and legal red tape that, where pay phones were concerned, took a minimum of several hours to accomplish. The same system established to protect a person's rights limited Boldt's ability to carry out his job.

Locke touched her finger to her earphone, listened, and then told Boldt, "It's a paging service. She would have keyed in a personal identification code, but the phone company's software doesn't trap any numbers dialed following line connection."

Boldt felt crushed by this news. Over his headphones, a woman's voice spoke incredibly softly: "The phone's ringing. Whoever she paged is calling her back." He could hear the ringing of the phone. It was the field agent at the bus stop, a few short yards from the suspect.

"Sergeant?" It was Billy. He directed Boldt's attention to the screen.

Cornelia Uli answered the phone.

Boldt said to Locke, "Get in touch with the —"

"Paging company," Locke interrupted. "Already on it."

Billy said, "Turn up your headphones, Sergeant. We're going to try something here."

Boldt adjusted the knob. He heard a raspy, steady breathing loudly in the headphones, and then in the background he picked up a woman's voice bitching about the "stupid car." In a pause, Billy explained quickly, "That background noise is the agent's breathing. We have a thirty-DB boost on her condenser." The suspect mentioned the bus stop. She paused. She said "okay" twice, and left the phone dangling as she approached the bus stop. There was a tremendously loud click in the phones, prompting Boldt to jettison his headset. It tumbled into his lap. Grinning, Billy said, "That was the agent turning off her mike." He added, "But we should thank her. If she had spoken she might have made us deaf."

"I'm going out there," Boldt announced. "Can

you communicate with the chopper?"

Billy said in that unnaturally calm voice of his, "Sergeant, Tech Services can do *anything*."

The chopper ride was brief, and a little terrifying at night. They stayed low, and the buildings swept beneath them with ridiculous speed, toylike in appearance. Boldt was left off in a school soccer field, seven blocks from the waiting bus, so that there would be no sound of a chopper anywhere near the suspect. He was met there by a field agent by the name of Nathan Jones, whom he recognized as King County Police. "We're all ready for you," the agent announced, showing Boldt into the car and racing down the streets, oblivious to any of the traffic signs.

As they approached the bus, it looked ominous to Boldt. It was parked alongside the road, its interior lights shining yellow. As he stepped aboard, there were seven people sitting in the various seats. He introduced himself, studied them briefly, and asked two to exchange seats and two to sit together. If she looked closely, Cornelia Uli might notice a similarity in age and appearance among several of them. Only one of them looked over fifty: another KCP detective Boldt knew casually, though he could not remember his name. "We're going to give her a lot of room," he announced. "If she signals early, then you" — he pointed to one of the three women — "will get off at the same stop. Don't follow too closely, but keep us advised. Remember," he said, addressing all of them, "we'll have support all around us, in every direction. My information is that she'll have to switch lines to head toward town. I think we can safely afford for four of us — me, and you three — to make that switch with her. We are going to make every attempt to have that be a dummy bus as well. Our people will be coming onto the bus at various stops. You two will disembark at the third and fifth stop, respectively. If we go the distance. If she holds off and stays on until the five-hundred block of Airport Way, when she stands, we take her. We do it fast and without fanfare, and she does *not* get off this bus. Any questions?"

There were none.

"Roll," he said, grabbing for a handhold as the bus door closed and the vehicle started off down the road.

They rounded a corner. Two of the agents were reading papers, another a paperback. Two stared blankly out the window. Boldt tried to settle himself. He leaned against the window and relaxed, feigning an exhausted man taking a nap — at any other time, something that would have required very little acting.

He had abandoned his radio earpiece, stuffing it down inside his collar. The bus and all its occupants, except for the driver, were now isolated from Billy the dispatcher, Sheila Locke,

Phil Shoswitz back at the department, and all the support vehicles in place and ready to assist them. They passed the disabled Datsun, the heads of several of the passengers craning to see it, and the bus slowed as it approached the stop.

The door hissed open.

Boldt recognized the agent from the live surveillance video. She boarded first, and took several seconds to come up with the right amount of money. Then Cornelia Uli stepped up and called out, "Excuse me!" to the woman agent. Boldt's heart pounded heavily. He wanted that door closed, and Uli trapped inside the bus. The agent turned. "Do you have change?" Uli asked. She waved a crisp twenty-dollar bill, and Boldt realized this had come from the cash machine. The woman agent seemed paralyzed.

Boldt silently urged the driver to shut the door.

The younger man sitting ahead of Boldt jumped up and said, "I do," fishing his wallet from his back pocket. He gave her an assortment of bills, accepting the twenty from her, and Uli fed one of the ones into the driver's pay machine. Uli asked the driver, a KCP man, about the route. Fortunately, someone had thought ahead to have a local in the driver's seat, and the man informed her about the line change that Boldt had just mentioned at the outset.

Everyone took separate seats.

The door hissed closed.

Boldt's sense of tension increased with every mile. His stomach grumbled noisily. He glanced up just once to look at her. *No staring.* She wore tight-fitting jeans and that black leather jacket. She had brown eyes, no makeup, and full, pouty lips. She scratched the back of her neck, and when she did this, Boldt's first reaction was that he had seen this woman before, somewhere other than in the surveillance video, and this continued to trouble him as the bus drove on.

The driver announced a stop, and handled the bus poorly as they slowed. Boldt faced himself so that he looked out a window, when in fact he was using the reflection to watch the suspect's profile. If she moved toward the rear exit door, he intended to follow. There was no one at this stop, and without a call signal, the front door never opened. The bus gained speed and continued on.

At the third stop, an agent disembarked. Another boarded, a pretty woman: FBI, with a simple face and inquisitive eyes. She sat directly across from Uli, who occupied one of the front wall benches. This agent took a look around for any leftover papers, then pulled out a nail file and went to work on her nails.

As a signal of their identity, all agents had been instructed to touch their left ear prior to boarding, which was why Boldt occupied a seat on the right side of the bus — and he was grateful that Uli had her back to this same side. In this way, Boldt knew ahead of time the status of his passengers. At the fourth stop, a civilian boarded: a portly, toothless man. He showed his pass and asked the driver, "So where's Danny tonight?"

The driver answered, "You're stuck with me."

"Never seen you before," the man said.

In the window's reflection, Boldt studied Uli's response. She seemed to take no notice. The driver handled himself well, though the bus poorly. He lunged ahead too quickly, sending the teetering newcomer charging down the aisle, barely keeping his balance. He smelled of cigarettes and booze as he passed. "Nice job!" he hollered. He took a seat immediately behind Boldt, which made the sergeant uncomfortable. He leaned forward over Boldt's shoulder and said, "Got a rookie behind the wheel, friend. I can drive blindfolded better than that. Hmm?"

Boldt made a point of not engaging in any conversation. This man had the feel of a nonstop talker, and that was the last thing he wanted at this point. One of the agents, sensing this, rose and came to this man's seat. "You mind?" he asked, and without awaiting a response, took the aisle seat next to this man and started him talking, taking him away from pestering Boldt.

The bus motored along, whining and hissing, one red light to the next. The following bus stop was again void of passengers. At the next, another agent disembarked. The one after that, two more boarded — both agents.

The bus driver announced the stop. He turned to Uli and said, "Here's your connection." Boldt hesitated. He did not want to commit to leaving the bus until he was sure Uli was also.

As the bus slowed, she rose. Boldt came out of his seat and headed for the front door. Three of the others joined him. They all disembarked, receiving transfers from the driver. They joined two others at this stop. Boldt guessed them both as agents though there was no easy way for either to offer the signal, so he could not be certain. The bus drove away.

The night was calm, the air warm. Above them in the darkness two white seagulls swooped over the street and one cried at the other, then they disappeared. Two of the agents discussed a Mariners game. The woman with the paperback found some street light and opened her book. Boldt said to one of the strangers, "Is this the line going into the city?" This man scratched his ear as he thought about it. "International district and downtown," he said. "You want the U, you gotta change downtown."

Boldt thanked him.

Cornelia Uli asked the woman next to her for the time. She looked restless, and the way she guarded her purse, Boldt assumed it contained the ransom money.

By now a police car would have pulled alongside Uli's Datsun. On the off-chance Caulfield was coming for the car while Uli headed home, this was handled in a straightforward manner. The patrolman wrote up the citation and called in a tow truck. The truck took ten minutes to arrive. It would be towed via a combination of the highway and streets — intentionally avoiding the bus route — to the police garage, where it would be given the full treatment by the grease-monkey division of Bernie Lofgrin's ID unit.

The bus pulled up to the stop. The driver was cleaning wax out of his left ear with his index finger. As Boldt climbed aboard and showed his transfer, the driver met eyes with him, revealing absolutely nothing in his face, but in the eyes themselves there was a keen energy.

Bobbie Gaynes was in the fifth seat back.

There were six others on the bus, all SPD. Seeing these familiar faces, Boldt felt an immediate sense of relief. No matter how much he respected the other agencies assisting him, nothing felt quite as good as seeing family again.

Uli took the first seat. It faced the front window. The bus bounced over broken roads and sagged through dips and rounded corners clumsily, cutting them a little too tight.

As it slowed to the third stop, Boldt looked out the window and felt a rush of heat up his spine. There were two people waiting for this bus. One of them was Digger Shupe, a retired

Major Crimes detective. He would recognize at least half the faces on this bus. The other man Boldt did not recognize, and there was no move toward the left ear. He carried a pair of grocery bags in his arms.

The doors opened and Digger Shupe climbed aboard. The driver shot Boldt one quick, intense look, and then averted his own face so that Shupe would not recognize him. An electricity sparked inside the bus. The two new passengers paid, and as Shupe looked up and saw Boldt he said, "Well, I'll be damned —" But the driver hit the gas, the brake, and the gas again, and sent the two newcomers sailing. Danny Levin feigned an attempt to help Digger Shupe to his feet, and in the process bent and pressed his lips close to the man's ear, and Boldt saw him say something. Shupe's head nodded, and when he climbed to his feet and collected himself, he walked to the rear of the bus, ever the professional, and took his seat.

The bus driver apologized profusely, especially to the man who had spilled his groceries. The groceries were gathered up, and this man took a seat by Bobbie Gaynes. The bus set off.

Two stops later Boldt saw LaMoia waiting in the shelter, and again felt a sense of relief to see one of his own people. There was a push to the back as several of the agents selected this stop to disembark.

LaMoia paid, walked right up to the suspect,

and sat down next to her. Boldt, two seats back, felt his stomach roll. Only LaMoia would hit on a suspect.

"Finally some nice weather," LaMoia said to her.

She offered him a weak smile.

"Of course, summers are the best anyway," he said.

No reply.

"You do any windsurfing?" he asked her.

She shook her head, but smiled a little at the attention he gave her.

"Terrific sport," he told her. "Better on the lakes because they're not as cold. Spend any time on the lakes, do you?"

She looked ahead, paying him no mind.

"Do you ride?" he asked. "The jacket . . . Is that a fashion statement, or do you ride?"

"A Sportster."

"A Harley. I can't believe this! You ride a Harley?"

Boldt turned to the window and smiled to himself. They passed another stop, the driver swooping in but not stopping.

Cornelia Uli peered out the window, reached up, and signaled the driver with the obnoxious electronic call.

Again Boldt felt the tension inside the bus, despite the passive faces and the casual expressions.

One hundred yards to go.

"This your stop?" LaMoia asked, indicating

by body language that he could get out of her way.

"Yeah, thanks."

LaMoia stood.

The driver's eyes caught Boldt in the rearview mirror. He gave a faint nod, gripped the stainless steel bar tightly, and reached in for his weapon.

The bus slowed toward the stop, then pulled a power turn to the left and sent Cornelia Uli hard up against the window and wall. LaMoia, reacting with the reflexes of a cat, planted his shield practically on her nose, spun her around violently, and pinned her, shouting: "Seattle Police! You are under arrest! *Do not move!* Don't do it!" he added, driving his knee into the small of her back to hold her steady.

The bus pulled off into a vacant lot.

Cornelia Uli screamed for help and glanced over her shoulder, only to be faced with the sight of a half-dozen handguns trained onto her. Some of the agents were shielded by the seats, some standing and fully exposed. A set of handcuffs clicked onto her wrist. "You fuckhead!" she shouted at LaMoia, wiggling to break free.

"The purse!" Boldt shouted.

An agent dropped to her knees and scouted under the seat.

"The purse," Boldt repeated, worried now. The evidence: the money, the cash card. He saw LaMoia, still holding the suspect, looking everywhere for the all-important purse. Two

522

others now searched the floor of the bus. One came up slowly, met eyes with Boldt, and hoisted it in the air. The purse.

A cheer went up spontaneously.

Boldt shouted out loudly, "Drive this thing downtown."

LaMoia added, "And watch the goddamn brakes!"

THIRTY-FIVE

Deputy prosecuting attorney Penny Smyth was on her third cup of coffee. She winced every time she sipped the police brew, but took it as medicine against the hour of 2:00 A.M. On the other side of the one-way glass, a handcuffed Cornelia Uli sat at the Box's cigarette-marred table between the NO SMOKING sign and the ashtray. The suspect looked restless and agitated. Looking at her, Daphne said, "She's going to talk, this one."

"You both know the rules," Smyth said. "I don't have to tell you the rules, and I'm sure as hell not coming in there with you, or you might have to observe them." The one area in which police were allowed a significant amount of latitude was in the interrogation of suspects. The interrogating officer could blatantly lie and make as many false promises as he or she wished, so long as the suspect kept talking. Silence and time were a suspect's only real defense in the opening twenty-four hours of confinement. A suspect could demand a court-appointed attorney, but the officer did not have to deliver that attorney for as long as the suspect continued to communicate. This being an arresting officer's only clear opportunity to quickly clear a case, many detectives had perfected the interrogation, promoting it to an art form. As a team, Daphne Matthews and Lou Boldt were among the best, and they were known on the fifth floor as "Sweet and Sour."

Smyth explained, "She has a long pink sheet, which at twenty-one speaks volumes. Convictions on gang activity, drugs, check kiting. Arrests, but no charges, on a handful of others, *including* second-degree murder. She has seen a lot of us. I'd keep that in mind. We've got her cold on this extortion, and with the connection to the threats and the murders, maybe on an accessory charge. If she *doesn't* talk, she may be going away forever. That's your carrot and whip."

The Box smelled of human fear. They could wash it, even repaint it, but within a week it smelled the same. Like an old worn-down railroad terminal, it was the end of the line, the last stop. For many who entered these walls, this was their last time in civilian clothes for years to come. The more experienced — the guilty — knew this. No matter his anger at what crime a suspect had committed, Boldt rarely entered this place without pity lurking somewhere in his heart. He had to wonder what events in people's lives had combined to deposit them here in this cheerless, vapid, dreary space, where a bulldog of an overworked public servant went to work on them like a butcher with a sharp knife.

She might have been pretty once, he thought. But the streets had aged her prematurely, drying her skin and creasing her eyes and placing torment and fear inside so that it bubbled out in a twitchy nervousness that kept Boldt on edge.

Daphne pulled up a chair. Boldt remained standing. Sweet and Sour got down to business. Daphne stared at the young woman. Boldt paced the tight room, in long, heavy strides, hands clasped behind his back. Neither spoke. They waited out their suspect, who finally said, "I want an attorney."

"An attorney?" he asked. To Daphne he said, "She wants an attorney."

"I'll make a note of that."

"Now."

"You want your attorney *now?*" Boldt asked.

"I just said so."

"Are you sure that's what you want? Because I was about to give you a chance to skate this whole mess you're in. And if you *insist* that I get you an attorney, well then, hey! that's all she wrote. An attorney is yours, and I'll see you in court. On the other hand, if you keep your wits about you, Ms. Cornelia Uli, I might turn out to be your knight in shining armor."

"Fat chance."

"She called me fat."

"You look all right to me," Daphne said.

"What? You're a comedy team? I want an attorney."

"And *we will assign you one,* Cornelia. It's taken care of." To Daphne, Boldt said, "You wrote it down, right?"

"It's right here," she informed him, pointing to her stenographer's pad.

"It's right there," Boldt told the suspect. "It's taken care of."

"Bullshit."

He slapped the table with an incredible force. Uli jumped back. Daphne did not flinch. "Listen to me!" he bellowed. "I am your *last chance.*" Effecting a noticeable calm, he said, "You play or you pay. It's that simple. You know what we've got you on? Do you *know* what we intend to charge you with?" To Daphne he said, "Go ahead, tell her." Boldt checked his watch. Two-thirty. He could not remember ever feeling this tired. Any minute LaMoia should have the preliminary results of the search of Uli's loft apartment. Boldt had been present when a SWAT team had kicked the place — hoping for Caulfield — but he had left the detail work for the ID unit and LaMoia.

Daphne read an incredible list of charges, including extortion and concluding with first-degree murder.

When this final charge was read, Uli's eyes flashed darkly between them and she said, "That's bullshit."

"She doesn't know," Boldt told Daphne. "We're supposed to believe that this woman is some innocent runner, some accomplice, when

527

in fact we *know* it was her all along." To Uli he said, "The account number is listed in one of the threats, young lady. That is a direct connection to you and these threats, to you and the poisoning deaths of *ten* individuals. Ten. And believe me, if you're thinking you will somehow get life instead of lethal injection, you have not been paying attention to what's been going on out at Walla Walla. This state is in the killing mood, Ms. Uli. And crimes like this are *exactly* the cases that I'm talking about."

"On the other hand," Daphne said, before Uli could issue the prerequisite string of denials, "if you have something to tell us, your co-operation *might* keep you off death row."

"It *might* let you walk out of here," Boldt said.

"She's not that smart," Daphne told him. "Girls like this always think they know better than us," and to Uli, "which is bizarre to me, since we spend *all* of our time putting people like you away. And people like you spend all of their time behind bars. Isn't that strange?"

"I want an attorney."

Daphne said to Boldt, "I told you she's not that smart. She can't even remember that I already made a note of that."

Boldt said seriously, "You can probably sell sex to the guards for cigarettes. I hear that oral sex is worth a pack. The real thing, a carton. At least for a couple of years you can.

You have a nice body. You're young. But others come along younger than you. And then it gets tough in there, because the guards are through with you. We try to police that, you know. We don't like it. But it's the prisoners who keep it going. They get a little desperate in there. Women liking other women. Are you into that stuff?"

"She's into it all," Daphne said.

"Fuck you!"

"She understands the topic," Boldt said.

"Definitely," Daphne replied.

Boldt looked at his watch again. "I'm tired, how 'bout you?" he asked Daphne.

"Exhausted."

"She's not going to cooperate."

"I think you're right."

"Who says?" asked Cornelia Uli.

Boldt told her, "You're not exactly being forthcoming here, Cornelia."

"Can I stand up?" the suspect asked.

"Please," Boldt said.

"I think better on my feet," she said.

"By all means, think better," Boldt encouraged.

She wandered the small room for a few minutes, and after a short time Boldt observed that Daphne was tracking her with an increased intensity and interest. Confusion knitted the psychologist's brow, and she squinted, saying suddenly to the suspect, "Put your arms over your head again. Like you just had them." Uli stopped walking the floor. "Clasp your hands over your head."

Uli looked to Boldt for support. The sergeant said, "Do as she asks."

Uli obliged, lifting her arms and lacing her fingers on the top of her head. "What's going on?"

She had small, high breasts that disappeared when she lifted her arms. She was thinner than Boldt had first judged her, and her neck was long and elegant.

"Turn around," Daphne instructed.

She did so, asking, "Come on. What's going on?"

"Turn around!" Daphne was out of her chair now. "Who gave you that ATM card?"

Facing the wall, the suspect said, "It was sent to me in the mail."

Daphne sounded angry. "No it wasn't. You *applied* for it by mail. You opened an account." Daphne produced the scanned copy of the account application provided by Lucille Guillard. "A handwriting expert will connect you to this application. We're confident of that. But who put you up to it?"

She began to lower her arms.

"Keep them that way. Turn back around." To Boldt she said, "Do you see it?"

He wanted to support her, but she had lost him. He looked at her inquisitively.

"Who told you to open that account?" Daphne asked.

Uli was looking down at the document on the table, blank-faced, her hands still held on her head. "I . . ."

"And don't hand me a crock of shit, Uli, because I'm running out of patience with you."

Sweet and Sour. They never really knew who would play which role. Sometimes they planned it out in advance: who would befriend the suspect, who would lean. Sometimes it evolved, and they found their roles as the interrogation wore on.

"I can't say," Uli said.

Boldt felt a spike of heat rush up his spine. By these words, Uli had just admitted her culpability in the crimes.

They interrogated her for another forty-five minutes, talking in circles.

Sometime after three, they elected to send her down to lockup. They would try again the next morning.

In the elevator, on their way to the garage, Boldt asked her, "What was the choreography about?"

A worried look about her, Daphne answered carefully: "It's not that I understand it, Lou, but I've seen that woman before."

THIRTY-SIX

Monday morning Boldt was physically awake at eight, but mentally he could not find his bearings. He drank a pot of tea and stuffed himself into his car. He turned on KOMO news on his way downtown. The plan was to meet Daphne and continue with the Uli interrogation.

But as the lead story for the morning news was read, Boldt nearly caused an accident. He involuntarily jerked the wheel, forcing another car to make a quick lane change that evolved into a skidding U-turn, and left Boldt's Chevy sandwiched diagonally in a parallel parking spot. The car's tail was protruding into the morning rush.

He had expected the Striker/Danielson shooting to be near the top, if not the lead itself, but instead the local report began with a pleasant female voice that announced "an unexpected development" in which Adler Foods had been ordered by the FDA, in conjunction with the CDC, to recall every retail product line from all grocery shelves by noon this day. The story suggested that an investigation had begun into the company's role in the "alleged" *E. coli*

532

contamination and in recent poisonings that had claimed several lives. It had yet to be confirmed, the listener was told, but "sources close to the investigation" also claimed that a major food product-tampering and extortion scheme had "held Adler Foods paralyzed" for nearly three weeks, and that local authorities, as recently as yesterday, had summoned the help and assistance of the FBI.

Captain Rankin and the bureaucrats had scored again: Knowingly or not, they had just challenged Harry Caulfield to Russian roulette.

The pulling of the products, the mention of the FBI — all forced Caulfield's hand. He had come to know his adversary. This reckless decision on the part of Captain Rankin drew detective and suspect closer. They shared a disgust at this decision. Boldt knew without checking that there would be a fax awaiting him when he reached his office.

In a strange way, he was glad he was right.

Daphne awakened late, having spent the night with Owen Adler. Feeling frustrated and dirty from the interrogation, she had shed her clothes and taken a moonlit swim, then joined Owen in his bed, where she fell into a deep sleep.

He had sneaked out of bed and showered and shaved, and as he was changing she came awake. "We have the estate under surveillance. Otherwise I wouldn't have come."

"I know," he said. "I'm glad you did."

"I haven't slept that well in weeks."

"I've missed you," he said. "So has Corky." He finished buttoning his shirt.

She pushed the pillow back and sat up in bed, the sheet down around her waist, and felt wonderful that she could be partially naked here without the sensation of violation. She felt none of what she had been experiencing in her houseboat. She decided not to voice her suspicions of Fowler. Not yet.

"Daddy?" It was Corky coming down the hall.

Adler did not want his daughter connecting Daphne to his bed. Daphne knew this, and she sprinted out of bed for the bathroom, making it only to his walk-in closet before being forced to hide. She felt like a teenager hiding from a parent, and she began to laugh at this notion — Corky as Owen's parent, not the opposite — and she gagged herself with the sleeve of a sport coat to keep from being heard.

"Your fax machine is going," his daughter reported.

"I'll be right there." Owen hesitated before saying, "Honey?"

"Why's Daffy in your closet?"

Kids. Daphne's mind raced. She called out, "I'm wrapping your birthday present, Corky."

"You are?"

"No peeking!" She looked through the racks of clothes for a robe to put on, and resorted to one of his man-tailored shirts.

"Are you coming sailing?"

"Maybe afterward," she said. "I can't promise."

"You'll miss Monty the Clown."

"Daffy's extremely busy, Honey, but she's going to try and make it to the party after."

"What kind of present?" she called out.

"No peeking," Daphne repeated, pulling on a pair of his underwear just in case. She started laughing again because the underwear would need a belt to stay on. She kicked them off.

"Meet you in the kitchen," Adler said.

"Okay," said the child, disappointed.

Adler rounded the corner of the walk-in. He said, "Don't even try for the party. I completely understand, and so will Peaches."

But Corky would not understand, and Daphne knew this better than her own father. "I'll catch up to you later. Save me some cake and ice cream." She waited a moment and reminded, "The fax."

D DAY.
FOR WHOM THE BELL TOLLS
IT TOLLS FOR THEE . . .

For the better part of the last thirty minutes, Boldt's attention had been divided between this fax and the situation room wall where eleven pieces of artwork printed by Grambling Printers were thumbtacked. All the artwork contained the three primary colors — red, yellow, and blue — and at least one foil — copper, silver, or gold. The products were as diverse as enchiladas and frozen yogurt, and just looking at them worried Boldt's fragile stomach.

It was nine o'clock in the morning, and LaMoia and Gaynes were home recovering from the ATM surveillance.

Following the advice of Dr. Richard Clements, Boldt had divided his team. Freddie Guccianno remained in charge of tracking down any truck farmer whose vehicle bore these same three colors. In the evening hours Freddie worked with a wall map, planning out the next day's coverage strategy. Although dozens of truck farmers had been questioned, Harry Caulfield remained at large.

Shoswitz was on the phone; he seemed always to be on the phone.

A uniform patrolman entered and crossed the room and handed Guccianno an enormous ball of aluminum foil that contained a sticky roll the size of a tree stump. "You get my receipt?" Guccianno asked. The patrolman produced the receipt, and Guccianno placed it in his top pocket.

Two women detectives, on loan from Sex Crimes, were sorting through the companies represented on the wall by product and affiliation, looking for a link to Adler Foods.

Daphne entered and walked up to the wall, stared at all the products thumbtacked there, and said to the Sex Crimes detectives: "Let's talk this stuff up." She stood there looking around the room. No one seemed to have heard her. "Lou?"

"I don't see what good talking is going to do."

"Which is why I'm the psychologist and you're the detective."

Guccianno oohed, seizing the opportunity to tease Boldt.

"Feisty," Boldt told her.

"Frightened," she answered honestly.

"Okay, so let's talk." He studied the board. "We got eleven companies. Nine of them have vehicle fleets bearing the company colors. Five of those companies utilize truck fleets."

"So we stay with those five companies for the time being," she agreed.

He pointed to the center row of artwork. "Top to bottom: noodles, frozen seafood, ice cream, jams and berries, smoked seafood."

Daphne asked the two women to read off some of the products. "Keep in mind," she told Boldt, "that Caulfield claims to be able to kill a hundred or more people with whatever product or method he's chosen. That has to limit the field."

"You're suggesting he intends to do this all in a single day, *before* we have a chance to issue a recall."

"*Clements* is suggesting so, yes."

Boldt knew that she only said this to attempt

to give it more weight. He then turned to one of the other detectives and said, "Denise, of those five, who has the highest product velocity?"

Boldt and Daphne met eyes while Denise checked through the papers. He acknowledged with a slight nod that Daphne's discussion did in fact seem to be clearing some of the cobwebs. And if she had not been so frightened, she might have smiled as a way of showing her thanks.

Denise said, "In dollar amounts, it's pretty much a tie between Chalmer's microwavable fish dinners and the Montclair ice-cream line. But in terms of sheer product volume, the Montclair ice-cream products far outnumber the dinners."

Daphne wandered over to Denise and borrowed her paperwork on Montclair for a moment.

Boldt knew her well enough to ask, "What is it?"

"That's a familiar name to me . . ." She looked over the paperwork.

Denise, checking more records, advised Boldt, "They also have the largest number of trucks — by *far* — of anyone we're looking at."

Boldt felt the bloodhound in him stir. He stood and began removing the other pieces of artwork, leaving Montclair in the center by itself. Studying it, he asked Daphne, "Familiar how?"

"It's probably a stretch," she said, not answering him.

Daphne flipped through the pages of fax paper detailing the Montclair products. She came across a large picture of a clown with the words *Monty the Clown* written beneath it. Her chest grew tight and her voice turned to gravel. "Then again, maybe not."

That comment drew Boldt's attention. To him she seemed to be in a trance. "Daffy?"

"Monty the Clown," she repeated, holding up the fax's black-and-white artwork for him. "It's an ice-cream bar with a gimmick. The kids love it," she quoted what Owen had told her when he warned her to expect an invitation to Corky's birthday party.

The birthday party was today.

"Ice-cream bar?" Boldt said, in a voice filled with concern.

He repeated it several times and began madly digging through the files stacked high on the table in front of him. "An ice-cream bar," he repeated.

"Lou . . . ," she called out, her voice stronger, her mind ruling out coincidence.

Guccianno raised his head, sensing the tension in both of them.

"It's here somewhere," Boldt mumbled. He found it inside the file, second from the bottom. "Got it!" he hollered, rattling Guccianno's nerves. Boldt tore into the phone book and found the phone number for the Broadway Foodland. Lee Hyundai was paged, and Boldt waited impatiently, finally looking up for the first time and seeing several pair of eyes trained on him.

He held up the receipt and reminded those in the room, "Four items purchased by a man in a greatcoat at express checkout lane, a man identified by Holly MacNamara as Harry Caulfield. Three of the items on here were Adler products — candy bars — and we lost those boys in the tree house, and after that, I never went back to the receipt, focusing on the candy bars instead."

He recalled the haunting words of Dr. Richard Clements: "He will try to deceive you." The Muzak stopped and the voice of Lee Hyundai came on the line. Reading the receipt, Boldt asked, "How much do you charge for a single Montclair ice-cream bar?"

His finger pointed to the receipt where it was written: 1.66. After a long pause, during which Boldt heard the clicking of a keyboard, Lee Hyundai reported, "That would be one dollar sixty-six cents."

Boldt hung up the phone and hollered, "We've got a match!"

Guccianno came out of his chair.

Daphne turned to Boldt and announced with difficulty, "No one may believe this, but I know what he's planning to do. And I know where to find him."

"Are there bells on these trucks?" Dr. Richard Clements was one of the eleven law enforcement personnel now assembled in the emergency meeting under way in the situation room. Department of Motor Vehicle records had been checked four times. No vehicles were registered to a Harry, or a Harold, or an H. Caulfield. Of the four Caulfields in the listings, two were senior citizens and two others in their late fifties.

A Be On Lookout had been issued for all Monty-mobiles, with orders to approach with caution. With urging from the prosecuting attorney's office, the company's legal counsel had agreed to open their employment records to the police, effective immediately. Although they could provide the general areas their trucks covered, there was no direct communication with the trucks, and the specific routes were left up to the drivers. The bottom line was not good: The ice-cream trucks would remain in circulation until late afternoon. The Be On Lookout seemed the only way to catch him.

Dr. Brian Mann had stated emphatically over the phone that strychnine was the perfect poison of choice for a frozen food. "Cholera wouldn't survive in that environment," he had added.

Clements repeated, "Are there bells on these trucks?"

There were three or four conversations going at once, and only by raising his voice in this manner did he draw the attention of those gathered.

"Bells on Monty-mobiles?" Shoswitz said. "Who knows?"

"Yes," answered one of the FBI men. "A least there are on Good Humor trucks back east."

"Well, someone find out," Clements ordered. He held up the fax for Boldt to read again.

FOR WHOM THE BELL TOLLS
IT TOLLS FOR THEE . . .

" 'It tolls for thee . . .' " You see? I am right about our friend. He would like for us to stop him, if we can, with our limited combined intelligence, and take him at his word. 'The bell tolls' for Mr. Adler, gentlemen. How can he be certain? Mr. Adler's daughter is a fan of Monty the Clown." He checked with Daphne, who nodded. She had remained sullen and silent for much of this, not understanding how — when she was so certain of Caulfield's whereabouts — that these *oafs* could call a meeting. Boldt could see the wait was destroying her.

"And Adler's daughter has a party scheduled, with an appearance by Monty the Clown."

"Which means a disguise," Shoswitz said.

"Precisely," agreed Clements.

"And we are assuming he *has* his own truck, rather than is planning to commandeer one — this because of the paint samples found at Longview."

542

"Agreed," Boldt said.

"Can we hurry this up?" Daphne snapped impatiently.

Clements glanced up at her. "Easy does it, Matthews. We understand your concern. We just want to do this correctly. Methodically. Mr. Caulfield is a worthy adversary — we must not underestimate him."

She boiled, crossing her arms defiantly. But she held her tongue.

Boldt reminded, "We have the registration tags for all the legitimate Monty-mobiles."

"One of which is expected at this sailing club — the party," Clements reminded. "But we *must* be able to identify his truck. That is imperative."

Bobbie Gaynes offered, "It would be easier to repaint an old truck than to make original art on one."

"An *auction* list!" Clements snapped his fingers at Gaynes. "Get on it! They *must* get rid of their older trucks!"

Gaynes ran from the room.

For the next twenty minutes they discussed the logistics of attempting to prepare for Caulfield at the sailing party.

Gaynes burst into the room and placed a fax down in front of Boldt. It listed the sixteen Montclair ice-cream trucks that had been placed on the auction block in the last five months.

"His name's not here," Boldt moaned, his hopes shattered.

"I suggest you try the name Meriweather," Clements directed, in that all-knowing tone of his.

Boldt ran a finger down the list and hit the name immediately. "Got it!" he announced. He whistled loudly. The door to the room swung open and a uniform blurred to him at a run. He circled the name and handed the man the sheet. "DMV title and registration. Go!"

"What?" Boldt asked, catching the expression of the psychiatrist, whose eyes immediately began to track back and forth in their sockets. He pointed to Penny Smyth. "Explain the situation."

The prosecuting attorney said, "I don't know how to put this."

"Quickly!" Boldt encouraged, watching the door for the return of the patrolman.

"None of us wants to see Caulfield duck these charges."

"What?" Shoswitz challenged.

She explained, "If you stop him now, you have a truck with poisoned ice-cream inside. You have *intent*, certainly." As she continued talking, Clements waved his pen high in the air and conducted, stabbing and punctuating her words. He was smiling thinly. "But *intent* is *all* you have — *we* have. Some good circumstantial evidence, certainly. Some good motivation that our expert psychiatrist can use to our advantage. I don't deny any of this."

"What is this shit?" Shoswitz asked.

544

Clements, eyes closed, answered for her. "This is the law." He opened his eyes now, sat forward, and placed down the pen. "She's right, of course. It's her job to be right about these things."

Shoswitz looked back at Smyth, who said, "We need to witness the actual passing of a poisoned item to an individual if we're to build any kind of case to carry a life sentence or greater. I'm not saying that what we have isn't good, but it is not enough, I'm sorry to say — not if you want this man on death row. You take him as is, and we'll put him away for ten or twenty. With a good jury, maybe twice that. But connecting him to these other deaths won't be nearly as easy as pinning down an attempted murder — delivery of a fatal substance. There are some holes in the narco laws we may be able to squeeze him into and put him away for mandatory life, which is what I think we all want." She looked at Boldt with sad eyes. She did not like this any more than the rest of them.

Boldt said, "So we sting him."

She nodded.

Checking the clock, Daphne reminded urgently, "Less than forty minutes."

The patrolman charged through the door waving a sheet of computer paper. "We've got the registration!" he announced.

A light breeze blew out of the west, filling

the nine white sails beautifully and causing each boat to heel slightly. Boldt was wearing a set of dirty dungaree coveralls, leaning on a shovel, where LaMoia used a pickax to dig a hole leading nowhere. They worked at the junction of an asphalt path and the parking lot that connected the dock with the parked cars. Boldt wore a flesh-colored earphone with an attached wire that led down between his collar and his neck. A hidden lavalier microphone was clipped below the coveralls' second button. He listened to the running monologue from the task force's dispatcher. By pretending to scratch his chest, Boldt could depress a button allowing him to transmit through the microphone.

The two men cleaning the pool were task force. So were all of a team of four — two men and two women, including Daphne Matthews — who were in the act of putting the finishing touches on the party. The hired caterer and her people were being kept inside the clubhouse and out of sight. Straddling the clubhouse chimney, a roll of tar paper at his side, an FBI sharpshooter pretended to be making repairs. Hidden inside the roll of tar paper, a semiautomatic .306 with laser scope awaited him. This man was capable of a hard-target kill at three hundred yards, and he had the blue ribbons to prove it. At the moment, he had sore ankles as well.

There was a party of three having cocktails in the cockpit of a twenty-one-foot ketch pulled up to the fuel dock. All were task force, all expert shots. The cocktails were ice tea in a bourbon bottle. There was a guy having engine trouble, and another helping him — both bent under the hood of a Chevy, where a pair of handguns remained within easy reach. Hidden inside the clubhouse were six Special Forces agents, and in the bathhouse, six more.

Twenty-four cops and agents in all, eight on radios. The dispatcher nimbly maintained constant communications with all elements, continually updating and informing, and ready to relay the latest input.

In the distance, Boldt heard the approach of the radio station chopper as it reported on traffic on the floating bridge. The Birdman was riding with this pilot and reporting on a separate frequency to dispatch. This was a man who could spot a fox in a thicket from a thousand feet up. If Caulfield's refrigerated truck was in the area, the Birdman would find it.

His efforts were aided by fourteen unmarked cars casually patrolling the seventeen streets that fed the two roadways that fed the dirt road at the end of which was this clubhouse. Phone line work was being conducted on these two feeder roads by FBI agents manned with communications and firearms.

The door-to-door salesman lugging his Naugahyde box from his backseat to the front door of every house on the approach street was in fact Detective Guccianno. He wasn't selling anything; he was informing all residents to get their kids into the house, lock their doors, and await an all-clear. He was also showing each a photo of Caulfield, in case the man had been staking out the neighborhood prior to today.

"Don't worry so much, Sarge," LaMoia said nonchalantly, digging the hole a little deeper.

Static spit in Boldt's ear. "The sailboats are about five minutes out and closing," Dispatch reported. "Alpha is four minutes ETA." That was Adler. "P-one and P-two, make your move, please." Parents-one. Parents-two. A 700 series BMW and a Mercedes sedan, both repossessed in drug convictions, turned into the final approach road, passing beneath the overhead phone line repair crew and pulling into the clubhouse parking lot — make-believe parents about to join their children at the party. For the last thirty minutes, police communications had busily sought out parents of the mostly girls in the sailing party. Of the eighteen kids, the parents of eleven had been contacted, and undercover police were to take their places. The whereabouts of the remaining seven were unknown.

The helicopter, displaying the station call letters, swooped low overhead and banked, as if to return for another pass over the floating bridge. Boldt glanced up. On the other side of the mirrored plastic bubble, the Birdman was scrutinizing the landscape through his binoculars. The Birdman, who could count

548

eyelashes on a flea.

Several more cars arrived — some police, some not. Boldt felt a stream of sweat trickle down his side. Civilians in the mix. He wished there had been a way to prevent that. "You okay?" he asked LaMoia.

LaMoia rested the pickax, looked up at his sergeant, and nodded gravely. "Digging holes is shitty work."

"You've got your line all memorized?"

"I'm ready, Sarge. Relax."

Boldt heard the barking of the dogs, but did not see them yet. There were three scheduled, all German shepherds. Diana, who ran the K-9 squad and trained the dogs, was dressed in jeans and a Bob Dylan T-shirt: out for an afternoon stroll, down to watch the boats come in. Down to wreak some havoc. Another actor in a play so hastily written.

In Boldt's right ear the dispatcher's voice said plainly, "We have hard contact. Repeat: *hard contact.*"

"Hold on!" Boldt whispered hotly to LaMoia, who stopped midswing and set down the tool.

Boldt listened and reported, "Birdman's spotted a gray roof of a decent-size truck parked in a stand of trees about a quarter-mile from here."

"He got here early," LaMoia said, "just as Clements said he would. I bet Clements was a Boy Scout." He added, "I always hated Boy Scouts. Now, *Girl* Scouts was another story

—" He swung the pickax again. A nervous LaMoia was a joke machine. Boldt longed for a switch. LaMoia said, "On second thought I could get to like this work. I kinda miss this physical stuff."

"Cut the chatter," Boldt said.

The chopper pulled up to a new elevation high over the bridge. Boldt assumed that from there the Birdman could keep an eye on the truck. Responding to a question from Shoswitz relayed through Dispatch, Boldt spoke into the radio, "No drive-bys. Nothing to rattle him. Copy?" He nodded and went back to leaning on his shovel.

Boldt pressed his ear and reported to LaMoia, "A second truck, just entering the road . . . Hold it! It has pulled off . . . Something's wrong. . . .Tires are out. Birdman has *all four* tires flat . . ."

LaMoia said, "He spiked the road."

Boldt said, "He spiked the road." And LaMoia grinned for guessing right.

"Take out the competition," LaMoia said. "Make sure the truck that was hired is a no-show. The guy is smart, Sarge."

"Tell me about it."

"You nervous?" LaMoia asked, his concentration fully on his work. "There's nothing quite like an operation, you think? But I never really recover. It's like putting too much postage on a letter, you know? You can never get it back." He added, "Your postman ever return

550

any money to you?"

He reminded Boldt of Liz's mother, who tended to rattle on when she became nervous or anxious, switching subjects randomly and somehow stringing them all together.

Boldt checked the roof. The sharpshooter had his hand inside the roll of tar paper. One of the two pool cleaners was scrubbing the steps of the high dive, making sure he had an elevated vantage point in case he had the only shot. All cogs of the same wheel. It rolled slowly toward Harold Caulfield.

"Boats are two minutes out," Dispatch reported into Boldt's ear. Then, after a spit of static, "Suspect vehicle is rolling." Calmly, he stated: "All stations, suspect is rolling. Good luck, everyone." SPD dispatchers rarely added such editorials, but Boldt was glad to have it.

The dispatcher traced the route of Caulfield's Monty-mobile as it passed under the first of the phone crews. "We have confirmation of vehicle registration."

"We're on," Boldt told LaMoia.

"Show time," said the detective. "Don't forget to smile."

Boldt heard the first sailboat thump against the float, and then the shrieks of excited, childish laughter. One of the parents passed by on the way down the dock, but rubbernecked the two cops, and Boldt realized she was looking at LaMoia's cowboy boots and probably wondering what a guy wearing a gorgeous pair of ostrich boots was doing digging a hole at her club. But she didn't say anything. She ran her hand along the rail, though she walked more slowly, apprehensively, and looked back one more time, her face still caught in curiosity.

Too many civilians, Boldt thought, tempted to abort. Tempted to let it be Penny Smyth's problem: Arrest now, figure out the charges later.

"Don't do it, Sarge," LaMoia said, reading his thoughts. "We've got this bastard. Five minutes and it's all over."

The inevitable question came into his ear; it was the voice of Phil Shoswitz. "Decision time. He's thirty seconds out." Hesitation as he awaited Boldt's signal to arrest now or play it out.

LaMoia stared at him.

The anxious mother, far down the dock, reached the arriving boats and grabbed hold of a line tossed to her. Other parents waited in the party area. Boldt caught Daphne's eye, where he saw both worry and concern, yes — but determination as well.

Boldt considered a sentence of twenty years — out in six with good behavior.

LaMoia, serious now and sensing Boldt's struggle, looked into the man's eyes and said, "Slater Lowry."

In the distance the jingle of cheap bells filled the air.

Boldt depressed the radio button hidden at his chest. "Go," he said.

Dispatch said into his ear, "All stations: green light." He repeated this and then added, "Suspect vehicle has arrived on-site."

Boldt glanced up to check the sharpshooter: The man had changed positions, and now hid behind the chimney where it would be easier to steady a rifle barrel. It occurred to Boldt that in the next few minutes they might kill a man — might get several more killed if they were not careful. For what? To appease the legal process?

The clanging bells grew louder, followed by the sound of a rough motor. Adler shouted not to run on the docks as a group of seven children sprinted toward Boldt and LaMoia.

Boldt recognized Corky from Daphne's description: third back in the pack. Bright-eyed and innocent. After today, regardless of the outcome, her life would be changed; in and of itself, a crime against persons.

The ice-cream truck, bells clanging noisily, came to a stop not fifteen yards from Boldt. The sergeant swung his head casually. The driver wore a clown's face, a bulb nose, and a yellow wig. He was dressed in a baggy jumpsuit of red, yellow, and blue. He reached to his mouth, withdrew a toothpick from his lips, and tossed at the ashtray. For Boldt, this confirmed it: It was Harry Caulfield.

Boldt felt hotter than just moments earlier: body chemicals. He could not allow himself to stare, and so he looked back at the *black hole* that LaMoia had dug, and the similarity to a child's grave was impossible to mistake. He took his first and only stab with the shovel and spilled a mound of dirt back into the hole like a widow at a funeral. He touched his breast pocket, LaMoia looking on nervously, and said for the benefit of the microphone: "Suspect confirmed." He heard the dispatcher repeating this as he plucked the earpiece from his ear and stuffed it down inside his collar, out of sight — out of contact now. Isolated.

The plan called for he and LaMoia to make the front of the line — to beat the kids to the truck and hence maintain their position closer to the parking lot than to the dock or the party area. Boldt took two steps toward the ice-cream truck and casually shouted over his shoulder loudly enough for the driver to hear, "What kind you want?"

"Get me an orange and vanilla," LaMoia answered loudly, delivering his one line just as he had been told.

Boldt quickened his step, sensing the approaching children coming up on him rapidly from behind. Everything felt sharp and crisp, and suddenly the sunlight seemed overpowering — blindingly bright. To his left, the cop on the high dive adjusted his position. To his right, high on the ridge of the roof, the sharpshooter could no longer be seen, but Boldt could imagine the black eye of the barrel looking down on him.

If Boldt pressed the switch hidden on his chest and uttered the words *Take him,* then Caulfield was a dead man — his sentence decided right here and now. The power of that possibility did not escape him. He was judge, jury, and executioner. Ironically, arrest was all that could save the man now.

In this moment of consideration, he moved too slowly. Two of the frantic children scampered past him and cut in line, beating him to the ice-cream truck. This was *not* the way they had planned it, and though his fallback position had been to take Caulfield before any sale of ice cream, that too was now no simple matter, given the two children — hostages — easily within his reach.

The safety release was Diana and her three shepherds. Boldt glanced over at her, seeing she was in position, just behind the ice-cream truck, kneeling and talking to her dogs: stalling.

Boldt could not make a play for Caulfield until these two kids were out of the way.

The first child in line ordered a Big Dipper with nuts, and Caulfield, looking uncomfortable and acting slightly awkward, moved to the side of the truck and checked two of the small doors before coming out with the order. "None with nuts," he said, handing the girl the ice cream. "I'm all out." She took it anyway and immediately handed Caulfield two dollar bills. Boldt recognized fear as it darkened the suspect's eyes: with all this preparation, he had neglected to bring change. He stuttered, "Ahh — I —," glanced into Boldt's eyes, and hurried back into the truck. He came out with change and handed the girl some coins. He looked into Boldt's eyes again — calmly — and Boldt thought that Caulfield somehow knew.

The second child in line ordered a Red Bar — frozen fruit juice on a stick — and it occurred to Boldt that as he stood here waiting in line, every Montclair frozen ice-cream product in a three-state region was being pulled from the shelves — every truck emptied and the product destroyed. If Caulfield had laid bigger plans, hopefully they had shut these down.

"Change?" the man was asking Boldt. "Any change?" Caulfield repeated. Boldt had been caught up in thought. "Any quarters?"

The coveralls allowed a snapped slit to access the pants he wore underneath, and Boldt reached into his pocket and found five quarters and several dimes. He extended his open palm to Caulfield, who thanked him, and picked his way through a dollar in change, exchanging it for a dollar bill.

He thanked me. I just helped him, Boldt thought. He stuffed Caulfield's dollar back into his pants, but it required of him an amazing amount of concentration and effort for so simple a task.

The girl with the Red Bar slipped out of line, and Lou Boldt stood facing Harry Caulfield.

"Help you?" the clown asked.

556

"An orange one with vanilla, and a Big Dipper, please." He was saying "please" to a murderer; it seemed inconceivable to him.

Caulfield checked two doors. The white vapor of the dry ice escaped, briefly concealing him inside a cloud. "An Orange-Up and a Big Dipper?" he confirmed.

"That's right."

Boldt heard the tearing of paper. The two kids were not waiting: They were ripping into their treats. He glanced hotly at Diana, and she released the trained dogs, who immediately bounded across the pavement and leapt at the girls, knocking them down and stealing their ice-cream bars. The panicked screams and piercing cries of the two girls cut Boldt to his core. Diana plunged into the fray, confirming that the ice creams were not in their possession, and then called off her dogs, making apologies. She reprimanded both dogs severely, all the while petting them — a trainer's game. As if on cue, Daphne and another of the fake caterers rushed to help the girls.

His backup was in place.

Boldt, pretending to be absorbed in the drama, kept one eye cautiously on Caulfield, who handled the disturbance quite well. And then Caulfield's head snapped and Boldt followed his line of sight: Inexplicably, the third of the shepherds was gobbling down one of the ice creams. It had sneaked in behind its trainer as she collared and controlled the other two dogs.

557

Seeing this, Caulfield seemed to panic.

Boldt tried to catch Diana's eye, but it was too late. *Snap, snap* — the Big Dipper was gone.

"Two-ninety," Caulfield said.

Boldt had not thought this out, had not figured on having to hold the two ice creams in one hand while searching for money in his pocket. This left him with no hand free for his weapon. As he rummaged back into his pocket and found several dollars, Corky Adler jumped line in front of him and demanded a Sno-Foam Fudge Bar. At this same moment, Owen Adler, right behind his daughter, looked first into Boldt's face, then Daphne's, and actually staggered as he realized what he had walked into. He straightened himself up, and in a moment of quick thinking said, "Corky, let's wait for the cake!"

At the sight of Adler, Harry Caulfield was unable to move. The air charged with hatred. Corky, oblivious to it, said to the clown, "It's my birthday, I can do what I want. Right, Monty?"

Boldt handed Caulfield the money, which snapped the man's momentary lapse. If he could just get Corky out from in front of him, it was over. His hand, free of the money, was now touching the stock of the handgun. *Move, Corky.* "Better listen to your father," Boldt said, trying to nudge her.

"Stop it!" she said precociously, holding her ground.

Move! He tried again.

"Quit it!"

"All out of Sno-Foam," Caulfield apologized to the girl, focusing on her briefly, moving to the freezer door closest to him. "But how 'bout a Big Dipper?" he asked. "Monty thought the birthday girl loved Big Dippers."

Adler stammered.

Daphne stepped forward, alongside Boldt, a face of cold stone. She took Corky's left arm, "Listen to your father, Corky."

"You made it!" a delighted Corky said. "Oh please. Oh please, Daffy!"

The other kids pressed in against Boldt, eager to be next in line. It was too crowded. It was all wrong. They could not take Caulfield with Corky where she was, and they could not allow this man to sell anything more.

Caulfield was distracted, and Boldt followed to see one of the shepherds whining and circling erratically, Diana consoling him. Boldt understood then that *all* of the ice cream was poisoned, not just selected pieces intended for Adler or his daughter. Another check of Diana's charge confirmed it. The dog stumbled and went down onto its front legs in a praying position. He collapsed twice and pulled clumsily back to his feet, wanting to perform for his trainer. But it was no use — he was dying.

Boldt turned in time to see Caulfield leaning toward Corky with the Big Dipper.

The little girl accepted the ice-cream cone

and tore at the wrapper.

"No, Corky!" Adler exclaimed, but not in the voice of a father worried about spoiling an appetite.

Caulfield reacted instantly, by reaching out for Corky — wanting a hostage. "Motherfucker," Caulfield muttered, looking at Adler.

Boldt went for his gun, but it hung up in the coveralls.

Caulfield took hold of the child. Daphne's purse came at his face like a wrecking ball, and as it connected, she yanked Corky away, threw her down onto the pavement, and covered her.

The children behind Boldt screamed.

Boldt charged the man. Caulfield went up hard against the side of the truck, and Boldt felt a knee implode into his gut, the wind knocked out of him. His head swirled as he heard more screams from behind him — screams of children — and the unmistakable sound of weapons being drawn from holsters as the voice of John LaMoia hollered, "Hold your fire!" Boldt was going down to the pavement in slow motion as LaMoia appeared in his peripheral vision, diving through the air.

He saw Sheriff Turner Bramm's shotgun then: It had been sawed off, the metal a fresh silver on the end of the barrels, and must have come from inside one of the freezers.

"Down!" he heard shouted in the midst of the pandemonium.

"Drop it!" came a stern voice from behind. LaMoia dove at Owen Adler and carried him down hard to the pavement.

Boldt, still falling toward the pavement in an indescribable slow motion, touched the chest of the coveralls and said, "Take him."

He heard a dull *pop* — like hands clapping together — and the side of the truck sprayed with Caulfield's blood. It was a shoulder shot, and though Caulfield's eyes rocked in his sockets and seemed to acknowledge the hit, the sawed-off never faltered for a moment. Mechanically, he pumped the weapon. Boldt, in midair, kicked out hard and caught the toe of his shoe under Caulfield's kneecap. Caulfield twisted and screamed.

The sawed-off blew the mirror off the truck and sprayed the front windshield into powder.

Two of Boldt's people swarmed on top of Caulfield.

Boldt's head slammed into the pavement and the lights went out. He heard the words, "Paramedics! He's hit." "Get these kids out of here!" Coming back, Boldt pulled himself up to sitting. Caulfield was buried under a pile of police. A pair of handcuffs sparkled in the afternoon sun as they disappeared into that pile. The Miranda was being spoken.

A moment later the pile parted slightly, revealing a clown without his nose and wig — just bright red cheeks and eyes filled with hatred. His shoulder was bleeding badly.

Daphne was hugging Corky and stroking her hair. Boldt could not see LaMoia or Adler.

But he did see Diana. She was weeping, her shepherd down and still. She held to it as a mother to a child.

Boldt's heart tore in two. Too close. Too big a risk. And yet the joy of triumph as well. The Tin Man was in handcuffs, his glassy eyes fixed rigidly on a point beyond Boldt, fixed on a man whose voice rose above all others as he called out joyously for his daughter.

THIRTY-SEVEN

While surgeons at Harborview Medical Clinic stitched up Caulfield's left shoulder, Boldt and six others went through several hours of debriefing. The Scientific Identification Division's second-floor lab, under the direction of Bernie Lofgrin, began testing each and every one of the sixty-one ice-cream products recovered from the freezer van.

Despite the fatigue of everyone involved, there was an ebullient bounce in the step of all those who walked the fifth floor. A press conference, scheduled so that footage could be included in the eleven o'clock news, was held in a conference room at the Westin, with over eighty journalists and news crew personnel in attendance. Captain Rankin, the police chief, and the mayor fielded questions, assuring the public that "this terrible man" had been apprehended, that a "nightmare of carnage had been avoided," and that Seattle's supermarkets were safe once again.

Bobbie Gaynes, John LaMoia, Freddie Guccianno, and dozens of others involved in the incident were given a six-hour break to go home and sleep. Some of them took it, some did not.

The emergency surgery took forty-five minutes, finishing up a few minutes before six o'clock. The chief surgeon allowed Boldt and one other detective to interrogate the suspect if the interrogation was kept to thirty minutes or less. Boldt pressed for and won a concession that the interrogation could involve three, possibly four people. A second, more involved session was tentatively approved for the next morning. Although Caulfield had already waived his right to an attorney, by morning a public defender would be assigned and the case would fall into the hands of the attorneys. With *black holes,* everything was done to the letter.

At ten-thirty that night, armed with a cassette tape recorder and a large tea, Boldt stood outside Caulfield's hospital room alongside two SPD patrolmen who stood guard. They were accompanied by Dr. Richard Clements and deputy prosecuting attorney Penny Smyth.

Boldt wanted nothing less than a full confession. They had attempted murder, they had enough circumstantial evidence to fill a courthouse, but a confession would finish things nicely. Clements wanted "a peek into that mind." Smyth wanted to make sure they conducted the interrogation properly.

"Before we go in," Clements said, stopping them, "his world has ended, and he knows it. He continues to blame Adler — not us, you will find — for *everything.* And that is *extremely* important, because it offers us a way to the truth. He will surrender the truth without meaning to. The more he tries to hide it, the more we can get from him. I see your confusion. You will understand as we proceed." He pushed open the door, and they entered the room.

Caulfield was awake, lying in bed, his head rocked up on a pillow, his eyes alert and sparking darkly with anger. The room, stripped down to the bare necessities, smelled of alcohol and disinfectant. The surgery had involved only local anesthesia, which meant medication would not interfere with or negate the results of the interrogation.

Boldt switched on the tape recorder and spoke clearly, listing the location, the time of day, and those present.

Caulfield's pewter-gray eyes ran over them. The man looked so *normal.*

Clements pulled up a chair beside the bed. Boldt and Smyth remained standing.

"I've got nothing to say," Caulfield informed them.

Smyth said, "The difference to you, should you cooperate, may mean life imprisonment instead of the death penalty."

"I want to hang," Caulfield said, stunning both Boldt and Smyth.

Clements smiled and said softly, "Of course you do."

Caulfield eyed him peculiarly.

Clements said, "But not before clearing Mark Meriweather's good name. Hmm? Think about it."

"You know about that?"

"We know about *everything,* my boy. We are very interested in Mr. Meriweather."

Caulfield looked at him curiously, wondering how far he could trust the man. "Bullshit," he said.

"Meriweather was set up, son."

"Don't call me that."

"Very well. What would you like me to call you? Mr. Caulfield? Harold? Harry?"

"Leave me alone."

"If I leave you alone, attorneys like our Ms. Smyth here will get their hooks into you and that will be that. You've been through this before, Harry. You know what I'm talking about. If you had wanted that, you would not have waived your right to an attorney."

"Attorneys suck," he said directly to Smyth. "No attorneys."

"Let's talk about your hanging for a minute."

"I want it over."

"I understand. But why so fast? What about Mark Meriweather?"

"He's dead. It's over."

"You loved him."

"He was good to me."

"They broke him."

"They lied."

"Yes. We know that."

Caulfield sat forward slightly, stopped by the pain of his wound, but his neck remained craned forward.

Clements said, "Oh yes. We know about it all. They laced the birds. They paid people off. They placed the blame on Mark Meriweather." He paused. "They made you kill the birds."

The pain on Caulfield's face cried out. The last thing Boldt wanted was to feel sorry for this monster.

"That wasn't easy, was it? Killing those birds."

Caulfield shook his head slightly. He seemed to have left the room.

"You had never seen Mr. Meriweather like that, had you?"

"So much blood," Caulfield whispered.

"He wasn't himself."

"He changed."

"Yes, killing the birds changed him, didn't it?" He added, "Changed you all."

Caulfield nodded.

"You loved those birds."

He nodded again.

"We need your help, Harry. If you help us, we will help you. Sergeant Boldt here knows all about what happened out at Longview Farms, but we need to hear about this soup. What you did to the soup."

"The birds were *not* sick."

"We know that. And you blamed Mr. Adler."

"They lied about us."

"What about the soup, Harry? Tell us about the soup."

"They poisoned our birds. I warned them. They didn't listen." He had a glazed look, no longer directed at Clements or Boldt or Smyth, but somewhere on the ceiling or the back wall. Off on his own. "I thought the cholera would convince them."

"You put the cholera in the soup?"

He nodded.

Boldt glanced over at the tape. *Still running.*

Clements saw this and said, "I didn't hear you, Harry."

Harry Caulfield just stared at the wall.

"We need your help, Harry."

"I did it because they did it to us. I did it to show them that they had better listen."

"Did what?"

"Poisoned the soup."

Boldt and Clements met eyes. There it was — and captured on tape.

Caulfield attempted to sit up once again, but was beaten by the pain. He pleaded, "Why didn't they believe me? Why did they let those people die?"

"Excuse me," Smyth said. She was pale and her lips were trembling. She walked quietly to the door and left the room.

"Tell me about the money," Boldt said.

"What are you talking about?" His eyes burned into Boldt.

"The extortion money," the sergeant reminded. But Caulfield's face went blank, and Boldt felt certain that this was no act.

568

"You're out of your mind." To Clements he said, "All cops are out of their fucking minds."

"Are you out of your mind, Harry?"

"Who is this guy?" he asked Boldt. To Clements he said, "A shrink, am I right?"

"How do you feel about these murders, Harry? Tell me about these murders."

"Ask Owen Adler. No fault of mine."

"Tell me about the murders."

"I didn't murder anyone."

"Yes you did, Harry. You have murdered twelve people, including two peace —"

"I didn't murder *anyone!* And I don't know *anything* about any extortion money, or whatever the hell it is you asked me," he said to Boldt.

Clements scooted farther forward, leaned in closely, and whispered intimately, tenderly, "We're listening, Harry. We want to hear whatever you want to tell us. Doesn't matter what." Caulfield's eyes brimmed with tears. "The world has not treated you fairly, have they, son?" This time, Caulfield did not object to Clements's using the term. Instead, the patient shook his head and tears spilled down his cheeks. Clements said warmly, but in a strangely eerie voice, "No one has listened, have they? *I know* what that's like, son. Believe me, I know. They just never listen." Caulfield shook his head again. "You told them about what happened at Longview, and did they listen? Is that *fair?* You told them about that drug charge — oh yes, I've read the piece. It's a brilliant piece of

569

writing, son. Something to be proud of. I've read it all." Caulfield groaned. "But no one ever listens, do they? They tell you to come back. They tell you to go away. They treat you like a child. But they never *listen*, do they?" He paused. "No one has ever listened like Mark Meriweather listened. And they took Mark away from you. They ruined him, didn't they?"

The cry that came from the man might have been heard across several of the hospital's wings. The patient's mouth hung open and he wailed at the ceiling, rocking his head on the pillow, and Dr. Richard Clements threw his own head back, closed his eyes, and listened like an opera patron enjoying an inspired aria.

"I'm listening!" Clements shouted in the middle of one of these cries, and it only encouraged the patient louder. Boldt glanced at the tape recorder — no one was going to believe this, he thought.

Before the male nurses threw open the door, Clements had already raised his hand to stop them and wave them off. Boldt had not heard their approach.

"We're fine," the doctor reported. "A little healthy release is all." He said to the patient, "They heard you, Harry. Do you see? We're listening now! We can hear you!"

Caulfield stopped and opened his tear-stained eyes, and Boldt thought he was witnessing a soul's final glimpse of sanity, that Harry Caulfield had made a fateful journey. But Clements did not seem bothered in the least. For the benefit of the troubled male nurses, Clements said to the patient, "We're fine, aren't we, son? Better now, aren't we?" To the nurses he said, "You see?" And he waved them off contemptuously, a move he finished by sweeping off the lapels of his double-breasted blazer.

"Now let's start at the beginning, shall we, son? Every action starts with a thought. Can you tell me, please, about the very first moment that you knew Owen Adler had to pay for his crimes? The very first inspiration. I have all the time in the world, son. All the time in the world."

Clements looked over at Boldt, beaming a smile.

Boldt was not certain who was crazier. "The money," Boldt repeated.

"I don't know anything about any money," Caulfield repeated angrily. For the second time, Boldt believed him.

He did *not* have all the time in the world. He grabbed the tape recorder and headed straight to the office to have it transcribed.

Boldt slept for fourteen hours, awakening at two in the afternoon. He ate a light meal, called the office, and fell back to sleep. At eleven that night, he found himself wide awake with a dozen thoughts colliding in his head. He kissed his sleeping wife, changed clothes, and returned to the office. DeAngelo's squad

571

was on rotation. Everyone congratulated him on the Caulfield raid and on the confession, treating him like a hero, but Boldt did not feel like a hero: The extortionist was still at large.

He checked with Lockup. He checked with Daphne — but could not find her. Cornelia Uli had a public defender assigned to her. She was in the system now.

With no evidential connection yet made between Uli and Harry Caulfield, no money found in Caulfield's possession, no ATM cards, and Caulfield's denial of extortion — while confessing to cold-blooded murder — Boldt felt compelled to believe that Caulfield had had no connection to the ATM scam.

He pulled out Uli's file and started through it once again, reviewing her past arrests: gangs, drugs, a prostitution charge that had been dropped. He looked at her earlier arrest photos. Sixteen, seventeen years old. A real sultry beauty then. Now, at twenty-one, the street had robbed her of her looks. The gangs were hardest on the young women.

Each time through, he had been reviewing the contents of the files, quickly passing over the form headings, the departments, the officers involved: the overly familiar information that any cop encountered repeatedly and with little or no interest. But the next time through, a number jumped out at him. One little number typed innocently years before into one little box. So easy to miss. One small piece of information left on a form. Over six years old now. By a cop making an arrest, filling out a blank: *Arresting Officer: 8165.*

The ATM PIN number. Boldt picked up the phone, his hand trembling, dialed Daphne's number again, and again she did not answer. He had to search his notebook to find Adler's unlisted residence. His fingers punched out the number. He waited seven rings before Adler answered and passed Daphne the phone.

"I need you," he said.

Chris Danielson was asleep when Boldt turned the light on in his room. Daphne and the male night nurse followed at a run. Boldt turned to this nurse, pointed to the other bed in Danielson's room, and said, "He's out of here — now."

The nurse opened his mouth to complain, but Boldt had already been through hell with him at the nurses' station, and he had had his fill. "Get that bed out of this room *now!*" The man mumbled something, but obeyed. Apologizing to Danielson's roommate, the nurse took him for a ride into the hall, and Daphne closed the door.

"I need straight answers, Chris."

He still appeared half-asleep. "Sarge?"

"And Matthews," Daphne announced herself.

"They're going to throw me out of here in a minute — we're still not allowed to see you

— and this can't wait until morning. Are you with me?"

"Go ahead." He rolled his head, blinked furiously, and reached for a paper cup of ice water with a straw. Boldt handed it to him and Danielson sucked in a mouthful.

"You took Caulfield's file from the Boneyard without signing it out — a day *before* we identified him. When we did, you returned it. I need to know why."

Any minute, that door would open.

The man had new lines in his face, and a combination of pain and exhaustion in his eyes. A tent frame held the covers off his abdomen, and two large weights held his legs in traction. His voice was dry. "I obtained a state tax record of Longview employees. Caulfield had a record. I pulled the file."

"But *why?*" Boldt challenged. "For money?"

"Money?" he asked incredulously. "To clear the *black hole*, why else?" The man was too tired, too medicated for Boldt to read his face well.

"You were offered a job away from the force," Boldt speculated.

"Not true." He met eyes with Boldt. "I wanted *your* job."

A flashing light passed below the window as a silent ambulance arrived. It pulsed light across all their faces.

"I wanted this one worse than you did. I've been going at this case night and day when I

574

wasn't handling *your* paperwork for you. 'Nice little nigger, sit behind the desk and let the white boys do the big, tough jobs.' Not this nigger, Sergeant. Bullshit."

"It wasn't like that, *at all*."

"Wasn't it?"

They both raised their voices simultaneously and began shouting. Daphne cut them off with a sharp reprimand and said to both of them, "Out of order!"

Unaccustomed to losing his temper, Boldt took a few seconds to pull himself together. He checked his watch — precious seconds.

Daphne said to the injured man, "Elaine Striker."

Danielson looked over at her. "Just one of those things that happened. It's nothing I'm proud of. She's lonely and she doesn't remember what love is."

"And then this *black hole* comes along," Daphne nudged.

"Like I said, it's nothing I'm proud of. Turns out Michael Striker is a talker, that's all. Turns out his wife knows everything there is to know about this case, and suddenly I'm a lot more interested in the romance — the pillow talk — and she isn't complaining."

"What a sweetheart you are," Daphne said.

"I paid for it, Matthews. You want to switch places?" He jerked his head toward the corner of the room where a collapsed wheelchair leaned against the wall.

Daphne stuttered.

"Listen, Striker was all messed up about Lonnie — Elaine. He wasn't thinking clearly. I came to him for a warrant to get the New Leaf bank records — the canceled checks — and it never occurred to him to clear it with you," he said to Boldt.

"You found the payoffs," she concluded.

"No, I didn't. They were more careful than that. It was a long shot was all: Hoping to find a paper trail to the bribe money. I had already guessed who had been paid off, but couldn't prove it. So I changed tack."

"We're listening, Chris."

"Check the transcript of Caulfield's trial. It was *not* a good case. But public sentiment toward drugs was bad right then — you so much as said the word *cocaine*, and in a jury trial the suspect went down for the long count. And what did the case hinge on? Some tip that the arresting officer received. The whole thing turned on this snitch — an anonymous tip. One anonymous snitch, and Caulfield goes away for four and change. Granted, that's how Drugs' busts go down: Narcs never reveal their snitches. But if you read between the lines of that transcript, the arresting officer — a cop named Dunham — was nervous as hell up on the stand. Why? Because he didn't have a legitimate snitch. It was a setup. Caulfield *was* framed."

"And?"

"And before I got to this Dunham, Striker

got to me. Must have followed Lonnie — Elaine — to the hotel."

"But you suspected someone."

"Wouldn't be fair. I never did prove it."

"Kenny Fowler," Boldt said, supplying the name. He mumbled, "Badge number eight-one-six-five."

Daphne stared at him, dumbfounded.

Danielson's eyes flashed. He hesitated, barely nodded, and explained, "Dunham's partner for five years on Major Crimes. Fowler goes private with a company called New Leaf. Dunham goes over to Drugs. He's floundering, can't get the hang of Drugs. Then he does this major bust: Harry Caulfield with a couple kilos of high-quality soda. Four months later, guess who he's working for? Double the salary, double the vacation. Double the fun."

Boldt sagged and leaned onto the frame of the bed. "Jesus." In a soft, apologetic, guilt-ridden voice, he confessed, "I got you shot, Chris." No one said a thing until Boldt spoke again. "I suspected you of stealing that file. I didn't want an IA investigation in the middle of this *black hole*. I asked Fowler to place you under surveillance for me. Keep it out of uniform. He lied to me about what he found out about you. Obviously, what he found out was that you were a little too close for comfort and that you were sleeping with Elaine Striker."

Another long silence as the sound of the circulating air and the hum of machinery seemed

deafening to Boldt. He wanted this man's for-
giveness, and he knew that was impossible.

"Her PD is on his way," prosecuting attorney
Penny Smyth informed them.
"But do we wait?" Boldt asked her.
"No one is forcing her to speak to you,"
Smyth pointed out. "You can push, but tech-
nically she doesn't have to talk."
"Understood."
Smyth was cautious not to give them her
outright approval. "You don't have much time."
She requested of Daphne, "Should anyone ever
ask: You loaned me your office, where I re-
mained while you two were in there with her,
okay?"
"Near as I can remember."
Boldt and Daphne moved quickly down the
hall. "I have an idea. Back me up in here,"
she requested, meeting eyes with him as he
reached to open the door for her.
"I'm there," he promised.
"We turn the volume way up and she's going
to talk. Bet on it. But it may get a little nasty."
"That suits her, I think."
He followed her into to the Box. Daphne
never broke stride. She burst through the door,
leaving it for him to close, and she hollered
at the suspect, "Out of the chair. Now!"
Dressed in an orange jumpsuit, Cornelia Uli
wore a haggard expression from her two dismal
nights in lockup. Uli sprang to her feet.

"Come over here," Daphne said, indicating the end of the table. "Right here."

Uli stood at the end of the interrogation table, looking concerned.

Daphne said, "Now let's get one thing straight: If you do not cooperate with us, your life just got ugly. You're going where girls do other things to girls that are not pleasant — things you've never *heard* of — and where the guards just do worse things, so no one ever says a thing to them. You keep your mouth shut, unless someone has use for it. That's option number one. Option number two is you open that same mouth for me, right now. This is *not* some two-year drug charge we're talking about. It is *not* some check-kiting scam. This is *not* some free ATM card that your pal set up for you. This is murder one. This is the end of your pitiful little life, Cornelia, if you do anything but *exactly* as I say."

"I've got nothing to say."

Daphne glanced once, hotly, at Boldt, turned to face the suspect, and said, "Lean against the table."

"I will not," Uli protested.

Daphne slapped the table hard, jarring the woman. "Lean against the table."

"Go ahead," Boldt said.

Reluctantly, Uli leaned onto her hands.

"Your forearms," Daphne said. "Good. Now open your legs. More. Move 'em. Good!"

"What do you think?" Daphne asked, stepping back to view the profile as she might a painting.

Having no idea what he was agreeing to, Boldt said, "I think you're right."

Daphne stepped up behind a nervous Cornelia Uli and reached around her, careful not to make contact, and leaned over her in a provocative position impossible to mistake. She rocked her hips unmistakably. In an intimate whisper she asked the suspect, "Remind you of anyone?"

"Get off me."

"I'm not on you. Neither was he. He was *in* you."

Boldt felt like an idiot for taking so long to see it: The woman in Kenny Fowler's apartment. The night Daphne had taken the hotel room and sat in the dark.

In that same intimate whisper Daphne said, "I saw you two up there."

Uli's head jerked. "I don't know what you're talking about."

"It didn't look like you enjoyed it very much," Daphne said. She added quietly, "Whatever he has on you is gone. We tear it up, burn it, whatever. We're not interested."

"All I do is squeal, right? Forget it."

The first crack.

Boldt said, "We're talking about extortion, accessory to murder. The rest of your natural life spent behind bars." He added, "We *know* it was you."

The door swung open and an angry male voice demanded, "Out of here now!"

It was Uli's public defender, and he left the door for them to close as he rushed to his client's side.

On the other side of the Box's one-way glass, Uli, her attorney, and Penny Smyth, were waiting impatiently for Daphne and Boldt, who had been talking it through for the last several minutes.

Wrapping it up, Boldt speculated, "Being one of the few insiders, Fowler knew how to word the extortion threat so that we would attribute it to Caulfield."

"But he blew it — the extortion demand neglected to blame Adler, something that bothered both Dr. Clements and me."

"We *expected* extortion demands. He simply gave us what we *wanted*."

Looking at Uli through the glass, Daphne explained proudly, "It was her body language that caught my eye. When she started prancing around the room like that, I knew I recognized her. I sat in that hotel room watching them for *hours*. It just took a second for it all to click."

Boldt said cynically, "Both of them in that apartment — right there across from us . . ."

"He was angry with her about something. Maybe she wasn't supposed to show up there. He took a quickie at the dining room table

581

for payment and sent her packing."

"He's such a prince," Boldt said, swinging open the door as they joined the others.

Uli's public defender was a young Jewish kid fresh from the law boards named Carsman. He looked like an unmade bed. He had a high, squeaky voice and he protested Boldt's every breath. Penny Smyth, looking the most dignified of any of them, dragged Carsman into the hallway for a conference, and when they returned to the Box, Carsman did not utter a single objection. He took notes furiously, and occasionally passed one to his sagging client.

Boldt passed Uli her arrest record. "Badge number eight-one-six-five. That badge number belonged to Detective Kenneth Fowler when he was a police officer. He arrested you in a gang situation, and you were charged with a second-degree homicide. The charges were later dropped for lack of evidence."

Daphne stated, "We saw you in his apartment that night."

"Shit," the suspect said, and she hung her head and shook her hair in defeat.

Boldt felt triumphant. His face revealed nothing. Impassive. Exhausted.

Daphne said, "What does he have on you, Cornelia?"

She mumbled. "A videotape. A surveillance tape. I was seventeen."

"Sex?" Daphne asked.

"A homicide," Boldt stated knowingly.

"Don't answer!" Carsman interrupted.

Boldt said, "Lester Gammon. Age eighteen. Stabbed seven times."

Cornelia Uli obeyed her attorney, though she locked eyes with Boldt. "He asks me to do stuff now and then. I do it."

"Like the other night?" Daphne asked.

"Go stuff it," Uli said vehemently. "What do any of you know about the streets? Let me tell you something — out there you do favors and people leave you alone. It's simple in the streets. It's basic survival. You and your perfect hair and your strawberry douche," she said spitefully to Daphne. "You make me sick."

Daphne blushed and held herself back in a formidable show of internal strength.

"You did Fowler favors," Boldt repeated.

"Like this ATM thing. Yeah."

"Do *not* say anything more!" her attorney advised.

"Shut up," Uli told him.

"I can't represent you if —"

"Shut up!" To Boldt she said, "I went where he told me to. I did what he said to do." To Daphne she said, "And yeah, he jumps my bones now and then. And no, I don't particularly like it. But it's not like it's something new, okay? He's been doing it since back when he was a cop. He had a lot of the girls doing it back then. If Kenny busted you, you went down on him. No charges. It was that simple. That's what I'm saying. You get why I'm afraid of cops? It started when I was fifteen and running with a gang. Kenny liked me. Too bad for me." She seemed to be apologizing to Daphne. "You get kinda used to the ones like Kenny Fowler. But it's better than the alternative, and that's the way it works out there. Doing favors for people beats the hell out of living under bridges in cardboard boxes. Getting gang-banged. Getting bad needles. You don't know until you've been there."

"You're right," Daphne said, overcoming her personal agenda and striving to establish rapport with the suspect. Daphne's friend Sharon *had* been there. Daphne knew all about it, but was not going to say so, was not going to defend herself. Boldt admired her for that.

"He gave you the ATM card," Boldt began for her.

"And the number. And he told me which machines to hit. Big deal. He gave me a hundred a night."

"Generous," Boldt said.

"It's a living," Uli replied dully.

"Sergeant?" It was Penny Smyth. She asked for a conference in the hall. Daphne stayed with the suspect.

Smyth said, "What I'm seeing here is that its going to come down to her word against Fowler's. Is there any other evidence tying them together other than this? Because I've got to tell you, a judge is not going to like her. Will Fowler have the money on him? No way. It's *long* gone — the minute you picked this girl up, it was gone. He was a cop, right? He knows the game. He'll have something planned; he used her for a reason. Am I right, or am I right? I'll run with this if you want. I can take it up the ladder and see what they think, but it stinks, if you ask me. She's young — she has reasons, serious reasons in her past to hate Fowler and want to do him harm, and that's going to come out in any testimony. It stinks, Sergeant. Matthews cannot say for sure it was this girl in Fowler's apartment that night."

Boldt countered, "We have the PIN number. We have the former arrest."

"The bank account was opened by her. She uses Fowler's badge number as a way of getting back at him, just in case she's caught, which she was. I'm showing you the spin that can be put on this. As a witness she stinks, I'm telling you. Your call. You tell me what you want me to do." She met and held eyes with him.

"I hate attorneys," Boldt told her.

"Me too." She smiled. "All my friends are cops."

He smiled back. "So what do you suggest, Counselor?"

"I suggest she wears a wire for us. We plea her down to six months in medium with good behavior. Carsman will do back flips to get that. We send Fowler to the Big House until he's gray."

Boldt asked incredulously, "Do you actually think that Kenny Fowler will get within a six-state region of this woman? No way in hell. Maybe to kill her, but not to —" He caught himself.

"What is it?" she asked.

"Maybe we let Fowler do our work for us. I think he owes us that."

Boldt had his car swept for listening devices before driving Daphne out to Alki Point, where he parked with a view of the water and a volleyball game being played out at sunset. Thankfully, no devices had been found.

A body had washed ashore here once, and had changed a case and their lives along with it. He had not chosen this place to park at random.

"I don't want to ask this of you, Daffy."

"Then *don't*." She knew already. But she had agreed to the drive, so perhaps he stood a chance of convincing her. She looked away from him, out her window. "Please don't," she repeated.

"You have to be living back there if this is going to work. We'll have to script some things for you and Adler to say. We have to chum the water, or he'll spot the hook."

"Do you understand what you're asking?"

"I know what I'm asking — I don't know what it would be like. I don't know that I could do it."

"And Watson and Moulder — they would see me, too, if all this works the way you have planned. On the toilet, in the shower . . . My God, Lou!"

"We gave him the mug shot, Daffy. We know he showed it around the processing plants, the warehouses. At some point someone must have recognized it. Caulfield delivered there on a regular basis. Fowler kept that information from us, all so that he could continue the extortion. He's as guilty as Caulfield is. If we're to put him away for that, we need a huge case against him. We need to build it from the ground up and show that Kenny Fowler, because of greed, allowed these poisonings to continue. But to do that, we have to have him dead-to-rights on the extortion. Honestly?" he asked. "I don't care much about the extortion. I care about these lives. I care about being lied to and strung out because of Fowler's greed. He deserves more than a slap on the wrist. And yes, it means that you have to take your clothes off. Yes, you have to do all the private things we all do every day of our lives. And yes, you have to do them as if there is no camera watching you, no microphone listening. And no, I don't know how a person does that. But I know you want him as badly as I do — otherwise, I couldn't have asked."

She sighed, and she scratched the dashboard with a fingernail. "Thank you for not saying that he's seen it all already — that he may have hours of me on tape — so what does it matter? And thank you for not saying that I'm strong enough to pull this off. That is a sentiment that would not be appreciated, I can tell you that. We won't know about any such strength until I try — *if* I try. And so that would only be manipulative garbage." She smirked and added, "More my territory than yours. I could blow this, Lou. And thanks also for downplaying the report on that witness from the loading dock. We *know* Fowler received confirmation of Caulfield's identity and did not act on it. I read that report. That makes him guilty of these crimes by omission."

Boldt did not realize that she had read it. "Whatever," he said. But his heart was pounding strongly, for it sounded to him as if perhaps she had made up her mind.

"They ask too much of us," she said, her lips tight as if fighting off her emotions. "We give too much, and we get so little back. The media tears us to pieces. The sixth floor rains hell on us. And all for what?"

"Cold pizza and Maalox," Boldt answered.

She sputtered a laugh. "Yeah. Job benefits."

"Right."

The wind blew across the water like a shadow, and sand swirled in the air, and the people playing volleyball shielded their eyes from it.

"As a teenager, like all teenage girls, I wanted to be a movie star. I thought it looked so *easy*. 'Be careful what you wish for. Someday it may be yours,' or however that goes."

"You have to do this willingly; it's not something that will work if you feel pressured into doing it. You have to sell him on the idea that everything you say, everything that goes on at that houseboat is for real."

"Business as usual," she said spitefully.

He was not going to touch that comment.

"I'm in," she announced. Facing him with hard eyes she said, "But for my own reasons, Lou. For my own damn reasons."

Everyone called the man Watson, and he ran Tech Services as if it were his own department, which it was not. He had been called Watson for so many years that Boldt did not remember his real name. He was a bald man with glasses and thick red lips, and was commonly mistaken for Bernie Lofgrin's younger brother. If it ran on electricity, then Watson could build it, modify it, copy it, or compromise it.

Watson and his prize technician, a man named Moulder, spent two consecutive days in a cabin cruiser anchored off of the Lake Union houseboats, alternating between running the gear and fishing off the stern — this "to keep up appearances." They were the envy of the entire department that week.

The two most difficult performances were turned in by Daphne Matthews and Owen Adler, who did everything short of making love for the cameras. According to script, they discussed the Uli case on occasion, with Daphne implying that the suspect was getting closer and closer to cooperating with the authorities. Daphne showered, shaved her legs, and brushed her teeth as usual, and Watson followed procedure to the letter, never connecting monitors to the cameras in the bedroom and bath.

The technology behind the ruse was explained to Boldt in layman's terms. Fowler's surveillance system worked off of infrared and radio-frequency transmission as opposed to hard wiring, which necessitated cables. The signals from the microphones and fiber-optic cameras were transmitted via the airwaves to a remote location that Watson estimated was within a quarter-mile of the houseboat. Another houseboat or a nearby condominium seemed the most likely location for this remote, but a vehicle or boat was a possibility. It was suspected that the incoming signals were recorded and videotaped at the remote site, although it was also possible that the signals were relayed over telephone lines from the remote to either the security room at Adler Foods or Fowler's apartment — they would not be able confirm this until they conducted a physical search of the various premises. It was no different from the surveillance techniques the police themselves used, except that Fowler was more thorough in his coverage of the houseboat, and he incorporated a state-of-the-art digital technology that required Watson to borrow some equipment from the FBI.

Watson and his people spent twenty-some hours identifying the various frequencies being used, and stealing onto the signals. Now, what Fowler was listening to and watching was also being recorded on the anchored cabin cruiser that housed two of the world's worst fishermen. More important, when directed to do so, Watson was prepared to jam Fowler's outgoing signals from the houseboat and transmit his own from videotape, leaving Fowler with false images of an empty houseboat, when in fact it would be bustling with activity. This deception had been the key element for Boldt's plan to work, and it took nearly seventy-two hours before Watson believed he was ready. No one could guarantee it would work.

On day four of the ruse, the morning headlines and broadcasts led with the story that Cornelia Uli had agreed to turn state's witness and to reveal to a grand jury the identity of the man who had run the ATM extortion of Adler Foods. Deputy prosecuting attorney Penelope Smyth was quoted as saying that with Uli's testimony, the state believed it had an airtight case, and that for "security reasons" the witness was being placed into hiding so that nothing could jeopardize her testimony — or the state's case.

At one-thirty in the morning the night before — well before the story hit the press — an unmarked dark-blue sedan pulled up in front of the dock that led to Daphne's houseboat, and two plainclothes policemen climbed out and walked the area for five minutes before returning to the car and giving the all-clear. The car's back door opened, and a figure small in stature, accompanied by a big bear of a man, walked quickly toward Daphne's home. The front door swung open and admitted these two without a knock or introduction. Moments later, the blue car sped away.

Daphne closed the door and locked it. "Everything go okay?"

"Fine," Boldt answered.

Cornelia Uli pulled back the hood to the sweatshirt and shook her hair free. "I thought we were going to a hotel," she complained.

"So will everyone else," Boldt said. "The press will be searching every hotel, motel, and inn within an hour's drive of the courthouse. A houseboat on Lake Union, five minutes from downtown? You're safer here than in any hotel. It has a brand-new security system, and —"

"A police*woman* to look after you and take care of you."

"What about television?"

"There's a television in the bedroom, and the bedroom is yours until this is over."

"Okay, fine." Cornelia Uli strolled the houseboat looking it over, touching some of the furniture, inspecting the view. "It's killer," she said.

"Let's hope not," Daphne answered. "And

let's get one thing straight: I am *not* your house-maid. We share dish duty, cooking, and cleaning."

"Forget it."

"This is nonnegotiable. You can go back to county lockup and take your chances, if you'd prefer."

Boldt began drawing the curtains and lowering shades.

"And you can't go outside," Daphne stated emphatically. "This is a small, closed neighborhood. We decided *against* putting any of our people around the area because we thought it would cause too much suspicion and probably force us to move you. We don't want to move you. We were also worried about leaks. Only a handful of people know you're here, all of whom can be trusted." Boldt continued with the shades. "You won't go outside, you won't use the phone, and you won't open any of the shades. We're taking no chances that you might be randomly spotted. And remember, this is for *you,* not us."

"Bullshit," the woman protested. "This is so I'll squeal. This is so Kenny Fowler goes to jail. Don't give me any of that shit."

Cornelia Uli had been told nothing of Boldt's ruse, and Boldt delighted in the fact that unwittingly she, too, played her role out to perfection.

For a day and a half, the two women lived

593

side by side — sometimes combative, sometimes in harmony, but with Daphne either wearing her weapon at her side or leaving it within plain reach.

Boldt and his team were equipped with some of the same digital communication technology used in the ATM sting, preventing any possibility of electronic eavesdropping. Officially, the police were completely out of this. In fact, an elite team of individuals including Gaynes and LaMoia were following a carefully choreographed script in which Cornelia Uli was the only unwitting participant. For the sake of possible surveillance, it had long since been decided that the trap would be baited after dark.

On the second evening of Uli's confinement, Daphne sat waiting for the woman to take a bathroom break. As usual, she wore a radio and earpiece.

Uli was a television addict, and remained virtually glued to the set in the bedroom during waking hours. Boldt used this against her in his plan: The diuretic slipped into the evening meal guaranteed frequent bathroom calls; at some point she would come down to the head — essential to the success of the ruse. More important, she would immediately return upstairs to her shows, where, true to form, she would remain. She would not be hanging around downstairs, checking coat closets. Crucial, because on this night, the closets would have more than coats inside of them.

But for Daphne the time seemed to stretch on forever. Finally Uli did come down from the bedroom, the sound of the television behind her, and crossed the room toward the head. Daphne, as per instructions, sprang into action.

She walked quickly to the front door and unlocked it. At the same time she keyed in the security code, deactivating the system, she also flashed a signal of three pops of the transmission button to her radio. Then she hurried to the back door, which she unlocked as well. All of this required only seconds to accomplish.

Thankfully, Uli always washed her hands after using the toilet. The running water was to serve as Daphne's warning signal.

Outside the houseboat, the three quick pops over the radio were the awaited signal. Boldt, LaMoia, and Gaynes, all dressed in dark clothing, hurried from the back of a panel truck and down the short dock toward the farthest houseboat, while through an earpiece Boldt monitored the monotonous drone of the dispatcher's voice tracking Kenny Fowler's every move. At present, Fowler was holed up in his water-view apartment across town.

On board the cabin cruiser, Daphne's radio signal instructed Watson to jam several of Fowler's transmission frequencies and to start the prerecorded videotapes playing. It was for this reason that Daphne remained standing close to the back door — there were no hidden surveillance cameras watching this back area of the house. One moment the hidden cameras were showing the real-time activity inside the houseboat; the next, only the camera and microphone showing Cornelia Uli urinating were live. The rest briefly displayed the images and sounds of empty rooms.

It was during these few precious moments of illusion that Boldt and his team slipped quietly inside the houseboat — Boldt and Gaynes through the front door, locking it behind them, and seconds later LaMoia through the back.

LaMoia took up position in the back coat closet.

Boldt stuffed himself into the front coat closet.

Bobbie Gaynes raced up the ladder and concealed herself on the small deck outside the bedroom.

Daphne heard the bathroom water running. She rekeyed the security code and the light flashed red.

She glanced into the living room. Boldt's jacket was caught in the closet door, cracking it open. He did not seem to notice.

No time. Watson had warned her that for the video to play correctly once the jamming was removed, she had to walk "on screen" from the same location where she had walked off. She could not suddenly appear in the middle of a room when the cameras went live.

Desperate to correct Boldt's coat, she had no choice but to return to her screened position at the back door, while at the same time clicking her radio three times successively. *Click, click, click.*

On the cabin cruiser, sweat clinging to his brow, Watson stood alongside his assistant, Moulder, each with fingers from both hands occupied, awaiting the signal. The radio sparked three times. Watson said, "Ready?" Moulder nodded. "One, two, three!"

In a synchronized movement, the men depressed the buttons simultaneously. The video of the houseboat was once again live. But now, there were three police inside.

Watson spoke calmly into the radio, "You're live."

Uli came out of the bathroom at the same time Daphne heard Watson's confirmation and crossed back onto a video screen somewhere in the city. The psychologist's heart was pounding ferociously. She had not realized how tense this would make her.

On cue, the phone rang, and Daphne answered it in her same bored manner with which she always answered a phone, fully aware of the electronic device listening to her every word.

"Hello?"

"It's me," said Lieutenant Phil Shoswitz. "We need you downtown. It's urgent — the grand jury has advanced the schedule. They've decided to hear her testimony tomorrow morning. Smyth wants to talk to you."

"But I —"

"Twenty minutes is all. I know you'll be leaving her, but it's better than us sending a replacement and making a scene. Lock it up tight and key in the security. You've done it before. She'll be fine."

"But I really don't think —"

"If we don't handle this tonight, we've got major problems in the morning. Get your butt down here." He added, "No one can bust in there without us knowing. I'm putting an un-marked car up on Fairview. They'll respond if needed, but I don't want them any closer than that."

"Yes, sir."

She hung up and told Uli, "I have to go downtown."

"Bullshit."

"I have to go. You'll be fine. I'll lock up and you'll rekey the security behind me. I won't be more than a half hour." She added, "I've gone out for food before." She turned around, and there peering from the closet was Boldt's eye, wide with urgency. Shocked, she quickly collected herself. Boldt could not spin around in the tiny space and free his coat without making noise. Nor could he pull the closet door shut without risking being heard.

"But not at night," Uli complained.

"It's orders. I have to go."

"A half hour, that's all," Uli stated as a requirement.

"I thought you didn't like cops," Daphne reminded her. She edged toward the closet.

"I like your gun. I don't suppose you would leave me that."

"You'll be fine." She reminded her of the code, although Uli had used the system before. "Lock up behind me."

"No," the woman snapped sarcastically, "I think I'll leave it open so Fowler can just walk right in."

Daphne stepped up to the closet door and said, "Oh hell, I don't need a coat," and smacked the door firmly, pushing it shut. A small triangle of Boldt's sport coat stuck out by the hinge like a tiny flag.

Boldt was not big on claustrophobic environments. He was large enough that even the front seat of a car seemed tight to him. The minutes ticked by interminably long. He monitored the time by pushing the button that lit the display on his Casio watch.

Four minutes after Daphne's departure, Boldt heard softly in his ear, "Suspect is departing his domicile. Repeat: Suspect departing." They had intentionally given Fowler only a few minutes in which to react, because they knew their operatives could not stand inside a coat closet remaining absolutely silent for more than thirty minutes, and because they hoped to force an urgency upon him that would require a quick, perhaps irrational, decision to act. This also accounted for Shoswitz's announcing to Daphne an advanced trial date.

"Suspect headed east on Denny Way," Boldt heard in his ear.

Boards creaked overhead — Uli was in the bedroom watching television, unaware of Bobbie Gaynes lurking in the shadows only several feet away.

The surveillance traffic crackled in Boldt's ear. Fowler drew progressively closer, and when he eventually turned north toward the lake, Boldt knew he was headed here. Seven minutes.

"Suspect has arrived at destination," came the dispatcher's bland voice. Boldt could not stand the lack of air another minute. He tugged on the closet door and cracked it open again, delivering fresh air, and leaving him a tiny slit through which he could see.

Somewhere around three minutes later, the back door came open, Kenny Fowler using a master key for locks that his own people had installed. He punched in an override code that circumvented a customer's PIN — supplied to alarm companies by the manufacturer in case a customer *forgot* his or her security PIN. Then he shut the door and reset the alarm.

Cornelia Uli's ears were aided by the fact that she had muted a commercial, and because Fowler proceeded to step on the same noisy board that had gotten him into trouble with

Daphne. Uli came charging down the ladder calling out, "Changed your mind?"

Boldt watched as Fowler came into view. He wore a dark-green oilskin jacket. Bold could not see Uli.

"Oh shit!" Uli barked out, seeing him.

"Relax! I'm not here to kill you." He sounded emotionally drained.

"Bullshit."

"*No* shit." He produced a fan of cash — twenty-dollar bills. "We're getting you out of here."

"What are you talking about, out of here?"

"I'm giving you a choice," he said calmly. "You can take a plane ticket and three thousand bucks right now, or you can get on that stand tomorrow morning —"

"It's *not* tomorrow morn—"

"Shut up! There's no time, Corny." Fowler evidently cared for the woman. Boldt had not anticipated this. "You get on the stand and you lose your memory. No ATMs. No Kenny Fowler. No testimony. It was all your idea. I can tell you how to make it sound convincing. You do that, and I'll give you thirty thousand when you get out."

"I'll *never* get out."

"Four years, maybe six. And thirty thousand at the other end. I'll deposit half in your name *before* you get on that stand."

"I take the fall for you."

"Something like that."

601

"Jesus," she said. Boldt realized she was actually considering it.

Boldt reached down and depressed the radio's call button twice: *Click, click*. Overhead, he heard Gaynes move. He saw Fowler turn as he must have heard LaMoia. Boldt swung open the door, his weapon already drawn.

Cornelia Uli screamed.

Fowler scrambled for his weapon, completely caught off-guard.

"Three of us, Kenny! Drop it!" Boldt announced.

"Hands high!" LaMoia warned from behind.

Gaynes leapt down the ladder and tackled Uli, shielding her.

Fowler shook his head. He sat down slowly onto the floor, only inches from the post where Daphne had struck her head. "But how?" he said, glancing toward the wall and one of his hidden cameras.

"We've got all the latest shit," Boldt said, quoting him.

Fowler remained dazed.

LaMoia said, "Hey, Sarge, get this: Tonight you and I came out of the closet."

THIRTY-EIGHT

At Owen Adler's recommendation they met at Place Pigalle because it was small and intimate and offered a stunning water view. Boldt noticed Daphne's new ring immediately, but he said nothing because he was not sure Liz had seen it yet. But of course, she had. Liz did not miss much when it came to Daphne Matthews. The ring was both handsome and elegant, though not showy, and Boldt admired Adler for that.

Boldt had accepted the invitation reluctantly, not wanting to leave his home for any reason, not comfortable with the idea of socializing with the two of them, but he had never been good at denying Daphne much of anything. She had gotten him into this investigation, and now, in her own way, she was letting him out.

Boldt asked, "How do you interpret Fowler's statement?"

In a plea bargain to lessen the charges, Kenny Fowler had agreed to cooperate by giving a written statement. One of Daphne's jobs was to analyze the psychology behind it. "From the day he left SPD he told all of us he was going to have his own agency. Working for

603

Owen, he spent as much money as he made — actually more most of the time; he lived beyond his means. He felt inferior — Howard Taplin's go-and-fetch-it. He claims that the Caulfield case brought all those feelings home. That he suddenly saw a way to make enough money to strike out on his own. He knew the look of the faxes, the language, and the tone — he could imitate the killer and extort money. If people kept dying, he could use this to apply more pressure."

"But he *withheld* information," Boldt reminded.

"He lied to *all* of us," Adler snapped. "If it was a matter of money —" but he cut himself off, clearly too upset to discuss it.

Daphne continued hesitantly, "The statement says nothing about the original New Leaf cover-up, or framing Caulfield on the drug charges. I suspect that his intention all along was to find Caulfield himself, *before* we did, and to take him out. That way he could continue the extortion while the New Leaf connection to the killings remained unproven, probably hoping it would fade away." She looked out at the view. "He exploited everything and everyone around him." She clearly included herself in this. Liz poked her husband in the leg, her actions hidden beneath the table. Boldt asked no more questions.

Liz changed the subject, asking questions about Corky, and Adler brightened and told a series of amusing stories.

He ordered champagne, and Liz changed hers to a San Pellegrino because of the child growing inside her. This announcement won several toasts and more talk of Corky, and naturally led into Adler's blushing, tongue-tied inability to speak, and Daphne's finally announcing their engagement. She confessed, "It may be the only engagement in history to be consummated not by a kiss, but a handshake."

Boldt and Daphne met eyes briefly, and he saw in hers a terrified joy that he had longed to see there. Far out on the water the ferries came and went, their lights blurred in reflection. Daphne drank nervously and started telling stories on Boldt, reminding him of things that he pretended to have forgotten.

Adler drank to Liz for the time-trap software, and to Boldt for everything he had done, and to his fiancée "for finding the truth." No one mentioned Harry Caulfield by name. Howard Taplin was cooperating with authorities, but he received no toasts that night. Boldt said a silent toast for Danielson and Striker — one recovering, the other facing a difficult trial and a messy divorce.

In all, it was an awkward evening for Boldt. He fought Adler for the check and lost, and this seemed significant to him. He drove home in silence with his wife napping in her seat, and when they pulled up to the garage, her eyes still closed, Liz said, "She'll always be your friend. It won't change that. You'll see."

He had no way to follow that. He got the door for her and they held hands on the way to the kitchen. After checking in on Miles, Liz paid the baby-sitter while Boldt tended to the day's mail piled by the kitchen phone. Among the letters was a brown package, and like a good cop, Boldt treated it suspiciously, chastising himself once he read the return address.

"I wondered what that was," Liz said, as her husband opened it carefully. "But I didn't touch it," she added. Boldt hated the precautions, he resented so much of his public service. The package was incredibly light and was marked FRAGILE, with a series of bright red stickers.

The note was on personalized stationery and read simply,

For your boy. I forget his name. Did you tell me it? I don't remember. It seemed a shame to let it go to waste. I know he's too young. But perhaps someday he can finish this. — Betty

Inside, he found the partially completed model of the Space Shuttle.

THIRTY-NINE

Howard Taplin took the stand for the third time in as many days. He had turned state's witness, and the convictions were piling up in a case that drew both Court TV and CNN updates. The succession of trials was nearly as exhausting as the investigation for the lead detective. It was in that horrible time of year for Boldt — between Thanksgiving and Christmas, when the sky was gray, the air cold, and there was canned Christmas music playing from fuzzy speakers on every street.

Kenny Fowler went down in flames, receiving three thirty-year sentences to be served consecutively. Amazingly to Boldt, Cornelia Uli was acquitted after the prosecution proved without a shadow of a doubt that she had served as Fowler's accomplice, had opened the phony bank account, and had made over twelve thousand dollars in withdrawals. Television reporters called it a sympathy vote, for Uli had been arrested seven years earlier by Fowler during a gang raid and had been forced to serve as his sexual partner ever since. The jury apparently bought the defense's position that she had been brainwashed. LaMoia had summed it up as far as Boldt was concerned:

607

"That's the law for you. Go figure."

Boldt still owed his wife that champagne dinner, but he had not forgotten, despite what she thought. He was in fact saving up to make it dinner in Rome, though that required another few months of happy hour at the Big Joke. Miles was in the terrible twos, and this, Boldt thought, was the only redeeming value of the endless series of trials.

He sneaked out of the courtroom the minute he was handed the note by the guard, and he knew what to expect despite its vagueness. Reporters' eyes followed him. These days, where Boldt went, the press followed. He was sick and tired of it. He wanted his life back. But they could not follow him down into County Detention where he was headed; the guards stopped them.

He walked and walked, down into the bowels of a system that failed at every turn. This was but one more example. He left his gun at the first station, and he flinched when the bars shut behind him, because he always flinched when he heard that sound. His shoes squeaked on the clean cement floor, though he avoided the center drain.

The guard was making excuses, but Boldt hardly heard them. He had argued; he had warned. He had heard the words of Dr. Richard Clements as he had seen him off at the airport: "You keep your eye on him. He's one determined fellow."

This was no place for Caulfield. He had been inside before, and the five years he had served for a trumped-up drug charge had helped to buy him a life sentence rather than death row. That was when Boldt had pressed for a suicide watch and had lost. The arguments had centered around transporting him back and forth for the trial, overcrowding, and expense.

They stopped in front of the cell. He hoped the guard was finished making excuses, but the man added, "I guess if you're crazy, you're just crazy."

Harry Caulfield had vomited, much as his victims had vomited. He was lying in the bed, his head cocked to one side, eyes shut. Perhaps it had been a peaceful death.

"You suppose he complained about the rats just so we'd put out the poison? I mean what kind of idiot would do such a thing? What the hell are we going to say?"

"That he got what he wanted." The morning paper open on the floor meant nothing to the guard. But Boldt saw it was open to the business pages. He knew the article: ADLER FOODS FILES CHAPTER ELEVEN. Besieged by lawsuits, Adler had folded his shop, though according to Daphne he vowed to return. Adler was not one to stay down long.

"Crazy bastard," the guard said.

Boldt turned and headed back for the entrance, passing cell after cell of human beings behind bars. They stood with their hands on the bars, staring out at him, envying his freedom to leave this place.

As he passed the front desk, the guard held out Boldt's weapon. He stopped, stared at it. The man wiggled it. It grew heavy for him.

Boldt accepted it. Snapped it into the holster.

He flinched as the cell door closed loudly behind him.

The employees of **THORNDIKE PRESS** hope you have enjoyed this Large Print book. All our Large Print books are designed for easy reading — and they're made to last.

Other Thorndike Large Print books are available at your library, through selected bookstores, or directly from us. Suggestions for books you would like to see in Large Print are always welcome.

For more information about current and upcoming titles, please call or mail your name and address to:

THORNDIKE PRESS
PO Box 159
Thorndike, Maine 04986
800/223-6121
207/948-2962